Beautifully Flawed

by

Laura Pavlov

Shine Design, Book Two

This is a work of fiction. Names, characters, places, and incidents are either the product of the author's imagination or are used fictitiously, and any resemblance to actual persons living or dead, business establishments, events, or locales, is entirely coincidental.

Beautifully Flawed

Contact Information: info@thewildrosepress.com

Cover Art by *The Wild Rose Press, Inc.*

The Wild Rose Press, Inc.
PO Box 708
Adams Basin, NY 14410-0708
Visit us at www.thewildrosepress.com

Publishing History
First Champagne Rose Edition, 2020
Trade Paperback ISBN 978-1-5092-3283-3
Digital ISBN 978-1-5092-3284-0

Shine Design, Book 2
Published in the United States of America

"Get your mangy mutt off me." She covered her mouth with her hand to keep Daisy's urgent kisses away.

Hell, he couldn't help but laugh; of course the spicy Southern prima donna disliked dogs. And who the hell wore white dress slacks, a white blousy tank top, and high heels to Lake Tahoe? It was like wearing a wedding dress to a campground. He doubted the little princess was one with nature.

"Daisy." He used a stern voice, which got her attention. Not the bitchy one on her back, but the non-human bitchy one who couldn't stop wagging her tail. His pup moved obediently to his side, and Maverick reached for Elle's hand to help her up.

"Why are you smiling?" she hissed.

He pulled her to her feet, and she tore her hand away as if the mere contact burned her. She dramatically brushed dirt from her pants.

"You all right, Peaches?"

"I'm fine, and you best call me by my name, seeing as I'm here for professional reasons." She stood straight, face flushed. "And why haven't you trained your beast of a dog? He probably ruined my outfit."

"She's a girl and just a pup. Still gets a little excited when people come over, but I will tell you, not the wisest move to wear all white in Tahoe. It's kind of an outdoorsy place, you know? I hope you brought other clothes, for your sake." He scanned her from head to toe.

Praise for Laura Pavlov and…

BEAUTIFULLY FLAWED

"The chemistry between Maverick and Elle is sizzling! I loved their banter. This book checks all the boxes for me."

~Willow Aster, USA Today Bestselling Author

~*~

Dedication

Greg,
Thanks for being the prince on the white horse.
Love you always.
xoxo, Laura

Chapter One

Elle's Tip of the Day

If someone doesn't accept you for who you are—they can suck it!

"I don't know why y'all think this is funny. I should be at the office, not driving to Lake Tahoe. I thought I'd fill you in on my disastrous romantic getaway in France over lunch, not be off to a job working for my nemesis," Elle said, her Southern twang more prominent as she ranted.

Dani and Peyton's laughter filtered through the Bluetooth of her Audi.

Elle scanned the water in the distance. Shades of turquoise and cobalt danced like diamonds on the surface. She focused on the winding curve before turning her attention back to her best friends.

She and her besties worked at the top interior décor firm in San Francisco, Shine Design, owned and operated by their powerhouse boss Camille Chadwick.

"There's our little Southern firecracker." Peyton's voice brought her back to the present. "Maverick is not your nemesis. He's a good guy. I've known him since we were kids. He's one of Jackson's closest friends. And for some reason he enjoys annoying you."

"He didn't seem to bother you at Peyton and Jackson's wedding." Dani's voice was all tease and sarcasm. "I found you lip-locked with Mr. Sexy out by the lake."

Elle's blood boiled at her complete lapse in judgment. Even though *make-out-gate* had happened more than a year ago, it still mortified her.

"Don't pee on my boots and tell me it's rainin', Dani. You know damn well I had one too many peach Bellinis that night. I'm not claiming the bastard isn't a sight for sore eyes, but he's so stuck up the man could drown in a rainstorm."

Hysterical laughter vibrated through the interior of her car as she approached a tight curve. Maverick Wallace was the last person on earth she wanted to talk about. She gripped the steering wheel. The magnificent body of water on one side, the massive Sierra mountains on the other; the jagged granite stone bordered the road covered in towering green pines. Splashes of yellow and white flowers took her breath away. The incredible beauty rivaled only by memories of summers spent in Savannah where she grew up.

"Hey, he did ask you out the next night, which is a first for Maverick," Dani said, reminding her of yet another memory she wished to forget.

Dinner with Maverick Wallace hadn't qualified as a date. He dazzled her at Peyton's wedding when she broke *golden rule number one*—no drunken public make-out sessions—he showed his true colors the following evening.

The man was as close to *sin-on-a-stick* as you got. Six feet, four inches of dark, chiseled gorgeousness, and she fell for his Greek-God good looks hook, line, and sinker. She'd forever blame those damn Bellinis. Maverick pushed to take her home after the reception, thankfully she refused. However, in another moment of mindlessness, she agreed have dinner with him.

"He's a crude, arrogant jackass, which is exactly how he acted on our date. Spending the next few weeks working with him is not high on my priority list. I don't understand why Camille is making *me* go."

"I can't leave Jojo. She's only three months old." Jojo was Ellie's goddaughter, Josephine Danielle Vance. Peyton and Jackson chose her middle name in honor of Dani and Elle. Elle adored the little green-eyed angel.

"…And Dani is in the middle of the project at the W-Hotel. Honestly, I'm glad you're going. I wish you two got along, seeing as both of you will be Jojo's Godparents. I know he pushes your buttons; he knows you hate him, and I think he feels bad about his behavior. You don't have to be best friends with the guy but maybe you can learn to tolerate him until you get to know him better."

She knew enough about him—she just didn't care for him. At all. He got under her skin. He never called her by her name. *Peaches.* Yep, he stuck her with the ridiculous title when she told him she was from Georgia.

Moron.

To add insult to injury, he was the quarterback for the San Francisco Miners, and everyone acted like the man walked on water. She was unimpressed. If he'd asked her to remodel his place in San Francisco it wouldn't be so bad, but no, he had to come to Tahoe, where he grew up.

She'd push aside her personal feelings and try to tolerate the guy. She hadn't slept with him. Thank God.

Just foolishly made out with him. Truth be told, he'd hurt her feelings, and like a true Southern woman—she never forgot.

"You're right. For Jojo's sake, I'll play nice. But I'm getting in and out of there. Camille said if I don't think the house needs a complete remodel, I can place the orders, hire a team to paint and help with necessary projects, and wrap up quickly. I'll be out of here in two weeks."

"Okay, now that you've agreed to stop hating your sexy nemesis, we're dying to hear more details about how things ended with Edward," Dani said.

The handsome Count Edward Efant whisked her away to the south of France last week. The man as close to a prince as she ever imagined finding. He split his time between his home in France with his children and his high-rise in San Francisco.

Five months ago, the man swept her off her feet, and they began dating. This past week he brought her home to meet his family, and they shared seven consecutive days together for the first time.

"It started out bad and went downhill with each passing day. We spent the first night at his family's winery. A winery in France should have been romantic, but he'd spent endless hours working, and the rest of the time he was tired. He still has the, um, *little problem* in the bedroom due to his medication. So no hanky-panky the entire time. It's not normal. Our time together is usually spent attending parties or going to fancy dinners—no real quality time," Elle said, glancing at her GPS. Only twenty-five minutes until she arrived at her destination.

"How did things end with the demon child?"

Peyton said, a hint of humor in her voice. Elle had phoned her girlfriends several times over the week in desperate need of support.

"Sophie, aka the *spawn of Satan?* Hmm, let's see, aside from the lovely nickname she gave me, the endless door slams and screaming freak-out sessions? Her meltdown on our last night, allowed her to go out with a real bang. She insisted Edward leave his *dirty little secret* at *home* or she wouldn't join him for dinner."

Dani tried to speak through her laughter. "Please tell me you went to dinner?"

"Oh yes. And what a lovely evening it was. Sophie refused to speak; she told Edward *I* didn't deserve to be graced with her intelligence. She *literally* would not eat in my presence, so she took her meal to go. I tried to bond with her. I thought we'd talk about fashion and school and boys. Nope. She called me a *teenage tart* when we left for the airport." Her two best friends' laughter filled the interior once again.

"What did Edward think of his daughter's behavior?" Peyton asked.

"Well, at first, he appeared appalled, but then backpedaled when he drove me to the airport. He insisted he shouldn't have flaunted our relationship in her face, and probably should have respected Sophie's wishes to have dinner without me." A pit settled in her stomach when the words left her mouth.

"Are you kidding me? He has some nerve," Dani said, not hiding her disdain.

"How did things end between you two?" Peyton asked.

"I broke up with him before I got out of the car. I

mean, the first half of the trip should have been amazing, but it wasn't. After spending a week together, I realized we have nothing in common. Throw in one vicious demon spawn, and a boyfriend with zero sex drive who doesn't have my back—it was an easy decision."

"I'm sorry. I know a part of you hoped the Count was going to be your Prince Charming," Dani said.

"What can I say? Another prince bites the dust."

Elle couldn't help but laugh along with her friends at the ridiculous situation.

"I'm guessing you haven't told your mother yet?" Peyton said.

Both Peyton and Dani were more than aware of Elle and Mama's strained relationship. Elle's mother had been over the moon since she'd started dating Count Efant. She craved her mother's approval, even if it were a rare occurrence. It didn't really matter now because it was over.

"No, I'm not ready for the wrath of Caroline Humphries yet."

"Are you sure she'd want you to be with someone who doesn't make you happy?" Peyton pressed.

"Yes. She'd be fine with it. The truth is, I've spent my entire life not living up to Mama's expectations, so she'll add this to the list of strikes against me."

"You know we love you exactly the way you are," Peyton said.

"We wouldn't change one hair on your adorable little Southern head," Dani added.

"I love you both. Thanks for always having my back. And now I have to go take orders from *Maverick Wallace*," she said, wanting to change the subject.

She felt the sting from the way things ended on the plane ride home yesterday, but she'd made peace with her decision. No more settling for anything less than the fairy-tale. And Edward Efant was not it.

"I wish you were here. Should I have Jackson call Maverick and tell him to go easy on you? I know he likes to give you a hard time, but if he knows you're upset he'll back off. He's a big teddy bear when you get to know him," Peyton said.

Elle couldn't respond quick enough. "*Hells to the no*. The last thing I'm up for is the manwhore knowing I'm single. I don't want his pity, nor do I need him trying to get me in the sack. No one knows Edward and I broke up, aside from you two. I'm certainly not telling Mama until I absolutely have to. This is the nicest she's been to me in years. I'll be home before you know it."

Determined to wrap this job up quickly, she hoped the project didn't require any major reconstruction. Maverick currently lived in the home he purchased a few years ago in South Lake. It included a guest cottage attached to the main home where she would stay. The new property sat a block away on the water.

"I totally understand," Dani said, and Peyton agreed.

"Oh wow, the street he lives on is nice." Elle turned down the final road per the British woman's instruction on navigation.

"Yeah, his home is gorgeous. Most of his family is still in Tahoe, and they all live within a few blocks of one another. I can't even imagine how amazing the new house will be," Peyton said.

"All right, well, I'm here. I better go."

"Okay, hurry back. We miss you," Dani said.

"I will. Love you both."

"Love you," they said together, in a singsong voice.

Elle inched down the street reading the house numbers before finding his. From what she'd heard, Maverick bought his lake home when he signed with his first NFL team, the Titans. He'd waited for property to come available on the water in the same neighborhood, and one finally did. According to Camille, he hoped to have the new home renovated before he returned to San Francisco in July for summer training. Elle could guarantee a quick turnaround. She did not intend to spend eight weeks renovating a lake house for an egotistical sex fiend. She would complete this job in two weeks or less and be on her way. Maverick must have paid a pretty penny for the short notice and to have her travel for this project. Camille would never turn down a local celebrity. One of her favorite mottos—the more famous, the better.

Turning into his residence, soaring green trees and striking lavender shrubs flanked as she drove. She put the car in park and took in the property. She always loved nature as a kid growing up in Savannah and forgot how serene it could be since moving to San Francisco five years ago. Rustic, dark wood and red brick accents made up the large structure. The oversized front door swung open, and a bronzed, shirtless Maverick Wallace stepped out and leaned against the doorframe. His gaze locked with hers as he lifted a red apple to his mouth and took a bite.

Sweet Jesus.

Her mouth went dry. She sucked in a long breath and took a swig of water.

This job could not be over soon enough.

Chapter Two

Maverick's Playbook
If at first you don't succeed, try, try, again!

The white Audi suited her. Pristine and haughty, like the woman behind the wheel. He requested to work with her knowing she'd be pissed. Camille obviously forced her to take the job, which was fine with him. They needed to put this shit behind them. They were both close with Peyton and Jackson and were going to be the godparents to their daughter, Jojo. He tried multiple times to make amends, but Elle proved to be stubborn. She avoided him. The few interactions they'd had since Jackson and Peyton's wedding, she'd barely acknowledged his presence, aside from a few smartass comments. They had hooked up, once.

Once.

More than a fucking year ago.

And by hookup, it was a kiss. Okay, probably the best fucking kiss he'd ever experienced. Could still taste her peach-flavored, bee-stung lips when he thought about it. But still—a kiss. He didn't bang her, per Jackson's endless warnings. No idea why the girl was so angry. He took her to dinner the following night and acted like a dick, but it was for her own good. Did what he needed. But it was goddamned time to move past it. This being the exact reason he didn't do relationships. They weren't worth the hassle. He preferred short-term, uncomplicated flings that revolved around fabulous sex. And there were plenty of women who wanted the same thing. But Elle Fiore was not one of them. He found out this past year, there was nothing uncomplicated about her. She was an uptight, pageant queen, with a stick up her ass. Yes, she happened to be hot as hell, and always got under his skin. He didn't know why he gave a shit if she hated him, maybe because it bothered Jackson and Peyton that they didn't get along, or maybe it bothered him. Hell, if he knew. But he wanted to fix it. She wouldn't make it easy, but he'd survived worse. Try pre-season NFL camp. Pushing yourself until you vomit, until your muscles ached so bad you couldn't move. Becoming friends with Elle Fiore would be a piece of cake in comparison.

She stepped out of her car as Daisy, his hundred-pound goldendoodle galloped past him, eager to greet their guest.

Shit.

"Daisy," he called tossing the apple core in the grass for the local chipmunks to feast on. Before he could warn Elle, his loveable mutt pounced, knocked her back on her ass, climbed atop, and pushed her to the ground. All while slathering her with wet kisses.

Jesus.

He adjusted himself beneath his sweatpants. His reaction to her left him—uncomfortable. He could only imagine the lashing from Elle if she noticed the raging erection currently straining against his pants. Sprawled out on his driveway she flailed, and damn if he couldn't look away. He wondered what it would be like propped above her, while she begged him for more. It wasn't the first time dirty thoughts of Elle Fiore filled his mind, but he had never considered taking her in front of his house on the pavement. It'd be a new fantasy he added to the list.

"Get your mangy mutt off me." She covered her mouth with her hand to keep Daisy's urgent kisses away.

Hell, he couldn't help but laugh, of course the spicy Southern prima donna disliked dogs. And who the hell wore white dress slacks, a white blousy tank top, and high heels to Lake Tahoe? It was like wearing a wedding dress to a campground. He doubted the little princess was one with nature.

"Daisy." He used a stern voice, which got her attention. Not the bitchy one on her back, but the non-human bitchy one who couldn't stop wagging her tail. His pup moved obediently to his side, and Maverick reached for Elle's hand to help her up.

"Why are you smiling?" she hissed.

He pulled her to her feet, and she tore her hand away as if the mere contact burned her. She dramatically brushed dirt from her pants.

"You all right, Peaches?"

"I'm fine, and you best call me by my name, seeing as I'm here for professional reasons." She stood straight, face flushed. "And why haven't you trained your beast of a dog? He probably ruined my outfit."

"She's a girl and just a pup. Still gets a little excited when people come over, but I will tell you, not the wisest move to wear all white in Tahoe. It's kind of an outdoorsy place, you know? I hope you brought other clothes, for your sake." He scanned her from head to toe.

So fun to look at. A gorgeous pain in the ass. Stunning. Her dark blonde hair trailed down her back, longer since the last time he'd seen her. Olive skin, mesmerizing golden topaz eyes, and pink full lips. She stood about a foot shorter than him even with heels on, but her presence was larger than life. Fierce. She didn't take any shit, and he liked it. No woman ever spoke to him the way she did, aside from his sisters.

Her body was designed to fuel any red-blooded man's wet dreams. Thin and feminine, with curves in all the right places. He'd fantasized what it'd be like to hold her perfect tits in the palms of his hands too many times to count. Every bit of her toned to perfection. He guessed her to be one of those women who took classes at a fancy gym to maintain her tight body. Working up a sweat didn't seem like her style. If she only knew how many time's he imagined her sweaty, desperate, and writhing beneath him. *Damn.* This happened every time he was around her. He'd screwed Brittney less than an hour ago. Imagining another woman naked while the other was still in his house getting dressed, seemed pretty-low, even for him.

Brittney had been a reliable booty call since high school, and any time when he came home since. He'd refused her during the few brief years she'd been married, though she'd been more than willing to cheat on her husband. Go figure, her marriage failed. Maverick didn't mess around with married women. He respected people willing to make those vows to one another, his parents and grandparents were examples of how it *could* be. His younger sister, Marley, married her longtime boyfriend Cage a year ago, and they were ridiculously happy.

Maverick's one true love was football. He'd never met any woman more important to him than the game. But he sure as shit had met a lot of ladies he enjoyed, both in and out of the sack. He didn't mind repeat visitors as long as they knew the score.

Catch and release—his motto when it came to the opposite sex. Don't stick around long enough for drama. Keep it short and sweet.

He was damn good at football and sex. No need to waste his talent.

"You're seriously giving *me* fashion advice while you stand here in nothing but dowdy sweatpants, half naked? How about the fact that your mutt has no manners? Apparently, the apple doesn't fall far from the tree, does it?" She moved to the back of her car in a huff, and he followed. He bumped her out of the way and reached for her hard-top suitcase in the trunk. He'd never seen luggage in this particular color and definitely never one this large. Jesus, how long did she plan on staying?

"You have pink luggage?"

"It's not pink. It's rose gold," she said. "Let me guess, people don't bring rose gold suitcases to Lake Tahoe either."

He chuckled because he'd never seen a rose gold suitcase anywhere—not just in Tahoe. Hell, he didn't know it was a real color. He kept that thought to himself since she was already irritated by his mere presence.

"Whatever you say, Peaches. By the way, Daisy here is harmless." He led her inside toward the kitchen.

"Well, you should at least warn a lady before you allow her to charge at people like she's running with the bulls."

"Yeah, sorry about that. Let me grab you something to clean yourself. I can give you a hand with your backside if you want?" He wriggled his eyebrows and handed her a dish towel from across the kitchen island.

"No, thank you. I don't think my boyfriend would appreciate it." A smirk pulled at her sexy mouth.

"Ah, yes. You're dating some sort of prince or duke, right?" He knew exactly who she was dating. He'd spent a lot of time with Jackson and Peyton, and the Count's name came up more times than he cared to acknowledge, but he didn't need to tell her that.

"Not a prince and not a duke. He's a Count." Her tone softened, and she gave up on cleaning her slacks and took a seat on a barstool.

"Well, no disrespect to the Count. Just trying to be helpful."

"Sure, you were."

"You thirsty? Hungry?" He moved to the fridge and pulled out a few bottles of water and a bowl of fruit.

"Sure, I'd love a water."

"Maverick, I'm about done." Maria's voice sang from the next room as he slid a bottle of water across the slick black counter.

Elle's topaz gaze grew wide, and she leaned over the island and whisper-shouted, "Oh my gosh, you have one of your bimbos here now? I've been here for what? Five minutes. What is this—some kind of sex brothel?"

She glared, like he'd committed the most heinous act. What the hell was her deal? She talked about her boyfriend, but he wasn't allowed to have women here?

She was exactly as he remembered—exhausting.

Maria entered the kitchen, and Elle's jaw dropped taking in the middle-aged woman. Maria stood five feet tall, her dark hair pulled back in a tight bun, and a wide grin spread from ear to ear. One of the sweetest people he'd ever known.

Yeah, Princess—you just called Mother Teresa a whore.

"Elle, this is Maria. She's practically a member of the family. Helps me out when I'm in town." Maverick introduced the two women.

Maria pinched his cheek. "Awwww, this is Maverick's kind way of saying I'm his cleaning lady. I've worked for the Wallaces for over twenty years. I knew this guy when he was a little tater tot."

Elle jumped from the barstool, all prim and proper, a pink hue spread across her cheeks. "It's so nice to meet you, Maria. I'm Elle."

"Yes, you're the designer for the new house, right? Maverick speaks very highly of you," Maria said, a smile spread across her face. Elle's questioning gaze met his.

"Yes. I'm excited to go see the new place."

"I'm sure you'll love it. I'll see you tomorrow. The guesthouse is stocked with waters and snacks for you. Nice to meet you, dear." Maria made her way toward the door.

"Thank you. Nice to meet you, too."

"Bye, Mav."

"See you tomorrow," he said, before the door closed.

Elle's stare locked with his, he shook his head, waved a disapproving finger, and made a tsking sound with his tongue.

"Did I seriously just call the most adorable lady on earth a bimbo?"

"You sure did, Peaches. Don't feel too bad. I mean, her five young children might be deeply offended, but I forgive you." He crossed his arms and leaned back against the counter. She was so easy to mess with and for some reason, he thrived on it.

"Five kids? Ohmigosh, what's wrong with me?" Guilt oozed from her sweet, sexy mouth. He should ease up on her.

Nah—too soon.

"You're fine. You can repent at church on Sunday if you want. Maria's husband Pastor Mike, is the closest thing to Jesus this town has ever seen. I'm sure he'd understand you calling his wife a dirty whore."

She choked on her water, and he burst out in laughter.

"Don't laugh. I'm going to hell."

"Well, at least it's always warm there. Although your all-white outfit might not meet dress code." She was quite possibly the most amusing woman he'd ever met.

"Mav, you in here?" Brittney waltzed into the kitchen in running tights that covered her hot little ass like a second skin. Elle's eyes widened to the size of saucers, and her mouth gaped open when she took in the tall, pretty brunette.

"Hey, Britt, this is Elle. She's designing my new place. Elle, this is Brittney."

His designer stumbled off the barstool once again, and the two women assessed one another with a quick handshake and a stiff greeting.

"Okay, I need to get going. Will I see you later?"

The question caught him by surprise. She'd never been clingy, nor inquired about their next meeting.

"Yeah, sure. I'll see you around. Let me walk you out." He followed her as she made her way to the front door.

He leaned in close to Elle's ear when he strode past her and whispered, "I believe this is the bimbo you were referring to." The smell of jasmine and vanilla flooded his senses, and she glared before he exited the kitchen.

"Your designer seems nice." Britt's face hardened, and her arms crossed in front of her chest.

"Apparently she's nice to everyone but me."

With a forced smile she nodded. "Okay, well, call me later?"

What? This was new.

He had one woman in the kitchen who hated him because he tried to sleep with her over a year ago, and another woman upset because he wasn't in a hurry to sleep with her again. He and Brittney had done this too many times to count. Always the same song and dance.

"All right, take care." She kissed his cheek before turning to leave.

Another first.

When he returned to the kitchen Elle broke out in laughter.

"Hey, I'm sorry for saying you had a bimbo here. My opinion's worth a hill of beans right now. I've been in France with Edward for the past week, and I got back last night. I'm definitely sleep deprived, and I shouldn't have talked about your girlfriend or your sweet family friend so disrespectfully." She ran a hand through her hair before taking a sip of water.

"First off, no one is offended. I was teasing you earlier. I don't think I've heard anyone use the word bimbo in a decade, not that it's a negative thing, because I love me some bimbos," he said, which earned him a chuckle and an eyeroll. "And Brittney is a friend, not my girlfriend."

"Please, you aren't serious? It's none of my business, but she definitely doesn't see you as a friend," she said with a knowing nod.

"I've known her for years, but we've never dated. Relationships aren't my thing, and she knows it."

"Well, she thinks it's a whole lot more than you do, trust me. She looked at me like she wanted to jerk me bald. And she had an after-sex glow about her. She didn't like me being here one bit."

"I said I wasn't dating her. It doesn't mean we don't bang every now and then. But I didn't plan on it happening right before you arrived. She was on a run and saw my car in the driveway. And you know, once she was here, she started looking at me all needy," he said, with a shrug of his shoulders.

Her hand came down on the counter and a laugh bellowed out. "And you had no choice but to bless the lady with some sex?"

Her Southern accent was cute as hell.

"What can I say, Peaches? I'm very philanthropic."

"Sure, you are. And for the record, Brittney was not out on a run. I'll bet you a hundred bucks her car is parked one street over."

"What makes you so sure?"

"Trust me. This is my wheelhouse, Wallace. She played the part by wearing her best Lulu leggings, and I must say, she wore them well. But let me assure you, a woman does not go on a run in full makeup, hair down and curled, and a slew of colorful, beaded bangles covering half her forearm. Most importantly, unless her feet are made of steel, she wasn't on a run wearing Michael Kors, metallic, slip-on sneakers."

"What are you talking about? Why would she say she was on a run?"

"She knows who you are. You like to keep it casual, unplanned. You were brilliantly played my friend." Her head tipped back with a chuckle. Elle Fiore was one cocky Southern diva.

"Why the hell would I care if she were on a run or not? It's sex. It doesn't require a work-out beforehand."

"So if she called and asked to get together because she heard you were in town, would you have been game?"

He thought about it, and his answer surprised him. He wouldn't have liked it. It didn't work that way. They ran into one another and one thing led to another. They didn't talk on the phone or ever plan to meet up. They never had.

"I wouldn't have invited her over."

"Exactly. That'll be one hundred fifty dollars for your session, playboy."

"You know, you're kind of a know-it-all, Peaches. You think you've got me all figured out, don't you?"

"You're textbook, Wallace. Now, let's get down to business. When can we go see the new house?"

The little spitfire thought she had him all figured out. She was bossy as shit, but he'd be lying if he didn't admit he kind of liked it.

A little more than he should.

Chapter Three

Elle's Tip of the Day
Always speak your mind!

Elle changed into leggings, a T-shirt, and tennis shoes. If Maverick weren't waiting for her, she'd explore the comfortable, yet stylish décor in the guesthouse situated next the main house. She joined Maverick, and they walked the short distance down to the water where the new house sat. The outside of the property was phenomenal, and she couldn't wait to get inside to check it out.

The three-story structure was similar to his current residence, but on a much grander scale. Sunlight brought out the rich brown and red hues in the wood planks, and the circular cobblestone driveway matched the stone on the home. Six wood-plank garage doors accented with iron hardware were situated on the right side of the house with windows cut out at the top. This home could easily grace the cover of any architecture magazine, and she hadn't even stepped inside nor seen the lake view yet.

Talk about curb appeal.

Maverick opened the oversized dark wood front door, and she followed him inside. Her gaze landed on the large wall, completely blocking any view of the water, at the back side of the aged home. Outdated pink tile floors covered the entrance. Walls to her left and right formed more of a maze instead of an open living space.

"The inside needs a lot of work, which is why I want to get a jump on it right away," he said as he closed the front door.

"Well, the outside is pretty spectacular, but from what I can see thus far, the interior needs some updating. Let's walk through and see what can be salvaged."

The kitchen was a complete gut job, as were all eight bathrooms. The home needed new flooring throughout, and the current layout did not make any sense. She photographed each space, the game-room in the basement, the six bedrooms, eight bathrooms, kitchen, great room, living room, and dining room. It appeared to be a much larger project than she'd anticipated. It required a lot more than nice furnishings and a coat of paint, especially when it had the potential to be amazing. They stopped in the kitchen and she stood in the center near the island and slowly turned in a circle, visualizing how to make the floorplan work.

Dammit.

She needed to take down walls and completely refigure the space, and her client had the financial resources to make it happen. But it wouldn't be quick.

"Problem, Peaches?"

She met his dark brown gaze, so easy to get lost in it. A chiseled jaw covered in a bit of day-old scruff, his bronzed skin and dark wavy hair left no question as to why most women dropped their panties at the door with the slightest show of interest. And the man's physique—he was a male masterpiece. His simple white T-shirt hugged his muscled torso and his biceps strained against the cotton fabric. Too bad Maverick Wallace was the best-looking man she'd ever laid eyes on, since the cocky-manwhore didn't respect the opposite sex. Immature, self-absorbed with a one-track mind of screwing as many women as he could get his hands on. It didn't mean she couldn't enjoy the sights—look and not touch, right? She hated behaving like a lust-driven, school-girl.

Lord, give her strength, because this was going to be a long couple of weeks. But if anyone had the discipline required, it was her. She prided herself on having control over all aspects of her life. Maverick Wallace was the exception. He caught her starry-eyed the first time they met, but she learned from her mistake, and kept him at a distance ever since.

The smell of sandalwood and mint flooded her senses as he moved beside her, leaving her no choice but to use the strategy she came up with over a year ago whenever forced to be in Maverick's presence. She called it *resistance-therapy.*

She concentrated on her childhood dog, the adorable Prince Albert. Mind over matter, right? The quick memory caused a dull ache in her chest, sad and weepy, all signs of lust diminished. It'd been tragic losing the beautiful basset hound due to kidney failure, as she spent the first twelve years of her life with him, and being an only child meant Albert was more than just a dog. He'd been her best friend and loyal companion. Somehow, revisiting the grief proved the quickest way to stomp out her ridiculous attraction to the man who played the lead in every sexual fantasy she ever had. Elle didn't have sexual fantasies, hell, she wasn't even a sexual person. At least not before meeting the manwhore.

"Are you all right? You look upset?" He touched her shoulder, snapping her from her daze.

"I'm fine. Just trying to figure out what we need to do." Elle backed away, pushing all thoughts of Prince Albert and his kidneys from her thoughts. Moving into the next room, she came up with a game plan. Her gut told her not to cut corners, not to rush it, and she'd most likely adapt to the sexual tension brewing whenever her annoyingly attractive client was around. She'd do what she had to.

God rest poor Albert's soul. She'd drudge up visions of the white and tan little guy with his stumpy legs, as often as needed if it helped to remain professional.

"Look, Peaches, I trust you, so whatever you say goes."

Why was he so nice? And since when was he so confident in her professional abilities?

She sucked in a long breath. "Well, I'm struggling with a few things."

"Let me hear it."

"They set this floorplan up backward, as these are the rooms you spend the most time in. The kitchen and the family room are in the wrong place," she said, moving into the next room as he followed. "If we transition both rooms to the opposite side of the house, and take out this massive wall at the entrance, you'll have a view of the water from all the main living spaces in the home. We could open this entire area and make it one large great room and separate the spaces with furniture instead of walls which will allow for views of the breathtaking lake. I mean, why have a lake house if you aren't going to utilize the water views?"

"Agreed. I like it. I have a contractor ready to go. What's the problem?"

Maverick was a straight shooter. She'd use the same strategy.

"Well, if we take on this much construction it means a much longer time commitment than I planned."

"Ah, got it. Listen, Peaches, if you don't want the job, I understand. But I want it done right, and I can hire someone local if it doesn't work for you. I chose you because I know you're talented, I checked out your projects on the Shine website, and you're obviously a perfectionist, which is what I want for my home." He crossed his arms and studied her. Waited for a response. She didn't realize he'd requested to work with her, specifically. She assumed Camille had forced her to do it because everyone else was busy. For some reason, she found it flattering.

"Thank you. No, I'll make the time frame work. I need to let Camille know it's a larger project than we anticipated. I'll go home on the weekends. It should be done right, and I'm confident my vision for the place will exceed your expectations. When do you need to be back for practice?"

"Eight weeks. I work with a trainer here in Tahoe until official practice starts. Are you sure you're up for the job?"

"Yes. I'm in."

"Good. Let's go eat. I'll take you to my favorite place, and we can lay out a plan and call the contractor." He led her out of the house.

****

“Hey, Mav. Good to see you buddy.” An older man greeted them at Pete’s Pub, a local place right up the street.

“What’s up, Pete. Just got back in town this morning. This is Elle, she’s designing the house I bought on the lake.”

“Pleasure to meet you, young lady. Beautiful property to work on, huh?”

“Nice to meet you, as well. Yes, I’m looking forward to getting started,” she said, as Pete led them through the waterfront brewery.

Peanut shells littered the dark floors. The simple rustic wood tables and chairs added to the comfortable appeal. Light flooded in from the large windows covering the back wall facing the lake, and the turquoise water showcased like a piece of art. French doors tied back with white twine held the entrance to the patio open and allowed the cool breeze to flow inside. She stepped out onto the patio, and the smell of pine and vanilla filled the air around her. Her chest tightened. Being surrounded by nature reminded her of home. Of a life she left behind to chase a career and a new beginning in a large city where she didn’t know anyone but her father. It was a dark time when she first left Savannah, and she’d worked hard to rebuild her life and follow her own dreams. She hadn’t realized how much she missed the beauty she left behind, until being enveloped by something equally magnificent.

“All right, you two enjoy. I’ll send someone out to take your order. Glad to have you back for the summer, Mav, and looking forward to seeing you around too, sweetie,” Pete said, a bright smile spread across his weathered face. She thanked the kind man.

"I take it Pete is the owner?" she said, once the older man stepped back inside. He had the same name as the restaurant, so it wasn't rocket science.

"Yeah, he's owned the place since I was a kid. My first job was bussing tables here."

"Wow. I think it's cool he still owns it. I can see why you want to build a home on the lake here. This view is—breathtaking."

"I wouldn't have guessed you a nature lover, Peaches." He set his menu aside.

"Have you never been to Savannah? It's nature at its finest."

"I assumed you were from the city."

"You know what happens when you assume, right?" She scanned the menu before placing it on the table.

"So you're a country girl. Interesting."

"Why is it interesting?"

"I guess I thought I had you all figured out."

A large man stepped onto the patio carrying a notepad and a resting-bitch-face frown. Disheveled sandy brown hair, but not the *I-just-rolled-out-of-bed sexy* kind—the greasy, overgrown kind. He moved at a snail's pace, as if his will to live had been sucked from him moments before. He looked to be a few years older than her—far too young to be carrying a chip on his shoulder one could spot from a mile away. He wore the same gray T-shirt as Pete, but the cotton fabric pulled against his wide midsection, and sported a large red stain on the chest.

Maverick looked up with a forced smile. "How you doing, Roth?"

"Well, I didn't lose the Super Bowl, so I guess I'm doing a hell of a lot better than you, Maverick." His tone matched his appearance.

"I imagine you're right, buddy. Glad to see you doing well."

Seriously? She looked between the two men, assessing what the hell was going on. *Roth-the-sloth* was slinging major attitude at Maverick, yet he handled him with kid gloves. She'd seen him interact with Jackson on a few occasions, and the guy was witty as all get-out. Her mind scattered for ideas, the only conclusion—Maverick must have slept with Roth's girlfriend? You know what they say—*once a manwhore*—what other explanation could there be?

"Is your team going to keep you around after your poor showing last season?" Roth said, launching yet another zinger.

Poor showing? He'd made it to the freaking Super Bowl. She didn't follow football, but she knew it was a big deal the Miners made it that far. Her friends had seen him play that day and said Maverick had played the game of his life. What was this guy talking about?

Maybe Maverick slept with the sloth's fiancée? Or wife? Or sister? Her brain continued to fire off possibilities as she waited for him to respond.

"You know, Roth, I think they are going to keep me around. I'll give it my best shot this next season, and hopefully I'll do better."

Do better? What? The only way to do better was to actually win the Super Bowl, right?

"Well, I'd start training soon. Looks like you've really let yourself go."

She gasped, glaring at Roth.

No.

He

Didn't.

She couldn't believe what she was hearing. Maverick Wallace was a lot of things, but an out-of-shape, half-ass football player was not one of them.

Roth turned to her. "And you are?"

She looked up to see Maverick's grin spread clear across his face. Why was he so amused?

"I'm Elle Fiore."

"Hmmm—haven't seen you around here before. You one of his groupies?" he said, and Maverick covered his mouth with his hand.

Elle lifted her chin and pressed a hand to her chest. "I assure you, I am nobody's groupie; however, I, too made the same assumption earlier with some ladies, so I can't very well hold it against you. But for the record, my boyfriend is related to the royal family. His name is Count Edward Efant."

Lies, lies, lies.

But she wasn't going to let him call her a groupie, and then admit to being single. She had a serious boyfriend forty-eight hours ago, so it wasn't a complete fabrication. Maverick's head fell back in amusement, and Roth stared at her blankly.

"Okay, cool. Well, I'm busy, so do you two know what you want?"

How did this guy work for Pete? He was quite possibly the worst food server she'd ever met. They quickly placed their orders, and Maverick didn't hide his surprise when she ordered a beer to go with her salad. But she didn't care to discuss her order once the sloth walked away. She wanted to know what he'd done to make the guy hate him so much.

"I'd never have guessed you a beer drinker," he said, when Roth disappeared into the bar area.

She waved her hand at him, "Yadda, yadda, who cares? Seriously? Yes. My dad's a fireman, and he loves beer. I guess it's genetic because I like it too. But it's sooooo beside the point right now. What the hell was that?"

"What? Roth?" His head cocked to the side and those chocolate brown eyes danced with mischief.

"Ummm, yeah? The guy hates you. He despises you. You slept with his girlfriend, didn't you?"

Maverick reached in the metal bucket sitting in the middle of the table, grabbed a handful of peanuts, cracked one open, and dropped the shells on the floor before speaking.

"You know, Peaches, you really have a poor image of me. I think it's good we're going to work together because I'm not nearly as bad as you think I am."

"Really. Well, we can discuss the reason I have a poor image of you another time. Right now, I want to know what you did to the sloth?"

His laugh bellowed around the patio, and he ran a hand through his wavy dark hair. He paused when Roth returned and set down the two beers in front of them. He didn't say a word to Maverick, but he smiled at her. "Here you go, Elle. You have great taste in beer. Stella is my favorite too."

Wowsers. The sloth smiled.

"I also ordered a Stella, Roth," Maverick said, with slight irritation.

Roth ignored him and walked away.

"Well, that was brutal," he said before taking a

long pull from his beer.

"Are you playing with a full stack, Wallace?" She took a small sip of her Stella. This was business, and she rarely drank alcohol with clients, but this gig would not be fast, so she'd bend the rules a bit. But alcohol and tingly lady parts never mixed well. She already experienced that disaster once and found herself lip-locked with the manwhore by the end of the night.

"Yes, I'm playing with a full stack. Why do you ask?" He rolled his eyes.

"The guy attacks your football skills. Which, excuse me if I'm wrong, because I certainly don't know anything about the sport, but from what Peyton and Jackson say, you're quite good. Yet you aren't offended when the man berates your ability and your profession? But he doesn't acknowledge your fine taste in beer—and that puts you off? Not playing with a full stack, just sayin'." She smiled knowingly.

"You seriously don't follow football? Did you know I played when we met at the wedding?"

She cringed at the mention of make-out gate. "Ugh. Definitely not. I was filled in the next day. And no, I don't follow it at all. But again, this is what you ask after what I just shared?"

He chuckled. "You are full of surprises, Peaches. All right, you want to know why Roth the sloth hates me?"

"Yes, please." She rubbed her hands together with anticipation.

"When he was a senior in high school, I was a freshman. He was the starting quarterback for three years, and they benched him his senior year and let me start," he said, leaning back in his chair. He took a pull from his beer, and she forced herself to stop staring at his mouth.

"And all these years later he's still angry about something that happened in high school? Are you serious? Why are you so nice to him?"

"His mom was my third-grade teacher. Best teacher I ever had. She passed away a few years back, after a lengthy battle with breast cancer. I feel bad for the guy. She was a special lady."

She watched as his gaze grew glossy, and he cleared his throat.

Well, hells bells.

The manwhore had a freaking heart.

"Looks like I'm not the only one who's full of surprises." She reached for a handful of peanuts.

"Moving on to a new subject, is your boyfriend's last name really Efant?" he said it slowly, pronouncing every syllable.

"Yes. Why?"

"Good luck if you marry the guy," he said, with a laugh. A cocky smirk spread across his face.

"What are you talking about?" She crossed her arms in front of her chest, prepared for an insult she could feel coming.

"Because you'll be the Countess Elle Efant. Say it fast three times, Peaches, *Countess Elephant*."

He hit the table with his hand and the corners of his lips turned up. She rolled her eyes. Of course, she realized the name issue the moment they started dating, but no one else ever mentioned it. Including Edward. Well, it wasn't an issue now. But she didn't feel like informing Maverick at the moment. Dating the Count sounded a hell of a lot more impressive than it turned out to be.

"You're sure putting a lot of thought into my married name. Why don't you focus on the fact that you just had a woman trick you into sleeping with her."

"Too bad I can't trick you, Peaches. I'm pretty sure I'd rock your world."

"What a romantic offer. Roth the sloth has a better chance of sleeping with me than you do, Wallace." She graced him with a fake smile, and he shook his head and chuckled.

Truth is—not everybody wanted their world rocked.

Chapter Four

Maverick's Playbook
Never underestimate your opponent!

He met his trainer at five a.m. the next morning for a grueling workout and parked his car beside the white shimmery Audi in his driveway. He'd asked Elle what the story was with the color of her car, and of course the question pissed her off.

Shocker.

As if he knew what the hell pearl-white was. He swore the girl made up these crazy ass colors. Glancing at the small guest cottage to the right of his house, he wondered if the princess had risen yet.

"Daisy." He walked into the kitchen. His goofy mutt liked to wait by the door for him, but today she was MIA. He grabbed a bottle of water from the refrigerator, and his gaze moved to the window. He choked on his water at the sight in the backyard.

Stepping through the back door onto the patio, he watched for a minute before making his presence known. The view so surprising, he needed to take it in. His debutante of a designer stood over Daisy—correction, straddled Daisy. Yep, one leg on each side of his ginger-colored doodle, who sat more still than ever before. Elle massaged suds into Daisy's body, the hose lay on the ground surrounded by the small puddle forming in the grass beside her.

Daisy didn't put up a fight, but who could blame her? Hell, he'd sit still if it meant Elle Fiore would straddle him and rub suds all over his body. He took her in, moving closer. Her cut-off jean shorts were sexy as shit, and her long sleeve light blue T-shirt was soaking wet. The cotton fabric clung to her skin, outlining her perky tits to perfection. Her hair was piled on top of her head in a messy bun, and her feet were bare.

Who was this laid-back, animal-caretaking chick? He glanced around in search of the giant stick she normally had shoved up her tight little ass, but there was no sign of it. A hard stream of water doused him in the face. He used his hands as a shield, and she set the hose back down on the ground.

"What the hell was that for?" He wiped his face with his T-shirt.

"It's what you get for acting like a peeping Tom, you stalker. Did anyone ever tell you it's not polite to stare?" She used the back of her hand to push a loose strand of golden hair back from her pretty face.

"I wasn't staring, I was a little surprised to find you out here washing my dog when you pretty much made her enemy number one yesterday."

"Don't be ridiculous. *You* remain enemy number one. Daisy here, I quite enjoy." She scrunched her nose before continuing. "You're quite friendly with the ladies, Wallace. Do you know many females who want to smell like urine and soy sauce?"

He couldn't help but laugh, and she rolled her eyes, appearing unamused.

"What are you talking about? Who smells like urine and soy sauce?"

"Miss Daisy here. She scratched at my door this morning, and I let her climb in bed with me. Lo and behold—a horrific smell engulfed me, hence the reason I'm out here cleaning her."

"You let her get in bed with you? I thought you hated dogs?"

She reached for the hose, and once again, the hard stream hit him right between the eyes before turning the hose back to Daisy. Maverick shook his head like a dog, water splattering around him.

"Focus, Wallace. Why in the hell do you think I hate dogs?"

He put his hands up in surrender. "You didn't strike me as an animal lover yesterday."

"I didn't like being knocked on my ass when I stepped out of the car. But I love dogs. Daisy here is the sweetest, but she smelled bad enough to gag a maggot."

Her Southern accent grew stronger, which never failed to amuse him. She turned off the water and towel dried the mutt. Daisy charged toward him and he bent down to greet her. She smelled like honey and coconut.

"What shampoo did you use?"

"Mine. She'll smell good, and her hair will be nice and shiny."

Damn, now his dog smelled like the woman who filled every dirty thought he'd had over the past year.

"Come on. I'm starving. Let's make something to eat before we meet with the contractor."

He pulled eggs and bacon out of the refrigerator and handed her a bottle of water. She crossed her arms in front of her chest, her gaze moving between him and the door. Holding the bacon up, he shook it in front of her face. "Come on, everyone loves bacon."

"Yeah, I don't eat it often, but I do love it. But um, I'll hit a market today and stock the fridge in the guesthouse. I don't expect you to feed me."

"Lighten up, Peaches. You're helping me out with the house, we're both here, no sense making meals in separate kitchens. We can share a meal, can't we?"

She narrowed her gaze, watching him. "I suppose so. It does makes sense."

Stepping around the island she moved beside him, reached for the eggs, and cracked them into a bowl before asking him where he kept the whisk.

"Third drawer on the right, but FYI, four eggs for the two of us won't cut it. You can go ahead and crack open four more."

"You're going to eat six eggs? You know that's half a dozen, right?"

"I'm pretty sure everybody knows six eggs is half a dozen, Einstein. And yes, I can easily put down six eggs."

She smiled, and an unfamiliar feeling resided in his chest. What the fuck was it about this girl that caused him to react like a little bitch? He noticed it the first time they met, and every time since. Maybe it was because she constantly shut him down. Women didn't reject him often. And this one in particular, not only rejected him, but his mere presence bothered her.

"Do you have siblings?" she asked, whisking the eggs with the intensity of a world-class chef.

"I have twin sisters. They're two years younger than me, and both pains in my ass," he said.

"Twins. Wow. What are their names? Are y'all close?"

He covered the bacon with a lid and turned on the

burner. She poured the egg mixture into the skillet and added a few seasonings before letting it sit on the heat for a bit.

"Yeah, we're close. Marley and Gigi. Marley got married last year, but Gigi's holding out for Mr. Right. How about you? Do you have a big family?" He set the silverware on the table, and she grabbed two plates.

"Nope. I'm an only child. Always wished for siblings."

Something vulnerable flashed in her eyes. It was gone as fast as it came.

"Your parents still live in Savannah?"

"My mama and stepfather, Winston, live in Savannah. My dad lives in San Francisco."

"He's a firefighter, right?" He remembered her mentioning him. He realized he didn't know much about her at all aside from being great at her job, and hearing something about her being some big pageant queen back in Georgia.

"Yep. I love going to the firehouse to hang out. It's like one big family."

"It's cool he lives close to you. Did he move out there after you did?" Flipping the bacon, he put the lid back on quick to stop the grease from splattering.

She didn't answer at first. Biting down on her bottom lip, she moved the eggs around in the pan.

"My dad lived in San Francisco first. We didn't find out about one another until I was eight years old. He moved to Savannah after he learned he had a daughter, and we've been close ever since. He went back to the West Coast when I graduated from high school, and I moved there after college." She blinked a few times.

He leaned back against the counter, stretched his legs out in front of him, and locked onto her golden topaz gaze. "It must have been tough, finding out who your dad was at eight years old. Tough for both of you. Why'd your mom keep it a secret?"

She swiped her tongue across her bottom lip, looking anywhere but at him. "Um, we both got over it, I guess. But yes, it was a bit of a shock. It was also hard on Winston, my stepfather. He thought he was my dad for the first eight years of my life. But honestly, it all made sense."

She'd been through something shitty, yet she stood there stirring the eggs, and spoke about it like it was a bump in the road. She was a hell of a lot tougher than he thought.

"How did it make sense?" He placed the bacon on a few layers of paper towels to absorb the grease, while she plated the eggs.

She sat down and set her napkin in her lap before continuing. "Well, I never felt like I fit in with Mama and Winston. I was the odd man out, you know? Winston is the sweetest man, and he really tried to be a father to me, the only way he knew how. He's very generous, always spoiling me and encouraging me to pursue my dreams. But the day I met my dad, it was like finding the missing piece of a puzzle. Ya know? We just clicked."

"Wow, that's amazing. Do you think Winston knew or suspected?"

"I think he subconsciously knew. I mean, she was a month along in her pregnancy on their wedding day. She'd obviously strayed during their engagement because she boasts about her Southern values and how she saved herself for her wedding night with Winston. She forgot it also meant you couldn't be with anyone else either." She paused to laugh. "Winston empathized with me, but he never goes against Mama. He's quite a bit older than her, and truly the kindest man. He loves us both in spite of everything," she said with a forced smile.

"And he and your mom stayed together after he found out she lied to him?"

"Yes, sir. You haven't met Caroline Humphries. Somehow, she was the victim in the whole thing. I don't know why I'm rambling on about this?" She shook her head, lips pursed, and tried to portray a girl unfazed. He didn't buy it. She was more complicated than he'd thought.

"Because I asked."

The phone rang and startled him from his thoughts. His grandmother's name, Mimi, lit up the screen.

"Sorry, I need to take this call." He put the phone to his ear, and took a swig of orange juice while Elle continued eating.

"What's up, Mimi."

"Mornin' sunshine. Can you come by and change out my air conditioning filters this morning? I tried to get on my step-stool, but I can't reach it."

"Jesus. What did I tell you about getting on a ladder? Call me or Dad, for fuck's sake." He knew the minute the words left his mouth he'd pay for it. He and his grandmother shared a very close relationship. Always had. He adored her. But she had no problem bringing the wrath of God on him when needed.

"Since when do you talk like a scoundrel? Don't make me sic your sisters on you. I can have Marley at your house in less than fifteen minutes." He heard the smile behind her voice.

"Sorry. I'll jump in the shower and head over. You can meet my designer. You'll love her, she's from your favorite city," he said, with a wink when Elle looked at him with a questioning gaze.

"She's from Savannah? You know that's where I met Poppy."

"You can tell her all about it. See you soon."

He took a few bites of eggs before speaking. "We need to swing by my grandmother's place so I can change her filters before we meet Tommy at the house."

"Does she live nearby?"

"Yep. One block over. You'll love her. Prepare to get your ear talked off." He stood and grabbed their plates and placed them in the sink before they both headed for quick showers.

Not together. Unfortunately. He wouldn't mind covering Elle Fiore's naked body in suds.

****

"It must be nice to just walk to your grandmother's house. Do you have other family livin' in Tahoe?"

He couldn't help but stare at the way her jeans hugged her ass just right. She wore a crisp white blouse tucked in, and some sort of fancy gold belt and matching shoes. At least she had on flats and not heels. They'd be on their feet most of the day.

"Yep. My parents live one block over and my sister Marley and her husband Cage, have a place less than a mile away. Gigi's in San Francisco, but she comes home often."

Taking the three steps up to Mimi's front door, he waltzed right in. It had been a few weeks since he'd last seen her.

"Where's my favorite lady?" he called out.

"Are you sure it's okay if we walk in?" Elle said, just above a whisper.

"She'll swat me on the head with a newspaper if I knock on the door, so yes, I'm positive."

"Where's my sunshine?" Mimi said. It was their shtick they always said to one another. She stepped out of her bedroom in her favorite white housecoat splattered with little pink roses. Her gray hair styled in tight curls close to her head, and ridiculous fuzzy pink slippers covered her feet.

Lifting the tiny woman off the ground, he hugged her tight, twirling her a little before he set her back down. She laughed, fixed her hair, and turned to Elle.

"Well, aren't you darling. What's your name?"

"Mimi, this is Elle. I'm going to go grab the new filters from the garage and let you two visit."

"Nice to meet you, Elle, please come sit down. I've a fresh pitcher of sweet tea," She said .

Still reeling from their conversation over breakfast—she'd surprised him with what she shared. In the past she'd always been closed off where he was concerned. Maybe he was making some headway with her.

He stood on the ladder and heard a loud ruckus down the hallway. His mother and sister, Marley were there, greeting his grandmother and Elle. Mimi must have called and told them he was coming over with his designer. *Traitor.* God forbid they didn't know his every move. As much as he loved his family, they were nosy as shit.

He finished and walked to the living room to find

the four women drinking tea and laughing. His grandmother's gaze grew wide when she noticed him standing there.

"Look who popped over." Mimi patted her curls in place around her face. A habit whenever she was up to no good.

"Hey, Mom. Hey, Mar. I was going to stop by after I met with the contractor today. Is Dad golfing?" He wrapped his arms around his mother and pulled her into a hug. He talked to his mom and grandmother most days, and his sisters almost as often.

"Hi, sweetie. You didn't tell me Elle was staying in the guesthouse. I'd be happy to bring cookies over and load her refrigerator with snacks."

Elle smiled wide as she took it all in.

His sister punched him in the arm, before giving him a side hug. "You told me you'd be home tomorrow."

"Changed my plans and came up yesterday. I wanted to get the house started as soon as possible. I didn't find out Elle was going to be here until yesterday. She was in France on vacation and just got back."

"Ooooh, I love France." Mimi rubbed her hands together.

"You've never been anywhere you didn't love," he said.

"Well, Miss Elle knows the story of how Poppy and I met in Savannah now." Poppy passed away seven years ago, but the love between his grandparents lived on through her.

"What a relief. I didn't know how I'd make it another minute if we didn't fill her in," he said, and all four women chuckled. "We need to get going. The contractor is waiting at the house."

Elle jumped to her feet and hugged his mom and his sister goodbye. When she reached Mimi, she hugged her the longest. "Thank you so much for the tea and the romantic story about your husband."

"You're always welcome here, dear." Mimi beamed.

Marley typed her cell number into Elle's phone. "I want to show you where all the good shops and boutiques are."

"I'll bring cookies over later," his mother insisted.

"Come by for tea in the morning," Mimi said.

He rolled his eyes at how quickly his family inserted themselves into one's life. They'd never met a stranger—and they took a particular liking to his designer.

"Your family is amazing," she said, as he led her down the street to the new house.

"They are, for a bunch of nosy-ass hens. Still a few you haven't met, but they're equally impressive," he said.

She giggled. "They're keeping you in line."

His family was such a presence in his life. Yes, they pushed the boundaries when it came to personal space, but he wouldn't have it any other way. It must have been lonely for Elle growing up as an only child, in a house full of secrets. Though he wasn't born a Wallace, they'd never treated him any different, and he'd be forever grateful. Maybe knowing that nobody's life is perfect would comfort her. He didn't share his personal life often, but somehow telling Elle about his, after what she shared, seemed like the right thing to do.

"Are you wondering why there's not much of a family resemblance?" he asked with a laugh. His mother and sisters were fair-skinned, with blonde hair and blue eyes. He stood out among the rest of the Wallace family like a sore thumb with his tanned skin, dark hair, and dark eyes.

She bit her bottom lip and looked up at him with a smile. "I thought maybe you resembled your dad?"

Running a hand through his hair, he chuckled. "Nope. My parents adopted me from an orphanage in São Paulo, Brazil when I was four years old."

She nodded. "Do you know who your birth parents are? Or how you ended up in an orphanage?"

"My biological mother was a prostitute. She overdosed when I was pretty young. My parents, the ones who raised me, were on a medical mission in São Paulo and somehow found their way into my orphanage. My mom said she knew I was hers from the moment she laid eyes on me. The rest is history."

Elle stopped walking and pulled her sunglasses from her face. "That's incredible."

"Looks like we have something in common after all, Peaches."

"What?" she said, her gaze glossy and full of emotion.

"We both found our families a little bit later than everyone else."

The corners of her mouth turned up, and he resumed walking, with Elle in tow.

"The way your grandparents met is so sweet. She was a nurse, and he was a marine. It sounds like somethin' out of a movie." She sighed and trailed behind.

"He was a few years older than her. Did she tell you he asked her out a dozen times before she finally gave in?"

"Yeah, she may have mentioned it." Elle laughed.

"It's her favorite part of the story. Apparently, it's a Wallace trait." He slowed until she walked beside him.

"What is?"

"Perseverance."

He watched her out of the corner of his eye, and she didn't hide the smile as it spread across her beautiful face. That feeling he got when he threw a winning pass to his receiver, a mixture of pride and satisfaction—it's what he felt right now. Why the hell Elle Fiore's smile was as good as a fucking touchdown, was a mystery.

And Maverick didn't care much for mysteries.

Chapter Five

Elle's Tip of the Day
Beware of handsome manwhores!

A loud bark outside the guesthouse startled her from sleep. It took a moment to get her bearings. She'd never slept better than she had this past week. The fresh air, the break from the hustle and bustle of the city, and the long hours they put in at the house left her collapsing into bed at the end of each day. Plus, having the world's sweetest dog wake you up every morning was—comforting.

Edward had returned to San Francisco, and she was glad she'd opted to stay in Tahoe over the weekend. Dani and Peyton missed her but understood. Edward not so much. He texted saying, *—I want to discuss things—*

She texted back, *—There's nothing to talk about—* They were through.

—Take care of yourself, Edward, I hope you find someone to make you happy, but it isn't me—

Having time to reflect, she knew without a shadow of a doubt it had been the right decision to end things with Edward. Sure, attending fancy parties and dressing up like a princess every time they stepped out together was fun. But it didn't constitute a relationship. Sadly, and maybe most importantly—dating Edward had impressed her mother, which still meant something to Elle, even now.

Astonishingly, she didn't mind being in Tahoe one bit and looked forward to spending time at the lake over the weekend. Maverick wasn't nearly as bad as she'd expected, and they worked surprisingly well together.

When he chose not to annoy her.

He'd opened up about his adoption, probably because she told him about her mother lying to her about who her father was. She didn't know why she told him something so personal. She rarely shared her childhood secret with anyone aside from her two best friends, but for some reason it was easy to talk to him. He'd somehow become more human to her over these past few days—but the man was still an egotistical, selfish manwhore. She hadn't realized he had a few redeeming qualities outside of his good looks.

She'd shared sun tea with Mimi, Maverick's grandmother, every day this week and looked forward to their daily conversations. Mimi reminded her of her own grandmother, Estelle, who had passed away a few months before Elle relocated to the West Coast.

Pushing back the covers, she hurried to the front door to let Daisy in. "Come on in, girl." She led her four-legged friend to the bedroom. Daisy jumped up on the soft white down comforter. Elle leaned down and wrapped her arms around the sweet pup. Thankfully, Daisy no longer reeked of urine and soy sauce.

"This coconut shampoo makes all the difference, Miss Daisy."

A loud bang on the door caused her to jump and nearly fall off the bed.

"Peaches, you in there?" Maverick's loud voice

bellowed from the front porch.

Jesus. Where the hell else would she be this early in the morning? He was awfully needy for a non-committal guy. Always walking over to see what she was doing when they weren't working at the house, which was basically the hours she slept. Rolling her eyes, she marched to the door, and pulled it open.

"What?"

He waltzed right past her, sporting basketball shorts and nothing else. His chiseled chest glistened with sweat, and his wavy hair dripped as he brushed it away from his handsome face. He crushed a plastic water bottle in his hand making a cringeworthy sound.

"Is this how you greet Daisy when she stops by?" He scanned her body from head to toe. Didn't even try to hide his slow perusal.

She hated how her body perked up every time he looked at her. She moved to the kitchen a few feet from the front door. The space was suddenly too small and intimate. The man had game. No denying it. He was obviously a natural at wooing the ladies—but she wasn't buyin' what he was sellin'.

"No. Daisy doesn't pound on the door and come over drippin' sweat. Maybe I need to take you out back and hose you off?"

She grabbed two water bottles out of the refrigerator and handed one to Maverick. His mother dropped off a plate of delicious cookies, which sat on the counter. Elle ate most of her meals next door at Maverick's house as they usually met before they started their workday and ended with dinner out, or at his place.

"Do you *want* to hose me off, Peaches?" A slow

smile spread across his face. His dark brown gaze was so intense at times, as if it could see into her soul.

She swallowed hard before taking a long drink of water to get her body under control. Her Prince Albert resistance-therapy was an epic fail. She'd never experienced anything close to the physical attraction she had to this man. Never. Of all the people to react to—why did it have to be to the most unattainable man on the planet? She wanted a prince who only had eyes for her, not a playboy with the libido of a teenage boy.

She crossed her arms over her chest, suddenly aware of the flimsy-white pajama top doing nothing to hide the way her body betrayed her in response to his words. She tugged on the matching pink and white pajama shorts, as they barely covered her behind.

"What do you need? It's early. I haven't even brushed my teeth yet." She didn't hide her irritation, a defense mechanism to keep him at bay.

"Just finished my run and thought I'd stop by and see if you wanted to grab breakfast before we get started today. A friend of mine owns this little diner up the road."

She tried not to stare at the script running across one side of his chest. Over his heart to be specific. She never noticed it before. God knows the man was shirtless every chance he got. She normally refused to look at him, but right now—it was impossible to look away.

"What does your tattoo say?" she asked before she could stop the words from leaving her mouth.

"See for yourself, Peaches?" He moved closer, and she worried he could hear her heart racing.

Flaunting her best dramatic eyeroll, she looked up,

inches from his sweaty, chiseled chest. "But without the dark, we'd never see the stars."

"Well, when you say it all breathy and sexy, it sounds like a line from a porno." He smirked and his gaze locked on hers.

"Shut up. I'm hardly breathy, you perv. I just woke up. But I like the sayin'. Not at all what I expected from you." She moved away from him. Needed to put some distance between them.

His head cocked to one side, "I can't wait to hear what you thought I'd tattoo on my body."

"Hells bells—I don't know." She flung her arms in the air. "Maybe somethin' like *sex me up*, or *I'm gonna get me some*." She purposely turned up her Southern twang with a side of sarcasm.

His boisterous laugh vibrated off the walls of the kitchen, and she couldn't help but join him. He tipped his head back and drank, every ripped line of his abs on display. Damn, his tanned skin glistened in the light pouring in through the kitchen window. My God. She needed space from the man. They worked together. Ate together. Practically lived together as the guesthouse sat only steps from the main house. Thankfully, it was only for a few weeks. She was doing this for baby Jojo after all. That's what she kept telling herself.

"You're insane, Peaches. And I'm fucking starving."

"Fine. Let me get dressed. Give me fifteen minutes."

"Cute jammies. Can I watch you change out of them?" His hot and hungry gaze made her belly flutter, and he playfully wriggled his eyebrows.

"Well, bless your pea-pickin' little heart. You're

quite the wishful thinker. Don't let the door hit you in the ass, Wallace."

"All right, see you out front in fifteen," he said, with a wink.

Elle hurried down the hall and splashed some cold water on her face, saying a silent prayer that this attraction would die down before being foolish enough to act on it. For a second time. Because if she were to ever kiss Maverick Wallace again, she was certain she wouldn't have the gumption to stop.

****

"I can't believe I let you talk me into this." She climbed into his truck. The stars lit up the night sky above like something out of a movie.

She'd joined him for breakfast, worked alongside him most of the day, shared a pizza after their ten-hour workday at the house, and now they were going to meet his friends at a country bar a mile up the road.

"Talk you into what? It's a bar. You'll meet a few people, have a beer, hear some good music. It's hardly a big deal. Don't worry, I told my friends you aren't single so no one will hit on you."

Great. Her ridiculous need to make him think she had a boyfriend meant she couldn't flirt with any single men. Even the non-manwhores.

Maverick wore a fitted white T-shirt which stood out against his deep bronzed skin and made her girly parts all tingly. The white cotton showed off his spectacular upper body the way it clung and strained against defined muscles. His dark jeans hung low on his hips.

Confident. Cool. And sinful.

"Well, it certainly hasn't stopped you from hitting

on me." She raised her brow in challenge.

"You haven't seen anything yet, Peaches. This is banter. I do it out of pity."

"What the hell are you talking about?" She was unable to hold back the snarl in her tone.

With one hand on the steering wheel, he used the other to reach for the water in the center console and flashed his panty dropping smile. "Your boyfriend is an old man. I figured his skills were rusty, so I thought I'd throw you a bone."

She rolled her eyes at the ridiculousness of his statement. "You're lyin' like a no-legged dog, Wallace. And Edward is forty. He's hardly old."

His head fell back, and his loud laughter filled the interior as he pulled into the parking lot of Willy's Brewhouse. "What's the deal with this guy? You have a thing for old dudes? Or do you have a thing for royals?"

Though he likely meant it as a joke—he hit a nerve. Why was she dating a guy who was more than a decade older than her, and not interested in starting a family or the kind of future she wanted? He put the truck in park and faced her. When she met his gaze, he studied her with an intensity that knocked the wind from her lungs.

"Shit. I was kidding. I didn't mean to hurt your feelings." He reached over and ruffled her hair.

She huffed and patted her hair back in place.

"You didn't hurt my feelings. It's a fair question. He's a friend of the family. Mama actually set us up." She swallowed hard as she took in his confused stare.

"Really? I don't know a lot of parents who want their daughters dating old men."

"Well, you haven't met my mama. Her husband is

much older than she is. Sadly, she's more concerned about the title and the bank account than the age." She lowered the visor to look in the mirror, needing an escape from his questioning stare.

Her mother would be appalled she was going to a country bar, drinking beers, and having fun. One more thing to add to the list of disappointments.

Why must you be such a Fiore? Mama's words rang in her ears, and Elle pretended to fumble for something in her purse. It was a sinking feeling she found overwhelming at times. Like fighting to hold your head above water when the current refused to offer a reprieve.

"You don't strike me as a girl who isn't capable of rebelling a bit. Hell, you're like a living, breathing firecracker waiting to ignite. You're not the kind of girl who dates a guy to make her mom happy. Or are you the one who cares about the title?"

Wow. Like fingernails on a chalkboard, he had a way of irritating her. He knew nothing about her. How dare he compare her to her mother? Her reasons for dating Edward were different.

"Nooooo. Mama introduced us, and Edward is a nice man. Charming even. And sure, him being a Count from France was appealing, but not for the reasons you think." She raised her chin and held her head high.

"An old guy with a royal title? What other reason is there than the obvious?"

He was no longer joking or teasing. He purposely pushed her buttons as he waited for an answer. They'd become friends over the past week. Sort of. And though she never had a friend who owned all her dirty fantasies, he genuinely seemed to want to know. But it wasn't something she even knew how to explain.

"It's going to sound really stupid."

"Like normal then?" He smirked. "Spit it out, Peaches."

"When I was a little girl, I was obsessed with fairy-tales. Mama always told me if you kissed a frog, you'd wind up with a frog. Her favorite saying was, *go out and find the man with the biggest castle, and call him a prince*. Terrible advice, right?" She paused as a lump formed in her throat.

"Yeah, not the best philosophy. Go on."

"Well, Louisa, our housekeeper slash nanny, she gave me all the classic fairy-tales, and I kept them under my mattress. I'd read them all the time as a kid. Somewhere along the way to being a drop-out debutante, an embarrassing disqualification from the pageant world, and thoroughly disappointing every dream my mom ever had for me—I held out hope my real-life prince was out there. And he'd see me for who I am. Imperfections and all. And love me, in spite of it. I know it sounds stupid, and maybe it is. But when I met Edward, he was so enamored with me. He likes who I am. He's a gentleman, very chivalrous, and I guess I like that. And sure, his home being a castle—it doesn't hurt the fantasy. And finding someone who isn't disappointed with your every move, is a fairy-tale in itself."

Why the hell did she have diarrhea of the mouth with this guy? Dammit. She'd never live this one down. She waited for the laughter. She'd just admitted to holding out for a fairy-tale. Hence the meaning of the word—magical and imaginary beings and lands. Ridiculous. Not to mention the fact her prince had already turned into a frog. Again.

His fingers landed beneath her chin and forced her gaze to meet his. The contact so unexpected and electric, she sucked in a shaky breath. He didn't smile or laugh. His dark brown gaze filled with kindness. Empathy. Understanding. Who the hell was this man, and where had he put the manwhore?

"I don't think it's stupid. You deserve the fairy-tale, Peaches. And I understand wanting to be accepted for who you are. I think it's what we all want. No shame in that. Is this guy the real deal?"

She wanted to tell him the truth, but something kept her from saying it. Maybe the safety of Maverick Wallace believing she were in a relationship helped to keep things platonic. At least outside her imagination.

"Too early to tell," she whispered.

A fist pounded against the window. She jumped.

Maverick rolled down his window. "Still assholes I see."

Loud laughter boomed from outside his truck and he chuckled. "You ready?"

"Yep. Let's go have some fun."

Maverick began the introductions as soon as they got out of the truck. "This is Nick. He teaches at the high school we attended and coaches football too, and Ryland here is the most successful realtor in Lake Tahoe. He sold me the lake house."

"Anything for Mav." Ryland pounded Maverick's back and grinned at Elle.

There was a comfort between them, which she recognized because it was similar to what she shared with Dani and Peyton. She sent them a selfie of the group, and Peyton and Jackson responded right away as they grew up with these guys as well. The night blew by in a blur as she was having a great time.

"Here you go, Elle." Nick handed her yet another beer. Her fourth maybe? Plus, the shot of tequila she downed with Nick and Ryland. Normally, she didn't indulge in so many cocktails, but being in this quaint country bar, up in South Lake Tahoe, with no expectations from anyone—she enjoyed the moment.

"I shouldn't." She giggled. "But I don't have plans tomorrow, so why not?" Usually her type-A personality didn't allow her to cut loose. Always so much to do, plans to make, and goals to achieve. She'd been chasing something for as long as she could remember. Approval, maybe? From someone incapable of giving it to her. The logical side of her knew it, but her heart—her heart wanted to mend things with Mama. Always had.

The renovation on Maverick's house was going well and she was confident in her design vision.

"That's the spirit." Ryland laughed and clanked her glass with his.

She played darts, laughed a lot, and ended up leading a line dance, per the crowd's insistence, but it had all been in good fun. She fanned her face when she returned to the table, sweatin' like a sinner in church. The place packed to the hilt, and the music filtered through the dimly lit bar with tables disbursed all around the rustic wood dance floor. The smell of sweet barbeque lingered in the air around her.

"Thank you for the beer, Nick."

"Are you kidding, you stole the show out there. Mav didn't tell us you were a professional line dancer," Nick said. "And having a gorgeous woman at the table instead of being stuck with these assholes, it's the least I could do."

Ryland balled up a napkin and threw it across the table at his friend. "Such a suck up."

They laughed and Elle's gaze landed on Maverick across the table. Is it possible for someone to get better looking while sitting in a chair?

The man was like a tall drink of—*fine ass.*

She burst into a fit of giggles at her jumbled thoughts, and how flustered he made her. Her head fuzzy and her hands tingled. His stare locked with hers, but not with the hunger she saw earlier. Now his gaze held a protective reverence. It left her warm inside. Or was it the booze?

"You doing okay, Peaches?" he asked, taking a sip of water.

She longed to feel those soft lips against hers. Setting his glass down, he smiled, as she stared at his mouth like her life depended on it. She didn't care. She was more interested in the things he could do to her with his mouth, than any judgment he could throw her way.

She shook her head and lifted her gaze to meet his. "Why aren't you drinkin'?"

"Someone's got to look after you, right?" His smirk so sexy, her lady bits were on overdrive.

"Mav here never has more than one beer. He's more of a boy scout than he lets on," Ryland said.

Elle leaned back in her chair and took a slow sip. Since when did beer taste this good? Like sweet tea on a sweltering hot day. Smooth and delicious. "I've never had such good beer before. Never ever. What in the world did you order me?"

Maverick's laugh boomed, and she tried to focus on his beautiful face, though it looked a bit blurry. She hadn't realized Ryland and Nick left the table. She and Maverick were alone for the first time since they arrived.

"You're drinking Coors Light, Peaches. I'm sure you've had it before."

"Hmmm—this must be a special kind of Coors Light. Imported from some sort of magical kingdom." She fell back in a fit of giggles.

"Must be."

"You never drink more than one beer? Then how have I seen you drunk before?" Were her words slurring? She stuck her tongue out and moved it back and forth to make sure it still worked.

"I can assure you—you've never seen me drunk." His elbows rested on the table where he sat across from her.

The haze of people moved around her. Most of the women sported short skirts and cowboy boots. There were more crop tops here than spring break in Ft. Lauderdale during her college years. She wore a fitted white tank top, cut off jean shorts, and her favorite cowboy boots.

"Duh. The first time we met. At Jackson and Peyton's wedding," she said, leaning forward to whisper her next words, "When we, you know…"

He leaned in close, his face so near she could feel his warm breath tickle her nose. She closed her eyes as he spoke. "We made out. That's your big sinister secret? And one of us was drunk, but it sure as shit wasn't me."

She opened her eyes and gasped at the sight of him.

She slowly pointed and counted aloud because seven sweet, chocolate, brown sugar eyes scattered around his face. She leaned back in her chair; her fuzzy vision cleared when she put distance between them. "Whew. No worries, you've got two eyes again." She swiped a hand across her forehead in relief. "You don't want to know how *ridiculous* you looked with seven of those beautiful eyes scattered around your handsome face."

He licked his lips, and she watched so closely she could almost taste it. She remembered how soft and minty his kiss had been.

Commanding.

Perfect.

"Why'd you assume I was drunk?"

"Because we wouldn't have behaved like fools if we weren't heavily intoxicated. I'm hoping you were three sheets to the wind the following night when you took me to dinner and acted like you were going to hell on a scholarship," she said, her temper rising. Thinking about their date still enraged her.

Maverick's head fell back, and a smile spread across his face. His eyes crinkled on the sides when he met her gaze. "You've got it all wrong, Peaches. I hadn't had a sip of alcohol either night. I was doing the opposite of what you think."

She pushed, sitting up straight, as she'd always wondered why he acted like such a pompous ass that night.

Focus.

Focus.

Focus.

"And exactly how were you doing the opposite of what I think?" She accepted the glass of water he pushed toward her and took a big gulp. Not as tasty as the world's best Coors Light, but fine for now.

"I was trying *not* to go to hell on a scholarship."

"Well, you weren't trying very hard," she said, before dipping her tongue right into the glass of ice water in attempt to get it to stop tingling.

"I think we better get you home, we can finish this conversation when you aren't icing your tongue," he said, a big, sexy smirk pulling at his mouth.

She lifted her face from the glass and used the cocktail napkin to dab the sides of her tongue to see if it worked.

"Me and my tongue are just fine."

Her gaze went wide as two arms wrapped around Maverick's neck and long brown hair cascaded down his chest, and someone leaned down and kissed his cheek. Elle swallowed hard and fought the need to dive across the table and scratch the woman's eyes out. When her head lifted, Brittney's stare locked with hers.

Brittney.

She'd been at Maverick's house the very first day she arrived in Lake Tahoe. It seemed like such a long time ago, yet it had only been a week. She hadn't seen any women at his house since, but maybe he smuggled his ladies in after she went to the guesthouse each night. Nick and Ryland slipped back into their seats beside Elle and neither appeared happy to see their new guest.

With her hands planted on Maverick's shoulders, and two skanky looking girls flanked on each side of her, she scanned the table.

"It's my lucky day. Ryland Nick, good to see you," Brittney said, oozing sarcasm before meeting Elle's gaze. "Oh, wow. I didn't recognize you outside of your *white linen* outfit. I can't think of your name, though? You're on Mav's payroll, right?" Her tone was half evil chuckle and half snarl. Her posse laughed behind her.

Oh, no, she didn't.

She was barking up the wrong damn tree.

Maverick removed Brittney's hands from his shoulders. "What the hell are you doing, Britt?"

Elle didn't need Maverick to defend her. She could take care of herself. Always had.

Elle snapped her fingers, and the other woman looked up, surprised. "My name is Elle Fiore. And if memory serves, I'm not the only one working for Maaaaav." She pushed to her feet and threw Brittney an exaggerated wink.

Ryland spattered beer all over the table. Nick fell back in his chair laughing. Clearly, these guys weren't fans of the she-devil, Brittney either. Maverick stood, tossed some money on the table. "All right, we're leaving."

Brittney glared, turned to look at Maverick as if he were a meal she was about to devour. "I'm sure the help needs a ride home. But call me later and I'll stop by, 'kay?"

"Not happening." His voice came out harsh.

"Hey, I have an idea. How 'bout I *help* you meet me out front," Elle shouted. She'd had enough of this girl's crap. She held up her arms in fight position. Peyton's husband Jackson happened to be one of the best MMA fighters in San Francisco and he'd taught her self-defense moves. Brittney gasped at the invitation to fight. Elle may be a lot shorter than her, but she was scrappy, and she'd taken on bigger opponents than this before.

All three men howled in laughter before Maverick wrapped his arm around her waist. "Okay, Champ. Let's get you home."

She hugged both Ryland and Nick, glared at Brittney over their shoulder, and moved toward the door. Maverick's hand rested on her lower back as he guided her through the parking lot.

"Sorry about Brittney," he said, his voice gruff.

"It's fine. The girl is slicker than snot on a doorknob, and she can kiss my grits."

He opened her door, helped her into the truck, and reached over and buckled her seatbelt. "So you don't like her then?"

She laughed and stared at him for a long moment before leaning back against the seat. He shut the passenger door. He'd surprised her several times this week with his kindness.

"I think we're actually going to be friends, Wallace." She fell against his shoulder.

He pulled out onto the road. "I think you're right, Peaches."

"You're not as horrible as I thought you were."

He wrapped an arm around her to keep her from sliding any further, and she nestled closer.

"Good to know." And though she wasn't looking at him, she could hear the smile in his voice.

"But you have terrible taste in women."

He parked in the driveway and helped her into the guesthouse. Her face hit the bed before her body, and though she desperately needed water and aspirin, she couldn't remember the last time she'd had so much fun.

Chapter Six

Maverick's Playbook
If all else fails—tackle your opponent!

"Where do you want the cooler?" Ryland asked. His girlfriend Tara walked behind him holding a pile of beach towels in her arms.

"Just leave it all here on the deck." Maverick whistled for Daisy to get out of the water.

"You don't want me to take these up to the house and throw them in the wash?" Tara said, dropping to sit on a chair.

This was the first time he'd taken the boat out from the dock at the new property. Though the house was going through major renovations, he could do what he pleased with the yard. Elle and Tommy had made some serious progress in a short amount of time, with most of the demolition completed. Elle, being a little drill sergeant, kept everyone on track.

"Nah. I'll take them up to the house later."

"Dude, your dog is a beast with the frisbee," Nick said, as he and Jen stepped onto the deck with Daisy in tow.

He glanced down at his phone for the millionth time today. "Yeah, she'll fetch anything. Frisbee's, balls, socks. If you throw it, she'll bring it back."

"I'm bummed I didn't get to meet Elle," Jen said,

sitting beside Tara.

"She's something else," Nick said with a grin. "You'll both like her."

Ryland nodded. "Keeps our boy here on his toes."

Nick and Ryland had gone on and on about his designer today. She made quite an impression on the two men last night, which he assumed was the norm for her. She was a captivating woman. She oozed charm, and her being hot as hell sure didn't hurt. The sight of her in those cut-off jean shorts and a thin white tank top clinging to her perky tits after she got all sweaty on the dance floor was engrained in his mind forever. Two cold showers later and he still couldn't sleep last night, struggling to think of anything else. Probably good she didn't answer her phone this morning when he decided to take the boat out, per his friends persistent nagging. The fact Ryland, Nick, and the girls showed up with four bags of groceries to fill the coolers, made it hard to turn them away.

Maverick stopped by and knocked on Elle's door before he left, but she didn't answer. Hell, even Daisy pouted for a good thirty minutes when she didn't open the door for her this morning. Her car still in the driveway, he assumed she was sleeping it off. She'd had a lot to drink last night, and the girl couldn't hold her liquor for shit, but she was cute as hell when her guard was down. The way she offered to step outside to fight Brittney nearly undid him. Small and mighty. They'd formed the start of a friendship working together this week, and the last thing he needed to do was piss her off by crossing any lines with her. Especially when she was drunk. It hadn't gone over well the first time around, and it took her over a year to move past it.

But shit.

He fought the urge to cover her sweet mouth several times over the night. And yeah, she had a boyfriend, but each time her gaze locked with his, he knew she felt the same attraction he did.

Sexy. Sultry. And needy.

"Yeah. You guys will like her. She's a lot of fun. I'm sure she'll go out on the boat one of these weekends. We still have a long way to go on the house, so there's plenty of time."

The sun faded into the horizon. Orange and red hues mixed with muted yellow. The turquoise water glistened beneath, looking like a fucking painting. Maverick never felt more comfortable or at home than he did in Lake Tahoe, where he'd grown up. A place where he wasn't just an NFL quarterback, but a regular guy who'd gone to school, worked his first job, and instigated his fair share of teenage shenanigans. Hell, with the older locals, he was best known for being Mabel Wallace's grandson than San Francisco's quarterback. Mimi was a legend. At seventy-eight years old, you could still find her on a pair of water skis or taking out the jet ski. He liked to think he got his love of adventure from her, maybe not biologically, but from the large presence she had in his life. He glanced down at his phone again, still no response from Elle.

"You sure are checking your phone a lot. It's Saturday, she has the day off," Nick said, razzing him like the asshole he was.

"Fuck off. We work together. Just making sure she's okay. She had a lot to drink last night." Maverick reached for the pile of towels as they all walked around to the front of the house where they parked.

"She had a couple beers and a good buzz. She was hardly drunk enough for you to be worried. Hell, maybe you should be more concerned about your psycho girl, Brittney. What the hell is her deal? Elle didn't take her shit at all. It was the best thing I've ever seen," Ryland said, with a chuckle. His car beeped as he unlocked the doors.

"Shit. When she put her fists up in challenge, I think Britt pissed her pants," Nick said, tipping his head back in laughter.

"Damn, I'm so bummed I missed it. I'd enjoy seeing Brittney put in her place," Tara said, pushing up on her tiptoes to hug him goodbye.

"She was a bitch in high school, and she's never changed. She thinks everyone's beneath her. It's about time someone stood up to her," Jen said, with an apologetic shrug before he hugged her as well.

"Thanks for telling me now," Maverick teased. He knew who Brittney was. She'd always been sugary sweet to him, but only because she wanted something from him. He'd witnessed the other side of Britt on occasion. But their families were old friends, and they'd grown up together. He wasn't dating her. They shared a bed; a couple dozen times over the past decade.

"See you this week, asshole. Thanks for today," Nick said, and they all shouted their goodbyes.

Maverick tossed the towels in the wash and took a quick shower. He ordered a pizza and pulled the garbage to the curb.

Daisy walked alongside him down the driveway, and the chirping of crickets filled the quiet night. Stars lit the sky above, and the water sparkled in the distance.

Daisy let out a loud string of barks and took off toward the guesthouse. Maverick followed, squinting to see the blur of movement through the pine trees.

Elle Fiore—hauling ass down the small path near the house. She all but jumped out of her skin when she noticed him and Daisy walking toward her. Crunching leaves and pinecones, along with Elle's heavy panting surrounded them. She reached for her earbuds and yanked them out.

"You scared me. What are you doing?" Her Southern twang full of irritation.

"The better question is what the hell are you doing?" he said, his arms crossed in front of his chest.

"I went for a run. What are you talking about?" She bent down to pat Daisy on the head, and the dog fell in a messy pile at her feet.

"You went for a run alone at night? While listening to music? Are you fucking kidding me?" What the hell was she thinking? And why the fuck did he care so much?

"I'm sorry, *Dad.* Did I break curfew?" She cocked her head to the side in challenge.

He chuckled. "It's called common sense. You shouldn't run alone at night with music blasting in your ears."

"Please. This is Lake Tahoe. Are you telling me you've never run at night while listening to music?"

His laughter echoed around them. "Yeah, I'm twice your size. I don't think anyone's grabbing me from behind."

"You're such a chauvinistic ass. I can take care of myself." An eyebrow raised as if she dared him to challenge her. Her running shorts barely covered her ass, showcasing toned, tanned legs which only pissed him off more. Her sweaty tank top clung to her body, and her face was completely bare of makeup.

Fucking stunning. And agitating at the same time.

"Really? Like it or not, Peaches, I could take you to the ground with no effort. If you want to be stubborn and claim you're some sort of hundred pound badass, suit yourself." He snapped his fingers for Daisy to follow and turned toward his house. He was done trying to talk sense into her. She had a stick up her ass once again.

"Hey." Her voice laced with anger.

He stopped and turned to face her. Two hard peaks formed beneath her wet tank top. Seeing as though it was hot as freaking hell tonight, either she had a thing for needy goldendoodles, or she was reacting to him. She put on this tough front like she was unaffected by him, but he didn't buy it. He saw her with her guard down last night, and her body was betraying her now.

"Did you need something?" His tone flat.

"First off, don't ever guess a woman's weight. And seeing as though you're a good twenty pounds off, you don't know what you're talking about, genius. Lastly, just because you're bigger than me, does not mean that you can take me down without a fight. You're so wrong."

"Am I?" He took a step toward her, and her chin lifted defiantly.

Maybe it was time to teach the little prima donna a life lesson about safety. Stubborn girl. Lost in her fairy-tale world.

Life isn't all rainbows and unicorns, sweetheart.

She raised an eyebrow and smirked, before shifting

on her heel and storming away. He took the opportunity to charge her from behind. She turned at the sound of pine needles snapping beneath his feet and gasped as he came up on her and wrapped both arms around her center. She reacted like a motherfucking caged tiger. She twisted to face him, unable to break free from his grasp. She flailed every single moveable body part with an unexpected force, and her knee came up and nailed him in the balls.

Son of a bitch.

He fell forward and braced their fall with one hand on her back, the other reaching for the ground as they went down hard. He landed above her. Her chest heaved against his, and she used her now free arm to grab his hair in her fist and pulled hard.

Jesus.

He planned to show her how easy it would be for someone to catch her off guard, but he sure as shit hadn't prepared for a high school girl fight. He'd underestimated the strength of Elle Fiore.

She was a motherfucking Tasmanian devil. Scratch that. She was a motherfucking kung-fu-ninja-Tasmanian devil. He'd fought with dudes growing up that didn't put up half the fight she did.

He wrapped his fingers around her wrists and pinned them above her head as she gasped for air, and continued to squirm, burying her face in his shoulder.

Was the little heathen surrendering?

Wishful thinking.

His shoulder wrenched like he'd been stung by a pack of bees. Not the case.

She fucking bit him.

He pressed her wrists harder above her head and

leaned more weight on top of her hot little body as she writhed beneath him.

"Get off me, you baboon." Her topaz eyes deepened with anger.

"Did you seriously just bite me?" He brought his nose above hers, mouths so close it'd be easy to graze her lips with his. He'd been in a constant state of want since the day she arrived at his house.

"You better believe I bit you," she said, still panting, though her body no longer fought to get free.

He eased his fingers from her wrists, still hovering above her. Enough contact to feel every curve of her gorgeous body pressed against his.

"You're a little scrapper, Peaches." He laughed, looking down at her. Her radiant face lit by the moonlight beamed with pride.

"I'm guessing your *balls* are feeling it about now," she said with a wicked grin.

If she only knew. His balls had been feeling it since the day her haughty ass pulled into his driveway. It had much more to do with her presence than the knee she nailed him with. No pun intended.

"You concerned about my balls, Peaches?"

She laughed, this vibrant sound that had his chest tightening.

For fuck's sake. First blue balls, and now her laugh had him reacting like a schoolgirl with a crush. She wasn't getting his goddamn man-card without a fight.

"Your balls are the least of my concern, Wallace." She smiled, and a pink hue spread across her cheeks.

Fucking adorable.

"Oh yeah? Well, you should be concerned about running alone at night. You get that now, right?"

"Fine. Can you get off me? I can barely breathe, you barbarian." Her words didn't match her body. She arched a bit, pressing herself closer to him.

"What does the Count think about you running alone at night?" He wanted to know more about her boyfriend. And while he had her full attention, he'd ask.

Her gaze darted away from his and her teeth sank into her bottom lip. The little vixen was nervous about something.

"Cat got your tongue, Peaches?" His voice gruff.

She faced him again. Daisy scampered around chasing her tail, paying them no attention.

"Edward and I broke up," she whispered.

Surprised, he watched her closely. "Today? Is that why you didn't answer your phone or the door?"

Her tongue darted out to wet her bottom lip and it took all he had not to nip at her plump lip. He waited for an answer.

"No. We broke up while we were in France. I didn't feel the need to advertise it," she said with an apologetic shrug.

Interesting. She sure as hell made a choice to lie to him. Was it to keep him at a distance?

"Well, at least you won't be the Countess Elephant. What a relief."

"It's obviously the reason I ended it," she said dryly.

"I thought we were friends. Do you lie to all your friends?"

She reached up and pulled a pine needle from his hair, her fingers lingered longer than necessary before she tossed it to the side.

"We weren't officially friends until last night,

remember? Which is why I'm telling you now."

He wanted to kiss the cocky smirk from her mouth.

"So why didn't you respond to me all day?"

She rolled her pretty eyes. "I needed a *me* day. We've been spending a lot of time together."

He knew their chemistry scared the shit out of her. The pull that lived between them. And it should scare her. Because if she ever wanted to act on it—he was all in. And they both knew he could never give her what she wanted.

Elle Fiore wanted a prince on a white horse. Maverick wanted her naked in his bed. Even still, desire surrounded them like a magnified force.

He turned to see headlights coming down the driveway.

"You hungry, Peaches?"

"What?" Her gaze filled with confusion, as he pushed off her and helped her to her feet.

"I ordered pizza. Delivery guy just pulled up."

"Oh, sure. I need to take a quick shower and rinse off first." She turned and started toward the guesthouse.

"See you in a while, *friend*," he said, walking the opposite direction.

"I bet I'm the first female friend you haven't slept with." She moved inside and shut the door.

She was correct. At least as far as all his single female friends went. But sleeping with Elle Fiore wasn't a good idea. Jackson warned him. Peyton warned him. Hell, even he had warning bells going off every time she was near. But damn, if he didn't want to.

He met the delivery guy in the driveway and dropped the box on the kitchen counter. Daisy followed him to his bathroom as he reached in and turned the water on in the shower.

He'd spent ten minutes on top of the woman consuming his every fantasy. He could still feel her warm, soft skin beneath him. He needed a cold shower like a dying man in the desert needed water.

He may as well turn off the hot water heater, because he didn't see anything but ice-cold showers as long as his designer was living next door.

Taking in the little bite marks on his shoulder as the water blasted him, he laughed. She didn't break his skin, but damn, if she hadn't marked him. And the crazy thing about it—he was proud of her. The girl was fierce.

The only thing more consuming than her was football. But Elle was turning his world upside down.

And that he couldn't allow.

Chapter Seven

Elle's Tip of the Day
Take what you've got and light it on fire!

The walls were down, and the refigured floor plan looked amazing. Tommy and his team worked hard to complete the demo quickly and get the new layout put in place. The floors were bare, and the kitchen and bathrooms had been gutted. The cement flooring was still covered with sawdust and remnants from the teardown. A chalky scent of drywall filled the air. The wood plank flooring had been delivered along with endless décor pieces Elle had ordered. Boxes were piled high in the center of the room.

Nothing beat a blank canvas for a designer. An opportunity to create something unique and special. The changes were already dramatic, and she and Maverick stood in the entryway and took it all in.

"Holy shit, Peaches. You were right about those walls." His hand landed on the top of her head, gripping it like a football.

"Is there some reason you continually palm my skull every time I make a design choice you agree with?" she said with annoyance. He chuckled and removed his unusually large hand. She combed through her hair with her fingers.

"I could always tackle you again if you prefer?" He

rested his hands on his narrow hips, shoulders back, and his strong broad chest on display. Proud as a peacock. He stared straight ahead at the incredible view of the lake and she took in his handsome bronzed profile. It was too difficult not to stare. A blind woman on a galloping horse couldn't miss his gorgeousness.

The memory of him lying on top of her left her all squirmy and anxious. In his quest to prove a point about safety, he damn near gave her a glimpse of every, last dirty thought she'd ever conjured up.

Damn Maverick Wallace and his hard, masculine body. And damn his manly smell. It had become her kryptonite. The man weakened her resolve faster than a hot knife moved through butter.

"If you ever pull a stunt like that again, I swear I'll slap you to sleep. You know, you're awfully touchy for a Neanderthal."

She moved toward the boxes, grabbed a pair of scissors, and opened the stack of packages. He reached for her notepad of sketches she'd drawn for the kitchen design.

"You can slap me to sleep anytime you want, Peaches. These drawings are impressive. You're more talented than you give yourself credit."

This was the thing about Maverick Wallace—he paid attention to detail and noticed the stuff most people didn't. Even her mama believed Elle just shopped for pretty things for clients. Maverick treated her like an artist perfecting her craft. He was smart, and genuine, and real.

"Thank you for appreciating the work…seeing something special," she said.

He winked and she rolled her eyes, but they both

knew she didn't mean it.

She hadn't met a man like him in a long time. Aside from her dad and Winston, of course. Maverick saw more than a pretty little package who'd competed in more pageants than she wanted to count. He saw more than the girl who shamed her family and lost their so-called legacy. Sure, Edward had been a gentleman. Chivalrous and charming in his sleek tuxedos each time they attended formal events together. He was regal and charismatic. But he'd never taken an interest in her career, or in her personally. They'd never discussed her childhood or that she'd learned who her biological father was at eight years old, or how hard her mama had pushed her to win every pageant she entered.

Though the manwhore strode into her life on a giant jackass in lieu of a white horse—he proved to be more of a prince than she wanted to admit. He wasn't capable of being with one woman long enough to invest in them.

****

"Are you looking forward to going home this weekend?" Maverick asked, as he settled across from her at a table at Pete's.

"I am. It's my dad's birthday. I'm excited to see Peyton and Dani, and of course, baby Jojo. How will you survive without me?"

Maverick Wallace weaseled his way into her circle of trust, which she never expected. Tomorrow she'd drive back to the city and put a little distance between her and her new bestie.

"I don't know, Peaches. Who would have guessed we'd become such good friends, huh?"

"Definitely not me," she said. "But with me out of

your hair the next couple days, think of all the ladies you can entertain at the brothel."

"How do you know I don't have women over now? It's not like you sleep at the house," he said, a frown took up residence on his face.

His demeanor changed. The man was normally all tease and charm. She'd obviously hit a nerve. But she always teased him about his lack of commitment, so why take offense now?

"I guess you're right. I have no idea what goes on after I leave." A tightness squeezed her chest. Why did she care? They were friends. Nothing more.

He raised a brow and gave her a nod and Roth approached the table. They'd been to Pete's four times in the past two weeks, and Roth was their server every time. He grew friendly with Elle, but his hostility toward Maverick hadn't dimmed.

"Hey, Roth."

"Hello, Elle. I see you're still gracing this one with your presence." He thrust his thumb in Maverick's direction, a look of disgust on his splotchy face.

Maverick rolled his eyes. "She sure is, Roth."

"I saw you guys running down the highway this morning. I'm surprised you can keep up with her, Wallace." The disheveled man frowned.

"I do my best," Maverick said, setting down his menu.

Country music trickled through the bar and the sweet smell of barbeque made her stomach rumble. The sun was going down, and golden orange hues seeped in through the windows cascading a warm light throughout the cozy room.

After the caveman, who currently sat across from

her, gave her a lecture about the safety of running alone at night, he convinced her to run with him a few mornings a week. He made this big deal for her not to stress about keeping up with him. You know, *because he was a professional athlete and all.* She enjoyed every second of his arrogant spiel about his speed and agility, because she knew it wouldn't be a problem.

And—it wasn't.

Maverick Wallace was in amazing shape, no doubt about it, and his pace was quick. But Elle had been running for as long as she could remember. Running to escape expectations she could never meet. Running toward a life she hoped to find far away from Savannah. It had always been an outlet—a break from her reality. She'd challenged him the whole time. They were both drenched in sweat and gasping for air when they finished.

"I suppose you have to if you want to keep your job," Roth said, and Maverick smiled with a nod.

Roth the sloth raised his pen to his pad. His movements so slow she grew impatient as she watched. She placed her order and waited for what seemed like a lifetime for him to scribble the words down on paper. Maverick copied her order. She wasn't sure if he wanted the same thing, or if he just couldn't bear to watch the man write down something different.

"He's such a jerk to you. It doesn't bother you?" she asked once the sloth walked away.

"Nah. He's got issues, so if throwing a few insults at me makes him feel better, have at it."

Instinct told her there was more to the story there, but he seemed a bit off tonight, so she didn't push.

"I heard Jackson's coming to see you this weekend.

You guys will have fun."

"Yep, they're finally starting work on their lake house. He wants to see what his contractor's got in mind. We're going to take the boat out and hang out with a few old friends tomorrow night."

Jackson and Peyton bought the old pizza place. Joseph, the man who raised Jackson, owned it when they were young. They decided to make it a family vacation home. The property held a ton of memories for them, not to mention it sat on a beautiful property on the water.

"You guys grew up here together, right? Were you always close?"

"Yeah. Jackson and I have been tight since we were kids. Lost touch for a while after everything went down with his sister. He shut everyone out during that time. But I found him a year or so later, and we picked up where we left off. Now that we live in the same city, it's like it was when we were kids. I'm looking forward to them having their own place up here too."

Jackson's sister, Chloe, had been caught in the middle of a violent fight between their drug addict mother and her drug dealing boyfriend the summer before they all left for college. Chloe lost her life in a horrific way, and it took Jackson nearly a decade to move forward with his own life.

"Yeah, Peyt's excited to get things going with the house. She can't wait to bring Jojo up for summer breaks like she used to."

"Man, Jackson used to count the days until summer when we were young. I remember we'd ride our bikes over to the Krofts' house, and wait for Peyton to arrive," he said with a laugh.

"They were destined to be together, huh?"

"I think so."

Roth set their food down, and they dug in.

"You don't think you're destined to meet your soulmate?" Curiosity got the best of her.

He thought about it before speaking. "I guess I found mine already."

"You did?"

"I found it on the field. Football is my center. Guess everyone's fairy-tale is different, Peaches."

Football was his fairy-tale? As in, his soulmate? Was he serious? He sure believed so and he was happy as a pig in poop about it.

"Interesting. So, since you play football you can't have a relationship? Do all football players feel the same way?" She took a bite of her salad.

"No. I think everyone's different. I have relationships. But my priority is the game. It's my job and my passion. It's what I do best—well, with the exception of one other thing." He wriggled his eyebrows at her.

He'd just compared his football skills to his bedroom skills. If he was as good in the bedroom as everyone said he was on the field, he had reason to brag. The man was clearly talented. And oh my, did it just get hot in here? Because right now, she was hotter than a goat's butt in a pepper patch.

"Have you ever had a girlfriend?" She wiped her sweaty hands on the napkin resting in her lap under the table.

"Of course," he said, licking the sauce from his fingers. Elle bit down hard on her bottom lip, fighting the urge to dive across the table and take a little sample for herself.

"You've had a *serious* girlfriend?"

"Sure."

"What's your longest *committed* relationship?"

"Does it only count if I was with the same girl the whole time?"

Her head fell back in laughter. "Um, yes. It's not a committed relationship if you're with multiple women."

"Says who?" He displayed his sexy smirk which continued to do crazy things to her lady parts.

"Says me and most of America."

He smiled and dropped his napkin on his plate. "Well, then I guess about six months."

Longer than she expected.

"You never cheated?"

He frowned. "Christ, Peaches. Do I strike you as a cheater? You seem to be confused."

"About what?"

"There's a difference between not wanting to be in a committed relationship, and not being capable of being in one. I'm very capable. It's a choice. My choice. So, no. I've never cheated on anyone I was in a relationship with."

So defensive.

"Sorry. I shouldn't have assumed."

"You know what they say about assuming…"

"I do."

"So how about you? Let me guess. You've always been a relationship girl?"

"Yep, pretty much."

"Let me hear about all your magical courtships."

"Well, I dated James Ratcliffe, correction, his formal name is James Ratcliffe the second. We dated all through high school. Mama was thrilled because the Ratcliffe family is well-known and respected in Savannah." She used her haughtiest voice and laughed.

"What happened to poor James and his highfalutin family?"

She closed her eyes and shook her head. "James really was the sweetest guy I've ever dated. He came to all my pageants and helped me practice for my talent on the weekends. He was such a gentleman too. Never tried to have sex with me either. And we dated for four years."

He choked, spatting water across the table. "You're shitting me right now. You dated the guy for four years during some of the horniest years of the poor bastard's life, and he never tried to have sex with you?"

"Correct. I always believed he was protecting my virtue. But sadly, it wasn't the case. James came out of the closet to me at our senior prom. I think he knew I expected somethin' to finally happen between us, so he confided in me." The memory made her cheeks warm. She hadn't seen it coming. She all but threw herself at the handsome boy, and the rejection had been a huge blow to her ego.

Maverick's head fell back, and his hands hit the table as loud laughter bellowed through the restaurant. "You're fucking serious? The dude dates what I can only guess was the hottest girl in the school for four years, and then tells you he likes dudes at your senior prom?"

"Thank you for not laughing," she hissed, and tried to cover her smile. It did sound ridiculous.

"Had you suspected? Let me guess, you thought he was your prince?" he said.

"Well, we were nominated prom king and queen earlier in the evening, so it sure seemed like a fairy-tale. I mean, aside from the fact my prince wasn't heterosexual, it could have been magical. We really were the best of friends. Still are very close. I took it hard at first, but we eventually got past it."

"You sure are full of surprises, Peaches. So, four years is your longest relationship, yeah? And there was no sex involved. Fascinating. I've had four-hour relationships that involved sex."

She rolled her eyes. "Nope. I dated Will Sanders all through college and another year after we graduated. It lasted a whole five years."

She wasn't proud of this relationship. Will Sanders was a snake in the grass. The worst kind of all.

"And what happened with our dear Will? Did he respect your virtue too much to sleep with you too?" he said with a grin.

She didn't laugh. Five years of her life wasted on a guy who wasn't worthy of a minute of her time. He took things from her she should never have given.

"He had no problem taking my virtue and promising me the world. He was an egg-suckin' dawg. A cheater and a scoundrel. I can't believe I stayed with him for as long as I did. Let's just say, he was a really good liar."

She swore she heard Maverick growl. His dark brown gaze filled with empathy. This big, rugged man was a teddy bear at heart. "He sounds like an asshole. Why'd you stay so long?"

"Great question. He was the master of manipulation. He begged and pleaded for me to stay even when I caught him in the act. He wanted to have his cake and eat it too. I had just lost the Miss Georgia Pageant, and everyone was so disappointed in me. He used it to his benefit. Probably the only time in my life I allowed insecurity to get the best of me. Not a proud moment."

For the first time in a long time, she felt undeniably vulnerable. Did he sense it? His gaze softened, as if somehow this beautiful, strong man had ever felt insecure or vulnerable a day in his life.

"Who was disappointed in you? Didn't you win a shit ton of pageants?" His stare locked with hers.

"Mama. My boyfriend. My coaches. Neighbors. Pretty much everyone in town, with the exception of both my dads, my grandmother, and a few close friends. My mother and my grandmother were both Miss Georgia back in the day. It was sort of my legacy. I'd won everything up until the one that mattered most."

"Are you fucking serious? You have no control over the judges or the competition. It's completely subjective. How could they be upset with you? Did you even like being in pageants? Was it your passion?"

"Isn't that the million-dollar question. I honestly don't know. It's just something I was expected to do from the moment I could walk. I think my passion was trying to please my mama. And even though you can't control all the outside factors, you can control your own performance. Mama believes I purposely messed up the talent portion of the competition. She thinks it cost me the title. And trust me, when Caroline Humphries isn't happy, she can be meaner than a wet panther." Elle fiddled with the napkin in her lap, twisted the corners into tight little points. The memory still stung. A time in her life she'd been worn slap out. Unsure what to do with her life.

"I'm glad you had your dads and your friends to support you through it. Shit happens sometimes. You can't always be perfect." A wicked grin spread across his face. "You've got to tell me what your talent was, Peaches. I'm dying here. So many to choose from."

"Well, it had forever been baton twirling. Me and batons—we've always been one. With the help of good ol' James Ratcliffe the second—I was the first person ever to use flaming-batons for my talent." She couldn't help but laugh. Her mama nearly collapsed when she'd shared her new skill, but the judges were taken with the daring talent.

"Flaming. Fucking. Batons. It's so you to take your skill and light it on fire."

The way he looked at her nearly melted her right there in her seat. He had a way of making her feel good, even when remembering the lowest point of her life. She took a sip of water, needed a distraction from their conversation.

"Did you drop the baton? Set the stage on fire?" he said with a laugh.

"I'd only had one serious accident in the two years of training with the damn things. I'd set the poor Ratcliffe barn on fire. But thankfully, we were able to free all the animals before the whole thing went up in flames. James' mama never did forgive me for it, though. But what happened at the competition was not my doing. It was out of my control. I dropped the baton because I was setup by my nemesis." Anger spewed, as an old fury took hold of her.

Thoroughly entertained, Maverick's gaze danced with excitement. "Who's your nemesis? Please tell me you both got naked before you whooped her ass?"

"I did no such thing. I could never prove it. I know Suri Sandemeyer put some sort of Crisco on one of my batons. The thing was slicker than a greased hog when I tossed it in the air."

Maverick laughed so hard his eyes watered, and his face flushed with an adorable pink hue across his cheeks. Everyone always found the whole thing ridiculously funny when they heard what happened. But at the time, the drama had consumed her life. In every way.

"Please tell me," he paused to pull himself together, "Sarah Sunflower did not win the Miss Georgia competition."

"*Suri Sandemeyer* certainly did not win Miss Georgia. She went on to trip and fall during her dance routine. The poor girl squirmed like a worm in hot ashes. And you know why, don't you?" She leaned in close to him from across the table.

"No, tell me."

"The guilt slapped her in the face like a redheaded stepchild. And Suri Sandemeyer was karma's bitch."

Neither of them could contain their hysterics.

"Amen to that. May little Miss Sandemeyer spend the rest of her days wallowing in shame," he said through his laughter.

For the first time in what seemed like forever, Elle found humor in her painful past.

"You know what, Peaches?"

"What?" She dabbed her eyes with her napkin.

"You just might be my favorite person," he said with a wink.

Her stomach did all sorts of crazy flips and twirls.

Because, truth was, right now—Maverick Wallace might be her favorite person too.

She tilted her head and smiled. "You're not so bad yourself, Wallace."

"Obviously."

"Am I really the first single female friend you haven't slept with?"

He thought about it for a minute. "Yes. I believe you are. But we could rectify that if you'd reconsider the value of meaningless sex. Friends with benefits. All that good stuff."

"Nope. I'm sticking to my guns and holding out for Mr. Right. What if he showed up here and found me in your bed being frivolous and carefree? He and his white horse might gallop on by," she said.

"Damn you and your morals, Peaches. I have a hunch you'd enjoy playing with my flaming baton."

Dear God. She could feel her cheeks heat.

"You can keep your flaming baton in your pants, and far away from me. Why don't you light yourself a fire with one of your ladies while I'm gone this weekend?" she said it in good fun, but her stomach wrenched.

Because the thought of anyone touching Maverick Wallace's flaming baton—it made her madder than a shamed beauty queen with a slick baton.

Chapter Eight

Maverick's Playbook
Don't be afraid to call a different play!

He walked along the property line where Jackson and Peyton were building their vacation home. His arms stretched above his head, intertwining his fingers behind his neck. He'd finished his workout when Jackson arrived at his house. They grabbed a quick breakfast and drove over to meet the contractor Jackson hired to start the remodel. He'd shared Peyton's drawings for their home.

Impressive as shit.

Peyton was a master at her craft like Peaches. The designers at Shine were a step ahead of the rest, which is why he'd hired their firm.

Well, mostly the reason.

He'd made amends with the woman who shunned him for the past year. Unfortunately, now he was in uncharted territory. Somewhere between *want* and *can't*. But goddamn if he didn't want this girl more than he'd ever wanted anyone. Anything.

Maybe even as much as he wanted football.

Maybe.

Never thought he'd say those words. He was going out of his fucking mind over this girl. Maybe it was because he hadn't gotten laid since the day the hot little firecracker showed up in his driveway.

They had a connection. No doubt. More than a physical pull living between them. A constant battle of self-restraint and desire. When she told him about her college boyfriend mistreating her, he knew if he ever saw the guy, he'd rip his throat out. And her mother—the person who was supposed to shelter her from the things that caused her pain. He guessed Elle's mom was at the crux of most of her hurt. Shaming her for not winning a pageant? Who the fuck does that? If his path ever crossed with Caroline Humphries, he'd take the opportunity to tell her how fucking amazing her daughter was.

Strong and vulnerable. Stubborn and sweet. Maddening and endearing.

What the fuck was going on? The girl had seeped beneath his skin. Like water flowing slowly through sand. Quietly consuming every granule. Taking hard grizzly edges and making them soft and smooth. And there wasn't a damn thing he could do about it. She wanted the fairy-tale. The prince on the horse. All the bullshit he didn't buy into. Hell, he couldn't if he wanted to. But damn, if Elle Fiore didn't deserve it all.

He needed to shake himself of this girl. She'd been gone for two hours and he was, antsy.

Anxious.

Irritable.

"What do you think?" Jackson asked as they walked down to the water.

An overcast sky hovered above as they stood on the beach. Grays and blues overpowered the golden hues fighting to bleed through. The weather matched Maverick's mood this morning.

Gloomy. As if the sunshine had gone away. Maybe it had.

"I think it's a phenomenal piece of land. Peyton's sketches for the place are amazing. I'm glad you aren't going to tear down the old structure. Too many memories, man. Tying the restaurant into the home is brilliant. Keep the history intact, right?"

"Absolutely. We want to build the main house closer to the water and away from the road. But making a little guest cottage out of the old building allows us to keep it for sentimental reasons. Shit ton of memories there."

"Yeah. I think we all grew up in there. You and I got into our fair share of trouble a couple times when we were young. Now you'll have a place for your kids to get into all kinds of shit when they get older," he said, before picking up a rock and skipping it across the water.

"Speaking of the guesthouse. How's it going with your guest? You two getting along?"

A slew of fucking butterflies hit his stomach hard. Fucking butterflies. He wasn't on his way to a goddamn middle school dance. But just the mention of this girl did crazy shit to him. What next? He'd get his period? Start reading blogs for fashion tips?

"It's going all right." He kept his voice steady. Unaffected.

Jackson reached for a rock, skipped it through the water. They took turns throwing stone after stone. They'd spent hours doing this as kids.

Out of his peripheral Jackson studied him. "Yeah? She doesn't hate you anymore?"

Jackson had always been able to see through his

bullshit.

"I don't think so. We got past it. We're friends."

Jackson narrowed his gaze. "Good. I think. You aren't messing around with her, are you? You can't fuck around with Elle, dude. No kidding. She's family. She's not that girl. Not like Brittney, or some of the other girls you fuck around with."

He let out a long, irritated breath. "Jesus, dude. I'm not a total dick. Trust me, I know she's not that girl. We kissed at your wedding, and she didn't speak to me for a year. Nothing's going on. We're friends. I like her. I wouldn't do anything to hurt her."

"That's a relief," he said with a chuckle.

But he didn't miss the undertone of what his friend said. Hurting Elle was not an option. Hell, he felt as protective over her as Jackson. Most likely in a different way. But still, the same common goal.

"I get it, man. I spend every waking minute with her. I'd beat someone's ass if they hurt her." And he meant it.

"Good to know. I guess Elle's ex-boyfriend, the Count, is trying to win her back. Dude took her to meet his family in France, and let his daughter shit all over her. I'm proud as hell she stood up for herself. The guy's too old for her anyway. I met him once. He's a tool. Who gives a shit if he's royalty, right?" He reached down and snatched another rock, sending it sailing across the water before continuing. "He knows he had a good thing, and he was stupid to let it go. He sent flowers to the Shine office every day this past week. Peyton brought them all home to save for Elle, and our house looks like a goddamn florist. Apparently, she hasn't responded to his texts, and he doesn't know she's still in Tahoe."

Maverick's hands fisted at his side. Was she going to see him this weekend? The fucker needed to stay the hell away from her.

"She's too caught up in this bullshit fairy-tale, and she keeps dating the wrong guys. Fucking pisses me off." He chucked the stone from his hand so aggressively, it bounced in a jagged pattern across the water.

Jackson turned toward him, his friend's stare burning a hole in the side of Maverick's face. Jackson didn't speak, just watched him.

Maverick kept his expression relaxed. "What?"

Jackson's head fell back, and the asshole's laughter bellowed and bounced around the tall pine trees surrounding them. His words came slow. "You. Like. Her."

The jackass kept his voice low making sure no one heard them. As if this were some sinister secret. They'd had their share of those. Jackson Vance was as trustworthy as they came. Loyal as hell. The guy always had his back.

"There's no one else here, asshole. Stop acting like you work for the goddamn FBI. I already told you I like her. We're friends." He raised a brow in challenge.

"I know what you told me, dickhead. But this is different. You like her. Holy shit. I always knew one day you'd get knocked on your ass. Should have guessed it would be a sassy Southern belle who didn't put up with your shit."

"You're insane. You're dreaming this up. Yes, she's hot as fuck. Funny as hell. Smart. Talented. Shit, Elle's the whole package. But I'm no prince, and I sure as shit don't have a white horse. I'm not looking to sweep anyone off their feet. Aren't you the one who's been warning me to stay away from her for the last half hour?"

Jackson shook his head. "No, man. Obviously, I don't want you to fuck around with her. She's not as tough as she portrays. She'd never get past it. But, Mav, you know I think of you like a brother. You're one of the best people I know. If you actually like her, want to give it a shot, that's a different story."

He ran a hand over his face. "Relationships aren't for me. Too complicated. Too much room for failure. And you and I both know I'd fail." There were things he couldn't even tell his best friend. Reasons he couldn't be in a relationship.

"If I had to put my money on anyone not failing, it'd be you, Mav. But I understand your apprehension. You don't want to mess this up. Don't act on it unless you're all in. At some point you're going to want more than meaningless romps. And you did date Madison for a few months."

"Yeah. There's a perfect example of why I don't do relationships. I had to get a goddamn restraining order when it ended."

He gave it a shot. Went without sleep for months, which affected his game. They fought constantly over things he couldn't explain to her. He didn't want to. And when he tried to end it, she went batshit crazy.

"Didn't she sneak in through your window, dressed in lingerie?"

"Yeah. Caught her in the bathroom poking holes in my condoms. I sure can pick 'em, huh?" He and Jackson both laughed, shaking their head at the memory.

"Yep. It was insane. Look, dude, I get it. Peyton and I went through a lot of shit. You know our story. And I promise you won't have a choice if it's the real deal."

"Why?"

"Because there's nothing more consuming than loving someone. Not even football. Trust me. You can't run from it."

"Jesus, dude. No one said anything about *love*. Not happening. Now you're acting batshit crazy. You aren't going to walk in my room dressed in sexy lady panties tonight, are you?" He wanted to change the subject. The conversation made him uncomfortable for reasons his friend couldn't understand. Getting Elle Fiore out of his head was the only viable option.

Jackson's head fell back, and a grin spread across the bastard's face. "You can be such a dickhead sometimes. Give yourself a break, Mav. You're a good guy."

"Okay. Do you want to run to the store and grab some tampons now, or are you done menstruating?"

He was done talking about it. Didn't need the distraction. Time to get his head on straight and get ready for the season.

Jackson rolled his eyes. "Dude, don't go there. If I've learned anything from being married—you never joke about a woman's cycle."

"You're such a chick. Now you're talking about *cycles*? I think we need to get you back in the ring."

He liked to give Jackson shit about the fact he hadn't had a fight since little Jojo came into the world. The dude was a badass MMA fighter before he got married. Hell, he understood why it was time to step away, but it didn't mean he wouldn't razz him about it.

"Don't make me kick your ass, douchebag. Becoming a dad made me realize I needed a break from fighting. There's more to life than getting punched and choked. Plus, Peyton worries too much about this pretty face of mine."

"Like I said, the drugstore is right up the street. I'll even get you an ice cream cone, unless you're feeling bloated?"

"Fuck off, dickhead. What time are we meeting Nick, Ryland and the other assholes to take the boat out?" Jackson asked as they walked toward the car.

"We've got an hour before we need to head back to my place."

"Good. Let's swing by and see my girl. I miss me some Mabel Wallace. She always liked me better than you anyway," Jackson said with a smirk.

"She did not. I've always been her favorite."

He pulled out onto the road and headed down toward Mimi's house as they bantered back and forth. Just like old times.

Maverick's phone vibrated in the center console and he reached for it, but Jackson slapped his hand away. "You do know that texting and driving is six times more dangerous than drinking and driving, right? Don't be a douchebag."

"Are you always this bitchy when you have your period?"

Jackson laughed and took it upon himself to read Maverick's text. *Shit. Here we go.*

"Awww, it's a text from Peaches. But I can see here she's responding to the needy, desperate text you sent earlier this morning demanding she text the minute she arrives in San Francisco. Who's the bitch now, asshole?"

Maverick rolled his eyes. "Dude, she's my designer. We're in the middle of a project on my house. Obviously, I want her to be safe."

He wasn't even buying his own bullshit.

"Right. Like I said, brother. All-consuming."

"Never going to happen. My day one is football."

He pulled into Mimi's driveway, and Jackson handed him his phone. "Keep telling yourself that. But you and I both know you're dying to text her back. You keep looking over at your goddamned phone like it's your lifeline. I'm going in to see my favorite lady while you text your *friend* back." He used two fingers from each hand to make air quotes like the dickhead he was.

Jackson pushed out of the car, while Maverick remained plastered to his seat and looked at his phone, reading Elle's message.

—Hey. Made it here safe and sound. How was your workout? Miss me yet?—

She had no fucking idea.

—Not the same without you, Peaches—

—You going soft on me, Wallace?—

His mind immediately went south—going soft would not be the words he would use to describe what was happening where she was involved.

—Never. You happy to be home?—

—Yes. Off to have lunch with Dani, Peyt, and baby Jojo. Birthday dinner with my dad tonight—

No mention of her ex-boyfriend. Or the flowers. Interesting.

—Sounds good. Have fun—

—You too. Text you later—

When he stepped inside Mimi's house, he found she and Jackson huddled on the couch like two schoolgirls gossiping. He let out an irritated breath to alert them both of his presence.

"Tell us, did she agree to go steady with you?" Jackson asked in a high-pitched voice.

"Has anyone ever told you you're an asshat?" Maverick said, before leaning over to hug Mimi. Jackson erupted in laughter and his grandmother pulled away and swatted him in the face with her hanky. Who the hell used hankies anymore?

"Maverick Wallace, you will not use that language in this house," Mimi said before sliding back on the floral couch she'd had since the pilgrims discovered the new world. Her lips turned up in the corners and she shook her head at him.

"It really is offensive, Mav. And to speak like that in the presence of a lady. *Shameful*," Jackson said with a dumb ass smirk on his face.

He shot Jackson the bird before he poured himself a glass of sweet tea and took a seat in the chair across from them.

"Probably quiet over at your place with Elle gone?" Mimi said.

He glared at his friend. Obviously, he'd encouraged her, and it would never end now. She'd be like a dog with a bone.

"She's been gone for a few hours. I've hardly noticed."

Fucking lie.

"Well, I've noticed. I enjoy my daily chats with her."

"She's back tomorrow night, Mimi. I'm sure you'll survive until then."

"So insensitive, Mav." Jackson's lips turned up in the corners and he wrapped an arm around Mimi's shoulders.

Maverick didn't hide his irritation, but in truth, it had a lot more to do with a certain someone being gone than it did with Jackson being a first-class asshat.

Elle Fiore was almost as consuming as football.

Almost.

Chapter Nine

Elle's Tip of the Day

What's good for the goose ain't always good for the gander!

Her heels clanked against the metal stairs as she, Dani, and Peyton made their way to the kitchen at the firehouse armed with loads of Chinese food, a cake, and birthday decorations. Of course, her dad chose to work on his birthday. So, she put on a dress and heels and brought the party to him. No one deserved a celebration more than Nick Fiore. He fought fires and saved lives, for goodness' sake. Most importantly, he was the most consistent, positive force in her life. Had been since the day he'd entered it.

"Well, look who the cat dragged in. Bring it in, Little Fiore," Billy Stark shouted. Everyone at the firehouse referred to her dad's best friend as Billy Goat. He took the bag of food from her and set it on the table before pulling her into a big, suffocating hug.

"Hey, Billy Goat," she said with a laugh, before he set her back down on the ground. "These are my besties, Peyton and Dani."

"Nice to meet you, ladies. Your dad's been looking forward to this visit all day."

Loud voices entered the room before their bodies followed.

"There's our girl," Axe and Westy, two of the older guys on the crew said.

They took turns lifting her off her feet, and she introduced them to her friends. Big Jim and Turbo helped set out the food, and she swatted Axe's hand several times when his finger dipped into the icing on the cake. The girls helped her tape up a few decorations before she ran up one more set of stairs to get the birthday boy. The guys called her dad, Hollywood, because of his good looks. They loved to razz him about resembling George Clooney.

She peeked in the doorway and found him sitting on the bed tying his boots. The room held six beds lined side-by-side with a small table separating each one. It always smelled like an odd mixture of Irish Spring soap and beef jerky. A peculiar smell, yet she'd grown used to it. A photo of the two of them at her college graduation sat on his nightstand.

"Happy birthday, Dad."

He pushed to his feet and made his way to her. "How're you doing, Short Stack?"

Elle's father, along with his three brothers, her uncles, were all tall men. Each one fell between six foot two and six foot four. She clearly took after her mother when it came to her blonde hair and her height barely reaching five foot four inches. He enjoyed teasing her about it.

"I'm good. Happy we get to celebrate you tonight," she said, and he followed her down to the kitchen.

Everyone sang "Happy Birthday" as they entered the room, and he greeted her two best friends with a hug.

She had enjoyed lunch earlier, catching up with

Peyton and Dani and spending time with Jojo. Between her trip to France and current job in Lake Tahoe she hadn't seen the little munchkin in nearly a month.

She'd gone to Peyton's house to see the slew of floral arrangements Edward sent to the office. He'd texted her a few times over the past few weeks, but she hadn't responded. There wasn't anything to discuss. They didn't have a future. It was important for her to be with someone who wanted to build a life together, and Edward Efant was not that man.

Her mind kept wandering back to Maverick. She wondered if he'd be out on the prowl with her being gone. The man was probably thrilled to have some freedom. Though she needed space from him, it wasn't because she craved it. They were growing too close. The lines were blurring, at least for her, and a little distance would help get her head on straight. Maverick proved to be a good guy, and she liked their friendship, but it couldn't go anywhere, so she'd need to keep herself in check.

"You still with us, Short Stack?" Her father pulled her from her thoughts.

"Yes, of course. Just a little concerned. It looks like your plate might not be able to hold that mound you have there." She laughed, noting he had enough kung pao chicken and sweet and sour pork to feed a small army. Her dad had a ferocious appetite, which made her think of Maverick, who ate as much as her father did.

"I think this will hold me over for a little while. Tell me how the lake house is coming along in Tahoe," he said, before they all started eating.

"It's going to be spectacular. The timeline is a little longer than I anticipated, but I don't mind being there.

It's peaceful. I spend most of my days down at the house with Maverick. The home sits right on the lake so it's not a bad way to spend your days."

Peyton beamed. "I told you he wasn't a bad guy."

"Yeah, no more nemesis talk, huh?" Dani flashed a wicked grin.

Elle rolled her eyes. "Turns out he's not so bad. We've actually become friends. I'm pretty sure I'm the first single female friend he hasn't slept with."

Her father choked on his Orange Fanta and she chuckled at his reaction.

"Well, let's keep it that way, okay?" Her dad forced a smile.

"Hey, why not date the guy and score us some free tickets to a game or two this year," Billy Goat shouted with laughter.

"You want me to date a manwhore just so you can score some free tickets?" Elle raised an eyebrow in question and Dani and Peyton fell back in a fit of giggles.

"What the hell is a manwhore?" Axe asked, around a mouthful of sweet and sour chicken.

"You know, someone who moves from woman to woman faster than a knife fight in a phone booth," Elle said matter-of-factly.

The dining room erupted in laughter. Dani leaned in and whispered, right after a text from Maverick came through. "The manwhore sure does text you an awful lot."

She scooped up her phone and dropped it into her purse so Dani wouldn't see just how often he really did text her.

"Keep your voice down. The last thing I need is

Billy Goat nagging me for tickets," Elle said, keeping her tone quiet.

"She's right, though. The man has been texting you all day." Peyton raised her brow in curiosity.

"I'm designing his house. He's just asking questions about…things." Her cheeks heated, and she caught her father staring at her with a smile.

"I thought you despised the guy," her dad said.

"I don't. He's fine." She shrugged. My God, what happened to a girl having the right to change her mind.

"Well, I vote for the *manwhore*. I love you, Li'l Fiore, but you know I'm the Miner's biggest fan. You need to work your magic and score yourself a date before the season starts," Billy Goat said in his boisterous voice from the other end of the table.

"You don't know dipshit from apple butter, Billy Goat," she hollered back. "He's the last man on Earth I'm going to date." The table exploded with laughter.

Her dad leaned in so only she could hear. "Short Stack, just because someone isn't settled down in their twenties, doesn't mean they never will. He's young, and he's a professional athlete. The man's got a lot of pressure on him. Nothing wrong with playing the field till he meets the right woman." Her dad hadn't settled down himself. He liked to say he only had room in his life for her. He'd had a few serious girlfriends over the years but never chose to marry. It made her sad. She didn't like the idea of him growing old alone.

"You don't even know him. Why in the world are you defending the guy?"

"He's a damn good player, and I've seen a bunch of interviews with him. He seems like a stand-up guy. Plus, isn't he a lifelong friend of Peyton and Jackson?"

her father said with confusion.

Peyton pushed right into their conversation. "He certainly is."

Elle rolled her eyes and reached for the phone in her purse as it continued to vibrate.

—When are you coming back? Daisy is depressed without you. She smells like soy sauce and urine again—

She covered her mouth to keep her laughter in check before noticing her father, Peyton, and Dani watching her.

Shaking her head, she said, "He's a very needy manwhore. He wants to know when I'm coming back because the dog smells like soy sauce and urine."

Her dad's gaze narrowed. "You're getting awfully friendly with this guy, huh?"

She waved him off. "He's a client. We have the same friends, and we're forced to spend a lot of time together. It's no big deal."

When her phone vibrated again, Dani reached for it before Elle could stop her.

"Ohhhh, now it's Edward. Looks like you've got two guys who want to see you tomorrow." She wriggled her eyebrows and handed the phone back to Elle.

—I'd like to take you to lunch tomorrow if you're available—

Her father went to get seconds, which was hard to wrap her head around. She typed a quick response to Edward.

—I'm going back to Lake Tahoe tomorrow and need to leave by noon, so lunch isn't an option. Thanks for the flowers. I'm sorry for not responding sooner—

—Breakfast? I'll meet you as early as you need. I am desperate to see you and explain a few things to you—

She tucked her hair behind her ear and sighed. "I don't know what to do."

"He wants to see you?" Peyton whispered.

"Yeah. I said I'd be leaving at noon, so I couldn't meet for lunch. He offered to meet for breakfast instead. Said he's desperate to see me and needs to explain a few things."

"What are you going to do?" Dani asked.

She typed out a quick response to say she'd meet for a quick coffee on her way out of town.

"It's not like anything has changed, but I'll hear him out."

"Well," Peyton said holding up her phone, "Jackson texted and said Maverick wants to know when you're coming back. Apparently, the dog *really* misses you."

Her dad smirked. "Careful, Short Stack. Sounds like you've got yourself in a game of tug-o-war."

"Sounds like one of those love triangles we see on those Lifetime movies Axe makes us watch. And you know which guy gets my vote," Billy Goat shouted.

She threw her balled up napkin across the table at him and turned her phone off. One of the men didn't do relationships, and the other had never made her a priority. There was no love triangle here.

****

"Hey, sorry I'm late. Just had to get a few thigs done before I get on the road," she said. Edward kissed each cheek before pulling her chair out.

She asked to meet at the cute café up the street

from her condo. The coffee shop took shabby chic to a whole new level, and she loved everything about it. Black and white designs were painted on shiny marble floors, with velvet couches and vintage chairs surrounding white round tables. A wall covered in floor-to-ceiling silk pink roses made the perfect focal point, and chalkboards decorated the walls behind the white counter, announcing the daily specials. Crystal chandeliers hung from above, and the elegant, feminine décor assured there was always a line out the door.

"No problem whatsoever, I'm thankful you agreed to meet," Edward said, his accent regal and elegant.

"Of course. Thank you for the beautiful arrangements. It wasn't necessary."

"I behaved poorly, and I want to fix things. I know I was wrong, darling," he said, as a woman approached and set down a cup of coffee for him and a black unsweetened iced tea for her.

"I hope it's all right I took the liberty to order you a tea?" His lips turned up in the corners.

Maybe he did know more about her than she'd given him credit for. Although anyone who knew her, knew she drank about four large ice teas a day. Still thoughtful.

"Yes, of course, and there's nothing to fix. I accept your apology."

"You do? You're willing to move forward?" His voice was full of hope and her chest tightened. She'd assumed he wanted to make sure they ended on good terms, not pick up where they left off.

"Oh, um, I meant I'm willing to put the whole episode behind us and end on good terms. I didn't mean move forward as a couple," she said.

"Why? Things were great until the episode with Sophie. I've spoken to her. Told her how important you are to me," he said.

Why now? Why not when the girl was hurling insults at her? What about the rest of the trip? He worked the entire time. They hardly spent any time together.

"Listen, Edward. I think we were a little caught up in the moment. Truthfully, we're in different places. You have grown children. One who blatantly doesn't accept me. I'm closer in age to Sophie than I am to you."

He reached for her hand. "It never bothered you before."

"Well, once I took the time to step back and reflect on everything, I realized how different we are. Yes, we have fun getting all dressed up and going to parties together. That doesn't make for a relationship though. I want to get married someday and have children of my own."

He studied her. His face appeared pained. He squeezed both her hands in his. "We can do all those things, darling. I'm not that old. Yes, I'm older than you. But men can have children much later in life than women can."

What in the Sam Hill? He'd considered leaving her at home for dinner per his daughter's request, and now he was talking about having kids? The man didn't know whether to check his ass or scratch his watch. They'd never discussed children because he'd already had two of his own. With someone else. Plus, he had some physical deficiencies which made her doubt children were even a possibility.

She leaned in and whispered, "Can you have children?"

Why was she even asking? She didn't want to get back together with the man. She hadn't experienced real heartache over the ending of their relationship. Disappointment, sure. Usually when she walked away from a boyfriend, she knew it was the right decision. Just like when she ended things with Edward.

His handsome face brightened. He leaned in closer, with a humored smirk. "I do have two children, so I'm quite certain I'm capable."

She looked over her shoulder to make sure their conversation remained private. "Right. But you know, we've had some, um, challenges in that area."

He stilled at her words, and her cheeks heated. But come on, how do you have a discussion about children without mentioning the sexual issues in your relationship? It wasn't like she'd had a ton of partners in her twenty-seven years. Go figure—she got a late start with her first boyfriend being gay and all. And honestly, James Ratcliffe was the best boyfriend she'd ever had. If only he'd liked the lady parts, she'd probably be married by now with a couple of kids. But even with her lack of experience in the bedroom, she knew that when someone said their parts didn't work more than half the time you were together, there's a problem. And when a man tells you his, um, what did Maverick call it, his *flaming baton*, was down, in the literal sense, *down*, he's about as useful as a steering wheel on a mule in the bedroom.

"Elle, I've told you my medication causes a few challenges for me in that department. But if we were trying to have a child, obviously I'd adjust things." He leaned back in his chair with confidence, his sapphire blue gaze never leaving hers.

They weren't together anymore, yet here they were talking about a future? They hadn't even said *I love you*, and if she'd felt it, she would have said it. Edward usually told her how much he adored her. Yet he'd sided with his demon spawn. The thought of spending her life with someone who didn't think she was enough did not appeal to her. She'd spent her childhood reminded of her shortcomings on a daily basis.

"Listen, I came here so we could both get closure. I'm not sure how we jumped to the topic of children when we aren't even together."

"Are you seeing someone else?" His gaze narrowed.

They'd been broken up for all of two weeks. How the hell would she already be seeing someone? Warning bells went off. This was exactly what Will Sanders used to do. Well, Will was worse. If his lips were moving, he was lying. But he was paranoid as all get-out. The man accused her of cheating on him every chance he got. In the end, she learned he was a serial cheater throughout their relationship. Edward questioning her was a red flag.

"Don't be ridiculous. We just broke up. Are *you* seeing someone?"

"I've been on two dates since you ended things with me, and the entire time I thought of you. I miss you terribly." He lifted his coffee mug to his full lips before taking a sip.

Well, *kiss my go-to-hell*—here the man talked marriage and kids and he'd already been out on a date? Two dates, actually. Obviously, France offered more opportunity than Lake Tahoe. She'd spent the past two weeks with the most unattainable guy on the planet, all while pretending to still be in a relationship, and Edward had been out on a dating spree.

"Wow. You don't waste any time, do you?" She reached for her tea.

"Do you want me to lie?"

It stung that she'd been so easy to get over. But at least he wasn't a liar. And oddly, she didn't care. She hadn't missed him. Taking a break from everything and everyone these past few weeks was delightful. Even spending time with Maverick—was nice. Fun, even. She'd laughed with him the way she did with Peyton and Dani. Edward rarely laughed. He was chivalrous, and gentlemanly, sure. But funny. Not so much.

"No, of course not. Were you on a date when you sent me all those flowers?"

"Listen, Elle. You ended things with me. I'm not a man who likes to be alone. I won't deny it. I went on two dates, setups, and I had a terrible time. They both ended with a kiss on the cheek. No fireworks. I missed my beautiful, brown-eyed girl." He reached across the table to clasp her hand.

He knew how to say the right things, but there were no fireworks. No passion. Maybe she was cursed to a passionless life.

"I appreciate the kind words, I do. But our issues are too big, Edward. We don't even live in the same country, for God's sake. The entire time we dated, we were on a vacation. It wasn't real life. As much as I love a good fairy-tale, this one isn't realistic. Your daughter despises me, and you're always going to side with her. And you should, you're her father. But I want a partner who stands up for me. A partner I will someday marry and start a family with, and that child becomes our priority. Together."

"I can give you all those things. I know you don't believe me, but I'm not ready to give up on you. I'm going to prove it to you. I spoke to your mother this morning. She didn't mention anything, so I'm guessing you haven't told her, which is a good sign."

It was not a good sign for the reasons he thought. Mama would chastise her for ending the relationship. She'd insist Elle look past Sophie's issues. Edward was a wealthy and powerful man, exactly what Mama wanted for her.

Her phone vibrated on the table, and she glanced down to find a selfie of Maverick and Daisy. She couldn't help but laugh. The caption read: *come back. We both smell like soy sauce and urine.* Her stomach did little flips.

She dropped the phone in her purse and faced Edward. "I appreciate the effort, but I really think it's best we move forward as friends. I haven't told Mama, because I'm not ready to hear what a disappointment I am to her."

He smiled and it reached his hopeful gaze. "Maybe Mother knows best?"

He meant it as a tease, but it rubbed her wrong. Edward fit in with her mother much better than Elle did.

"We can agree to disagree," she said.

"Okay. Friends it is. I'm going to be the best friend you've ever had."

She forced a smile. "Okay. I really do need to get on the road. I have a crisis at the house."

"Okay, darling. Thank you for taking the time to meet with me. I'll call you this evening to make sure you made it there okay. You know, a friend checking in on a friend." He winked as they both stood.

She gave him a hug and he kissed both her cheeks, holding her stare for longer than usual.

"Drive safely, darling."

As she pulled away from the curb, she looked in her rearview mirror. Edward watched her drive away. And now he was in her rearview, exactly where she intended to keep him. She looked ahead and merged onto the freeway. Surprise hit her when she realized how excited she was to get back to Lake Tahoe. The place where she had one amazing house to design, one stinky dog, and one charming manwhore waiting for her.

And there was nowhere else she wanted to be.

Chapter Ten

Maverick's Playbook
Keep your eye on the prize!

Fucking Peaches. The girl would be the death of him. Why did she insist on rising to any challenge that came her way?

"Get off the goddamn ladder." His tone made it sound like a command.

She stood on the top step of the ungodly tall structure, wobbling about like she was moments from plummeting to the ground, yet her stubborn ass stayed put.

"Don't tell me what to do, Wallace. Thomas said it was fine," she said, placing one piece of stacked stone against the adhesive on the wall. He turned to glare at Thomas but remained beneath the ladder in case he needed to catch her.

"Hey, she told me it was good luck for the designer to contribute a little." Thomas held his hands up in front of him in defense.

"Who exactly is she quoting? Who in the hell says it's good luck for the designer to stand on a twelve-foot ladder in high heels and put the last piece of stone on the highest point of the wall?" he said, unable to hide his irritation.

Her head tipped back, causing him to reach for the

ladder, but she was just taunting him with laughter. "These are not high heels." She lifted one foot and dangled her leg in the air. "These are wedges, you fool. I could run your ass into the ground wearing these. Just like I did this morning."

He rolled his eyes. She'd hardly run his ass into the ground this morning. Maybe he'd thrown up a little in his mouth at the end, but it was because he'd done a full workout with his trainer before they'd gone on their run. He was undoubtedly in the best shape of his life, and he'd be lying if he didn't admit his decorator was contributing to it. They didn't go on leisure runs—they were full on five to six-mile all-out races. Now the little tartlet wanted to join him with his trainer to see what all the hype was about. She had no idea what she was in for. She may be some sort of freakishly fast runner, but his workouts were for top-notch NFL players.

"For God's sake, Peaches. Get your ass down here so we can call it a day." He ran a hand through his hair.

The woman was exhausting, yet he couldn't get enough of her. Since she'd returned from her trip home, they'd been inseparable. Putting in long hours at the house, working out, and everything in between. Today he offered to take her for a ride on his boat. She hadn't been out on the water yet. Mimi insisted on making them sandwiches so they could eat dinner on the lake.

"Well, bless your pea-pickin' heart. Is that concern I hear in your voice?" She took one step at a time and made her way down. Shaking her hot little ass in his face the whole way down.

"Don't mistake concern for irritation," he said dryly.

"All right, well done, Elle. Sorry, Mav. The guys

and I are taking off. You two be careful out on the boat and try not to kill each other," Thomas said with a wink.

"Thanks for trusting me with the final stone. I feel like I've blessed this house in a way now. Like I gave this place its own little baptism," Elle said with a cocky smile.

"Are you drunk? Now you're a pastor?"

Damn, he loved messing with her. They laughed and bantered, and hell if he didn't enjoy it. He'd never had a relationship like this with a woman. They'd grown so close, there wasn't much he couldn't say to her. Only his dirty thoughts were off-limits. God knows she'd cut off his tongue if he voiced all the things he wanted to do to her.

With her.

For her.

Fuck. He was horny as hell. The worst part of being platonic besties, as Peaches liked to call them—he hadn't been with a woman in three weeks. It had to be some kind of record. Hadn't so much as touched a woman. Her crazy ass had put some sort of *no sex* spell on him, and he didn't want anyone else. He'd take no sex with Elle Fiore over sex with anyone else. How fucked up was that?

"Why? Do you need to repent? God knows you've sinned. But I think you're going to need some sort of exorcism, which is a bit out of my expertise."

His laugh echoed through the empty house. "I didn't think anything was out of your expertise."

They walked up to the house to change clothes and grab the sandwiches at his grandmother's. Even being away from Elle while he changed his clothes made him anxious. He found himself rushing, so he could get back to her. He'd become Elle Fiore's bitch. He didn't do this with women. He didn't even really date. Not the traditional way at least. Dinner. Sex. And catch ya next time.

No sleepovers.

Ever.

He knocked on the door to the guesthouse. Daisy scratched frantically. Damn if his dog didn't have it as bad as he did. When the door swung open, his jaw hit the ground.

"What the hell are you wearing?" he said.

She strode past him in white short-shorts which showed off her tanned, slim, running legs, a white tank top with a blue anchor in the center, and the icing on the cake—a goddamn navy-blue captain's hat. Sexy as fuck, but there was no yacht in sight.

"Aren't we going on your boat? This is my boating outfit," she said with a shit-eating grin, and something fluttered in his stomach. He didn't do butterflies. He didn't get nervous. Maybe it was infatuation, the hell if he knew. But Elle Fiore was the most beautiful woman he'd ever known. Inside and out. She tried so hard at everything she did, and he loved it. Correction. He *liked* it. He liked it a lot.

"Well, the Skipper called. He wants his hat back," he said.

She laughed as they walked down to the water. "Ah, thanks, Gilligan. I'll return it when we're done."

They climbed aboard, and Daisy sat beside Elle while he drove the boat out to his favorite place to watch the sun go down. When she looked out at the water, he stole a glance. She pulled off her captain's hat and held it, and her long blonde hair blustered in the wind. The sun shone down on her olive skin, causing it to glisten and sparkle. A few freckles scattered along her nose and her pink lip gloss accentuated her plump lips. He cut the engine and reached for her hand.

"Come sit over here. It's the best spot on the boat," he said, and she dropped down on the white leather bench beside him. Daisy liked to stand on the nose of the boat once it stopped moving and look out for anything fluttering in the water.

He grabbed the picnic basket Mimi made and set it between them.

Elle opened it and laughed. "This is her idea of a few sandwiches?"

He rolled his eyes as he took in the packed basket. Sandwiches, chips, fruit, cookies, and two large bottles of Pellegrino.

"Yeah, she's something else. You sure spend a lot of time with her, huh?"

"I love Mimi. She's a wealth of knowledge. She's teaching me how to make homemade pies tomorrow after work. Marley's coming too," she said.

His family took to his decorator like they'd known her their whole life. Usually it would've bothered him, but he liked it. He wanted her to be comfortable here. She didn't have a good relationship with her own mother, and he got the feeling she craved it.

"Yep, she's an amazing lady."

"Sure is. Wow, it's beautiful out here," she said. Specks of gold and amber danced in her topaz gaze when she looked out at the turquoise water.

"It's my favorite place."

"Thanks for bringing me out here." She looked up

to meet his stare. "Honestly, thank you for everything. Letting me stay in your guesthouse and introducing me to your family."

She played with her napkin. Fucking adorable. Sometimes she exuded confidence and other times her vulnerability caught him off guard. The girl was real. What you see is what you get. It was a rare quality these days, and he admired it.

"Of course. I'm glad you don't hate me anymore."

She sighed. "I'm sorry about that. I mean, I was bitter about our so-called date."

He wanted to explain why he behaved like such an ass, and what better time than the present? "I deserved it. I know it wasn't what you expected. Asking you to dinner was a mistake."

She leaned back and studied him. "Why did you even ask me out?"

"You want the truth, Peaches?"

"Always," she said.

"Well, I'd had a hell of a night with you at the wedding. I mean, that was some kiss." He shook his head at the memory.

She buried her teeth in her bottom lip and nodded for him to continue.

"I didn't want it to end, and you weren't even considering taking me home with you. I wanted to see you again, so I asked you to dinner the following day. Then Jackson pulled me aside at the end of the reception and told me you were like family to them. You weren't the kind of girl to put up with my shit. I'd need to go all in or call it off."

"So why didn't you just call it off?" she said, her voice just above a whisper.

"I wanted to see you again. Guess it makes me a selfish prick. A part of me hoped you'd be okay with the way I am. I don't know." He took a bite of his turkey sandwich and gave her a chance to respond.

"You thought I'd be okay with dinner and a quickie?" She lifted her chin in challenge.

"Well, come on, Peaches. You don't ask someone for their life's plan on a first date. You weren't exactly helping the situation," he said. The words came out more defensive than he planned.

"I asked you where you saw things between us going. Keep in mind, I also got the lowdown on you at the end of the reception. I was on edge. I didn't want to be used. I'm not a one-night stand girl, it's just not who I am."

Her honesty was refreshing. Even when she said crazy shit. She didn't care what anyone thought of her. He respected it.

"I know. I don't even remember what I said to you, but I remember being an asshole."

"Let me replay the conversation for you. I asked where you saw this going," she said, motioning her hand between them. "You replied *I see this ending with you naked in my bed. That's as far into the future as I like to go*." She stared at him with disapproval.

His laughter bellowed off the water and his head tipped back. "Well, I sure laid it all out there. I really did want you naked in my bed. You know, there are a shit ton of women who enjoy that sort of arrangement."

"And then, what? You could just kick me to the curb after? Sorry, but that dog won't hunt. You made me feel like some sort of prostitute," she hissed.

He couldn't help but chuckle, but something in his

chest tightened because he knew he'd hurt her feelings. "Jesus, Peaches. I wasn't offering to pay you for sex. Why would you think that?"

"Well, you bought me dinner and expected sex, did you not?"

Goddamn, she was adorable. Even when she acted batshit crazy, he found her charming as hell.

"I never *expected* sex from you. But yeah, I wanted it. I guess I hoped you'd want it to. Once I realized it wasn't your thing, I knew you shouldn't waste your time with me. I mean, I'm no prince, Peaches. There's no white horse. And knowing you the way I do now, I'm glad I walked away that night," he said.

"Why?"

"Because you're so—good. You deserve all the things you want, and then some." He wanted her to know because it was true. He wished he could be that guy because she'd be worth changing for. But he sure as hell couldn't tell her the whole reason he'd drawn a line in the sand. After Jackson's little talk, he knew he couldn't up and leave her if she'd invited him back to her place. So fate decided for him.

Her pretty gaze welled with emotion, and she blinked a few times. "That's the nicest thing you've ever said to me. You're not so bad yourself, Wallace. I think we can call it even. I believe I racked up a pretty hefty bill that night if memory serves."

He reached over and caught a single tear as it made its way down her cheek. "That's an understatement. Not to mention the hour and a half you sat there in silence, refusing to speak to me while you ordered one of everything on the menu."

She laughed. "It was a great exit though, wasn't

it?"

"Ah, yes. You took the last bite of cheesecake, tossed your napkin on the table, pushed back, and faced me. I can still picture you in the gorgeous pink dress with the spaghetti straps. Fucking beautiful. You had your hair in a cute ponytail, and you pointed your little finger in my face. So close, I wanted to bite it. I believe you called me a *manwhore*, turned, whipped me in the face with your hair, and stormed out the door. I'm surprised you didn't drop the mic before you left. It was very gangster, Peaches."

Her mouth fell open. "Wow. You've got quite the memory. I can't believe you remember the color of my dress."

"Trust me. It was memorable."

She wrapped her arms around her body, and he didn't miss the tremble in her shoulders. The air had cooled over the last hour. He leaned back, wrapped his arm around her and pulled her close. She didn't acknowledge his hand as it rubbed up and down her arm to warm her. Her skin was soft and smooth.

"Well, thanks for explaining. I'm glad we've put it behind us. We are going to be Jojo's godparents after all, so it's best we don't hate each other."

"Agreed." He tipped his head back to see the sun as it dipped below the distant horizon. The water lapped against the shore and made for a perfect night out on the boat.

"So you never did tell me if you opened the brothel when I was gone. I'm sure Brittney couldn't wait to come back over." Nervous energy radiated from her as she leaned into him and waited for a response. He didn't understand what was happening between them.

Her anxiety over him being with other women was as crazy as his reasons for not being with other women since the day she arrived.

"Nah. I hung with Jackson. We took the boat out."

"Really? You're completely blowing your reputation as a manwhore, you know," she said, her voice borderline giddy.

"I guess I am." He chuckled. "What about you? I hear the Count is trying to get you to take him back?"

"Yeah. I had coffee with him before I left the city. He wants a second chance. I told him I think we're better as friends. He called this morning and asked me to come back next weekend to attend some gala with him. *As friends*."

His entire body tensed. He didn't want her to go back to attend jack shit with Count Asshat. He didn't like the guy. He had his chance and he blew it. He didn't deserve her.

"Do you want to get back together with him?" He tried to hide his agitation from his tone. He didn't even know if he wanted to hear the answer. He couldn't stand the idea of her being with someone else. But what the fuck did it even mean? They were friends. So basically, he couldn't have her, and he didn't want anyone else to either. *Who's the asshat now?*

"I don't know what I want."

"Bullshit. You know what you want more than anyone I know. Is he the guy?"

"I don't think so. I feel like I'd know, right?" She paused and leaned forward to take a sip of water. "Obviously, I like dressing up, and I enjoy fancy parties." She hesitated, as if she were holding something back.

"What? Trust your gut."

"I feel like I'm a showpiece for him sometimes. But I could just be ultra-sensitive to it. My mama never saw me as more than a pageant queen. Not someone who enjoys art and running and school. She never *saw* me. I don't think Edward does, either." She paused to look up at the sky.

"You shouldn't settle for anyone who doesn't see you for who you are. You're fucking awesome, Peaches," he said, wanting to hear more. He understood it. Hell, most people didn't see much more than a football player when they looked at him.

"I think my college boyfriend, Will, sort of treated me the same. He loved telling people I was Miss Savannah. He never took an interest in my schoolwork, the design projects I took on, the fact I was tired of doing pageants. He didn't see me. He saw what he wanted me to be. He said I embarrassed him when I lost the Miss Georgia pageant. He didn't console me or take my feelings into consideration. I think Edward may fall into the same category in some ways, so I'm hesitant. Go figure, I seem to date men who treat me the way my mama does," she said.

"There's so much more to you though, Peaches. I mean, you're a mad woman when it comes to working out. I had no idea you were so tough. You're an awesome friend, loyal as shit. Your design skills are off the chart. You have a vision, and you know how to bring it to life. You have a great work ethic. I think you're going to have a very successful career. You are so fucking talented. I see you in all your beautiful, ferocious glory."

A smile spread across her gorgeous face. "Thanks.

I have some pretty big career aspirations. I've only shared them with my dad, Dani, and Peyt."

"Are you teasing me, or are you going to tell me?" He loved the way she stretched out and leaned her back against his chest, her head nuzzled in his neck. Her knees bent, and her feet rested on the bench. She fit there perfectly. Almost like she belonged there. Their comfort with one another had grown into something he'd never experienced with anyone.

"Someday I want to have my own firm. Be my own boss. Build something I can be proud of," she said the words so softly he dipped his head down closer to hear her.

"I think it's a great plan. If anyone can do it, my money's on you."

"Thanks. That actually means a lot."

She sat forward and turned to look at him, sinking her teeth into her plump pink lip once again. His gaze locked with hers and his hand acted on its own recourse when his thumb traced over her bottom lip and released it from her teeth.

"You can't do that, Peaches."

"Can't do what?" Her words were breathy and sexy as hell.

"Make me want things I can't have." He wanted to take her bottom lip between his teeth and tug it free. Kiss her senseless. Taste her. Brush his fingers across her silky skin.

"Do you?" she whispered.

"Do I what?"

"Want things you can't have?" Her stare locked with his and her arms wrapped around her chest for warmth. Little goose bumps spread across her bare skin.

He pulled her close against his body, hugging her in his arms. Her back to his chest. Looking at her was not a good idea. "A whole lot, lately."

"Me too." She peeked up at him, before tucking her head beneath his chin again. He'd wondered if she felt the strong pull between them the way he did. But knowing she wanted him too—it sure as shit didn't make things any easier.

Wanting and needing were two different beasts.

He wanted Elle Fiore.

But he needed football.

Chapter Eleven

Elle's Tip of the Day

Mess with the people I care about and I'll smack the stupid out of you!

Pete walked them outside to their table and leaned forward, his voice low. "Listen, Mav, I don't know how long I can keep Roth around. He's quite possibly the worst server I've ever had. Customers keep complaining about the guy."

Her gaze moved back and forth between the two men. She and Maverick ate here often, and she'd never seen Pete so frazzled. Why would he discuss Roth's poor service with Maverick?

"He's not costing you anything, can't you find a different position for him?" Maverick asked.

"All right, let me see what I can come up with. I'll never understand why you help the guy so much," Pete said, before hurrying off to greet a couple as they walked through the door.

She watched him with an impatient gaze. "I'm waiting."

"For?"

Sometimes his cocky attitude bugged the hell out of her. He knew exactly what she was waiting for. "Why do you want Pete to keep Roth employed? And why did you say it doesn't cost him anything for Roth to work here?"

"I cover Roth's paychecks, and I need Pete to keep him employed because no one else will."

Falling back against her seat, she let out a long sigh. "You know, Wallace, I'm always sharing every detail of my life with you, but sometimes it feels like I'm pulling teeth to get you to tell me anything. This is not how friendship works. Have you ever heard the term, two-way street?"

He laughed. "I just told you what you wanted to know."

"Okaaaaay. So why in the world are you payin' for his employment? It. Makes. No. Sense."

She was in a foul mood. Their relationship confused her. They had somehow become the best of friends with a burning attraction neither would act on. He made her all squirmy and uncomfortable. Add this to her epic fail in the kitchen with Mabel last night. She set poor Mimi's oven on fire and then burned a hole through one of the pie tins by accidentally turning on the burner on the stove top. She didn't have the energy to drag every bit of information out of this complex man today. Could he not throw her a bone now and again?

He seemed hesitant but finally spoke. "Fuck it. I cover his pay because the guy can't get a job anywhere. You know he's an asshole. I convinced Pete to hire him as a favor to me."

"Because?" Sweet baby Jesus, this man liked to make things difficult. "Spit it out already."

"I told you his mom was my favorite teacher, right?" He avoided her gaze and fiddled with his napkin. He was nervous. Almost vulnerable. Maverick

Wallace was many things, but nervous and vulnerable were not the norm.

"Why was she your favorite teacher? You didn't sleep with her, did you?" she said, trying to lighten the mood. His face fell, and she immediately regretted her words. "Kidding, Wallace."

"Mrs. Jones was my favorite teacher because she believed in me. I have a learning disability. It's not my favorite thing to talk about. She was the first teacher who didn't get frustrated with me. She stayed after school to help and encouraged my parents to get me tested to find out why I struggled so much."

A dull ache settled in her chest. This big strong man was human like the rest of us. No one would look at Maverick Wallace and think he ever had a day where he wasn't on top of the world. Here he was trusting her with something he obviously didn't like to talk about.

"What did you find out when you got tested?"

"I'm dyslexic. School wasn't easy. Between my parents and Mrs. Jones, and a shit ton of hard work, I made it through. Thankfully, I found football in middle school, and it became my focus, built my confidence."

"Wow. She was the teacher who affected your life the most, and you show your appreciation by helping her son," she said.

"Something like that. After she passed away, Roth spiraled. She was a single mom, and he didn't have anyone else. The guy doesn't have many friends. Obviously, his charming personality doesn't help." He chuckled.

She took in the amazing man across from her. She'd underestimated him.

"What?" The corners of his mouth quirked up.

"You're full of surprises, Wallace."

She thought about the things Roth said to him the many times they'd come to Pete's. He taunted him about his football skills, which she'd laughed off as ridiculous. But she remembered a few comments about him not being able to learn the playbook or understand the scoreboard. The little shit was referring to Maverick's dyslexia. Her anger was unexplainable. She wanted to give Roth a tongue lashing.

"I can see your wheels turning, Peaches. Roth doesn't bother me. His mother was the one person in school who stood up for me, and I can thank her by helping her son."

Such a good man. So much more to him than she ever knew.

The sloth approached the table with a friendly greeting for her, but she simply nodded. She needed a moment to process things. They ordered food and Roth made a snide remark about Maverick always ordering the same thing on the menu as Elle because he didn't want to take the time to see what else they had. Was it a dig about reading the menu?

Breathe. Calm down. The need to protect this man was startling.

"I can fight my own battles, Peaches," he said after Roth walked away.

"I'm aware."

"What else do you want to know? You said I don't share enough."

She perked up. "I just give you a lot more than you give me."

"Okay, then. Ask away."

She didn't expect him to concede. She rubbed her

hands together with excitement,

"Okay. Tell me about the one relationship you had for six months."

"Really? You want to know about Madison? It isn't a very exciting story." He popped another peanut in his mouth.

"Try me."

"Hmmm, met her in a bar the summer before my junior year of college."

"And she knocked you on your ass, so you pursued her?" she said, curiosity getting the best of her.

"Nope. We had a one-night stand, and she was persistent as hell. We hooked up a few more times. The girl showed up everywhere I went. Should have recognized her eagerness as odd. But I liked her enough, so I gave it a shot. But nothing I did was enough. She wanted to spend every minute together. Didn't understand I had class and practice. I don't do sleepovers, so every day was a fight. Eventually the relationship crashed and burned," he said, as if this were all a common occurrence.

"I don't know where to start. It sounds like you dated your stalker." Her jaw hung wide open.

"I haven't even told you how I found her in my apartment after we broke up. She smashed a window to get in. I found her in the bathroom poking holes in my condoms."

Elle rested her forehead on the table. This made her relationships seem tame. He dated his stalker, so obviously she wasn't going to take the breakup well.

"I have a question."

"Shocker."

"Well, first, good job on the condoms. I'm glad

you practice safe sex. What's with no sleepovers? You never spend the night with a woman? You give manwhore a new name. You can't even stand being in the bed with them for a few hours after the dirty deed?"

He ran a hand over his face. "Will you please stop calling me that? Have you even seen me with a woman since you've been here?"

"Touché. I'll drop the manwhore handle. But what's with no sleepovers?"

"Jesus. I don't do them. Never have."

"That's your answer? *I don't do them.* It's not open for discussion? What woman is going to be okay with that explanation?" She rolled her eyes.

"You underestimate my flaming baton."

She flushed at the mention of his—baton. The man was so sexy and full of innuendos. It was hard to stay focused. Something was up with his no sleepover rule. Maverick was a sweet guy. Always hugging her and touching her. He was warm. Thoughtful. Something didn't add up.

"I don't want to talk about your flaming baton, Wallace. Remember, I know what happens when a baton goes up in flames. It takes everyone down with it."

He laughed and shook his head, but she actually wasn't kidding.

Roth approached the table and set down both plates.

"I thought I ordered this without cheese and mustard?" Maverick said, and he'd be correct. He specifically said to hold the cheese and mustard, as he did every single time he ordered a burger.

"Did you read the menu? It's how the hamburger

comes? Or you still can't read?" Roth the sloth must have a death wish because she was on her feet and in his face before she could process what was happening.

"You better give your heart to Jesus, Roth Jones, cause your butt is mine," she shouted and waved her arms wildly.

He stepped back with surprise. "Sorry, I was kidding, Elle."

"Don't you ever kid with him again, do you hear me? You have no idea how much he's done for you." She pointed her finger in his face.

"Peaches, sit down." Maverick's voice remained calm and cool.

She didn't care. Here he was paying Roth's paycheck, and the guy was a total ass to him. She wasn't having it.

"I didn't mean nothin' by it. I thought you got all that stuff fixed when you worked with my mom," Roth said, his voice cracked a bit when he spoke.

"It's all good, buddy. She gets a little defensive."

"*You thought he got all that stuff fixed?* Are you kidding me? How dare you make light of it. *Let's call a spade a shovel*, okay, Roth?" She glared.

"Okay? I don't know what that means."

"It means, you best change your attitude. You don't just fix a learning disability, you work your ass off, all the while dealing with people like you who don't understand how hard it is. This guy is the best friend you've got, so you best rethink how you treat him."

Maverick chuckled. "I think he gets it. Please sit down and eat."

"Are you and me good, Elle?" Roth said, his gaze

full of concern.

Did the guy not get it? He should be apologizing to Maverick, for God's sake. Not to her.

"You're apologizing to the wrong damn person, Roth. Of course, we're fine. Just watch your P's and Q's, got it?" She took a bite of her salad in a huff.

"Sorry, Maverick," he said, moving quicker than she'd ever seen before. He was off the patio and back in the dining room before she set her fork down.

"You're like half Southern belle, half fucking gangster, Peaches. But you do realize I don't have an issue with Roth."

"Well then, it's a good thing you have me looking out for you."

****

Howling and barking woke her. Daisy? She nearly fell out of bed, scrambled for her phone on the nightstand, and pushed the hair away from her face to see the time. It was two o'clock in the morning. What in the Sam Hill was going on?

Loud, relentless scratching at the door followed by more loud barks.

She tripped as she rushed down the hall to the front door. Daisy ran in frantic circles on the porch. Elle tried to get her to come inside, but the dog wouldn't budge. She grabbed her phone and tried to call Maverick, but he didn't pick up. Daisy started *howling*. Elle put on her robe and some flipflops and followed Daisy toward the main house.

"What's going on, Daisy?" she whisper-shouted.

The dog ran forward, turning back every few strides to make sure she followed. Once at the front door, she rang the bell and peered through the windows, but there was no movement. She couldn't call because she set her damn phone down when she grabbed her robe.

What the frick was she supposed to do? She could crawl through the doggy door. Daisy continued to bark and run from the front door to the garage. Elle hurried to the garage when she spotted the keypad. She remembered he'd given her the code the first day she arrived, but she'd never used it. She quickly typed in the numbers and hit enter. Daisy followed her inside and she heard Maverick screaming for help.

Her heart raced, pounded so loud she thought it might burst from her chest. Daisy stopped barking and ran inside ahead of her. More shouting. He was fighting with someone. Adrenaline kicked in, and she moved swiftly to the kitchen, grabbed whatever she could find to use as a weapon.

A butcher knife.

A rolling pin.

No rhyme. No reason. They both seemed like they could do some damage.

"Stop. Stop. No," Maverick shouted.

Her hands shook, and she tiptoed to his bedroom door. She gripped the knife and the rolling pin hard in each hand prepared to either swing or stab. She didn't know, but she'd figure it out. He needed her.

One. Two. Three.

She jumped like a ninja in the doorway, ready for battle. A loud gasp escaped her when she saw Maverick on his bed, pressed against the headboard yelling. Screaming. She scanned the room, thankful for the light coming from the hallway. No one else was there. His arms flailed wildly, his skin glistened with sweat, and his hair damp.

"Maverick," she whispered. No response.

Daisy paced around the room. Maverick's dark gaze was distant. Empty. His skin a bit pale. His eyes were wide open, but he didn't see her standing there. He was far away. Fighting someone off. Tears streamed down her face as she stood frozen at the foot of his bed. He continued to yell for another two or three minutes, until the room went eerily silent. He stopped yelling. Sat completely still. She wondered if he would acknowledge her now, but he didn't. He moved down on the bed, placed his head on the pillow, and closed his eyes. He returned to sleep as if he hadn't just been fighting for his life. She'd heard of night terrors before, but never actually experienced one. This was terrifying.

She dropped down on the floor and Daisy walked over and sat beside her.

"Good job, girl." She patted her.

Well, now what? What if it happened again? She wanted to make sure he was safe. She grabbed a pillow off his bed and went to the couch. Using the throw blanket, she made herself a little makeshift bed and stretched out. Squeezing her eyes closed, she pulled the blanket up around her shoulders. Tears streamed down her face. She couldn't shake the image of Maverick screaming for help and fighting off whatever haunted him.

She didn't know what it was, but she made a promise to herself to find out. Then she made herself another promise: she'd fight his demons for him if she needed to.

Chapter Twelve

Maverick's Playbook
If you know it's right—go after it!

The alarm startled him from sleep, his arm heavy when he turned it off. He pushed up, stopped in the bathroom to brush his teeth, and went to the kitchen to get the coffee going. Hitting a few buttons on the coffee maker, he saw movement out of his peripheral.

What the hell?

He walked to the couch and saw a wild mane of blonde hair. "Peaches?"

She stirred, moaned, and finally rolled over to face him. Pushing her hair out of her face, she peeked out from under the thin throw blanket. "Oh, hey."

"Oh, hey? You want to tell me why you're on the couch?" He pushed her legs aside and moved to sit beside her.

She sat forward and rubbed her eyes. "Daisy woke me up at two in the morning. She was frantic. Howling, and barking, and running in circles. I followed her over here and tried to call you, but you didn't pick up. I rang the doorbell," she said, her voice raspy.

"How'd you get in?"

"I remembered the garage code." Her gaze darted around the room. She was nervous. What the hell happened? A sinking feeling hit his stomach.

Fuck.

He glanced at the coffee table and noticed a large knife and a rolling pin. Was she afraid of him? "Did I scare you? What's with the knife and the odd baking utensil?"

She laughed a little, her stare locked with his. "Oh my gosh, no. Not at all. I was worried about you. I heard yelling. I thought someone was attacking you."

"And you didn't call the police? You grabbed a knife and a *rolling pin* and charged the tundra, huh?" He couldn't look at her. Didn't want her pity. She thought someone was inside threatening him, and she ran to help? If he couldn't defend himself, how the hell did she plan on defending him?

"Of course, I came to help you. I'd never leave you alone if you were in trouble." Her hand landed on his back and moved up and down slowly.

He put his face in his hands. She'd seen him at his worst. He fucking despised being weak. "Shit, Peaches. I'm sorry you had to see that."

She moved closer. "Don't be ridiculous. I don't care. It's a night terror, right?"

He cleared his throat. "Yeah."

"Do you have them often?"

"I don't know when I have them. My arms felt a little heavy this morning, sometimes I suspect I had one when I wake up feeling a little off. I don't think I have them often, but I can't say for sure."

"Is this why you don't do sleepovers?" Her soft voice soothed. She wrapped her small arms around his middle and squeezed before tucking her head under his arm and settling her cheek on his chest.

"Yeah. I mean obviously my family knows this is

something I deal with because I've had them since the day they brought me home. It's not something I really want to share with people, you know?"

She lifted her head and looked at him. "I would never tell anybody. But I don't know why you won't talk about it. Everyone has *something*, Wallace. Night terrors aren't uncommon. Have you ever seen a doctor about it? Tried to figure out why you have them?"

He leaned back against the couch, not the conversation he planned to have first thing this morning. "Yeah. My mom took me to several doctors when I was young. It's pretty basic. I went through some shit the first few years of my life. I guess it's buried in there somewhere. But at this point, their only solution is medication. I can't take meds and play football. So, I don't do sleepovers. Problem solved."

"It's not a solution. It's a bandage."

"Well, it works for me. But I'm sorry you got pulled into this shit. I'd never want to scare you. You want a cup of coffee?" He pushed up and walked to the kitchen.

"Sure."

Peaches wasn't the quiet type, so he knew she was stirring over something. He settled back on the couch with two cups of coffee. "Here you go."

"You didn't scare me. If you're worried you did. I wanted to help you." Her voice soft, tentative.

He moaned. "I don't want you to worry about me."

She studied him but didn't say a word.

"What?" He raised his hands in question.

"This is why you were a jerk the night you asked me to dinner after the wedding."

"You've got *cuddler* written all over you,

Peaches." He wanted to lighten the mood. And yeah, he'd been a dick because there was no way to explain his situation to her. Hell, he'd never even told Jackson about his night terrors, and he'd known him most of his life.

"I'm not a one-night stand girl, sure. But this is different. You should have told me." Her gaze filled with empathy and understanding.

Not what he wanted.

"It's not really first date conversation, you know."

"Well, you dated Madison for six months. It never came up?" she said.

"Nope. Not something I talk about." He took his empty mug to the sink.

"Hey, Wallace…"

"Yeah."

"We had our first sleepover, and it wasn't so bad." She followed him to the kitchen, set her mug in the sink, and bumped her hip into his playfully.

"You slept with a butcher knife beside you. I wouldn't call it a huge success." A heaviness settled in his chest. She'd seen him at his weakest, and he fucking hated it.

"Nah. I was just afraid you'd bring out your flaming baton." She winked before walking out the door.

****

"Are you done ignoring me? It must be my lucky day," she said with complete annoyance and stormed past him to drop on the couch.

"I'm not ignoring you." Yeah, he was. He'd kept his distance since she found him screaming like a little bitch in his sleep two nights ago. "I texted you to come over. I have something for you." She knew about his nightmares. It was why he'd stayed away from her in the first place. She was fucking beautiful. Long blonde waves cascaded down her back. Her tanned skin shimmered against a white silk tank top, and tight jeans emphasized her toned shape. Her arms crossed over her chest and she glared at him.

"What? We're just fine now?"

"Yep."

"You've been MIA for two days. And now you text me saying you have a present for me?"

"I'm sorry, Peaches. I had some shit to work out." *More like hiding.* He missed running with her, but he'd bailed the past two days. He avoided work at the house.

"You know, Wallace, excuses are like backsides. Everyone's got one, and they all stink. The jig is up—I know you have nightmares. *So what?* It's not a big deal. We all have flaws. I don't expect you to be perfect, God knows I never considered the idea for a moment. Not when you're always acting like a stubborn ass."

Damn if she wasn't sexy when she was pissed off.

"Jesus. Could you insult me more in one breath? Thank you for pointing out how imperfect I am. You found something out about me I haven't shared with anyone aside from my family. Ever. I needed to process it. So I stayed the fuck away. I didn't enjoy it. I missed the hell out of you and I'm happy to see how much you missed me, Peaches." He smirked.

Her features softened and she covered her smile with her hand. The girl could bring him to his knees with just a look.

"Fine. I forgive you."

He dropped down on the couch. "It won't happen

again. Can I give you your present?"

"Yes. I can't even imagine what you got me."

"Come on." He led her out to the backyard. "Take a seat and close your eyes."

With her eyes squeezed shut, and a smile spread across her face, she held both hands out. "I'm ready. You better not be naked."

He laughed, placed the package in her hands, and took the seat beside her. Daisy ran out to play in the grass. "Open it."

She tore at the paper, like a tiger mauling its prey. She blinked several times and looked up at him. "Nooooooooo."

"Yes." He laughed.

"No. How?"

"I'm that good. And it's as much a gift for me as it is for you. I'm dying to see you twirl some fire, Peaches." He sat back in his chair, stretched his legs out, and crossed his ankles.

"A freakin', flamin' baton," she said.

"Come on, let me see you do your thing."

"You're serious?"

"Dead serious." The thought of Elle Fiore flinging her flaming baton in the air—it was something he had to see.

She walked over to him and snatched his phone. "I need music. You can't do a routine without music."

"Obviously," he said, and prepared for the best thing he'd ever seen.

She pulled an elastic from her wrist and tied her hair back in a low ponytail. She hit play on some techno, fast-paced beat, and stood fifteen feet from him. She lit the baton on both ends using the little lighter it came with, and in a matter of seconds, she transformed into a full-fledged professional baton twirler. Flames blazed on each side.

"Holy shit." And he swore something lit inside him.

Her face flushed and her gaze in full concentration—the most magnificent thing he'd ever seen. Her moves were as good as any professional cheerleader, but with the added thrill of launching a blazing stick into the air and catching it. Over and fucking over.

She caught it while down in the splits.

Balanced it on her head.

Twirled it while doing a cartwheel.

"You're like a fucking Las Vegas Cirque De Solei show," he whispered. A fiery fucking acrobat, who had somehow weaseled her way into his heart. Hell, he'd been consumed with her for longer than he wanted to admit. Long before he hired her, back when she hated him. He wanted her. Even when he pushed her away. But something had shifted. She knew about his secret and she didn't care. He'd spent the last forty-eight hours analyzing the shit out of it. And for the first time in his life, there was something worth going out on a limb for, and it didn't involve football.

By the time the flames burned out, she panted from exertion. Her wide smile lit up the night's sky. He swore she got more beautiful each time he saw her.

He clapped, slow, deliberate, and took her in. "Fucking perfection, Peaches."

Her head fell back, and laughter bellowed from her hot little body. "You really liked it?"

"There are not enough words to describe how

much I liked it."

She bent over her knees to catch her breath. "I can't believe you found a flaming baton for me."

"You should never be without one," he said. "Come on, let's go in and grab you a water. That was some serious cardio."

She followed him inside. Her phone vibrated on the kitchen counter, and he glanced down and saw Edward's name.

Fucker.

"Count-Pain-in-the-Ass is calling. Again." He didn't hide his irritation when he handed her a glass of cold water.

"What's your problem with him?" she said before guzzling her drink after she spoke.

"I don't like him. I don't think you should go tomorrow." He followed her into the family room, and she plopped down on the couch.

"Yes, you've mentioned it. But you haven't said why. I can't read your mind, Maverick. You ignore me for two days, and now you don't want me to go home for the weekend?" Her gaze locked with his.

He ran a hand through his hair. He didn't know how to do this. Didn't know how to tell her he wanted her all to himself.

"Do you want to get back together with him?"

"No. I'm going as a friend."

"But you know he wants you back, so why go?"

"Why do you care?" She licked her lips, arms crossed in front of her chest in challenge.

"Well, what happens to us, you and me, if you get back together with the guy? Hell, what happens when we go back to our regular lives?"

She sank her teeth into her perfectly plump bottom lip. “What do you want to happen?”

Shit. What did he want? He wanted her. “I don’t know how to do this.”

She rolled her eyes and stood. “Don’t ask me not to go, and not to see him, when you don’t have a damn clue what you want.”

She stormed toward the door, but he was on his feet before she got far. He wrapped his fingers around her wrist and turned her to face him. He may not know how to say it, but he damn well knew how to show her what he wanted.

“Why is it only up to me? What do you want?” His eyes were hard on her.

She squared her shoulders and shook her head. “You know what I want.”

“Bullshit. Tell me.” The words more of a command than he intended.

“I want everything,” she said just above a whisper.

“I don’t know what that means.” He wanted to be honest, but she shook her head and yanked her arm away.

“Let me go. You’re a coward, Wallace. You know exactly what it means.” She marched toward the front door.

He reached for her arm once again, his voice louder now. “Oh no you don’t, Peaches. You don’t get to run away and hate me because we aren’t the same. We don’t all have goddamn unicorn blood running through our veins and believe in fairy-tales. I don’t have a white horse, and I’m not perfect, as you so happily pointed out earlier.”

She stilled, her back pressed to the wall beside the

door. Her breaths came fast. “Well, excuse me for knowing better than anyone what an ass you are.”

“Then you know what you’re getting into. What’s the problem then?” He studied her.

Her words were angry, but her body leaned closer to his. Her face flushed, she licked her lips and he closed his eyes to control the raging erection beneath his zipper.

“The problem is, you don’t know what you want.”

“There’s never been a doubt about what I want.” He moved so close, her breath heated his neck.

“Humor me.” Her gaze searched his.

“I want you. I’ve always wanted you.”

“Just for sex.” She crossed her arms in front of her chest.

He moved closer. Crowded her. “Not just for sex.”

Her teeth sank into her bottom lip again, almost undoing him.

“Then for what?”

He took his thumb and released her lip. Traced it back and forth while he stared down at her. “I want you so fucking bad, Peaches. I don’t know what it means. I’m not good at this. I know it’s more than sex because I can have sex with plenty of women, but I only want you.”

She gasped and pushed her hands hard against his chest. “Is that supposed to impress me?”

He moved into her again, trapped her between the wall and his big body. “You know that’s not what I’m saying. I love being with you. I love talking to you. Running with you. Eating with you. Watching you work. Hell, I love watching you twirl a fucking flaming baton. I don’t want to have sex with anyone else, I only want you. Only you, Peaches."

She didn't speak. For the first fucking time since he met her, the girl was speechless. He took advantage of the moment and wrapped his hand behind her neck and pulled her closer. Her head fell back, she arched her chest toward him, and tangled her hands into his hair.

His mouth covered hers, as an electric current surged through his body. Every muscle coming to life as desire flooded his veins. A need and hunger so unfamiliar, it was almost blinding. Her tongue tangled with his, so sweet and perfect. He tipped her back, deepening the kiss. Her hot breathy pants against his mouth only fueled him more.

She grinded against him mercilessly. My God, this woman was made for him. She fit perfectly against his body, her soft, sensuous touch lighting him on fire.

"Fuck, Peaches. I want you so bad."

She pulled his head down further and tugged his hair as their kiss grew urgent. She nipped at his bottom lip, and he growled, pressing her deeper into the wall. Making sure she felt how bad he wanted her. Needed her. One hand slipped under her thin tank top, desperate to touch her. He'd fantasized about this since the day he'd met her, yet this far exceeded anything he could have imagined. He teased her, as his fingers grazed over her bra.

A moan escaped her sweet mouth, and she pressed harder against him. They'd been holding back far too long. He pulled away from her mouth and kissed his way down her neck.

"Maverick," she whispered, the word a silent plea.

Digging her hands into his hair she pulled him closer. He reached around her back and unsnapped her bra. She arched into him. Hungry and needy.

"So beautiful. Fucking perfect." He whispered along her neck as both hands cupped her perfect tits. Running his thumbs over her hard peaks, he reveled in the way her body responded to him. Lifting his head from her neck, she pulled him to her mouth again. Kissing him hard, as if her life depended on it.

She continued to grind against him, and he didn't know how long he could hold on before all hell broke loose. He'd never been so hard, so desperate. He reached down, unbuttoned, and unzipped her jeans. His fingers traced the hem of her panties, in desperate need to touch her. Make her feel good. He slipped his fingers beneath the delicate silk—his head whipped back as a sting settled on his cheek. Startled, he looked down at her. Her hand still in the air from where she'd slapped him.

Slapped him.

What the fuck?

Her hair wild and disheveled. Her gaze filled with desire. Her breath still came fast, and her chest heaved up and down in frantic rhythm. She reached down and buttoned her jeans, adjusted her tank top, turned on her heels, and walked out the door.

He couldn't even process what just happened. Had he misread her signals? Well, he certainly hadn't misread his own because he had a painful erection and was in desperate need of relief.

Hell, he'd told her he only wanted her. No one else. Maybe it wasn't what she wanted to hear. Maybe he'd scared her off? Came on too strong? But she'd pulled him closer, tried to take charge of their kiss—it made no sense. This was exactly why he didn't do relationships. He didn't understand this shit. Had no idea what he did to offend her. He'd actually opened up to her, told her how he felt about her. Didn't he?

He walked in the bathroom and dropped his shorts at the shower door, turning on the cold water. This time she'd have to come to him. He'd put it all out there, and she ran away.

****

He tossed and turned all night and checked his phone no less than twenty times. Nothing. In the morning, Daisy ran over to the guesthouse and continued to bark and scratch at the door to no avail. Her car wasn't in the driveway. She'd left? She'd fucking gone to the event with Count Asshat.

He'd never been one to pout and sulk. He made shit happen. But here he was. Pouting and sulking like a little bitch. The girl he wanted didn't want him. And now, she'd ruined him for all other women.

He needed to workout. A kickass, push-till-you-puke workout.

He sent his trainer a text.

—Hey, I know it's not my day, but can you get me in for a workout?—

He responded less than a minute later.

—Meet me at the gym in an hour.—

Thank fucking Christ. He needed an outlet. He stopped by Mimi's house to change the batteries in her smoke detectors, and she grilled him about Elle.

"Did she go back to see Edward?"

"To hell if I know, Mimi. You'll have to ask her yourself."

"Ah, someone's in a foul mood." She smiled, as if she held all life's secrets under her little housecoat.

"I'll stop back by later. I'm going to work out." He kissed her cheek and was out the door.

The gym was seven minutes away, and he turned up the music to distract his thoughts.

No luck. He wondered if it would be awkward now, after he'd dry humped her in his entryway. Maybe she'd quit and never talk to him again. Seemed to be her M.O.

He turned left into his gym. A flash came out of nowhere. A car barreled toward him at full speed. He swerved. His tires screeched. He jerked the wheel to stop skidding. Too late, the car's rear end fishtailed, and pavement surrounded him, before everything went dark.

Chapter Thirteen

Elle's Tip of the Day

If you find your prince, don't let the white horse get away!

She twirled in the mirror, and the lavender gown moved in waves around her legs. She hoped getting all dressed up and ready for the gala would put her in the party mood. Wrong. She didn't know which way was up right now. And Maverick Wallace was to blame.

My God.

Her cheeks heated every time she thought of the way he'd kissed her. They'd practically had sex in the entryway of his home. She stared long and hard in the mirror, shaking her head. God knows she'd done a whole lot of crazy things in her pageant days. But losing control? Never.

She grabbed the Cosmo magazine on her nightstand and fanned her face. Thinking of the man left her hot and bothered. Hot more than bothered. His mouth owned hers. She squeezed her eyes shut to calm her breathing. *Crazier than a sprayed roach.* She'd all but stripped him naked right there against the wall. And oh Mylanta, he was hardness at its finest.

Hands over her face, she dropped onto her bed. The man wasn't even sure he could do a normal relationship, so what had really changed from the first time they met? Thankfully, she came to her senses when he undid her jeans. Would they have had sex in the middle of the foyer? They weren't even dating. She'd never done anything like that with the men she dated. No. There were rules, and she liked to follow them. Leave the shenanigans in the bedroom, not out in the open like two wild animals.

A loud groan escaped her. She didn't know how to fix this. She ran away like a chicken fleeing her coop. Her feelings for Maverick were too powerful and out of control. She didn't want to get used, nor did she want to get hurt. He'd take what he wanted and throw her away, and she'd never be able to look at him again.

Sometimes a woman just needed to get away. Clear her head. And she'd promised to join Edward for the gala this weekend. Maverick had pouted about it all week. The man didn't want to date her, but he sure as hell didn't want her to date anyone else. Well, he could sell his crazy somewhere else, because she was all stocked up. Obviously, she wasn't interested in dating Edward, and maybe a part of her liked making Maverick jealous. She wanted him to want her the way she wanted him. She'd make sure Edward knew they were nothing more than friends, but Maverick didn't need to know that.

She was startin' to regret the way she left. She should have at least explained why she needed to get out of there. She'd sent him a text when she arrived in the city, but he hadn't bothered to respond. Was he mad at her for leaving?

The doorbell rang, and she pushed to her feet. Her strapless lavender gown fit like a glove through the bodice and was long and elegant. She pulled her hair into a loose bun, with some of the waves falling around her face. She dabbed a little pink gloss to her lips and made her way to the door.

"Wow. You look gorgeous, darling," Edward said, clad in a black tuxedo. The man could dress. His hair was gelled neatly in place. All she could think about was the dark mess of hair her fingers were tangled in last night. The way she'd pulled him closer, desperate for more.

"Are you okay? You look flushed?" he asked, his voice full of concern.

"Oh, yes. I'm sorry. Just been busier than a one-legged cat in a sandbox today." She hoped he'd buy her lame excuse.

"Well, tonight you can relax. I'll be at your beck-and-call."

"Sounds good," she said, lying through her teeth. She glanced down at her phone, frustrated Maverick still hadn't replied. How dare he ignore her. The man would have stripped her naked right there in the foyer if she hadn't stopped things.

Edward escorted her to the car, and his driver pulled from the curb. She sent another quick text to Maverick while Edward spoke to the driver. Even when he'd gone MIA after his nightmare, he still texted her constantly to see where she was. This was out of character. Panic settled in a tight knot in her chest. What if he wanted nothing to do with her now? She couldn't imagine not seeing him every day. Not talking to him every hour. She sent one more text.

—Why are you ignoring me? I thought we were friends—

Traffic backed up on the highway, and they moved

at a turtle's speed. Edward rambled about a business trip to Japan and asked if she wanted to join him.

"I can't just up and leave work whenever I want." Her lips pursed, she continued to check her phone for a response every thirty seconds.

"I'm sure you could work your magic with Camille. Hell, if it comes down to it, you can quit your job. Move in with me," he said.

What the hell? Quit her job? A job she loved, and a career she hoped to build into a business of her own someday. Did the man even know her?

She should give Edward a piece of her mind. Unfortunately, her bat senses were going off elsewhere. Maverick Wallace always responded to her. Something didn't add up. She didn't like the way her chest constricted. Her stomach twisted. Something was off. She knew it in her gut. Hell, she knew it in her entire body.

She sent a quick text to Marley. She needed to know he was okay.

—Hey, I'm in the city, but I can't reach your brother. Just checking to make sure everything is okay—

She met Edward's curious gaze. "Sorry. There's some issues with the house."

"All right. What about Japan?"

"First of all, we aren't dating, so suggesting we move in together is completely irrational, don't you think? Secondly, asking me to walk away from a career I've worked hard for—well, it's insulting, Edward." Her arms crossed in front of her chest.

She stared down at the annoying bubble waiting for Marley's text. Waiting as if her life depended on it.

Maybe it did. Maybe her feelings ran deeper than she wanted to admit. Being away from Maverick made her feel all sorts of needy. She didn't like it. She wanted to be in Lake Tahoe with him. On the boat. At the house working. At Pete's. On a run. Anywhere, as long as he was there.

"I'm terribly sorry I offended you. I wanted you to know I'd be happy to take care of you, if you so wished."

A month ago, this might have sounded chivalrous, although still offensive. But something had shifted. Even her forever fairy-tale picture had changed. She didn't want this. She didn't want the Count on a white horse. She wanted the brute, rugged football player who said what he wanted. The man who made her laugh. The man who somehow understood her and liked her anyway. The man who saw her. Really saw her. He may be a bull in a China shop, but she'd ride that bull off into the sunset any chance she got. No pun intended. Even if just for a short time. She missed him.

"I'm not looking to be taken care of, Edward. I can take care of myself."

She could throw a flaming baton over her head like nobody's business. She didn't need a man to take care of her. She needed a man who believed in her. And it wasn't the man sitting beside her.

"I understand," he said, stepping out of the car and offering his hand to help her out.

By the grace of God, her phone vibrated. She read the text from Marley.

—Maverick asked me not to text you. He didn't want you to worry, or to ruin your weekend. He was in a car accident. His car rolled and ended up in a ditch.

They said he's going to be okay. They're keeping him here as a precaution. I'm at the hospital with my parents and Mimi. I will keep you posted. His phone was smashed in the accident, so text or call me anytime. I'll keep my phone on. I'm sorry I didn't call you when it happened. My brother is a stubborn ass sometimes—

Her feet were glued to the pavement. She covered her mouth, barely stifling a gasp.

"Darling, are you okay?" Edward said, crowding her personal space.

Shaking her head, she closed her eyes and fought back tears. She left Maverick last night without an explanation, and now he lay in a hospital bed. She'd left him to go out with her ex-boyfriend. All because she wanted to make him jealous.

Her bottom lip trembled. "No. I'm not okay. Maverick's been in a car accident. I need to leave. Right now."

"Is he all right?" If Edward were genuinely concerned, he hid it well.

"I don't know. His sister said they're keeping him for observation. I need to get out of here, Edward. Please." She bent over, placing her hands on her knees, attempting to catch her breath. There was no holding back the tsunami of emotion. Tears streamed down her face.

"Do you have feelings for the man? I thought he was only a client?"

Anger took over. "He's not just a client. May I please use your driver to take me back to my place?"

"Of course. But be straight with me, Elle. Should I be concerned about your feelings for him?" His gaze locked with hers.

Impatience built. She needed to leave now. She didn't have time to get into the details of their relationship, but she knew she couldn't leave without some sort of answer. "Yes."

Staring down at her, he leaned in the car and asked the driver to take her back to her place.

"Go take care of what you need to. But I'm not giving up so easily. Let me know when you make it to Tahoe safely, please."

She nodded, slid into the car, and pulled the door closed. Making quick calls to Dani and Peyton, both insisted she call once she started her drive to Tahoe. She phoned Marley to let her know she was on her way. His sister told her they'd been kicked out for the night, as visiting hours were over. She'd deal with it once she got there. One hurdle at a time. Right now, she needed to see him. She didn't change clothes or stop at her apartment. She jumped in her car and got on the road.

Fear spread through every part of her, and the tears continued to fall.

She needed him to be okay.

Nothing else mattered.

****

Her heels tapped against the laminate flooring in the hospital. The hospital was a ghost town, quiet and eerie at midnight. Marley told her to go to the second floor and wished her luck getting in. Well, she'd be pitchin' one hell of a hissy fit if they tried to stop her. She glanced in the mirrored wall in the elevator. Her reflection caught her off guard.

Holy hell.

A rejected prom queen stared back at her. She swiped at the mascara beneath her eyes and tucked the loose waves behind her ears. The elevator doors opened, and she sucked in a long breath, ready for battle. Wild horses couldn't keep her away. She'd made it here, and she wasn't leaving without seeing him.

The *click, click, click* of her nude colored stilettos made it impossible to sneak in quietly. The stuffy corridor smelled of bleach and disinfectant. Above the double doors a large blue sign labeled the areas of the hospital. Maverick was just beyond those doors. She pressed the button and the doors swung open, all but inviting her in. Just as relief spread through her body, the hope of getting in without a fight quickly dissolved.

A woman in what looked like her mid-forties, stepped in front of her. Seriously, she may have entered the *Twilight Zone* because the lady was Nurse Ratched's doppelganger. Brown shoulder-length hair, resting bitch face, and eyes full of judgment.

"You can't be in here. Visiting hours ended *long* ago," she said in a whisper-shout, arms crossed in front of her light blue scrubs.

"I understand. But this is an emergency. I just drove several hours to get here, and I need to see Maverick Wallace. I'm not leaving until I do," she said.

Nurse Ratched's eyes softened, which surprised her. "Well, dear, we really aren't supposed to let anyone in after hours. Can you come back in the morning?"

Her tears started again, no stopping them now. The dam burst and a tsunami of emotion followed. "Please. You don't understand. I can't wait until tomorrow." She sobbed. "I made a mess of everything, and I just need to see him. You can call security. You can call the police. But they will have to drag my lifeless body out of here because I'm not leaving until you take me to his room."

She squared her shoulders to let the other woman know she wasn't backing down. Her hands fisted at her side before she reached up to swipe the falling tears, as Nurse Ratched quickly looked around to assess the situation.

"No one is calling security or the police, but I do need you to keep your voice down. I don't want to wake the patients."

"Peaches?" Maverick's voice called from two doors down. "Come on, Carla. Do me a solid."

"Oh, for God's sake. Follow me. You two are going to wake the whole floor. I swear if Mr. McNichols asks for another sponge bath, I'm having you do it."

"I'll do whatever you need, just please let me see him."

Nurse Ratched led her to Maverick's room and pushed the door open.

He lay in a hospital bed, vulnerable and helpless, and she could no longer hold back. Sobs and whimpers be dammed. "Oh, my God. Wallace. Are—you okay?"

"Dear, you really need to calm down. He's fine. We kept him overnight because apparently he's a very important man in San Francisco," she said with a wink.

Elle threw her arms around the older woman. Ashamed she ever thought her evil. "Thank you so much. I'll be quiet. I promise."

"Peaches, what in the hell are you wearing? Why are you crying?" Maverick pushed to sit up. He thanked Carla, before she pulled the door closed behind her.

Elle rushed to his bed and wrapped her arms around him. "I'm so sorry for leaving the way I did."

He pulled her beside him on the bed and used his thumbs to wipe the tears still pouring down her cheeks. “You worry too much. Everything’s fine. Coach Romero insisted they keep me as a precaution. I can leave first thing in the morning. Who even told you I was here?”

She placed a hand on each side of his face and shook her head, finally able to speak without sobbing. “You weren’t responding to me, so I texted Marley.”

“Ah. So, you did text me, huh?”

She stroked the hair back from his handsome face. He had a bruise on his forehead, and she lightly traced it with her finger. “I’m sorry for running out on you last night.”

“I’m sorry if I took things too far. If I misread the signals in any way—”

“—No.” She stopped him. Scooting closer, she whispered, “You definitely didn’t misread my feelings. How could you even think that?”

He moved back and pulled her to lie beside him. Turning on his side, he faced her. “Hmmm, let’s see. You slapped me in the face, ran out the door, and left town to go meet up with your ex-boyfriend.”

She laughed. Couldn’t help herself. It did sound ridiculous. “Well, you know I love a good exit.”

His face sobered, and she didn’t miss the concern in his gaze. “What happened, Peaches? Why’d you run?”

She didn’t know where to start. She buried her face in his neck—exactly where she wanted to stay.

For as long as he’d let her.

Chapter Fourteen

Maverick's Playbook
If you want it bad enough—make it happen!

He held her close, letting her bury herself in the crook of his neck, giving her a minute to pull herself together. She had shown up at the hospital in the middle of the night, like fucking Cinderella trying to get back home before her spell wore off. Her light purple gown hugged her perfect breasts, and then flowed down to the ground covering her sexy legs. Layers of silk surrounded her gorgeous body. He'd never been so happy to see someone in his life.

Her hair, wild and unruly, she'd never looked more beautiful.

Raw and vulnerable.

"You done hiding yet?" He chuckled against her hair. Honey and coconut awakened his senses.

She pulled away just enough to look up at him. "Hey."

"Hey." He wanted answers. Wanted to know what happened with Edward. He didn't fight insecurity often when it came to women, but damn if he didn't feel it right now. Wanting her the way he did.

She sucked in a long breath. "I've never done anything like that. I guess I just freaked out."

What the fuck? She wasn't a virgin, was she?

"You've had sex before, right?" he said.

Her cheeks flushed pink again, clearly uncomfortable talking about sex. Hell, it was his favorite topic. He'd need to help her get past it, because he not only planned to talk about it with her, but he planned to have a shit ton of it with her too.

Her head fell back with a laugh. "Yes, of course. That's not what I mean."

"Explain." He fought the urge to kiss her again. Her mouth so close. Her body invading his in every way.

"Well, I've never done anything like *that*." Her gaze darkened when it locked with his.

"Peaches, you're going to have to help me. I don't know what you're talking about? You've never made out before?" He didn't laugh. He sensed her vulnerability and wanted her to talk to him.

"Of course I have. I've never been, *like that*, with anyone though. You know, so out of control. I could barely stop myself. If I hadn't, we may have ended up having sex in your entryway," she said.

He could barely stand it. She was fucking adorable. Innocent, yet she hid behind this confident mask.

He stroked her pretty face, moved closer, occupying the space around her. "Why is that a problem? I want to have sex with you everywhere. In the entryway," he paused to kiss her forehead, "on the boat," he kissed her cheek, "in the bathtub," he kissed the tip of her nose, "anywhere you'll have me."

A nervous smile spread across her face. "I've never been so wild with someone the way I was with you last night."

"Do I turn you on, Peaches? It sure sounds like it,"

he said.

Her face flushed. So, fucking sweet.

"Oh my gosh." She buried her face in her hands, but he pulled them away. He needed to see her. "Well, I guess, maybe, you're right. Because I've never felt like that before. It's not like I've had many partners. Three in total. But sex has always been sort of planned, more structured, I guess. Never so…er…spontaneous."

Three men. Three lucky fuckers he now hated. He searched her gaze, wanted to understand how these men hadn't ravished her. The girl was so sexy and full of fire.

"Sex shouldn't be planned or structured. It should be natural. I swear to Christ what happened between us last night was *all natural*. I used as much self-control as I could muster, or you would've been naked beneath me on the tile floor. That's what you do to me." He lifted her chin to meet his stare.

"And then you'd be out the door today? Done with me?" she said, lips pursed.

"Why would you think I'd be done with you? Have I done anything to make you feel like I'd use you and walk away?" He studied her. Needed to understand where this was coming from.

Her fingers stroked his face gently. He'd never liked women showing affection like this. But somehow, Elle Fiore touching him—he fucking loved it. Craved it.

"No. But you've made it clear your number one is football, and you don't have room for anything else. Or, anyone else." Her teeth sank into her bottom lip. Pink and plump. Determined to bring him to his knees.

He fought the urge to roll her beneath him and feel her soft curves press against him. But he needed to clean up the mess he'd made with his big fucking mouth. He'd meant what he said at the time, but somehow, everything had changed since.

"Look, Peaches, football is a big part of my life. Has been for as long as I can remember. And my one attempt at a relationship with Madison was a disaster. But this, what we have—it's different. It's special. You know about my nightmares, which was the main reason I held back with you from the beginning. I don't know what I'm capable of giving, especially with the season starting, but I want to try. I don't want to be away from you."

Her watery gaze met his. "No other women, Wallace. If we try this, it's just you and me. I don't share."

He chuckled. She was as possessive as him. He loved it. Because he didn't fucking share either. Not when he wanted something. And he wanted Elle Fiore more than he'd ever wanted anyone.

"I haven't been with another woman since Brittney, the day you arrived in Tahoe. No one. I don't want anyone else. But this goes both ways. I don't want you going with Count Asshat to events. I'm not sharing you with any other man. It also means telling your mom, you and Edward aren't together." His thumb traced her bottom lip as he spoke.

"You don't know her. She's meaner than a wet panther when she's mad." She groaned.

"She'll get over it. Are you in?" he said.

"I'm in."

"It's not going to be easy when we get back to the city. The press will be all over it, so we need to keep things as private as possible. But let's enjoy the last few weeks of peace up here together. I think it calls for lots of sex in the entryway."

"Pace yourself, Wallace. We're taking this slow."

"I don't do slow, Peaches." He kissed her gently. Not like before. Softer. Slower.

They were in a goddamn hospital room. And he'd agreed to give this a shot. He didn't feel panic. He was—relieved. He'd wanted this woman for so goddamned long.

"You also don't do relationships, so…" she said, pressing herself against him as he kissed her again.

"So full of yourself." He smiled against her lips.

"Do you think I need to leave? I'm afraid of Carol. She reminds me a little of Nurse Ratched," she said, just above a whisper.

"The resemblance is uncanny, but she's harmless. All bark and no bite. You're not going anywhere. But if you don't stop rubbing up against me, we're going to have a problem."

She pulled back to look at him with confusion. "What do you mean?"

"I've told you I want you everywhere, Peaches. I'd prefer our first time not to be in a hospital bed with Nurse Ratched outside the door. But I'm not above it. Rub your hot little body against me one more time, and I'm not holding back." He played with her silky hair.

"You're so crude. I'm not having sex with you in a hospital bed." She laughed and a pink hue covered her cheeks.

"Maybe not today. But the next time I'm in the hospital, I won't hold back. Not to mention, you're wearing a fucking ball gown, so I have no access." He tugged on the top of her strapless dress, attempting to sneak a peek.

She slapped his hand away. “Go to sleep, Wallace. You’ve got to be achy from the accident. You need rest.”

“You better rest up, too. You won’t be sleeping once I get you back to the house.” He tucked her head beneath his neck and wrapped his arms around her.

“Promises, promises,” she said, her lips tickled his neck as she spoke.

“You have no idea, Peaches.”

****

“You’re such a control freak. It’s my car. Why do you have to drive?” Elle huffed when he pulled out of the hospital parking lot.

“I like being the driver. Even if it means driving this girly car.”

They’d spent the night in his small hospital bed. His body screamed with anticipation as he drove toward the house. Hell, he’d been in a constant state of want for the past month. He needed her so much he was willing to give this relationship thing a try. Because he didn’t want anyone but Elle. So, call it what you want. He was all in.

She snorted. “Girly car? You’re ridiculous.”

They bantered back and forth on the short drive. She glanced out the window after he pulled in the driveway. Still wearing her fancy ball gown, her skin glowed, her makeup free from her tears, and she managed to look gorgeous with no effort at all.

Nerves settled in his stomach when they stepped out of the car. He didn’t get jitters when it came to women. Nor did he get anxious about having sex. At least not before now. But somehow, with her admitting her lack of experience, he didn't want to push her or scare her off. Hell, a make-out session in the hallway had her running back home. He'd need to go slow. It wouldn't be easy. But nothing about her ever had been. And he wouldn't change a thing about her.

"Where do you think you're going?" He wrapped his fingers around her wrist when she walked toward the guesthouse.

"I'm going to shower." Confusion filled her gaze.

"The hell you are. You're coming with me. No pun intended."

Her face flushed at his words. "You're unusually bossy today, and don't be so crude," she said as he led her toward his house.

His fingers intertwined with hers, an act he normally despised, but not with her. Not with this girl. Her hand fit perfectly in his. He pushed through the front door and dropped the keys on the console table in the entryway. Daisy was still at his parents' house, and they'd bring her over later. No distractions. He had one thing on his mind, and she was standing right in front of him fidgeting with her fingernails.

Slow.

"Listen, Peaches. I've wanted you since the first day I met you. This last month—being together, it only made me want you more. All of you. I sure as hell don't want to scare you off again, but I'm going out of my fucking mind. I've been fighting this for weeks. Seeing you every day and wanting you the way I do. So I'm going to try like hell to take this slow. But if you think you're going next door to bathe—I'm here to tell you it's not happening. You can shower here." His breath came hard and fast as he looked down at her.

Her face flushed and her gaze searched his. “You want me to shower here? Why?”

He rested his forehead against hers in frustration. “I want you to shower with me.”

A gasp loud enough to wake the dead escaped her. “No way. Have you lost your mind?”

“Give me one reason.”

She licked her lips before pulling her bottom lip beneath her teeth. “I’ve never showered with anyone.”

How the fuck was it even possible? She’d had a five-year relationship. The dude never showered with her? Looking how she did? Hell, he’d never shower without her now that she was his. Wasn’t that the benefit of being in a relationship? All the fucking togetherness?

“We’ll take it slow. But I need you trust me.” It was all he could say.

“I do.” She looked up at him.

“Come with me.” He led her to the master bathroom.

He turned the water on in the tub and poured in bath salts his sister gave him. She wanted to bathe. Fine. She didn’t want to do it together. Fine. He handed her his white robe.

“Here, put this on.”

“You think taking a bath together is taking it slow? How is this different from showering together?” She clutched the robe as if it offered her protection. How was this confident, beautiful woman so insecure when it came to intimacy?

“Because we aren’t bathing together. You are taking a bath, and I am going to sit right here and talk to you.”

Her laughter a melodic rhythm. "You're going to watch me bathe?"

"Yep."

She shook her head and raised a hand to cover her mouth. "Why?"

"Because I want to."

They stared at one another for a long moment before she spoke, "What's the robe for?"

"I assumed you wouldn't get naked in front of me, not yet, at least. So you can go change into the robe and wear it until you step in the water. But I will see you naked either way. This is me meeting you halfway. I'm trying to make you more comfortable."

Her gaze softened, and she turned on her feet and walked into the closet. He knew she wanted this as badly as he did. Felt it when they'd kissed. The way she pressed her body against his, rubbing greedily. Needy. So complicated he didn't know what she was thinking most of the time. He leaned over and turned off the water and sat beside the tub. She sauntered out of the closet in a robe that nearly swallowed her whole, her hair tied in a big, messy knot on top of her head, and her feet bare as she shuffled on the white marble floor. She never looked sexier. So vulnerable and sweet.

She lifted her arms out to the sides. "Okay, boss. Now what?"

He could barely pull his stare from hers. "Get in the water, Peaches."

She sucked in a sharp breath, wrapped her arms around her chest. "Turn around."

"No," he said, one brow raised in challenge.

"Why?"

"I agreed not to get in with you. I'm giving you as

much space as I can muster. And it's fucking killing me. Do you have any idea what it's like to have blue balls for a month? No way in hell am I looking away. I've imagined you naked a million times. I'm not missing this." He held his ground.

"You know this makes you a bit stalkerish. Just sitting there all creepy, watching me step into the bathtub."

"I'm totally fine with it." He leaned his back against the wall, taking her in.

"Stop grinnin' like a possum eatin' a sweet tater," she said, her Southern drawl exaggerated. She bit down on her plump bottom lip again, making it hard for him to see straight he wanted to kiss her so badly.

He knew she wasn't going to run this time. She wouldn't have put on the robe if she weren't all in.

"You're fucking beautiful, Peaches. You don't need to be shy with me. If I had my way, you'd never wear any clothes." He held her gaze, wanted her to see how much he meant what he said.

"I'm not being shy. I've pranced around on stage in a bathing suit too many times to count. This just feels so—intimate. It's not helping you staring at me all intense with your blue balls and your cocky grin." She huffed before tugging at the white belt and squeezing her gorgeous eyes shut, before looking back up at him again. It was like unwrapping a present. She pushed the fabric off her shoulders, and it fell in a heap at her feet.

Holy. Fucking. Shit.

She was even better than he'd imagined. At least in the one point five seconds she'd allowed him to look before she hurried into the water and blanketed herself in the clear liquid. But he could see her. He'd always seen her. She was never more beautiful than right here in this moment. Her face clean of makeup, youthful with a few freckles scattered across her nose.

"Did you really just reference my blue balls?" he said.

She rolled her eyes and chuckled. "Stop looking at me like that, Wallace."

He couldn't help himself. He dropped down to his knees beside the tub. Wanted to get closer. Take her in.

"Looking at you how?"

"Is this how you seduce all your ladies?" It was part tease, part serious.

He knew her fear that he'd take off after they were together was real. He couldn't blame her. His track record was less than impressive. But he wasn't going anywhere. She'd be the one who'd break him. He'd never felt like this with anyone.

"I can promise you, Peaches, I've never watched any other woman bathe. Never wanted to. Not before you." It was the truth. Sure, he'd showered with plenty of women over the years. It was another place to have sex. Nothing more. Not like this.

She searched his gaze, and leaned her head back against the tub, sinking down low in the water. "So I'm your first."

"Yep. And it's fucking amazing." He rested his elbows on the side of the tub and leaned his face closer to her.

She laughed. "You know you're crazy, right?"

He examined the water, trying to make out the beauty beneath, but the details were blurred. He couldn't wait to get her out of the tub and into his bed. And not for the usual reasons. Of course, he wanted her. But he also wanted to memorize every curve, every detail. Wanted to make her feel good. Make her feel *everything*.

"You know you're beautiful, right?"

She rolled on her side like a mermaid the way she moved around in the water, as if she had all the space in the world. Her face close enough to feel her warm breath on his lips, her skin flawless and gorgeous. And those fucking eyes. Gold, amber, and topaz penetrated straight to his soul.

"When do I get to see *you*?" Her voice teased, but her hands trembled when she rested them over his.

"All you have to do is ask. I'm all yours, Peaches."

She hit the drain with her foot and wiped a few water droplets from her pretty face. He pushed to his feet and reached for a towel. She stood before him, lifted a shaky hand out for the towel.

"How about I dry you off?" His voice gruff. The thought of touching her had his body reacting in all sorts of crazy ways.

"All you have to do is ask. I'm all yours, Wallace," she said, mimicking his words. He took her hand and she stepped out of the tub. She stood there on the bathmat, water dripping from her gorgeous body.

Looking like everything he'd ever wanted.

Chapter Fifteen

Elle's Tip of the Day

You've got to kiss a lot of frogs before you find your prince!

She'd read plenty of sexy romances in her day. Watched every rom-com ever made. Hell, she'd even indulged in the whole Christian Grey phenomenon. But nothing, *nothing*, prepared her for standing before Maverick Wallace as he towel-dried her body. The way he looked at her. My God. The man was hotter than six shades of hell. Desire radiated from him. His nearness so overwhelming. She'd never felt so wanted. So desired. Yes, she'd been completely self-conscious at first. Never stood in front of a man so bare before. But she trusted him. There was an unexplainable bond between them. One she couldn't explain. A force stronger than anything she'd ever experienced.

He dropped to his knees and began drying her legs. Her whole being flooded with desire. His lips grazed her abdomen as he raked his gaze over her. She bit down hard on her lip and pushed away the need building inside her. Her fingers twisted in his thick dark hair.

"So gorgeous," he said, his lips grazed her thigh.

Oh.

My.

God.

Her breaths came hard, and he'd barely touched her. He pushed to his feet, towered over her, and his fingers traced the back of her neck. He took her hand and walked backward toward the bedroom, his gaze never leaving hers. She reached for the towel on the side of the tub, needing something to cover herself. He tugged it from her hands and tossed it on the floor.

"Let me see you."

Butterflies fluttered in her belly. Her heart hammered in her chest as they slowly made their way to the bedroom. "I don't like being undressed when you're fully clothed," she whispered.

He didn't miss a beat. He reached over his shoulder and tugged his shirt off, tossing it on the floor. One hand still in hers, he guided her until the backs of her legs hit the mattress.

"You want to see me, Peaches?" His voice gruff.

"Yes," she said, the word barely audible.

His thumb came up and traced her bottom lip. She all but panted, so desperate and needy for this man, he had her all spun up. He pushed his joggers down dropping them to the floor. His boxer briefs followed. Not an ounce of insecurity. A loud gasp escaped her as she took him in. She was too enamored to be embarrassed by her reaction. Maverick Wallace was all man. Bronzed and beautiful. Every single muscle and movement big and hard. She'd never seen anything so magnificent.

"Oh, my God. You're—perfect." Her hand trembled as she reached out to trace the lines across his abdomen.

A sexy chuckle rumbled from his chest, and he

moved closer. Crowding her. Consuming her. His hands explored and teased, as they moved up the sides of her body, he eased her back onto the bed.

"Fuck, Peaches. I could look at you all day. I want to take in every inch. Know what you like, what you need." He lifted her like she was a pillow he could easily maneuver and moved her back further on the mattress. He pressed a knee on each side of her, and hovered above, and she settled on her back beneath him.

Her pulse raced, and her heart pounded so hard she could hear it. Her mouth dry, and her body needy. His nearness. His touch. Her feelings for him had intensified with each passing day. This out of control feeling was foreign and unfamiliar.

"Relax, Peaches. Let me make you feel good." His mouth came down over hers, and she buried her hands into his unruly hair, urging him closer.

He pressed his body to hers, his desire hard against her most sensitive spot. A moan escaped her, and she reached up to cover her mouth. He wrapped his fingers around her wrist gently and pinned her arm above her head. Running his lips down her neck, she arched in response.

"So sweet." His lips grazed her skin.

His mouth covered her breast, and his hand moved up her thigh, touching and teasing, exploring her body. It was too much. Too overwhelming. More than she could handle.

"Oh, my God, Maverick." She gasped.

He pressed up and hovered above her, studied her, before pushing away a loose strand of hair from her face.

"I want you to feel everything. Do you trust me?" He reached across the bed to his nightstand. She heard him tear open the foil packet. She squeezed her eyes shut, needed to breathe. She wasn't dreaming. This beautiful man wanted her as much as she wanted him.

"Yes."

"Open your eyes. I want to see you." He pushed up on his knees and slowly covered himself. She was burnin' up. Never had she seen anything so sexy.

Her gaze locked on his. "Please, Maverick." She couldn't wait another second to feel him. Couldn't get close enough.

"So fucking beautiful, Peaches."

He settled between her legs, teasing, and torturing her needy body. His mouth covered hers, possessive and greedy. She arched toward him instinctively, pleading for more. She gasped as he filled her inch by inch. Slow and torturous. He watched her as they moved together, connected in every sense of the word.

"Elle," he moaned as their bodies danced in perfect rhythm.

A building, consuming need.

"Let go, baby."

A soul-shattering sensation ripped through her body at his words. Pure and explosive. Her senses spun. He followed with a bone deep growl of pleasure, his face in her neck. Her trembling limbs clung to him. Gasping, he rolled on his side, pulled her with him, and she buried her face into the corded muscles of his chest.

Her heaving breaths and racing pulse returned to normal in long, slow increments as she slowly peeked up at the man heaving beside her. A sexy grin spread across his handsome face, as his dark, heated gaze locked with hers.

"What are you doing to me, Peaches?"

"I don't know. But I sure hope we do it again." Her voice came out breathy and raspy.

"Oh, trust me, we're going to be doing this as often as possible." He kissed the top of her head, and his arms came around her even tighter.

And for the first time in her life, she wasn't anxious about planning out the next step. She was exactly where she wanted to be.

****

The floors were in, the walls painted, and the window coverings hung. This was always her favorite time of any project but doing it for Maverick only magnified the entire experience. Not to mention they were together, and she couldn't ask for more. She made a conscious effort to keep her expectations low. Maverick hadn't been in a relationship since dating his crazy ex years ago. But as far as boyfriends went, the man set the bar high. Sure, it had only been a week and they were existing in a little bubble away from the real world, but she'd never been happier.

He understood her. Listened to her. Encouraged her. The friendship they'd built only intensified their bond, and the man set her body on fire.

Every. Single. Day.

They couldn't get enough of one another, which was a first for her. Before Maverick Wallace, she'd pretty much dreaded sex. It had always been a chore. But this—she couldn't put it into words. She fought hard to keep her emotions reined in. Her heart couldn't take it if he tired of her.

"All right, darlin', we're all finished," Sam said

with a wink.

The man was a shameless flirt. It bordered on annoying as the day wore on. He owned the shutter company she chose for this project. They'd only met twice—first when he came up to the house to take measurements and gave her a bid, and today to oversee the installation. Both times he'd come on strong. Like the stink on a skunk kind of strong.

"Well, everything looks great. Thank you." She stood in the great room, admiring the gorgeous wood shutters.

"I thought I was going to meet your famous client today?" He moved beside her, close enough to press his shoulder to hers. The overpowering smell of self-tanner and musk surrounded him like a dark cloud. She breathed through her mouth to keep from gagging.

"He's at the gym, unfortunately I think you're going to miss him." She gave a sympathetic smile, hoping he'd follow the rest of his team out the front door.

"I hear you two run together most mornings? Everyone thinks it's funny, a woman keeping up with a football star, but I guess it explains why you look so fine." Sam stood just under six feet tall, his shoulders too wide for his build. His buzzed head was too small for his body. Skin tinged slightly orange, and his too-white teeth stood out against his complexion. His sexist comment rubbed her wrong. She could handle a harmless flirt. But don't insult her athletic abilities, and *fan girl* all over her boyfriend, all while hitting on her.

"It's been a pleasure doing business with you, Sam." She plastered her best fake smile on her face.

"Shit, Elle. Didn't mean to insinuate you weren't in

amazing shape. I mean look at you. But, Wallace is one of the most competitive athletes in the league. The dude is a badass. It's obviously how he scores a shit ton of women, right? I'm sure he gets the pick of the litter." He placed a hand on her shoulder, and she shrugged it off and took a step back.

The porch light was on, but no one was home. The man just compared all females to a bunch of newborn pups. More like *bitches*. The guy was completely clueless at reading social cues. How dare he talk about the *shit ton of women* Maverick scored. Jealousy flooded her. The feeling so foreign she didn't know what to do.

"There is something I wanted to ask you," he continued, while she fought the anger he incited.

She nodded. "What can I help you with?"

"That's a loaded question, sugar. There's a lot I'd like you to help me with." His sleezy smile caused a chill to run down her spine. "I was wondering if you'd like to go to dinner with me?" He crowded her, cocky and confident.

"Thank you for the offer, but no thank you." She stepped away.

"Ah, someone likes to play hard to get. Give me one reason why you won't go out with me, gorgeous?" He moved closer.

Irritation engulfed her. She'd happily kick this moron where the sun didn't shine, but she wanted to keep things professional if possible. She'd handled plenty of guys like Sam.

"I can give you more than one reason," she said, stepping back again, chin up, ready to give this guy a piece of her mind if he pushed much further.

He chuckled. Did he actually think they were flirting? Had he never read a social cue in his life?

"Ooh, you're feisty. Let me hear your reasons, and I'll tell you why you're wrong."

The nerve.

Two protective arms wrapped around her middle from behind. Mint and sandalwood. Maverick. His chin rested on her shoulder, and the scruff around his jaw grazed her cheek. Intoxicating. Her hand instinctively came over his.

"You want a reason? How about she has a fucking boyfriend. You going to tell me why I'm wrong?" Maverick's voice remained steady, calm, but his body was anything but. Tension radiated from him, as he enveloped her in his hold.

"Oh, dude, I'm sorry, man. I didn't know. I'm a huge fan," Sam stuttered, holding his hands up in apology. The pushy, cocky guy from moments earlier completely evaporated before her eyes.

"You know who I'm a fan of?" Maverick rubbed his scruff against her cheek, affection brimming.

"Who?" Sam looked confused and awestruck at the same time.

"My girl right here. And I'm pretty fucking sure I heard her tell you she wasn't interested—more than once. That shit won't happen again. Now I suggest you say your goodbyes and go find your own fucking woman."

"My bad, man. I'm sorry, Elle." Sam made his way to the front door, and Maverick followed him.

"Take care, Sam," she said, relieved to see him leave.

Maverick shut the door behind Sam and stalked

toward her, his expression laced with concern. “What an asshole. Did he touch you?”

“Don’t be ridiculous. No. I would have kicked him in the balls if he’d tried anything.”

“Don’t talk about that fucker’s balls, Peaches,” he said, brooding as he ran his hand through his hair.

“You’re ridiculous. You do know I can take care of myself, right? I have been for a long time.”

“Yes. You’ve mentioned it a couple hundred times. Why didn’t you tell him you had a boyfriend?” he said.

She chuckled, seeing Maverick jealous was entertaining. “I didn’t know if you’d want me to. I wasn’t sure we were telling people.”

He rolled his eyes. “Of course, we’re telling people. I don’t want to be your dirty little secret.”

Relief spread through her body. They hadn’t discussed how public they were going to make this. Being tucked away in Lake Tahoe allowed them to keep their relationship private. Of course, her two best friends knew everything, but she didn’t know who he’d told.

“Come on, I want to show you something.” He took her hand and led her out back and down toward the water.

“Where are we going?”

“Down to the sand.” A mischievous smile spread across his face.

She paused to slip off her shoes. They dropped down on the warm powder and she adjusted her sundress around her and tucked her legs beneath her body. A pit settled in her stomach at the seriousness of his gaze. He said he wanted to tell people they were dating, but now he seemed nervous.

She sucked in a slow breath. “Out with it, Wallace.”

“Well, I want to talk to you about the last few weeks we have left up here.”

Holy hell. Did he want it to end when they went back to the city? Was she just a Lake Tahoe fling? “Okay.”

“I don’t know why you insist on keeping your stuff in the guesthouse. I told you I was all in. I want you to keep your clothes and all your girly shit at my house. With me. I don’t like when you leave to get ready next door in the morning.”

A chuckle escaped her. Not what she expected. He’d been relentless about her moving her things to his place for the past three days. The man did everything with a force, and she didn’t want to be left in the wreckage if he lost interest.

“Why do you care where my stuff is?”

“Because you’re always leaving. I want you with me.” The sun shone down and his bronzed skin glistened. His warm chocolate gaze settled on hers, a white T-shirt stretched across his toned chest, and his dark wavy hair tousled around his handsome face. Butterflies fluttered in her belly every time she looked at him.

“This is all new for you. There’s no need to rush it.” She knew him well enough to know something else was on his mind. Something more than moving her suitcases next door. He fiddled with the hem of her dress.

“Let’s put our feet in the water. Come on.” He took her hand and led her down the sand. She held the bottom of her sundress up to keep from getting wet.

The cold temperature startled her at first, but her feet quickly adjusted. He stared out at the horizon, the sun beginning its descent.

"You're acting weird. Is something wrong? Is this really about me bringing my stuff over to your house?"

"I have to tell you something." His body stiffened next to hers, and a sinking feeling settled in her chest.

"What?"

Her legs came out from under her, and before she could process what was happening, he threw her over his shoulder. She couldn't have stopped him if she wanted to. His hand slipped under the back of her dress and landed on her bottom.

"Maverick Wallace," she wailed, slapping at his hand as she tugged her dress back down. "What in the hell do you think you're doing?"

"Do you trust me, Peaches?" His voice smooth and sexy as he walked further into the water.

"How can I answer you when you're holding me over your shoulder, and you have your hand on my ass? Take me back to the sand now," she shouted, pounding her fists against his lower back. Her hair hung down, the tips almost touching the water.

On a gasp, they crashed into the ice-cold water. Shock and surprise made it hard to breathe but two strong arms held her close and pulled her to the surface. His laughter ricocheted across the lake and she sucked in long, labored gasps.

"What the hell, Wallace." She slapped at his hard chest before finding her footing on the rocky lake floor. Her shoulders barely above the surface, he pulled her close again and wrapped his arms around her. He shook his dark, wavy hair like a dog, and water droplets flew all around.

"I said I have something to tell you." He lifted her up and wrapped her legs around his waist. It was much easier to stay above water.

"Well, this lake is colder than a penguin's balls. I'm not sure why you had to drag me into the water." She wrapped her arms around his neck and tried to hide her smile.

"Why must you talk about everyone else's balls?"

"Spill it, Wallace."

"I wanted to take you somewhere you couldn't run away when I tell you this. You have a habit of running away, you know?" The tender look in his gaze made her heart race for this beautiful man. Even when he annoyed the living daylights out of her.

"I'm not going anywhere.".

Licking his lips, his gaze bounced everywhere but her direction. She placed her hands on each side of his face and forced him to look at to her.

"You can tell me anything," she said, and she meant it.

"There's a reason I want you to bring all your stuff over to the main house. With me." His tone serious.

"There's an opening at the brothel?" She laughed and pushed the hair away from his handsome face. Her fingers grazed over the scruff shadowing his chiseled jaw. Her dress pooled around her waist. She'd never felt freer.

"You know, I'm sure to you this seems fast. We only decided to give this a shot a week ago, I get it. But I've known how I felt about you since the day you showed up on my driveway. Hell, to be honest, I think I knew how I felt about you the first time we met, at the wedding. It scared the shit out of me, Peaches."

Emotion nearly choked her. "How did you feel?"

He let out a long breath. "I love you. I think I have for a long time."

Her fingers tangled into his wild, unruly hair. Long black lashes framed his gorgeous dark stare, his beautiful face so striking it nearly took her breath away. Tears broke from her eyes and streamed down her already wet face. Emotions so powerful, she just might drown in them. But he had his arms around her to keep her above water. In more than just the literal sense. His thumb swiped at the falling tears and he studied her.

"How can you be sure?" Her voice trembled. She needed to know this was real.

He chuckled at her question. "I don't say things I'm not sure of. I've never told a woman I loved her. And I've never been more sure about anything."

She buried her face in his neck and whispered in his ear. "I love you, too."

"No way. You don't get to hide." He pulled back and forced her to look at him.

Nervous laughter escaped her lips. "So bossy."

"Only when I want something."

She placed a hand on his cheek. Her body pressed against all his hardness. God, how would she ever survive this man if he left her? It didn't really matter because she didn't have a choice. She was in too deep. There was nowhere to run.

"I love you, Maverick Wallace."

His mouth came over hers.

Water splashed around them.

She'd read every fairy-tale ever written—and not a single one came close to comparing to this moment.

Now, if only he could promise her the happily ever after, too.

Chapter Sixteen

Maverick's Playbook
You can't always play it safe!

Three days. Three fucking days until they returned to reality and left this peaceful little bubble they'd existed in for the past eight weeks. They worked out, double workouts for him. They spent long hours remodeling the house. Dinners on the patio beside the lake and boat rides. He was surprised how much he enjoyed their lengthy conversations about their childhoods and their jobs. Nothing compared to lots of fan-fucking-tastic sex, everywhere an opportunity presented itself—the old house, the new house, the guesthouse, the boat, the lake, the patio, he couldn't get enough of his girl.

Hell, he missed her the brief parts of the day they weren't together. Dating the same girl was new for him, and their strong physical connection was new for her. It blew his fucking mind. How she hadn't experienced pleasure from sex before? He'd be lying if he didn't admit he liked being the one to ignite a fire in her.

The only one.

She'd been convinced they'd get arrested if they had sex on his boat last week. She even insisted he Google the laws for boat sex and sure as shit, there was a law about indecent exposure. He didn't tell her that.

He explained it was private property, and they were out in the middle of the lake with no one around. He tried to convince her the good people in law enforcement encouraged boat sex. The girl was a walking contradiction—innocent and naïve, yet strong and fierce. And sexy as shit all at the same fucking time. He loved everything about her.

His gaze locked with hers as she sipped her wine once they took their seats at the reception for his cousin Brynn's wedding. Elle's lacy peach dress clung to her body like a glove. He sat back in his chair and scanned her from head to toe. Nothing beat a slow perusal of his girl. She'd pulled her hair back in some fancy, twisty knot at the nape of her neck, and a few loose waves fell around her gorgeous face. She unknowingly commanded the attention of everyone in the room. People stared, gawked, and admired. Mostly men, but women were entranced with her as well. He didn't give a shit, as long as they all knew she was his. When it came to Elle Fiore—he was possessive as hell. He'd never been that way before, but with her, it was primal. Instinct.

Maverick's entire family came out to celebrate the happy couple, including the other half of the wonder twins, his sister, Gigi, who seemed far more entranced with Elle than their cousin's nuptials. She'd heard about his girlfriend all summer from the rest of the family, who made a big deal that he was actually dating someone. They all loved her, and they weren't the easiest bunch to win over. The girl was a living, breathing metaphor for a glass half-full. While most people were both dark and light, Elle Fiore was all light. All goodness, with enough sass splashed in to keep her human.

He didn't know what they'd face when they got back to the city, when their days didn't revolve around one another. She'd go on to the next job, move back to her condo, and he'd do the same. And hopefully they'd find their place in one another's lives back home. Hell if he had a clue how to be in a relationship during football season. He'd never met anyone worth trying for. Not before now.

Elle leaned back in her chair, her gaze full of lust and want locked with his.

"Something on your mind, Peaches?" he said, leaning in close to her. He didn't want to invite his family into their conversation.

"Just thinkin'."

"Yeah? Are you thinking about what I did to you before we came here?" He grazed her ear with his lips. A pink blush crept up her neck and spread to her cheeks. He fucking loved the way she responded to him. And he knew exactly what she was thinking about, because he was too.

She pushed back a little, and her eyes darted all around the room, making sure his family couldn't hear their conversation. Which would be a first for his sisters if they kept their nosy asses out of his business.

"We're at a wedding, Wallace," she whispered, all flustered as her pretty face flushed again. Fucking adorable.

"No one can hear us over "Pussy Monster" blasting through the speakers. Do you see how hard my father is concentrating right now? He's convinced he's hearing the lyrics wrong. Gigi is moments away from going on a #MeToo tirade about how inappropriate this song is by referring to female body parts, and my mother is three glasses of chardonnay in and believes she's dancing along to a Disney Halloween song."

Elle's head fell back in laughter and she scooted her chair closer and leaned into him. "Fair enough. So, tell me. What are you thinking about?"

"Well, I spent the first half of this wedding thinking about how I took you in the shower before we got ready. Now, I've moved on to what I want to do to you next."

Even as the thumping beat pulsed around them, he heard a little gasp escape her. Her puzzled gaze studied him. "I don't think there's anything left to do?"

"Not true, Peaches." He adjusted himself beneath the table. Her nearness mixed with the conversation did crazy things to him.

Gigi's fist hit the table and the glasses shook, startling them from their conversation. She made this grand announcement about it being the year of the woman. This was her big epiphany. He was all for it. Power to all women everywhere. Hell, his entire family, aside from his father were females. He was all about empowerment; however, right now, he was more enthralled with one woman in particular. His sister's tirade could wait until tomorrow.

He rested a hand on Elle's thigh, returning his attention to his girl. She took a long sip from her glass before setting it down as her eyes searched his. "Okay. What haven't we done? Humor me."

He reached for her. Couldn't wait another minute. He pulled her to sit on his lap and wrapped his arms around her small body, taking in her gorgeous scent of honey and coconut. He grazed her ear again and whispered, "I haven't *tasted* you yet."

A gasp he heard over Fifty Cent belting out "In Da Club" which blared through the speakers. She pushed back enough to look at him. Her eyes the size of saucers. "Oh my gosh. No. I've never done that."

What kind of selfish pricks did she date before him?

"You haven't?" He ran his thumb over her bottom lip, memorizing this new expression on her beautiful face. Concern? Fear?

"No. I've never wanted to, and no one's ever suggested it."

"Jesus. Where the hell have you been, Peaches?"

The thought of being the first to make her feel pleasure like she'd never felt before caused even more of a strain against his zipper. He shifted her on his lap to save his out of control erection from even more torture, as her ass pressed against him. Surprise hit her when she realized what he was doing.

She leaned close to his ear. "I've been waiting for you my whole life, Wallace."

"Well, thank Christ. Let's go." He pushed to his feet and set her down beside him, shoving the chair back abruptly.

"What? They haven't cut the cake yet, we can't leave." A mischievous grin spread across her face.

"Mom, Dad, we're leaving. I have a migraine," he announced to his family. His dad who sat completely enthralled with the gangster rap, gave him a thumbs up. His grandmother leaned into Marley and asked her to repeat what he'd said about a migraine, and his mom jumped to her feet, reaching for her purse.

"Oh, no. Let me get you some Excedrin Migraine,

sweetie."

Marley and Gigi both made their way over to him. Let the ten thousand twin power questions begin.

"Bullshit, Mav. You were fine five minutes ago. You don't have a migraine," Gigi said making sure only he could hear as she narrowed her gaze.

He didn't have time for a lengthy debate with her. She had a gift for arguing, and he nor his erection had the patience for it right now. "You're right, G. I don't have a migraine. But I do have a raging boner, and no amount of Excedrin is going to help me."

Elle buried her face in his chest and groaned with embarrassment. She'd be groaning for a different reason in about fifteen minutes if the wonder twins would stop cock-blocking him.

Marley burst into hysterics. "Who are you and what have you done with my brother?"

"He's still a pig. Sorry you have to deal with him, Elle." Gigi rolled her eyes in disgust.

"Yeah, but not with one woman. Look at him—all needy and desperate." Marley laughed along with her evil twin, and his girlfriend joined in. Obviously these three never experienced the discomfort of sporting wood in public.

"Not needy. Just horny."

"What's so funny?" His mother pushed in front of Gigi, pressed the back of her hand to his forehead and handed him two capsules. "Here, sweetie, take these. There's nothing funny about migraines."

"Thanks, Mom. Sorry to cut out early." He kissed her cheek, and Gigi gave him the finger as she stood behind their mother.

Marley giggled. "Yeah, we don't want your

temperature to *rise*, Mav."

"Don't worry about my temperature, Nosy Smurf." He palmed the top of her head and tousled her waves.

"Elle, please take him home and get him right in bed. He needs a good night's sleep." His mother insisted.

"I'm sure she'll tuck him right in, Mom." Gigi winked at his girlfriend.

"Is it possible for this Hallmark moment to end?" he grumped.

"Yes, sweetie, you go. I'll check on you in the morning." His mom patted his cheek before his father pulled her out to the dance floor. Watching his parents dance to "Baby Got Back" might be the antidote for a boner.

He yelped when the skin under his arm twisted in his sister's fingers, as she pinched him hard. "You have Mom wrapped around your finger, Ferris Bueller." She rolled her eyes and chuckled. "Take your girl home, but you better plan on hanging out with me tomorrow before I drive back. I want more time with this one." She thrust her thumb at Elle.

You're preaching to the choir, naughty twin.

"For a tiny human, you sure are strong." He laughed and rubbed beneath his arm where she accosted him.

"So dramatic. Love you, brother." She pushed on her tiptoes and kissed his cheek. Marley did the same, and they both hugged Elle and made plans for the following day.

"Love you too," he said, before hurrying his girl past the crowd. The universe was working against him as they were stopped by every intoxicated relative on their way out.

When they made their way to the parking lot, Elle continued to move at a snail's pace in her heels, careful not to fall. He had zero patience left. He threw her over his shoulder and jogged to his truck.

She slapped his hand away from her ass. "What in the hell is the rush?"

"You're about to find out. And you're welcome in advance, Peaches."

Laughter rumbled from her chest against his back, and he swore on all things holy, this woman was going to be the death of him. Because his sister was right. He was needy and desperate.

He set her down in the truck and she shook her head, falling back in a fit of laughter. "You are ridiculous, Wallace. Looks like your migraine isn't too bad, huh?"

He pulled the seatbelt across her chest and kissed her mouth hard. "Oh, I've got it bad, all right. And you're about to have your world rocked."

A nervous smile spread across her face because she knew what he had in mind. He jumped in the driver's seat and pulled onto the road. When he parked in the driveway, he helped her from the truck, once again, fireman style. He had her sprawled out on his bed within seconds.

As he pushed her dress up to her waist, she grabbed his shoulders and stopped him.

"I need to tell you something?" She panted, her face flush and lips swollen from his mouth on hers.

"You can't get arrested for this, Peaches. But I think your ex-boyfriends should be under arrest for being selfish pricks." He pushed the hair back from her face to look at her.

"No, I don't know. I'm self-conscious about this. You know—you doing this." She covered her face with her hands.

He pulled her hands down and stared at her. "What's to be self-conscious about? You're fucking perfect."

She smiled and looked away, before meeting his gaze again. "I don't want it to be gross."

His head tipped back with laughter. Was she serious? "Do you honestly think I could find anything about you gross? I can't get enough of you. Trust me, I'm going to love this as much as you are," he said, wanting to wipe the worry away. He continued, "Okay, tell me something you think is amazing. The most delicious thing you've ever tasted."

She rolled her eyes. "Ummm, let's see." She wound her fingers into his hair, making his need for her more urgent. "Best thing I've ever tasted? A mint chip milkshake."

"Ah, got it. Do you know where one gets a mint chip milkshake? Well, they start by milking a filthy, fucking cow. The milk comes from the teat of a large beast, Peaches," he said, nuzzling her neck with his lips and rubbing his scruff against her the way she liked. Her laugh filled the space around them, and he continued. "And then they probably squeezed the teat into a filthy bucket before taking it to the dairy, which is where your shake comes from. It might be gross if you thought about it, but once it hits those lips, it's the best goddamned thing in the world."

She shook her head and smiled, licking her lips as she searched his face. "I'm going to have to take your word for that."

"Do you trust me, Peaches?" His voice gruff, the anticipation of burying his face between his girl's thighs was slowly killing him.

"Yes," she said just above a whisper.

It was all he needed to hear before he made his way down her body. She writhed and moaned, and it took all he had to take it slow. Because this girl was every fantasy he never knew he wanted. Everything he never knew he needed. And as he watched her come apart before his eyes, he swore for the first time in his life that pleasing her was better than pleasing himself. The most beautiful thing he'd ever seen.

And that alone scared the living shit out of him.

Chapter Seventeen

Elle's Tip of the Day

Find yourself a man who makes you grin like a possum eatin' a sweet tater and hold on tight with everything you've got!

Well, stick a fork in her.

She.

Was.

Done.

Every positive Southern saying she'd ever heard played on fast track through her mind.

She felt finer than a frog hair.

If she were any peachier, she'd be a cobbler.

Someone cue the confetti because this girl had a whole lot to celebrate.

Maverick Wallace managed to set her world on fire in every sense of the word. And lying here, naked as a jaybird, her body may as well be floatin' above the mattress. Sure as cornbread goes with greens—the man was a livin' dream.

Thoughts like this weren't good. But for the love of Pete she couldn't stop them. She stretched her arms over her head. She'd never slept naked. Never. Didn't believe in it. But right now—you couldn't pay her to put on a stitch of clothing. And hells bells, if it wasn't a slice of heaven being wrapped in Maverick's arms all night. Well, they hadn't slept much. The man kept her up half the night.

He walked back in the room. Her bat senses on high alert where he was concerned.

"How are you feeling, sleeping beauty?" His navy joggers were slung low on his hips, his chest bare. The man was a walking GQ ad. All ripped and manly. He handed her a glass of water and dropped down on the bed to lie beside her. Mint and sandalwood wrapped her in a warm hug.

"Never better," she said, her voice raspier than she expected.

He chuckled. "Same here. You're sweeter than any mint chip milkshake I've ever had, Peaches."

"Oh my gosh. Stop." She pulled the sheet up over her face. Her entire body flushed.

He pushed the sheet away and nuzzled her neck, propping himself above her. "I love waking up with you. We need to talk about what we're going to do when we get back to the city."

Maverick was driving back tomorrow, but she'd stay a few extra days. Her boss, Camille was coming to walk through the finished project in two days and oversee the photo shoot by *Interior Décor Magazine*. They were a huge national publication and Camille pulled a lot of favors to get this feature story. Everyone wanted to see how the famed quarterback lived.

She scheduled movers to take large pieces over to the new house, and handpicked everything else from custom furniture, to beautiful artwork, and loads of accessories. They'd get to spend one night at the new place before he left tomorrow. Official practice for Maverick started the following morning.

"Okay. Well, at least we don't live far from one another." She chuckled and ran her hand through his hair wavy hair. She liked their little world here at the lake and worried about all the changes they were about to face.

"I want you to stay with me when we get back," he said, and his lips made their way down her neck.

Gasping, she pushed him back and moved to sit up with her back against the headboard. "I can't be logical when you're kissing me."

"Then say yes. Stay with me, and there's nothing to discuss."

"You've lost your marbles. I'm not some *kept woman*. I have a home, and a job, and a life back in the city." She pulled the sheet around her body. There'd be no way to have a conversation with him if she didn't cover up. The man had some kind of VIP pass to her lady parts, and right now she needed to focus on the conversation. Things were going to change, and they'd both have to be flexible.

"I know. But with my practice schedule and you working, I want to have our nights together." He tucked a loose strand of hair behind her ear.

"I do too. I think we should take turns staying at each other's place. It's called compromise."

"You live in a high rise. What about Daisy?"

"Nice try, Wallace. People have dogs in my building. There's even a cute dog park on the main floor."

He rolled on his back and looked up at the ceiling. "So stubborn, Peaches."

"I'm not being stubborn. I'm meeting you halfway. You're the one who doesn't want to bend."

He rolled on his side and faced her, and his gaze locked with hers. “Move in with me.”

She laughed. Assumed he was kidding. Once she realized it wasn’t a joke, she shook her head. “Maverick Wallace, you could drive a preacher to drink. We can’t move in together. We’ve only been dating for a few weeks. That’s not how this works.”

“Why does it have to work a certain way? We can make our own rules. I know how I feel about you. You know how you feel about me. What’s the hang up?” He ran his knuckles gently down her cheek, and it took all her strength to think logically.

“What’s the rush?”

“I want to be with you.”

Her entire body warmed. He loved her. Really loved her. In a way no one ever had. She loved him so much she felt like her heart might explode sometimes.

“We should exchange keys.” Once again, she was compromising. He was used to getting his way. But relationships were about give and take. They’d need to be flexible and meet in the middle.

He rolled his eyes. “Do you have a rule about shacking up? Please don’t tell me you have to be married before you move in with me?”

“Well, sure. I’d prefer to be married. I mean it’s the long-term goal, right? And why do you assume I’m moving in with you? Maybe you’ll move in with me, you stubborn ass.”

“Semantics, Peaches. But I wouldn’t marry someone I didn’t live with first,” he said, and her stomach twisted in a knot. Not what she wanted to hear. What was the purpose of living together first? To wait and see all her flaws and then decide if he still wanted her? Marriage was about unconditional love, not a safety net or a way out when things got rough.

Been there, done that.

"See, Wallace. These are conversations one normally has before shacking up. If you aren't sure about me, then we certainly aren't ready to live together. We've never discussed children, or what we both want out of life."

"Yes, we have. You want the fairy-tale. I think we already have it. I'm crazy about you, which makes me the perfect prince. And as far as not being sure about you—you couldn't be further from the truth. I've never been so sure of anything. I just don't think we need some piece of paper to be together. At least not now. I'm not saying I'm against it. Not if it makes you happy. But I want you to live with me now. And we have Daisy. She's kind of like a kid, right? Minus the shit diapers and lack of sleep. The only reason we're having sleepless nights is because I can't keep away from you."

His chuckle rumbled against her lips and his mouth covered hers. *Sweet baby Jesus.* Maverick sure had a way of distracting her. The conversation could wait. Her fingers tangled into his hair. Would she ever tire of this man?

Doubtful.

****

Camille arrived prompt as always. Elle worked late into the night and the house looked incredible. Maverick left for the city less than twenty-four hours ago, and she missed him already. He'd insisted on christening as many rooms as possible. The man was insatiable, and she enjoyed all of it.

"Oh my, this view is breathtaking." Camille exuded confidence as she stepped out of her champagne colored Mercedes, her white linen suit similar to the outfit Elle wore the day she arrived in Lake Tahoe. So much had changed in a short period of time.

"Yes. It's spectacular. How was your drive?"

"Eventful. I just booked your next gig, and you're welcome," she said, as she walked up the driveway, pausing to look out at the turquoise water.

"Wow. I've barely wrapped things up here. Does the new job start right away?"

"It does. I'll fill you in after you show me everything. Did Maverick make it back to the city?"

"Yes. He left yesterday." And dammit to hell if her chest didn't tighten at the mention of his name.

"What's the story there? Your two partners in crime are very tight-lipped, but I've heard whispers in the office about a little romance between you and your client. Maverick also phoned me, gushing about your talent. It sounds like he's as impressed with the woman as he is the design." Camille crossed her arms in front of her chest, but her smirk carried a hint of humor.

"I mean, it's new. But yes, he's amazing," she said, and she could feel her cheeks heat.

"I guess it's too late for the *don't mix business with pleasure* speech." She chuckled and tucked one side of her white, shoulder-length bob behind her ear. "You're an adult, I trust this won't interfere with your work."

"Of course not. I'll let my work speak for itself."

She led Camille through the front door, pausing in the entry to take in the great room, the magnificent views, and every detail in between.

"Wow, your work is certainly doing the talking

now," she said on a gasp.

The dark wide plank flooring set the tone in the masculine, yet classic cabin. The design screamed comfort, homey and cozy; however, it also managed to be rustic, modern, and stylish at the same time. Not the easiest design to pull off.

Slip-covered couches and oversized chairs sectioned off the great room. There was a mix of fabrics with coordinating color palettes in plaids and solids throughout the space. Soft cottons donned some of the pieces, and velvet and chenille covered others. Tan and sage green were the predominant colors, with splashes of blues and creams adding detail in the accent pieces. Large shaggy cream area rugs warmed the dark floors. Rustic wood beams with dark metal brackets ran along the ceiling, while three large rustic chandeliers hung from the center of the ceiling in the main room.

Camille was rarely speechless, but she didn't say a word as she walked through the home, her gaze wide and a smile spread clear across her face. She bent down to run her fingers along the large farm-style coffee table.

"Magnificent pieces. I love how you sectioned these areas into two different living spaces without using walls, which provides a view of the lake from everywhere you stand in the room."

"Yes, it's exactly what I envisioned the first time I stood here. The home was one big maze when we started, and the walls blocked the lake view from the entrance, family room, and kitchen. It's so much better open."

"Where did these couches and chairs come from? I love the way the mismatching fabrics warm the room.

Rustic yet still chic and classic."

"Most of the furniture is custom. Every piece was made specifically for this home. A talented woodworker who grew up with Maverick made all the tables. I drew what we wanted, and it took some time to find the correct finish. He's a talented carpenter, and he nailed it. Our timeline was longer due to all these factors, but I think it was worth the wait to have everything sized and selected specifically for this space."

"I could not agree more. The magazine is going to eat this design up. We may have a new clientele for cabin design," Camille said with a chuckle, while she scanned and studied the details in each room.

Elle's favorite room in the house was the kitchen. The custom cream cabinets and the oversized island finished in distressed black stain, boasted an elegant farmhouse design.

"Oh my. This counter is magnificent." She ran her manicured nails along the smooth surface.

"Yes. It's quartz. I liked the cream with the black and tan specks. There are some pops of gold in there when the natural light comes through the window. It all ties together well."

"Agreed. These appliances are definitely chef worthy." She checked out the top of the line oven and stovetop. The dishwasher and the refrigerator were custom as well, covered in the same wood as the cabinets.

Camille made quite a fuss over the details in each room. A den filled with Maverick's trophies and awards and footballs from the games he'd won over the years were displayed in glass boxes on the shelves. Framed photographs of his journey from childhood to this point in his career hung on the walls and were a collection his mother helped Elle put together.

The doorbell startled her from the tour. Camille continued to rave about the incredible game room which held a pool table and several vintage pinball machines, as they made their way to the foyer to greet their guests.

"Elle, you've outdone yourself. This is your best work. I'm floored. I see why Maverick is blown away."

"I'm really happy you're pleased. I had a lot of fun with this project."

"I think your client did as well." Camille winked.

On the other side of the door stood a slew of people here to photograph the house. The next few hours were exhausting and exhilarating. They took shots of every room in the home, the gorgeous lakefront yard, and asked endless questions about the design choices. Her boss let her take the lead.

When the last person waved goodbye, Camille fell back on the chair, kicked off her heals and propped her feet on the oversized coffee table. Elle followed suit and let out a long breath.

"Impressive stuff, kiddo. I'm proud of you."

"Thank you. I'm glad you came up to do this with me."

"Of course. I wanted to see it in person. Facetime doesn't do it justice. Take the rest of the week off, get yourself settled back in the city, and then you start your next project."

"Okay. What is it? Another home?" She enjoyed doing homes, getting to know the clients, and transforming residential spaces. But she was eager to take on larger commercial projects as well. She needed to spread her creative wings if she hoped to someday own a firm.

Her boss looked down at her phone and typed a message to someone, before looking back up to meet her gaze. Something unfamiliar crossed her expression. Concern? Apprehension?

"It's not a house. It's a large project. And they'll only sign with us if you are the designer."

Elle sat forward, rubbed her hands together. "Okay. It sounds great."

"I hope so. The project is Efant Capital. They want a full renovation of their San Francisco office. Is it a conflict for you? They won't work with anyone else. It was their one stipulation."

Her chest tightened. Why in the world did they want a full renovation? The building was in great shape and had been renovated two years ago. Edward never mentioned the idea of revamping it to her. He'd reached out a few times over the past few weeks and sent flowers to her in Lake Tahoe after prying the address out of her mother. She called to let him know about her relationship with Maverick, per her boyfriend's insistence. They hadn't talked since. She wanted to remain friends but needed to put some distance there. Maverick didn't like Edward and didn't hide his irritation over the flowers. But Edward didn't live in the city full time, and they didn't run in the same social circles aside from Mama and Winston. Maybe Edward's father requested the remodel, and they were throwing it her way out of respect.

"Who is the contact on their end?"

Camille paused. "Edward Efant. He'll be staying in

San Francisco permanently until the renovation is complete."

She and Maverick's safe little bubble was fracturing, and she hadn't even made it back to the city yet.

"You know he's only doing this because he doesn't like the idea of me being with someone else."

Camille nodded. "Keep it separate. This is where you need to put on your professional hat and get the job done."

In other words—*put on your big girl panties and deal with it.*

"Yep, I get it. If you can't run with the big dogs, you should stay under the porch. I've got this. You can count on me."

If Edward Efant thought he could rock the boat, he had another thing comin'. The man didn't know dipshit from apple butter when it came to her and Maverick. She wouldn't allow anything to come between them.

Chapter Eighteen

Maverick's Playbook
You don't always get to call the plays!

His first week back in the city was a shit storm. His training this summer prepared him well, but two-a-day practices were a bitch, no matter how good of shape you were in. He and Elle dove back into their busy lives headfirst, and though the outside noise proved challenging, they remained solid.

Even when she told him her pain in the ass ex-boyfriend hired her to design his offices.

"He's dangling his family fortune over Camille Chadwick's head to get his way. Like they say, once a douchebag—always a douchebag. I don't like this, Elle."

He'd even tried calling Camille to ask if there was any way around the loophole, but she insisted there wasn't. She'd keep her eye on the situation and make sure the Count behaved professionally. Naturally, he hadn't told Elle about his call with Camille.

"He's doing this to get close to you. You know that, right?"

"Shine will only get the contract if I agree to design the space. Trust me, I can handle Edward."

"I trust you." There was no question she was loyal as hell. But he sure as *shit* didn't trust Edward Efant.

****

The Miners hosted a family practice a few days ago to welcome everyone back and encouraged their significant others to come out and meet one another and cheer on the players. He never understood the hype before but having Elle there this year—he loved it. Loved showing off his girl.

Today, he met with Coach Romero after practice to discuss plays.

"Your pre-summer training is going to pay off when we're deep in the season, Mav. Well done. Now we build on it, and you put your head down and grind these next few weeks. Let's focus on those passing plays with Brent and Big Joe." Coach stood and drew on the white board, made a few suggestions to tighten things up and offered a few different pass options. He knew the game inside and out.

"Sounds good. Yeah, you know, I'm all in. Whatever it takes to get where we need to go come February." The guy was a brilliant coach, and they got along well.

"Amen. Keep your eye on the prize and let it push you through these next few grueling weeks. I like the leadership I'm seeing from you out on the field. Being your second season, the guys respect you now, look up to you."

"Honored to lead this team any way I can," he said, and he meant it. He stood and shook the other man's hand before they stepped out to the waiting area.

He did a double take. Elle sat poised on the leather chair, and he had no idea what she was doing there. They were supposed to meet at his place after work, per her strict rule about switching off where they slept every night. Weren't rules occasionally meant to be broken?

"Oh, hey. Hope you don't mind me dropping by, Coach Romero." Her tone sugary-sweet. More so than usual.

She kissed Maverick's cheek but didn't meet his gaze. Also not the norm.

"Of course not, Elle. You're always welcome. Beverly went on and on about you after family day. She wants to redecorate our entire house now, so I guess I have you to thank for the hit our bank account is going to take." Coach chuckled.

"Well, that's part of the reason I dropped by. Beverly and I realized we both share a weakness for the butter cookies at Frenchie's Bakery. My girlfriends and I happened to have lunch there today, and I grabbed her a box of sugary goodness. She mentioned she was having foot surgery tomorrow, so I thought these might help her through her recovery." His girl was charming as shit when she wanted to be. But something was up. She still hadn't look at him and her attention lie fully on Coach Romero.

"Aren't you thoughtful. She'll appreciate this. Thank you," Coach said.

"Of course. Send her my best. While I have you here, do you mind if I ask you a quick question?"

"Not at all. What can I help you with?"

"Well, I just wondered how you'd feel if one of your players *better-halves* told you which plays to call during a game?" She flashed her megawatt smile that left men in a puddle at her feet.

Coach coughed on the water he'd just sucked down. Christ. What the hell was she talking about? She knew nothing about football. She caught the man completely by surprise, and it took him a minute before he recovered and pulled himself together.

"You mean if a girlfriend or wife of a player tried to call plays for the team?" He studied her.

"Yes, sir." She nodded, with an oversized grin on her pretty face.

"Well, without being part of the team and knowing the players, I can't imagine anyone would attempt to do my job for me." He watched her curiously.

Maverick slyly tapped his foot against hers, an attempt to get her to look at him so he could figure out what her crazy ass was up to. She picked up her nude high heel and stomped on his foot, making a scene in the process. Coach coughed again, but this time to cover up his laughter at Elle's apparent anger. What the hell was her problem? He stuck to her ridiculous sleepover schedule and hardly fought her on it all week.

She turned back to face the older man. "Agreed. It's outrageous for someone who knows nothin' about what you do to poke their nose where it doesn't belong. *Like a cowboy trying to ride a pig bareback in the wild, wild west.* Ludicrous, right?" Her twang was on full display and Coach chuckled, only encouraging the angry little heathen to continue.

"I've never used this particular analogy, but I think it's a fair comparison, yes."

Her anger was out in the open, and clearly Maverick was the pig in this scenario. Camille must have mentioned their chat. *Fuck.* Elle came here to make a point, and she didn't appear to be done making it.

"Well, thank you, Coach Romero. You've been

married to your lovely wife for a long time now, right?"

Coach smirked, as if he were happy to assist in Maverick's demise. "Yes, ma'am. Twenty-seven years in April."

"How amazing. Seeing as you're practically an expert and all, how important do you think it is to trust your partner when you're in a relationship?" Now her gaze landed on Maverick. The sugary-sweet little Southerner was nowhere in sight. She was downright hostile. If fire shot out her ass in the next thirty seconds, he wouldn't be surprised. He'd never seen her this angry. And considering how often he'd pissed her off over the past year, that was saying something.

"Trust is essential in any relationship," Coach responded and nodded at Maverick with a dumbass grin.

Elle returned her attention to Coach Romero. "I couldn't agree more. Which is why I would never go behind Maverick's back and talk to you about how he should do his job. Only a scoundrel would do something that disrespectful."

Jesus. Now he was a fucking scoundrel? Coach couldn't contain his hysterics any longer. His head fell back in a fit of laughter before he pulled it together and faced Maverick.

"Yep. I think Beverly would have my balls in a sling if I went behind her back and talked to her boss. I'm a lot of things, but a scoundrel is not one of them," Coach said, still chuckling.

Nothing like getting schooled by your five-foot nothing girlfriend in front of your coach. He wasn't about to point out the obvious—Beverly was retired. She currently didn't even have a boss. He had a hunch

Elle would have his balls in a sling of her own if he tried to get technical with her.

"Ah, Beverly is a wise woman. Thank you so much for your time. I appreciate it." She patted Coach on the shoulder and whipped around and stormed toward the elevator.

"Anytime, Elle. See you at practice tomorrow, Mav." He leaned in and whispered, "Trust me. Start with an apology."

The elevator doors shut in his face by the time he got there, and he ran to the stairs and hurried down to beat her to the ground level. When the doors opened, she marched right past him. Chin pointed up and refused to give him so much as a glance.

He chased her, as he imagined he'd be doing for the rest of his life. "Peaches, stop."

She didn't. Her stubborn ass stormed toward her car. He ran ahead of her and used his body to block her.

"Get out of my way, you pompous ass," she said, loud enough for anyone within a few miles to hear. Her face flushed, hair wild, and never more beautiful.

"Peaches, come on." He placed his hands on her shoulders gently and met her fiery gaze. "I'm sorry. I should have told you I talked to Camille."

"Maverick Wallace, you're actin' crazier than an outhouse rat. You shouldn't have talked to Camille at all. I'm not mad you didn't tell me about the conversation. I'm mad you had the conversation at all." She poked her finger at his chest hard.

"Now I'm the rat? What about Count Dickhead who's having his entire building renovated so he can spend time with you? He's the one you should be calling names. I'm the one trying to protect you. Protect us." His anger hit a boiling point, and it was time she saw his side of this.

Her gaze softened and she stepped closer. "You don't need to protect me or us. But you do need to tame the green-eyed monster, Maverick. If I wanted to be with Edward, I'd be with him. I'm not. I want you. Only you. I've never felt like this with anyone. Don't you know how much I love you?"

He pulled her against his body. "I'm sorry, Peaches. I love you. I don't want him around you. Don't you understand why this is a problem for me? Would you like it if I was hanging out with Brittney every day?"

She looked up at him. "Of course not. Don't you think it bothers me when I read comments online where women are throwin' themselves at you? Once the season starts it will only get worse. Trust me, I understand how you feel. But you can't go to my boss and try to control my workplace. It's not okay. Do you remember the guy who cheated on me multiple times?" She paused and turned away for a minute.

"I'm not a cheater."

"I know you're not. What I'm saying is, he was a cheater. He accused me of cheating all the time. Never trusted me. I didn't understand it at the time, but it all made sense in the end. He didn't trust me because he wasn't trustworthy himself. He put his guilt on me." Her topaz gaze locked with his.

"But you can trust me."

"Right. And you can trust me. I'm not a cheater either, Maverick. It's not who I am. And this won't work if we don't trust one another."

"Christ, Peaches. I trust you. It's the douchebag I

don't trust."

"What he does, doesn't matter. It's what we do that's important. I'm appalled by this stunt Edward pulled. But you're letting him win by acting on it. In the end, you're doubting me and my loyalty to you."

He let out a long breath and nodded. "You're right. I shouldn't have gone to Camille. This is all new for me, and I swear I'm trying not to fuck it up. I don't like you working with him every day. It makes me fucking crazy."

"I've been completely upfront about you and me with Edward. He knows how I feel about you. My God, my mother isn't even speaking to me because I told her about us. Can't you see how invested I am in this?" A single tear ran down her cheek, and his gut wrenched.

He sure as shit was the rat. And the pig. He'd behaved like a jealous asshole.

"I do trust you, Peaches. It won't happen again. I'm sorry." Shit. He wished they could go back to the lake and get away from all this noise.

She swiped at her cheek and smiled. "From here on out, it's you and me, Wallace."

"You and me. I promise."

****

"See, this isn't so bad, right?" She pressed her forearms on his chest and looked up at him.

He agreed to take a bath with her. Hell, he'd do whatever it took to get his ass out of the doghouse. He'd hurt her, and if soaking in a hot tub cheered her up, count him in. She'd tried to get him to join her at her house for a bath the night before in her Barbie doll-size tub, it wasn't happening. His oversized jacuzzi tub easily fit two people with room for more. He'd never understand all the fuss over a small bathtub with no jets, the damn thing barely had room for one person—but because it had some weird shiny feet holding it up, women made a big deal of it?

"Anytime I have you pressed against me naked, it's never bad." He pushed the hair away from her pretty face.

"Tell me a secret," she said, her voice soft. The lights were dim, and a candle burned beside the tub.

"Like what?" He remained perfectly still in the hot water. He wasn't big on secrets. If he didn't share something it wasn't because it was a secret, it was because he didn't want to talk about it.

"I don't know. I just want to know more about you. I'll tell you one if you tell me one." She drew little circles on his chest with her finger. He couldn't remember the last time he was this relaxed.

"Okay. Ladies first."

"So chivalrous. Hmmm, let's see. Oh. I have a good one. I stole something once. When I was eight years old. It was the one and only time I found myself on the wrong side of the law."

He chuckled and shifted her body so he could wrap his arms around her. She fit perfectly between his legs, her chest pressed against his, and her head rested beneath his neck. "Yet I'm the scoundrel? Let's hear it. What did you take?"

She paused for a minute and sucked in a deep breath. "It was shortly after I found out about my dad. I was so mad at Mama. But I couldn't talk about it because she didn't think it was my place being a kid and all. So, I never ate candy when I was a kid because Mama didn't allow it. The woman dreamed of me being

Miss Georgia from the moment I took my first steps. She said junk food was the kiss of death. Well, you know those bins with the bulk candy at the grocery store?"

"You're not going to tell me your one time on the wrong side of the law was eating a piece of bulk candy?" His laughter echoed off the walls in the bathroom.

"I didn't eat just a piece. Have you ever met an eight-year-old who wasn't allowed to eat candy? Well, let's just say one piece wasn't enough. I went crazy. Lost my marbles. I ate so much I actually threw up in the grocery store. Right in the middle of produce. Those poor zucchinis were covered in gummies and red dye."

She sighed, as if the confession was a load off her mind and he tried to contain his laughter. "What did your mom do?"

"Mama wasn't there. She never went to the grocery store. I was with Clara, our housekeeper, slash nanny. She covered for me, of course. Always had my back. Mama never found out, thank goodness. But every time I go to the grocery store, I feel like I'm going to see my face on a WANTED poster, you know? So, there you go. The skeleton is out of the closet." She lifted her head to meet his gaze and he leaned down and covered her mouth. Needed to kiss her.

She chuckled against his mouth. "You're not getting out of telling me something, no matter how hard you try to distract me."

Her head settled against his shoulder again, before he spoke. "I can't help it. It's pretty hot—you being a grocery store thief and all. I knew somewhere under the Type-A, rule following, perfectionist lived a candy snatching bandit. You don't fool me, Peaches."

She chuckled and flicked a little water in his face. "I'm waiting, Wallace."

"Okay, it's not as scandalous as your grocery store robbery." He kissed the top of her head. "Do you remember the night we met at Jackson and Peyton's wedding?"

"Yes, of course."

"Well, the next morning I called Mimi. I told her I met the girl I was going to marry the night before."

She gasped. "You're lyin'."

"Nope. I speak the truth, Peaches."

"How did you know we'd be together?" she asked.

"I thought you were beautiful, obviously, couldn't stop staring at you. But when we were introduced…"

"Yeah?" she said, just above a whisper.

"All the hair on my arms stood up. Never felt anything like it before. My dad always told me he knew with my mom right away, and I never understood it. Not until the night I met you. But it scared the shit out of me, feeling so strong about someone I didn't even know. And then I was a dick the next night. Wanted to push you away. It tortured me every time I saw you."

"Damn, Wallace. Your secret is so much better than mine," she said, looking up at him.

He laughed. "Damn straight."

"Thanks for telling me. You knocked me off my feet the night I met you, too. But then I hated you for a long time." A grin spread across her face. "Until I realized I love you."

"I love you too, Peaches. Am I out of the doghouse yet? Anything else you want to know while you have me by the balls?"

Her fingers intertwined with his and settled on his chest. "Do you remember your birth mom? Or your time at the orphanage before you were adopted?"

Fuck. She wanted to know things he tried to forget.

"I remember what my mom looked like. She was pretty. I have vivid memories of being alone. Scared. Can't place where I was or why I felt the way I did, but I remember a lot of chaos and fear. Shit I don't like to think about or wish on anyone. My mom was a prostitute, so you can paint yourself a picture of what life was like for me. Thankfully, I wasn't old enough to fully understand what was happening. My mom lost her life to an overdose, but it most likely saved my life. The orphanage was the first time I remember feeling safe, before being adopted, of course."

She pushed up, rested her forearms on his chest, her gaze watery and full of emotion. "What a life you've lived, Maverick Wallace. You beat all the odds."

He used his thumb to wipe away a stray tear running down her cheek. "I just told you my mom was a prostitute and died of an overdose, and you act like I'm some sort of hero?"

"You're such a good man. I want to know everything about you." She rubbed her nose against his. The girl so sweet it made him want things he never knew he wanted.

"Everything?" he teased.

"Yep."

"Well, if you move in with me, I'll tell you more. We could spend all our nights in this tub if you want."

"It's too soon."

"So many rules."

"You have no idea." Her laugh trickled around them and he closed his eyes, savoring the moment.

So peaceful.

So perfect.

So Peaches.

Chapter Nineteen

Elle's Tip of the Day

You'll never please egg-suckin' dogs—but you can please yourself!

"You know you have sex hair, right?" Dani said.

Elle sat on the couch in Peyton's office with a big grin on her face.

"Well, hells bells, it must be all the good lovin' I had before I came to work." She grinned and patted her hair back in place. Dani and Peyton fell back in a fit of giggles.

"Who are you and what have you done with our prim and proper bestie?" Peyton said, her tone all tease.

Elle gasped. "I'm still me."

"Sure, but now you're all sexed up and relaxed. You went from English Duchess to *Girls Gone Wild Spring Break Edition* in a few short weeks," Dani said.

She laughed right along with them. The light coming in through Peyton's office window highlighted the pretty space. Clean and modern. Elle named their three offices after famous women when they first started at Shine Design. She based her choices on individual office décor.

Peyton's style—all white. White couch, white rug, white chairs, white desk, and black and white fashion prints on the walls. It screamed Victoria Beckham.

Dani had her own unique style. Classic and elegant. Dark woods, scholarly accolades decorated her walls, dark shelving, and no fluff. All business, which donned her the office name of Ruth Bader Ginsburg.

Elle preferred bright colors. The space splashed with hot pinks, bright greens, and turquoise. Her shiny white desk held colorful picture frames, fresh flowers, and pretty décor, emulating her Lilly Pulitzer dresses. Obviously, her office name was Reese Witherspoon.

"Is he still trying to convince you to move in with him?" Peyton pulled her from her thoughts, and Elle settled on the white shaggy rug in front of the couch.

"He sure is. I thought he might propose last night when I got to his place after work. He dropped down on his knees after dinner, and I swear my stomach dropped. I mean, it's too soon, right?"

"It's not too soon if it's right. But if he didn't propose, what the hell was he doing down on his knees?" Dani leaned closer and Peyton scooched down to sit on the rug and pressed her elbows on the coffee table to get closer.

"The only other thing a man drops to his knees for," Elle said, wriggling her brows, before the room erupted in a fit of giggles again.

"Amen. It's about time men dropped to their knees for women," Dani said, with pursed lips.

"Thank you, *hashtag me too*, but there's no political agenda here. Just a man pleasing his lady," Elle said in a singsong voice.

"I think *hashtag me too* should be Dani's new nickname. It's very fitting," Peyton said, shaking her head and chuckling. Dani rolled her eyes at the suggestion.

"How are you feeling about your mom meeting Maverick tonight?" Dani asked.

"Well, Winston set this up, Mama and I still aren't speaking. We are gonna mix if she takes a shot at Maverick."

"Is he nervous about meeting her?" Peyton set her tea on the coffee table.

"He keeps telling me not to worry. He isn't the least bit concerned. He doesn't know who he's dealin' with, though. Mama can be an egg-suckin' dawg when she's angry. And Maverick's family is so different. They're always callin' me to see how I'm doing. They're so genuine and real. I don't know how he'll deal with her, ya know? I hope he doesn't look at me differently."

"He loves you. Hell, the man is crazy about you. Nothing is going to change that. He begs you daily to move in with him. And look how close he and your dad have gotten. He's not going to judge you by your mom's behavior," Dani said.

"I know. She's my mama though. I just want her to be nice to my boyfriend. It's not like I'm asking for world peace."

"I know. Go tonight and give her a chance. Maybe she'll come around. God knows, the man is charming. Even you couldn't resist him," Peyton said.

"He's such a good man, and an amazing boyfriend. I want her to be happy for me. Like my dad is."

"Jackson said your dad and a few guys from the firehouse went to practice the other day to watch him play." Peyton smiled.

"Yeah, my dad loves him. Speaking of football and the first game next week—Maverick gave me one of his jerseys to wear to the game. But it's kind of, I don't know, plain? I told him I wanted to get his number covered in Swarovski crystals, and the man all but fell over laughing. He said you can't put jewels on a jersey. Apparently—it's sacrilege. He makes fun of all *my rules* but try to add a little sparkle to his jersey and he's up in arms. What does one even wear to a football game? In college all the girls wore cheerleading skirts to the games. Those are pretty cute."

"I will literally drop your ass at the curb if you get in my car wearing a cheerleading skirt on gameday. Because guess who wears cheer skirts?" Dani clucked her tongue.

"Who?"

"The *cheerleaders*, you fool. This is the pros, not college. It's T-shirts, jeans, and baseball caps. You eat hotdogs and drink beer." Dani looked at Peyt. "Um, feel free to jump in anytime."

Peyton chuckled. "Take it easy, Bader Ginsburg. No one is dropping anyone at the curb. You could bedazzle a baseball cap. Put a little sparkle on your head. And we know how much you love hotdogs and beer."

"Okay, I can work with this." Elle nodded. Her stomach rumbled at the mention of hotdogs.

"Jackson said we're all going to be up in the box with Maverick's family for the game?" Peyton asked.

"Yes. Even Mimi, his grandmother is coming. I can't wait to see her. The whole family will be there. My dad and Billy Goat are coming too. Should be lots of fun. And an oversized jersey may not be the most fashionable thing but being wrapped in Maverick's number makes up for it," Elle said.

"Good Lord, you're like a living, breathing fairy-tale," Dani said, with a big grin spread across her face.

She didn't know if it was true, but she sure seemed to be living one these days. But everything could all change tonight depending on how open Mama was to meeting Maverick. He wouldn't be the first person to turn tail and run.

****

"You look gorgeous, baby," Maverick said, coming up behind her and wrapping his arms around her middle.

She leaned back against him. Mint and sandalwood enveloped her senses. Something about his nearness always settled her. "Thank you. I'm glad you're coming with mc."

"Nowhere else I'd rather be."

"You're not nervous about meeting them?"

"Nope."

Damn, the man never let things get to him.

"How do you not let things stress you out?"

"Because I don't give a shit who likes me, as long as you do," he said against her ear, and her lady parts went into overdrive.

She turned in his arms, kissed his neck just beneath his throat. Her lips ran along his rugged scruff. Her breathing came hard and fast. It didn't take much with this man.

"Well, lucky for you, I'm crazy about you." She pushed on her tiptoes and kissed him.

"Crazy about you, too, Peaches." One hand tangled in her hair and the other dropped beneath the hem of her dress. His hand settled on her leg, teasing, and taunting as it moved further up her inner thigh.

"We need to go. We're going to be late." Her head fell back on a gasp.

"They can wait. Let me make you feel good, baby. I don't like seeing you so stressed." His mouth covered hers and his fingers slipped beneath her lace panties.

Oh. My. God.

They were going to be late to meet her mother and Winston, yet she didn't move. Couldn't if she wanted to. Maverick's touch soothed her worries—amongst other things.

****

"We're so late. My mother despises tardiness," Elle said, pulling him along the sidewalk toward the swanky restaurant.

"Well, if Winston did to her what I just did to you, she might not mind being a few minutes late to dinner." The man loved to tease her. Her face heated at his words. She swore he had a playbook for her body. Knew what to do, all the freaking time.

"Hush it, Wallace. You can't use your dirty mouth in front of Mama. She finds sexy talk inappropriate." Her heels clicked against the sidewalk. Thankful she chose her white eyelet spaghetti strap dress in this unusual heat wave. The setting sun decorated the sky in red and orange hues. The street bustled with people heading out for the evening.

He laughed, and his hand snaked around her waist. "It's a good thing I won't be doing any sexy talk with your mother then."

"Thank goodness. The woman is not easy to please."

"You guys have been on the outs since the pageant?" He intertwined his fingers with hers which calmed her fury.

"Honestly, ever since my dad took Mama to court when I was twelve years old and filed a request to change my name legally, our relationship was forever damaged." A lump formed in her throat. The memory a dagger to her heart.

"What do you mean? Why did she blame you?"

"The judge asked my opinion on the matter. I said I understood my father's desire for me to legally be Elle Fiore. I suggested my middle name become Humphries. Elle Humphries Fiore. It seemed like a fair compromise. It allowed my dad one small victory against my overpowering mother." Her pace quickened when she spotted the restaurant a few feet ahead.

"Seems fair. You honored both Winston and your dad."

"Yeah, seems logical. Keep in mind I was only twelve. I answered the judge honestly. But back home, the last name Humphries means something. Winston comes from old Southern money, and his lineage holds a lot of clout. When I was supposed to be presented as a debutante years later, all sorts of gossip broke out about my father's lack of Southern roots. Being a fireman with the last name Fiore didn't impress the haughty women in Mama's social circle. She fought to have Winston present me to society, but it would have been a slap in my dad's face. I chose to walk away and went back to college without my Savannah debutante cotillion title, which was the beginning of the end for Mama and me. And then I lost the Miss Georgia contest—you can't imagine the disappointment."

He held the door open for her, and as she walked in, he stopped her. "You're a flame thrower, Peaches.

You're not afraid to stand up for what you know is right. No one should be disappointed about that."

He kissed her, nipped at her bottom lip, and led her inside. The hostess ogled her boyfriend before guiding them to their table. Soft classical music played in the background, and the smell of French bread and garlic filtered through the air. Mama and Winston set down their wine glasses when she and Maverick approached. Her stepfather's face lit up. Winston had always treated her like the brightest star in the sky. Maybe it was to overcompensate for Mama's disappointment. Winston sent her two arrangements of fresh flowers every month. Like clockwork. One to her office and the other to her condo, all because after graduating from design school she told him how every room needed something living, something fresh, to bring it to life.

He jumped to his feet. Standing only a few inches taller than Elle, her stepfather wasn't a big man. His gray hair combed back neatly; his black suit fit to perfection. He came around the table and embraced her. "So nice to see you, my darling."

"You too, Dad." The way she saw it, she was lucky to have two great fathers in her life. "Maverick, this is my dad, Winston."

"Nice to meet you. I've heard a lot about you, sir," Maverick said, shaking his hand.

"Thank you, young man. Please, call me Winston. I look forward to seeing you play this season. Always been a Falcon's fan, but I reckon it's time to change things up." Winston's grin spread clear across his face.

"Nonsense, if we switch who we cheer for every time Elle has a whim, we won't make it through a season." Her mother stood and raised a brow in challenge.

Her boyfriend stiffened beside her.

Buckle up, handsome. We haven't even scratched the surface.

Maverick was striking in his gray button up and dark jeans. He'd made an effort to be here tonight. She knew he was exhausted from two-a-day practice. His wavy hair tousled around his handsome bronzed face. His concerned gaze locked with Elle's. She wanted to lean into him and let him wrap her up in a safe little cocoon. Instead, she straightened her shoulders. "Hello, Mama. I see you still have a sense of humor."

"I don't have much of a choice keeping up with you, now do I?" She leaned in for a quick hug, followed by an air kiss. Heaven forbid she smudge her ruby red lipstick showing real affection. Her blonde hair was pulled back into a perfect chignon. Always polished. Always poised. Her black cocktail dress fit her slim frame like a glove and ended beneath the knee.

"Mom, this is my boyfriend, Maverick Wallace. Maverick, this is my mama, Caroline Humphries."

"Pleasure to meet you." Maverick extended his hand.

"Ah, yes, *the boyfriend*," she said. Elle cringed at her rude tone.

They took their seats and Winston spoke first. "I hope you don't mind I took the liberty of ordering a nice bottle of red."

"Of course not, thank you." Elle licked her lips, tension crackling around them. Mama clearly didn't want to be here. Winston must have forced the issue.

"You didn't give us much of a choice with you showing up late," Mama said, and Elle reached for her water glass.

"My apologies for being late. It was my fault. I needed to give Elle a *hand* with something, and I think I slowed her down in the end."

Elle spattered the large sip of water all over the table and coughed uncontrollably. Maverick remained calm and collected and patted her on the back until she gathered herself.

"You okay, Peaches?" His hand settled on her thigh beneath the table. The bastard was going to torture her until she relaxed.

She leaned back against her chair. "Never better."

"It's a bit soon for nicknames, no?" Her mother's tone full of judgment and disapproval, yet so familiar she almost laughed.

"Yes. We've been together for a while now, but Maverick actually called me Peaches before we started dating." Elle smiled, meeting Mama's icy blue stare.

"It suits you. Peaches, I mean. It's sweet." Winston winked, and gave her mother a stern look.

"All right, then. Maverick tell us about yourself. We know you play football. Where are you from?" Mama extended a bit of an olive branch, yet her tone always managed to sound condescending.

"I grew up in Lake Tahoe, most of my family is still back there. I have a house in South Lake. Elle actually transformed the place over the summer. We'll have to show you some pictures."

"Well, that's a surprise." Mama gaped.

"That I have a place in Tahoe?" Maverick didn't hide his confusion.

"No. I assume football players make good money while they're playing, so I'm sure affording a lake house right now isn't a problem. But I wouldn't have guessed you were from Lake Tahoe."

"Really. Why?" Her boyfriend's voice clipped. Serious.

Mama's gaze slowly perused him in all his beautiful glory. "You're—very tan. I assumed you were from another country. You know, a foreigner."

Elle's back stiffened. She wanted to climb over the table and strangle the woman. Mama was deliberately trying to make him uncomfortable.

Maverick took a sip of water and his hand found hers under the table. "I'm actually from Brazil. My family adopted me when I was four years old. But you didn't ask where I was born, you asked where I was from. And like I said, I'm from Lake Tahoe."

The waiter approached the table and they ordered dinner.

"Our girl is talented, isn't she?" Winston lightened the mood.

"Unbelievably. At everything she does." The way Maverick looked at her melted her heart. Literally. On one side of the table it was all shade. Cold and gray. But beside her, pure heat. Fire and warmth.

"Did you know she was Miss Savannah? Has she shared her pageant days with you?" Mama asked, and Elle stiffened. She avoided this topic with her mother whenever possible. It always ended in a fight.

Her boyfriend didn't miss a beat. "She sure did. She's even twirled flaming batons for me."

Winston chuckled. "Only Elle could light two batons on fire and toss them in the air without a care in the world. I loved watching her perform. She commanded the attention of everyone in the room without even trying."

A dull ache settled in her chest. He'd always been proud of her. Both Winston and her dad celebrated her successes. Mama used to, at least where pageants were concerned, but she couldn't remember the last time she encouraged her at anything.

"Oh, lovely. She didn't drop them when she performed for you, did she?" Any opportunity to go high or low, the woman always went low.

"Caroline." Winston's tone stern beneath his breath. Something was different between them. Her stepfather always showed Elle kindness, but he'd never gone against Mama. At least not in front of her.

"Of course, I didn't drop them. There was nobody there to slick them with oil," Elle hissed. Would Mama ever get over it? My God, it had been years.

"Ah, yes. The great setup. Who did you blame for the mishap? The Sandemeyer girl?"

"Suri freaking Sandemeyer, Mama. You remember her, don't you? You pitted me against her most of my life." She had two glasses of wine in her system now—if Mama wanted a fight, she'd damn well get one.

Chapter Twenty

Maverick's Playbook
Protect what's yours!

Christ, he'd never seen anything like this before. It was a shit show. Elle's mom took shots at her daughter every chance she got. Anger radiated from the woman. Not to mention the way she sized him up. Like he was the dirt beneath her manicured fingernails. Women never looked at him with complete disgust, but she clearly wanted her daughter dating a preppy, polo playing, royal—and Maverick was anything but. All this discourse because of a pageant? It was like a bad reality show.

"So Maverick. Adopted at four years old and playing professional football now. I suppose when you look at where you started, it's actually an accomplishment, right?" The ice queen spewed.

He laughed. Loud. Hell yeah, it was an accomplishment. Any way she wanted to look at it. "Less than one percent of kids who play ball and dream of making it to the pros, actually do, so yeah, it's an accomplishment."

"I wonder what the statistic is on kids not born in the United States playing professional ball? You obviously were adopted into the right family." Her venomous words did nothing to him. He'd dealt with worse than Caroline Humphries in his life. But her being Elle's mom complicated matters. He knew it hurt his girl, which bothered him.

"Enough, Mama." Elle stood up, planted both hands on the table, and stared down at the older woman.

"It's fine, Peaches. Don't let it get to you. Sit down with me, baby." He kept his tone calm and even. Elle took her seat beside him, her face flushed and spirit damaged. He could see it in her topaz gaze. He turned toward her mother before speaking again. "As far as your question, maybe you can write to the NFL and ask them to research the statistics of adopted kids making it to the pros. Especially us tan ones." He winked and gulped down his water.

"I think what my wife meant to say is what an accomplishment it is to play professional football, Maverick. I was never any good at sports. Always the last one picked in P.E." Winston chuckled. The poor guy seemed desperate to lighten the mood.

"Well, we all struggle with something, right? School didn't come easy for me, so I know how it feels to work hard and sit the bench, metaphorically," Maverick said.

Winston held his wine glass up and Maverick clinked his water glass in what he assumed was a toast to overcoming obstacles.

"Ah, so what happens when you're done playing football. I mean, you can't play forever. You'll play a few years, and then what? You have no income, and you'll have to find a career at some point. Is there a plan for you and—Peaches?" Her condescending tone matched her offensive question.

"I have a plan, yes. But it doesn't strike me as the

appropriate time to discuss it, not with all this animosity. When you want to have a civil conversation about your daughter and me, give us a call." Maverick locked stares with Caroline Humphries. The odd thing, she looked impressed for the first time tonight.

"Fair enough." She nodded.

He glanced over at his girl, and a heavy weight settled in his chest. She was a vision in her white lacy dress. It hugged her bodice and flared out a bit at her waist, ending just above her knees. He knew exactly where her hem stopped because he'd been beneath it an hour ago. But here she sat, all prim and proper. Looking like some sort of angel. He held her hand beneath the table. Wanted to support her. She'd done so much for him in the short time they'd been together.

Hell, he'd never spent the night with a woman before her. Not the way he did with her. All night, every night. The way he liked it. He'd had one nightmare since they returned from Lake Tahoe, and seeing there were no secrets between them, they'd discussed it. They had a deal. She'd go to the guest room and not attempt to wake him. Not put herself in danger as they didn't know what his reaction would be. He'd found her in the guest room the next morning, and she said it wasn't as bad as the one at the lake house. She'd found a therapist she wanted him to see, some sort of doctor who specialized in night terrors and traumatic incidents. He hadn't gone yet, had his hands full with practice and the team, and wanted to come home to his girl when he was done.

The waiter set their plates down and damn if it didn't smell delicious. He and Winston made small talk about San Francisco's current heat wave. Elle and her mom were quiet. It was the calm before the storm, because her mother set her utensils down and cleared her throat like she was getting ready to make an announcement. Maybe she'd apologize for being a raging bitch.

"We had lunch with Edward today. Such a lovely man." Caroline's gaze locked with his and she picked up her wine glass and took a long sip. So much for an apology. Jesus, she was ready for round two.

If she wanted to provoke him, she'd found his kryptonite. He fucking hated Edward Efant and the way he manipulated the situation to keep Elle around.

"You saw Edward before you saw me? I thought you flew in this afternoon?" Elle's voice trembled. She was always strong, so seeing her vulnerable cut him deep. He wanted to attack anyone who came at her, but this was her mother, and he needed to tread lightly.

"We've been here for a few days. I don't know why you assumed we just got here." Her mom beamed. She appeared to get off on hurting her daughter. It made him sick, and he'd had enough of it.

"I guess I just thought you'd want to see me as soon as you got here," Elle said quietly. Her fork rested on her plate and she sat back against the brown velvet chair. He noticed her glossy gaze and his hands fisted beneath the table. How long did they have to sit here and endure this?

"Don't be silly. You have *Nick* here in town. We've always played second fiddle to him, haven't we?" A fake ass smile plastered across her mother's frozen face. There wasn't so much as a line on her forehead. Caroline Humphries was all ice, and somehow her daughter was all warmth.

"Nick? You've never played second fiddle to my dad. I love you all the same. It's why I wanted to see you. To fix this, Mama. Whatever this is between us." Her voice wobbled and tears streamed down her gorgeous face.

He fought the urge to throw her over his shoulder and get her the hell out of here. It was like watching a scorpion play with a kitten. No wonder Peaches dreamed of princes on white horses whisking her away. Life with her mom was like a dark fable. The non-happily ever after kind. No, his girl had unicorn blood pumping through her veins and it sure as shit didn't come from her mother.

"If you loved us the same, you would carry the Humphries last name. Instead, you chose to shame your family as a drop-out debutante, for God's sake, Elle. I'm the head of the Savannah debutante cotillion, and you quit when the going got rough. Do you know what you've done to my reputation? All the work and money we put into your pageants, and how did you thank us? Oh, yes, by making us the laughingstock and dropping the batons in your ridiculous performance. It was your legacy, and you let it all go up in flames. Then, finally you date Edward Efant, a man worth bringing home, and what do you do? You throw him away. You want to know if I'm disappointed in you? The answer is yes. You are my greatest disappointment."

A gasp escaped Elle, and her skin paled. Winston's jaw dropped, and Maverick felt the anger radiating from the older man. And Maverick? He'd had enough. He could sit beside his girl through a horrific dinner if it helped her, but no way in hell was he going to allow her to be disrespected like this. He pushed to his feet, his chair made a loud screech against the dark, wood floor, and he reached for his wallet.

"Winston, it's been a pleasure meeting you. But we're leaving." He put his hand out to Elle, who remained completely bewildered. She took his hand and moved to her feet. Tears streamed down her pretty face, and he made a silent promise to never let anyone hurt her like this again.

"Caroline, wish I could say it was a pleasure, but it would make me a liar. And a liar I am not." He tossed five bills on the table, more than enough to cover dinner. "I know it's not old money, but as far as I can tell, most places accept new money."

Elle's mom shook her head with disapproval. "You can't leave dinner. We haven't even had dessert."

The lady was seriously insane. She was concerned about etiquette, now? Elle gathered her purse and looked up at him with her big trusting gaze. He turned back to her mother. "Well, this ain't the cotillion, lady. This is real life. And if you ever talk to my girl like that again, it'll be the last time you speak to her if I have anything to say about it."

A cold laugh escaped her. "Please. You won't be around long enough to hold that promise. You may not understand tough love, Maverick, but my daughter is in need of a reminder of how her actions have hurt our family name."

Elle shook her head in disbelief and threw her arms in the air in frustration, but Maverick wasn't done yet.

"You want to talk tough love? You're shaming your daughter for using the name of her biological father. The man you lied to and hid his own child from—and now you shame her for acknowledging him?

As far as I can see, the only one disrespecting Winston is you. Elle loves him. She isn't the one who betrayed him. So, if you want to pass judgment, take a long look in the mirror. You've done some evil shit to your daughter, and in spite of it, she's still trying to repair things. Shame on you."

Her mother pushed to her feet. "How dare you speak to me like that," she hissed. "Elle's paychecks sure won't cover her expensive condo, will they, dear? You better watch who you cross, or you can start paying your own way."

"Sit down, Caroline. Those aren't your checks paying for her condo either. Stop this nonsense now." Winston kept his tone in check, but his anger was impossible to miss. His wife finally dropped down in her seat.

"Let's go. I've had enough." Elle tugged at his hand.

He led her out of the restaurant, like they were escaping the gates of hell. Once out on the street he turned to look at her and she fell into him. Crumbled into a million little pieces. So much more fragile than she wanted anyone to know.

"I'm sorry, baby," he whispered against her head.

Standing out in the street, with his arms wrapped around her, she broke down. Let it all out.

When she finally pushed back, she wiped her face and straightened her shoulders.

"I'm sorry she was so awful to you, Maverick."

"I don't give a shit how she treats me. I'm concerned about you." He placed his hands on either side of her face, forcing her to meet his stare.

"Thanks for defending me. No one ever stands up

to her. Not even Winston." She grabbed his hand and started walking toward the car.

"She doesn't intimidate me. She's a wolf in fancy clothes. Her reality is so skewed. She should be the one apologizing to you, your dad, and to Winston. Yet she blames everyone for her mistakes. I don't know how Winston stays quiet about it," he said.

"I can't believe the things she said tonight. I've always known I was a disappointment to her through her snide remarks, but she's never actually come out and said the words."

Once in the car, he merged onto the freeway. "Listen, baby, don't let her get to you. Her threats won't work here. I will pay off your condo, you don't need her money. Better yet, we could sell it and you could move in with me." He turned to her and winked.

She sniffed and leaned back against the seat. "I make decent money. Not enough for my condo, obviously, but the money I bought the condo with is in my name. Winston set up a trust for me when I was a kid. I don't think he'd let her take it back. I don't want the reason we move in together to be because I can't afford my condo. I want us to do things right, okay? When we're ready. But thank you for the offer. It means a lot."

He hated the sadness in her eyes. The pain written all over her face. "Well, you say the word, and I'm in. I'm ready to have you with me all the time. But I meant it when I said I'd pay off your condo. The offer stands whether you move in with me or not. Tonight was a lot, so we can talk about it later. Right now, I want to know you're okay."

She gave him a half smile and leaned back against

the seat, staring out the window. "I'll be fine."

****

The first two games of the season were in the books, and the Miners were off to a fan-fucking-tastic start. With two W's, things were looking good. The press dubbed Elle Fiore his lucky charm, snapping pictures of them leaving the games. Hell, maybe she was. He liked knowing she was there, wrapped in his jersey and cheering him on alongside his friends and family. Unfortunately, their first away game was on Monday night, and Peaches had to work. The dickhead found every reason in the book to keep her from taking the day off. He wanted her with him, but he had to respect her career as she did his.

They'd grown even closer after the visit from her mom and Winston. She and her mother hadn't spoken since, but Winston called several times to check on her. He apologized for her mother's behavior and assured her the trust fund was her own to use as she wished.

He told his own mom about what transpired, and she'd really stepped up to support his girlfriend. His family really took Elle under their wings. Aside from attending the games together, his sister Gigi joined Elle and her friends for happy hours in the city. Mimi and Elle had a special bond, and they talked almost daily. For the life of him he didn't know what they rambled on about, but he liked his family being there for her.

He'd arrived in Minnesota last night. Hated being away from his girl. He'd grown used to having her sprawled across his chest. Elle Fiore was a rule following, proper, etiquette-crazed woman by day—but when she slept, she was out of control and wild. He loved it. He always woke up with her attached to him.

Like two magnets, even during sleep, they were connected. Coach sent a text letting him know it was time to head over to the stadium. There was a knock at his hotel room door, and he pulled his bag over his shoulder and stepped out in the hall.

"You ready?" Big Joe, his go-to receiver was always serious on game day.

"Hell, yeah."

"Let's go kick some Minnesota ass," Brent, the leading running back in the league, and also the team prankster said.

His phone vibrated as the elevator took them down to the ground floor. A text from Peaches.

—Wish I was with you. Good luck. I love you so much. I will be cheering the loudest from here. Of course I'll be wearing your non-bedazzled jersey while doing so—

He laughed. That was his girl. He shot off a reply.*—I miss your face. I miss your body. I miss you—*

Damn, he had it bad for this girl. Twenty-four hours apart proved torturous.

"Damn, dude. You've gone from playboy to pussy-whipped all between seasons." Brent laughed so loud the elevator shook.

"Get your head in the game, fucker," Maverick said as they boarded the bus.

****

To say the game was a shit show would be an understatement. They'd had two interceptions, and their first loss. The flight home was long and tense the following morning. When he got in his car, his phone vibrated, and Jackson's name flashed across the screen.

"What's up, buddy," he said, through his

Bluetooth.

"You back in town?"

"Yep. Just got here. Driving home now."

"Sorry about the game. You'll get 'em next time," Jackson said.

"Yeah, I played like shit. Need to get back to work and tighten things up."

"Everyone has off days, Mav. It wasn't only you, there were a bunch of fumbles and mistakes."

Jackson always had his back, but Maverick knew he hadn't led his team yesterday. Hell, those were the worst stats he'd ever put down. "Well, it's on me. I didn't make it easy for anyone. But we'll put our heads down and get shit done."

"Did you see what's trending on social media?" Jackson said, and Maverick didn't miss his hesitation.

"No. I'm menstruating, so I've been off social media. Did you and the girls already go to the pep rally?" he said dryly.

Jackson cackled, which caused him to laugh for the first time in two days. "Shut the fuck up. Peyton called and filled me in. Apparently, Elle's being blamed for the team losing. They're saying you didn't have your good luck charm, and she should have been there."

His fingers tightened around the steering wheel. "Where the fuck do they come up with this shit?"

"Who knows. You know how crazy the fans get. But I wanted to give you a heads up. She probably won't tell you, but her car got egged at the office and someone wrote something on the windshield."

His head fell back against the seat in his truck. Could this day get any more fucked up? "What did they write?"

"Support your man, bitch." Jackson said, and started to laugh. "Dude, I can't make this shit up. These are some messed up super fans, right?"

Jesus. People were batshit crazy when it came to football.

"I've talked to Peaches a few times today, and she never said a word. Why the hell doesn't she tell me shit?" The girl could be so damn stubborn sometimes.

"She doesn't want to stress you out."

"All right, well, thanks for telling me. How's little Jojo? I hope you didn't let her watch me play yesterday. I don't want her seeing her godfather take a loss."

Jackson laughed. "She fell asleep in the first quarter and seeing she's not even a year old yet, I think you're safe."

"Good. Peaches said I need to wear a suit to the baptism. I told her you said I could wear a polo shirt and nice jeans, but she insisted it was out of the question." He ran a hand through his hair and laughed.

"Dude, she's going to have you dressed nicer than me, and it's my kid being baptized. You've got a few weeks to change her mind." Jackson chuckled.

"Have you ever seen her change her mind? I swear she makes most of these rules up as she goes."

"Well, you're a persuasive guy. You'll figure it out. You heading home?"

He was going to, but instead, he pulled off the freeway and parked in front of the Efant Capital building. "I'm going to stop by and see Peaches at work first. Make sure she's okay."

"All right, brother. Call me later."

He texted her and asked where she was. The building was massive, and she had already completed the lobby renovation. It looked modern and sleek with marble flooring and gray modern accents. She only had a few more floors to finish before this project wrapped up. Couldn't happen soon enough for him.

The elevator doors opened, and Peaches rushed out and lunged at him. She threw her arms around his neck and hugged him.

"Hey. I said I'd come up." He grazed her ear with his lips.

"I couldn't wait. I'm so happy you're home," she said with a big smile.

She wore a pink blouse, and he couldn't wait to take it off her. He lifted the fabric near the buttons and peeked down her shirt, and her head fell back in laughter.

"Missed you, Peaches."

"Missed you more. Sorry about the game." Her head cocked to the side, studying him.

"Yeah, I played like shit. I heard you're taking a little heat for it?" He wrapped his hand around her waist and tugged her closer.

"It's fine. I like being your good luck charm." She tried to make light of what happened, but he knew better.

"Can you leave work now?" He looked down at her. Wanted to take her home.

"No. I have a few more hours. I'll make dinner tonight though, okay?" She pushed up on her tiptoes and pressed her sweet lips to his.

"Elle. My father wants to see you." Count Asshat's voice pulled them from their moment.

His girl straightened, ran her hands down her front to make sure everything was in place, and Maverick glared at the older dude.

“All right, I’ll be right there,” Elle said, with a fake smile plastered on her pretty face.

“I’ll ride up with you.” Edward stepped onto the elevator and held the door open. He was one impatient douchebag.

“Oh. Okay. I’ll see you at your place in a few hours.” She pressed one more kiss to his lips.

“See you soon, Peaches,” he said, as he watched her walk toward the elevator.

“Sorry about the game, Maverick. Tough loss for our city,” the asshole said. His French accent almost made it sound polite. But he knew better. The guy was being a dickhead.

“Well, since you don’t live here, I’m sure you’ll get over it.” He kept his tone calm, but he felt anything but.

Chapter Twenty-One

Elle's Tip of the Day
Stand up to squirrel turds!

"Those chairs go against the far wall." She led the two men carrying the furniture across the room.

"Right here?" The older man asked.

"Yes, perfect. Thank you."

"Darling, there you are. I've been looking for you."

Why Edward still called her darling was beyond her. She avoided him at all cost and made it clear on several awkward occasions how fully committed she was to Maverick. The man never gave her this kind of attention when they dated. His little games were getting old. Edward found endless reasons to extend the project, and there wasn't much more he could add to the list. If this was a ploy to get her back, it had failed miserably.

"What do you need? I'm heading out in a few minutes." Her tone snippy. Maverick was frustrated with the situation, and honestly, she couldn't blame him.

"I was going to order in. I wanted to go over some new design options for this last stage." He leaned against the wall, his gray suit tailored to perfection, and he oozed confidence. But these were exactly the games she wasn't partaking in.

"Edward, we've already ordered everything for the final phase. My workday is over, and I need to get home." She crossed her arms in front of her chest and met his stare. She felt nothing for her ex, aside from irritation.

"It won't take long. We can have a bite and go over a few quick things."

"No. I'm having dinner with Maverick. He has a game tomorrow, and I need to get going. I don't know how many times we need to go over this. I have a boyfriend, and I'm very happy with him," she said in a huff. The man was relentless.

"You can't blame a man for trying. I spoke with your mum today. She mentioned the two of you aren't speaking?" Edward followed as she walked to get her laptop and her purse. Of course, her mother was speaking to her ex-boyfriend, but not to her own daughter. It had been a few weeks since their blowup. She expected an apology at the very least, but none came.

"I'm glad she feels the need to call you and discuss our relationship. Or lack thereof." She shoved her computer in her bag.

"She believes you're dating the football player to make me jealous and to get a rise out of her." His arrogance grated on her nerves.

"She also thinks I purposely dropped two flaming batons at the Miss Georgia pageant. The woman isn't exactly playing with a full stack. I assure you I'm head over heels in love with Maverick. Mama knows nothing about my relationship." She turned and pointed her finger at Edward. "You nor my mother entered my thoughts when I fell for him. Don't insult me or my boyfriend again. From here on out, no more games or trying to extend this project, or I walk."

She stormed to the elevator, but he followed right behind her. "I'm sorry, darling. I didn't mean to offend you. Your mother said it, not me," he said, with a chuckle.

She stepped on the elevator and did a half nod. "You and Mama shouldn't be discussing me or my relationship with Maverick. Have a good evening."

Mama phoning Edward Efant to discuss her relationship stung. Though she and Winston still spoke, he'd never stand up to her mother. No one would. Well, Maverick did, and he didn't even break a sweat doing so.

Their bond was undeniable. They were under a considerable amount of stress, yet it only brought them closer together. The fans were hot and cold with Elle on social media. Some days she was the hero and other days she was Satan's spawn. Maverick hated it. But it came with the territory of dating the city's golden boy. Thankfully, they'd only lost one game and won five, so she'd received more love than hate. But the closer they were to the end of the season, the more intense the attention on their relationship grew.

"Hello?" she called out when she arrived at her condo.

"Hey, beautiful." He came out of the bedroom in navy joggers slung low on his hips, no shirt and wet hair. The man so striking, he took her breath away most days.

She dropped her purse right on the floor and stepped into his arms. "How do you look this good after taking a shower?"

She soaked in his manly scent. Sandalwood and mint. Her arms wrapped around his middle and her head rested on his chest.

"Missed you. Did he let you leave without a fight this time?" He kissed the top of her head, and she forced herself to push away and head to the kitchen. She wanted to make a healthy dinner for him, as he had a big game tomorrow.

"Same ol' thing with him."

"You want me to step in? Just say the word. I'd love to knock some sense into the guy." He leaned against the counter, his abs chiseled and cut. She licked her lips and tried to focus on the chicken she pulled out of the fridge.

"Thank you, but I handled it. Apparently, Mama called him and told him we weren't speaking." She left out the condescending comment about their relationship. He had a game tomorrow and didn't need to give it a thought.

"Here, let me pound that for you." He took the meat tenderizer from her. "Though I'd rather be pounding you."

"Oh, you will be tomorrow night, Wallace." She chuckled and wriggled her eyebrows. "Once the game is over, you're all mine."

"I'm always all yours."

Her stomach did little flips and she tossed the salad in a bowl and dropped the pasta into the boiling water.

"I'm sorry about your mom, Peaches. It can't be easy knowing she calls him."

"Mama's heart is a thumpin' gizzard. There's no talking sense into her. Until she apologizes, I have nothing to say."

"Good for you. Stand your ground. I think she's so used to walking on everyone she expects people to roll over. I can't imagine your mom and dad ever being together. They're so different."

"Yeah. It was a short summer fling, I guess. Two good looking people who had nothing in common."

"Well, they have one thing in common, and you're the best thing that ever happened to me."

A dull ache grew in her chest. It was nice to hear him say she was the best thing to ever happen to him. She felt the same about him. But she'd be lying if she didn't admit it hurt knowing her own mama didn't feel the same way about her.

****

"Pass the ball, Wallace." Billy Goat screamed in the box so loud she swore the floor shook.

She paced off to the side, couldn't stand by Maverick's family or her father, or her friends. It was anyone's game in the last few seconds of the third quarter. He carried a lot of weight on his shoulders being the quarterback. She didn't know a thing about football a few months ago, and now she could recite stats, and understood the difference between passing and throwing plays. Hell, she liked to study the footage with him after his games.

Wrapped in his jersey, she closed her eyes when he threw a Hail Mary down the field. Everyone in the box went crazy when Greenly caught the pass and scored. While their friends and family celebrated, panic coursed her veins. Something wasn't right. She knew it before she even realized he was down on the ground.

"Hush it," she snapped.

While all the spectators watched the perfect throw

move down the field to its receiver, her eyes never left Maverick. He landed on his head, with two gigantic men on top of his back, and he wasn't getting up.

The booth silenced. Her fingers formed a teepee and rested at her mouth. Anxiety built. Every awful scenario played out in her head.

"He'll be all right, Elle," Gigi and Marley assured her with hopeful smiles. How the hell did they know? Did they have six hundred plus pounds take them down? No. None of them did.

Dani and Peyton stood beside her, and her dad paced as he watched the field. Maverick's parents were quiet, but obviously after years of watching him play, they remained calm. Thankfully, Mimi wasn't at this game, because she tended to be a nervous Nellie also. Minutes felt like hours as the clock moved in slow motion and everyone waited. Her heart raced, and she squatted down on the floor, resting her elbows on her knees as she tried to catch her breath.

The crowd cheered when Maverick moved to his feet, coaches and trainers surrounded him, leading him off the field and out of the stadium. The last thing she heard the announcer say was they were taking a medical timeout. Her feet moved of their own volition. Like running from a dangerous situation or fleeing for your life—the strongest need to get out of the box and find him.

She sprinted down the long corridor, hit the stairs, and took two at a time down to the ground floor. Her heart pounded in her ears, labored breathing the only audible sound until a voice from behind mixed in. Jackson, Peyton's husband wasn't far behind, and continued to yell her name. She didn't slow down or turn around. Three more flights of steps to go. When her feet hit the cement floor, she took a sharp right in the direction of the locker rooms.

"Christ, Elle, you need to stop. He isn't in the locker room," Jackson said, his voice loud.

She turned and gasped, "What do you mean? Where is he?"

Jackson caught up to her and bent over to catch his breath. "You're fucking fast. They don't take him to the locker room. They will do a few tests to check for symptoms. He's in the middle of a game. Don't embarrass him by storming into whatever room they have him. If anything is wrong, we will know right away, and then we can try to get back there."

She bit down hard on her bottom lip, annoyed at his sensible words. "I can't go back up there and do nothing. I want to be close if he needs me."

She hadn't experienced this kind of anxiousness even when she competed in pageants. This feeling was foreign—her heart raced, her mind spun, and she couldn't stand still.

"All right. You need to relax. We can stay down here and see what happens. This is part of the game, Elle. You have to trust them to do their job. It's a tough sport, but they have topnotch trainers and doctors, and they know what they're doing."

She paced and looked at the field through the opening at the end of the hallway. They'd put in the backup quarterback temporarily. And there had been no further update on Maverick. She reached for the white brick wall to stable herself and slid down to sit on the floor. Nausea made it impossible to stand. She was completely helpless.

"I need to get in there with him, Jackson." She buried her face in her hands.

He dropped down on the filthy ground beside her in a corner near the hallway leading to the locker room. Of course, she'd need someone to let her in since it was blocked off, but she'd cross that bridge when she got there. Maverick insisted she meet him outside the locker room after every home game, but getting back there right now, might prove a challenge.

"You need to breathe. You have your phone. If it were bad, he'd have someone call you. He's okay. They're just checking him out." Jackson rubbed her shoulder and tried to comfort her.

She flipped her phone over, and scanned the texts from Dani, Peyton and Maverick's sisters asking where she went. No word from her boyfriend.

"I need to know he's okay, Jackson. I'm freaking out."

"You don't have to tell me—I'm sitting next to Elle Fiore on the disgusting floor of a football stadium which says it all." He snorted.

Loud cheers came from the stadium, she pushed to her feet and hurried to look out on the field to see what was happening. Maverick jogged onto the field, and the fans went crazy with excitement.

"Why is he going back in?" She gasped over the ruckus.

"They must have cleared him. Let's get back upstairs so we can watch the last quarter."

The last quarter would go down in history as the longest quarter ever. Not due to actual time, but because time seemed to move backward. She sat off to the side in the private box again, hands clasped together, making an effort to calm her breathing. Peyton and Dani came over and sat beside her. They didn't speak, because they knew her. They knew if she started talking, all those emotions would come flowing out. This wasn't the time or the place.

Maverick's mom approached. "Are you okay, sweetie?"

She shook her head because she couldn't find the words to explain her worry. The odd thing—Elle might not know everything about football, but somehow, she knew Maverick Wallace better than she knew anyone. And something wasn't right. Maybe it was all in her head, but there seemed to be a pause when he threw the ball. Hell, maybe she'd just gone three sheets of crazy town over this man, and everything would be fine.

Isabel reached for her hand. "Honey, I know how difficult it is to watch him get hurt and not worry. But I promise you, they won't let him play if he isn't okay."

A sob escaped her throat, and even she was surprised by her lack of ability to contain her emotions. "He just seems off, and it scares me."

Isabel turned to face her and scooted her chair closer. "It's frustrating because you have no control over the situation. But you have to remember, this is what he loves to do. It's a part of who he is. A big part. Honestly, up until meeting you, it was everything. I am so happy to see him open himself up to more than just football."

Elle swiped a tear running down her cheek, fighting to rein in all these feelings—like holding back a dam on the verge of bursting. "I don't even know why I'm so emotional. It's just, he was down for too long, and then when they took him out, I assumed he'd sit out the rest of the game. If he's hurt, he needs time to heal."

"You know Maverick though. If the doctors cleared him, he wouldn't want to miss the rest of the game. It's who he is, honey. It's a competitive sport and playing for the Miners has been a longtime dream of his. You have to trust he knows what he's doing. He's a stubborn man. Lord knows, he was a stubborn boy. There's no telling him what to do. But he's not going to do anything stupid, not when he has someone else to think about now." Isabel's glossy blue gaze locked with Elle's.

"Thank you." She smiled, before they both turned to watch the final play. Maverick passed the ball to Big Joe, who ran it in for a touchdown. While the room erupted in cheers, her gaze landed on her boyfriend who was once again down on the ground. He moved to his feet slower than usual. People probably didn't notice how rigid his neck movements were, but she did.

While their friends and family celebrated the win making their way out of the stadium, she waited outside the locker room for him, along with endless press agencies. She was anxious to see him and make her own assessment about whether or not he was actually okay.

Big Joe was the first player to step out, and he winked at her when he saw her standing amongst the crowd. Yelling over all the chatter, "He's finishing up an interview, and then he'll be out."

A few reporters spewed questions his way, and he took it all in stride. Players streamed out one at a time until Maverick waltzed through the double doors and into the hallway. All attention turned his way, and he answered every question while his dark gaze found hers, numerous times. He finally put his hands up, an almost pleading expression on his handsome face. “Come on, guys. My lady’s been waiting, and if you don’t mind, I’d like to take her home.”

Everyone made room for him to move her way. She pushed off the wall, a surge of emotion erupted, and she threw herself in his arms. Her face buried in his chest. He pulled her close and wrapped her in a safe little cocoon.

“I’m fine, Peaches. Let’s get out of here,” he whispered in her ear.

She linked her fingers with his, and they made their way toward the exit. A man standing right outside the door shoved a camera in Maverick’s face, so close it almost hit him.

“I don’t know, Wallace, you were down for a while today. You think you’re tough enough to make it through the rest of the season?”

She reacted on instinct. No time to think. Her hand came up and smacked the camera hard. “Get out of his face, you egg suckin’ dawg.” Her Southern twang on full blast.

Maverick chuckled under his breath and stepped forward, tucked her behind him a bit, shielding her with his big body. “Interviews were inside, pal. The show’s over.”

The dirtbag laughed. “You’ve got yourself a live one there, Wallace.”

“Quit talkin’ with your tongue out of your shoe, you squirrel turd,” she shouted. All the angst of the day finally barreling out. The *squirrel turd* apparently found her quite hilarious, as his laughter echoed through the parking lot.

"Baby, stop engaging him." Maverick's stern tone didn't hide the exhaustion behind it.

"Sorry," she said. "I don't like how he stuck his camera in your face."

"Are you my protector, Peaches?" He smirked and opened the passenger door for her.

"If I need to be, yes."

He smiled and shook his head. "You've taken heat in the press when we lose a game, but it never bothered you. Why are you all worked up about this?"

They merged onto the freeway, and she sighed. His question struck a nerve. It didn't bother her in the slightest when they blamed her for a lost game. But her blood boiled when anyone spoke ill of Maverick.

"Well, I guess it's because you always defend me when they say stuff about me. Honestly, you're the first man who's ever had my back outside of my dad."

"What do you mean?" His brows pinched together, as he pulled the car in his garage.

"You see me. And you love me in spite of my flaws. God, knows I have a lot of them. You can just ask Mama if you need a list," she said. "And I see you too—in all your beautiful glory. I won't let anyone ever make you feel less. If this makes me your protector, then I guess I am."

He clicked to release her seatbelt and effortlessly pulled her onto his lap and buried his head in her neck. "I'll always have your back, Peaches. I love you so damn much."

"Love you, more."

And she meant it. There wasn't anything she wouldn't do for him.

Chapter Twenty-Two

Maverick's Playbook
The goal is always to score!

He stepped out of the shower and toweled off. Elle hadn't joined him. She'd been quiet since they left the stadium. Well, aside from her attack on the douchebag photographer waiting for them out in the parking lot. When you played professional sports, you got used to people poking at you when they could. It came with the territory, and he'd sure as hell opened himself up to it today. But the way she blocked the camera from hitting his face and jumped to his defense like a badass wolf protecting her territory. He fucking loved it. Something was off with her though, since his ass kicking on the field today. First bad hit of the season. He knew she worried, but it was inevitable—came with his job description.

Dropping the towel in the hamper, he walked into the bedroom. His beautiful girl lay under the covers, her head on the pillow and blonde hair tumbled all around her. He slipped into bed, her eyes squeezed shut, and a single tear ran down her cheek. She pretended to be asleep, but he knew better. He turned the light out on the bedside table and moved closer to her. He loved getting wrapped up in her warmth and lost in the smell of jasmine and vanilla. He pulled her into his arms, and she tried to muffle her giggle.

"Why are you fake sleeping?" He wanted to get her to relax and tell him what was bothering her.

"How do you know I'm not sleeping?"

"Because you're talking?" His lips grazed her cheek.

"Maybe I'm talking in my sleep. It's a real thing."

"Tell me what's wrong." His tone more serious now. Her hands settled on his chest and she pulled her head back and faced him. His hands tangled in her pretty hair. He needed to touch her, comfort her.

"I didn't like seeing you get hurt today. You know when those two baboons were on top of you. You didn't get up at first, and it scared me." She shook her head and tears sprung from her eyes like they'd been held back too long.

He moved closer, his nose almost touching hers. "I'm fine. It happens. It's not a big deal, I promise."

"It's a big deal to me. You're the most important person in my life. I don't want you to get hurt. And then they took you off the field, and I…I didn't know if you were okay."

He'd never seen her like this. Even when her mom had been cruel, she'd cried a little bit and moved on. This was different.

"I'm sorry, baby. They checked me out, ran a few tests and made sure I didn't have a concussion. It's part of the game. I promise, I'm fine."

"You weren't fine though. You threw different after you got up. Your neck was rigid. I could tell, Maverick. You weren't okay." Tears streamed down her face. And damn, if the girl wasn't spot-fucking-on. She'd never seen a football game before this season, yet she had the lock on how he moved on the field. She was different from everyone else. She noticed things, especially when it was someone she cared about. He'd taken a bad hit, no doubt about it. And fuck yeah, his movements weren't as quick afterward. He made the plays, put the ball where it needed to go. But he was in a shit ton of pain in the last quarter, and he worked through it. His girl noticed, because somehow, they were tied together in a way he couldn't explain.

"You know when I'm off, or when I'm on." He wrapped his arms around her tighter as he spoke.

"Yes, I do. And you were hurting. I know it."

He pushed back. Her gorgeous face illuminated with moonlight shining through the window, highlighting her flushed cheeks, and her gorgeous gaze clouded with worry.

"Hell yeah, it hurt. But it's not a bad thing. If it were, I wouldn't have played after. You've got to work through the pain sometimes." He pushed the hair back from her face, using his thumbs to swipe away the moisture falling down her cheeks.

"It worries me. I want to grow old with you," she said, her voice just above a whisper.

He liked hearing her talk about their future. He was always the one pushing for her to move in with him. She lived by a set of rules. They made no sense to him most of the time, as they had time restrictions and order. He tried to be respectful, but he wanted her with him. All the fucking time.

"Tell me about us growing old together," he said, studying her. The tension in her face not as prevalent. Her tears almost dry.

Her fingers traced his jaw, leaving him hazy and

relaxed. “Well, I see lots of big, bronzed beautiful boys running around our house someday.”

“Ah, future football players, huh?”

“Hmmm, I think they’ll play golf or tennis,” she said, her voice laced with humor, but there was something serious behind her gaze. Hell, he didn’t care what their kids did, as long as they were passionate about it.

“You’re going to dress them in pink polo shirts and plaid shorts, aren’t you?”

Her head fell back in laughter, and he loved seeing her all light and happy again. Her smile straightened, tone more serious. “So do you see why I worry about you getting hurt? Our future doesn’t work without you.”

“I promise not to do anything to hinder putting as many babies in you as you’ll allow.”

She smacked his chest and laughed. “You better put a ring on it first, Wallace.”

“So many rules, Peaches,” he teased, but he already had the ring.

He was waiting until the season was over to propose the way she deserved. With his full attention. Mimi had offered him her wedding set. She told Maverick to use the stone, or the band, take it apart, whatever he thought Elle would like. She wanted to pass on some of the love she and Poppy shared. He knew his girl would appreciate the sentiment behind it, she was all about tradition, but he’d give her something that was her own at the same time. Peyton and Dani went with him to the jeweler, and together, they designed the perfect ring. He used the platinum band engraved with the words: *forever mine*, which his grandfather gave to his grandmother more than seventy years ago. A brilliant cushion cut diamond with pave diamonds surrounded the band. Classic and beautiful, like Elle. He made the stone from his grandmother's ring into a pendant for her so Mimi could wear it around her neck.

He stopped by the firehouse last week and asked her father for his blessing. Thankfully, Nick was on board. He knew he wasn't going to have her mother's blessing.

"I'd break every rule for you." She moved closer and rested her cheek against his chest. "But you still won't let me wear a polo shirt to the baptism, right?"

Her laughter rumbled against him. "No, way. That one I'm not breaking. I found you a gorgeous modern gray suit, and a pretty, pink dress for me. They complement one another, just like we do."

"You complement me, Peaches, no question there. So, what's with you only mentioning boys? What about a few little firecracker girls, with blonde hair?"

She let out a long sigh, her warm breath tickled his skin. "Yeah. A little girl would be nice too. I'd let her find her own path in life."

"Of course, you would. You're hesitant about a little girl, but fine with a pack of wild boys?" He ran his fingers down her arm.

"I'd need to protect a little girl from Mama. She'd want her to carry on the family legacy. You know, the one I lost." Her tone a mix of tease and apprehension. "God, I just hope I'll be a good mom someday."

"Are you kidding me? You're the most empathetic person I know. You'll be a natural. And most importantly, you twirl flaming batons, for fuck's sake.

All the other moms are going to hate you," he said with a laugh.

"I'd want our kids to have a real childhood, you know? I honestly think Mama resents me for being born sometimes. But since she was stuck with me, she made me her toy. And when I didn't have the same dream as her, she had no use for me."

His chest tightened at her words and he pulled her closer.

"Well, my mom definitely didn't plan for me, nor did her maternal instincts kick in after I was born."

"I'm so glad your parents went to Brazil and found you."

"Me too. And think about it. If our moms had been different, we wouldn't have ended up here. Together."

"I never thought of it that way. I ran as far away from home as I could get."

"And it led you to me." He ran his fingers through her silky hair. "So, do you feel better about everything else? I don't like seeing you upset, Peaches. But this is what I do, and I wish I could tell you I won't get hurt again, but I'd be lying. I'll probably get hurt a shit ton more this season, so you need to be prepared."

"Yeah. I mean, I don't have much of a choice, right? This is part of who you are. Of course, I'll support you."

"Well, if it's any consolation, it hurts a hell of a lot more thinking of you working with Count Asshat every day than getting tackled by large men."

Her hysterical laughter trickled around them.

"You're ridiculous, Wallace. I actually can't wait for this project to wrap up. Just a few more weeks."

He tensed. "Is he doing something to make you

uncomfortable?"

"No. No, not at all. He's fine. It's just an awkward situation, and I know it bothers you. You do know there's nothing to worry about with him, right? You trust me, don't you?"

"I do. But he wants what's mine. My instinct is to fight. I'm trying to taper the urge because you've asked me to."

"Taper what urge?" Her fingers grazed the scruff on his jaw.

"To knock the asshole out. It's my nature, Peaches. I'm not the *sit back and watch* type of guy. Hell, my profession is a perfect example. I don't sit on the sideline waiting for something to happen. If someone tries to take the ball from me, I fight with everything I've got to hold on to it. And there's nothing more important to me than you. It's not easy for me to sit back and—trust. I'd rather hold on tight and call the plays," he said with a smirk. He wanted to be honest with her, but she'd had a rough day, and he didn't want to add to it.

"You trust your teammates, right? Think of me as the catcher, or the runner."

Fucking adorable. "Do you mean receiver and running back?"

"Potato, po-tot-o."

He rolled her onto her back, propped himself above her and pressed his hips against her. Needed to take her mind off things, and he knew exactly how to do it.

Her head fell back, and he paused to look at her. Damn, she was perfection.

"You're insatiable. Don't you ever get tired? You had a game today."

"I never tire of you." There were no truer words. He'd never spent the entire night with another woman. Never stuck around after sex. Elle was the first, and she'd be the last.

"I love you," she said, and a long sigh followed.

"I love you too."

He covered her mouth with his. Loved the little moans she made when he kissed her. He pushed up and reached for the foil packet in the nightstand. He tore it open, sat forward and covered himself. She watched in fascination.

"You like what you see?" he asked, his voice gruff.

She wriggled her brows. "Like a pig in sunshine."

"I can't wait to stop wearing these things. Just you and me. Nothing between us."

"Don't put the cart before the horse, Wallace. It's not happening till we're ready to have kids. I'm not doing what our mamas did. No unplanned pregnancies."

"I love when you talk about pigs in sunshine and unplanned pregnancies when I'm hovering above you," he said with a laugh, before rolling on to his back and pulling her on top of him.

"You know what I love?" Her smile reached her beautiful gaze, as she pushed up, straddling him.

"What?"

"I love how much you love me in spite of my flaws. My irrational worrying, endless rules, believing in fairy-tales—throw in my mean mama, who treated you as poorly as she treated me, and you've got yourself a long list right there. Not to mention me working for my ex-boyfriend and my unusual gift for pre-love-making banter," she said.

He pulled her down, his lips grazing hers. “If those are flaws, then you are the most beautifully flawed person I’ve ever met.”

Her fingers intertwined with his. “Perfectly imperfect?”

“Perfectly mine.” His mouth captured hers.

She ground against him and he deepened the kiss. His hands tangled in her silky hair pulling her closer. Needing more. She broke their kiss, reached for the hem of her tank top and lifted it over her head. The move so sexy he lay motionless, watching her, taking in his girl.

“You’re so fucking beautiful.” He pulled her back down to him. Couldn’t wait another minute to bury himself inside her.

Elle shifted and took control. He loved it. Her topaz gaze glittered in the moonlight, tousled, sexy blonde hair falling all around her, like some sort of angel. Almost undid him right there. He lifted her hips before pulling her down. Inch by glorious inch.

And this is where he wanted to stay.

Forever.

Chapter Twenty-Three

Elle's Tip of the Day
Never trust an egg-suckin' dawg!

A high pitch sound startled her from sleep. Daisy? Why was she barking? The mattress dipped, and she rolled toward the center and reached for her boyfriend. Her gaze sprung open, struggling to see through her sleepy haze. Maverick sat up, his back rigid against the headboard, and his fingers clenched a pillow in front of him. The sound he bellowed matched the terror in his distant stare.

"Go away, go away," he shouted over and over.

Daisy continued to bark, and Elle hurried off the bed and crouched down on the floor.

"Stop," she whispered to the pup.

Maverick shrieked, begging whoever haunted him to leave him alone. To go away. He called out for his mama a few times, and a pain tore through her heart. What had happened to him? He'd been so young at the time. Who could hurt a child? A beautiful child. Tears streamed down her face. This big, strong man was just a child. Small and frightened. She sat with her back against the wall so she could watch him. Damn to hell if she'd leave him in the middle of a night terror. He could hurt himself.

After what felt like forever, the room went eerily

quiet, and he slipped back down on the pillow. She waited a few minutes and watched him sleep as if nothing had happened. Grabbing her phone, she set the alarm for five fifty in the morning. Maverick woke up like clockwork every day at six fifteen. She'd promised to go to the guest room if he had a nightmare, but she wasn't leaving him now. Lying to him wasn't an option because he'd never agree to see someone about it if he didn't think he was still having them. She wanted him to see the world-renowned doctor she'd found through a lot of research. But leaving Maverick now? Not happening. She needed to know he was safe. She reached for her pillow, grabbed a throw blanket, and settled on the floor beside him. Tears continued to fall. Her heart ached for him.

When her alarm vibrated beside her, she hurried down the hall and climbed into the guest bed.

"What happened?" he said, sitting on the edge of the bed. She must have dozed off again because she jumped when he spoke.

She rubbed her eyes before sitting up and wrapping her arms around his middle. "You had a nightmare. It wasn't bad."

"You left immediately, right?" The concern in his gaze caused pain to settle in her chest.

"Yes," she said, because sometimes white lies were necessary.

"I'm so fucking sorry."

"You have nothin' to be sorry for. I don't know why you insist on me sleeping in the guest room. Your nightmares don't scare me, baby. I want to be there for you."

"Because I can't risk your safety. I don't know

what the fuck I'll do. I don't remember anything. Promise me you'll leave every time. No matter what," he said, dropping his head in his hands. Her gut wrenched. She hated seeing him like this.

"I promise," she said. And then followed her statement with a few silent words of her own.

But I promise to make sure you're safe first.

****

"It looks perfect," she said, to Jess and Brandon, the two guys hanging artwork for her.

"Yeah, it's really come together these last few days." Jess straightened the last print.

By the grace of God, this project was finally wrapping up. She'd finished all eight floors, and there was nothing left to do. Saturday was the unveiling of the new space to the public, and between Edward and Camille, there were going to be a ton of influential people in attendance. Maverick didn't have a game this weekend, so the timing worked out well. She made sure Edward knew Maverick would be attending to support her as they were very much together. In every sense of the word.

The mid-century modern space came together even better than she had imagined. The gray office furniture featured clean lines, with splashes of geometric, colorful art on the walls. This was not her typical design style, and it proved challenging to step out of her usual upscale glam décor projects. She liked expanding her horizons when it came to being creative.

"There's the lady of the hour. I need to speak to you for a moment," Edward said, as he stepped off the elevator into the large open space. The other two men appeared notably uncomfortable any time Edward was around. He was their boss, and he did carry himself with a certain arrogance.

"What do you need?" She turned and reached for her briefcase.

"There's a slight problem. Nothing major. However, the opening will be moved to next Friday evening, instead of Saturday. My father wants to be present, and he needs to leave for France on Saturday morning due to family business. I've already spoken to Camille, and an email blast has been sent out to all the guests."

Her stomach dipped. Would he do this on purpose? No. Going to all the trouble of rescheduling a large event just to mess up her plans? No. She was being paranoid. This was just bad timing.

"Is there any flexibility?" Her voice cracked as the words left her mouth.

"No. The date has been changed and the emails have already gone out. What's the problem?" He didn't look at her as he continued to study the new art on the walls.

"Well, um, Maverick is receiving an award on Friday evening for the work he's done with a national children's organization. It's a huge honor, and I want to be there to support him, just as he planned to be here for the opening for me," she said.

He turned to face her. "Ah, I do recall hearing something about him winning some award. I'm sorry to put a wrinkle in your plans, Elle, but this is business. My father wants to be present to see your work and congratulate you. Besides, I'm sure you support him enough by attending his soccer games. He can survive one night without you."

His smug, cool demeanor rubbed her wrong. “He plays football, not soccer. Thanks for the advice, but I wasn’t asking for it. I’ll figure it out. Have a nice night.”

She moved to the elevator, anxiety coursing her veins. He was all too pleased about messing up her plans with her boyfriend. A large hand wrapped around her bicep, stopping her in her tracks.

“Stay. Have a drink with me,” Edward said, pulling her back against his body. His lips grazed her ear.

Repulsed, she yanked away and faced him. “Unless you want to get slapped, you best not touch me again.”

He placed two hands on her shoulders and completely ignored her request. “Stop behaving like a child. I’m simply requesting two friends have a drink together.”

“And I’m simply requesting you get the fuck away from her. Now. Am I making myself clear? She shouldn’t have to ask you twice. I don’t give a fuck who you think you are.” Maverick’s voice startled her, and she whipped around to see him standing behind her.

Edward stepped back and a cocky smirk spread across his face. “How did you get past security without a visitor’s badge?”

Maverick reached in the back pocket of his dark jeans and tossed the plastic badge across the desk. He wrapped two arms around Elle and pressed her back to his front. His warmth soothing, but the anger radiating from him sent off alarm bells. With the project almost completed, the last thing she needed was the two men to get in a fight.

“You touch her again and I won’t need a visitor’s badge to hunt you down,” Maverick said.

Edward chuckled. Arrogant and taunting. "It's a good thing you won't be able to attend the opening, with the date being moved, because you are no longer welcome in my building. I'll alert security immediately. I suggest you be on your way. You must have a ball to kick around, right?"

"Is that the best you can do? Don't you have an Ivy League education, and all you can say is for me to go kick a ball?" Maverick taunted and Edward crossed his arms in front of him, smug.

Elle glared at Edward before turning to meet Maverick's gaze. Dark and angry, yet still protective and loyal. The man owned her heart. And her soul.

"Let's go," she said.

They took the elevator down in silence. He kept a firm grip on her hand. Once outside, he finally spoke. "You're driving home with me."

"I'll ride home with you, but you don't need to be so bossy. There are nicer ways to ask."

He opened the passenger door, his tone serious. "You're driving the fuck home with me. Thank you. Better?"

She laughed, buckled up, and waited for him to get in the truck. "You're making this a way bigger deal than it is."

"It's a big fucking deal. In fact, I'm calling Camille. He crossed a line. You're done there." He pulled the truck onto the highway, veins bulging from his chauvinistic neck.

"You're being ridiculous. Since when do you tell me what to do? And if you call my boss *again*, Maverick Wallace, we are going to have a serious problem. Did you learn nothing the first time?" Her blood boiled, and she rubbed her temples as the onset of a migraine beckoned.

"Yeah, I learned I should have insisted she pull you off this goddamn account before you even got started. You don't see what a problem this is? He put his hands on you. Twice." His voice boomed in the cab of his truck. She'd never seen him so worked up.

"And I handled it. I told him to take his hands off me, and I walked away," she said, angry she had to defend herself to her boyfriend.

"Oh yeah? And how did he respond? From what I could see, he did it again. You're damn lucky I walked in when I did."

"You're a pompous ass."

"I call it as I see it."

"You're such a hypocrite. There are women lined up just waiting for our relationship to fail so they can get their hands on you. They wear your jersey and talk about you on social media like you belong to them. But guess what, Maverick? I trust you. And it's not easy keeping my own green-eyed monster at bay. Most days it makes me madder than a wet hen. But one man asking me to have a drink with him puts you over the edge? A man I'm not interested in whatsoever. Because I'm in love with you."

He pulled in the driveway and turned off the engine. Wind whistled outside the truck, and the trees swayed and swooshed from side to side through the windshield.

"He's not just any guy, Peaches. He's your ex-boyfriend. And he wants you back. He doesn't give a shit about our relationship. He proved it tonight. You aren't the one I'm concerned about. And as far as other women go, there's no one I want but you."

"And there's no one I want but you, either. You're allowed to be upset about what he did, but don't flip it on me. Don't doubt me because you don't like him. I don't care for him either, but I'm able to separate my feelings and do my job. I hope you respect me enough to do the same."

"It's more than *jealousy*. Why was he grabbing you? Has he gotten physical before?" He faced her, and for the first time she saw fear when her gaze locked with his. She hated it. Hated Edward for causing it.

"No, he's never touched me. I've been straight with him since day one. He's an entitled man, not used to hearing the word *no*. But it doesn't mean I haven't said it repeatedly. I love you." Her voice cracked as the words left her mouth.

He reached for her and pulled her close. "This isn't about me not trusting you, I do. I'm trying so fucking hard. But this prick is getting under my skin. You went after a photographer for sticking a camera in my face, Edward had his *hands* on you after you asked him to let you go."

She breathed him in. Being with Maverick made her feel safe. And loved. He loved her more than she'd ever thought possible. "I promise you there is nothing to worry about. I've repeatedly told him I'm in a committed relationship and I'm very happy." She climbed onto his lap, putting her hand on his cheek. "I love you. Only you."

He pushed the hair back from her face. "I'm sorry for telling you what to do, and I won't call Camille even though every instinct in my body is screaming for me to do it. What did he mean when he said the date for the opening changed?"

"Apparently his dad wants to be there, and he has to leave town Saturday morning, so they moved it to Friday evening. They already sent the mass email to everyone without checking with me," she said, her gaze locked with his.

"Did he know you were attending an event with me on Friday?"

"I never told him. But I did brag about your award at the office, and he didn't seem surprised when I told him I had a conflict. But I don't think he'd change the entire opening just to mess up our plans, either."

"He's a manipulative prick. I wouldn't put anything past him. But I'm sorry I can't be there to support you. Promise me you won't be alone with him. I'm not fucking around, Peaches. I don't trust him."

"I promise. I don't have to go back until Friday evening, and I'll drive with Dani and Peyton. There's no reason to be alone with him. But I'm disappointed I won't get to see you receive your award." She pushed his unruly hair back from his face and kissed him.

"I'm sorry I won't be there for you. You know how proud I am of you, right?"

"Yes. Do you have any idea how much I love you?" She nipped at his bottom lip, before he lifted her out of the truck and threw her over his shoulder.

They say girls find men like their daddies, and Maverick Wallace sure had a thing for carrying her fireman style. She slapped his butt. "Why do you insist on carrying me everywhere?"

"Because it's faster. And I'm starving."

"What are you in the mood for?" she squeaked, as his hand slipped beneath her pencil skirt and landed on her bottom.

"The same thing I'm always in the mood for. Some sweet Peaches." Maverick howled the last three words, tossed her on the couch and settled above her.

The man was insatiable.

And she thanked her lucky stars he was hers.

Chapter Twenty-Four

Maverick's Playbook
Don't get distracted by the outside noise!

Daisy whined at the side of the bed, and though he wanted to ignore her, he knew she wouldn't go away. He and Elle got to sleep in later than usual. Yes. Her going back to Efant Capital for the opening bugged the shit out of him, but she'd be done with Count Asshat soon. It took all the restraint he had not to beat Edward's face in for touching her yesterday, but he knew better than to play into the guy's hand.

He stretched one arm and gazed down at Elle sprawled across his chest. Blonde hair strewn around—the girl slept the way she lived. Wild and full of life. He pushed golden hair back so he could look at her pretty face. The irony wasn't lost on him. Six months ago he wouldn't spend the night with a woman, and now he woke up every morning with Elle Fiore attached to him. Like a second skin. Just the way he liked it. This invisible force lived between them even when they slept. She was warmth and sweetness, softening his rough edges.

Daisy scratched the side of the bed again. He shifted Elle to slide her off his body, trying not to wake her while adjusting himself as he sported major morning wood. Her nearness did it to him every fucking time.

A little moan escaped her. "Where are you going?"

"Go back to sleep, Peaches. I've got to take the cock-blocking four-legged ginger out."

She didn't open her eyes, but her plump lips curved up at the sides and she chuckled. "You've got a one-track mind, Wallace."

"You're naked under those sheets, can you blame me?" He pulled his sweatpants on and made his way out the door. When he returned to the bedroom, Elle walked out of the bathroom wearing one of his T-shirts. Or it was wearing her because it hit her right above the knees and practically swallowed her whole.

"You're wearing too many clothes," he said, dropping back down on the bed.

"I want to show you something. I lose focus when we aren't dressed," she said, grabbing her laptop from her bag before settling beside him.

He sat up with his back pressed to the headboard and watched her speed type on her keyboard.

"What are you working on? You aren't going to try to film me naked with your laptop, are you? Because, it'll cost you, Peaches. I don't drop the drawers for just anyone," he said with a laugh.

She settled beside him and rolled her eyes. "I'm not making a porno, you perv. I like to keep you all to myself."

"Good to know. Then, what are we working on?" He loved to tease her.

She'd come a long way over the last few months. When they were first together, she wouldn't get undressed in front of him. Now she slept naked, and they talked about anything and everything. He loved seeing her confidence grow. Loved how she asked him for what she wanted. There was nothing sexier than a woman who told her man what pleased her. And there was no one he liked to please more than her.

"I need your opinion."

He noted the pink hue covering her cheeks. She was up to something.

He studied the computer screen. There were pictures of furniture. Not his favorite activity when his girl was barely clothed beside him in bed, but her work was important to her, so he'd play along. "I like it. Is this for your next project?"

"Yeah, it's sort of a side job. Camille doesn't have anything for me right now, so I have a little down time between gigs." She scrolled down, pausing to show him specific pieces.

"What do you think of this one?"

"It's a cool couch, if you take all the ridiculous throw pillows off."

"Well, throw pillows bring in a ton of character. I'd never have a couch without throw pillows," she said, appearing offended. Why the hell was she asking his opinion then? He didn't know shit about decorating.

"You know this isn't my area of expertise." He kissed her neck, making his way down to her collarbone.

"Oh yeah. What is your area of expertise?" Her words came out all breathy.

"Football and Peaches."

She fell back in a fit of laughter. "Good Lord, you make it hard for me to concentrate."

"Then stop trying so hard," he said with a smirk.

"Focus, Wallace. What do you think of this table?"

She pushed back up and turned her computer toward him.

He focused on the table. “I think it’s great. I’d like it better if you were naked and sprawled across it.”

She set the laptop aside and pushed up on her knees to face him. “You have a one-track mind.”

“Is that a problem for you?”

“Oddly, no. It’s not.” A grin spread across her gorgeous face.

“Yeah? So, who is the furniture for?” He snaked an arm around her waist and tugged her closer. He grazed her lips playfully.

She tangled her fingers in his hair, her warm breath tickling his neck. “It’s for us.”

He sat back and pulled her onto his lap. “Spill it, Peaches.”

“Well, I thought about what you said. We do spend every night together. And I don’t want to be away from you.”

“So, you want to buy more furniture?” he said with a laugh.

“I want to redecorate this house. Make it ours. I realize my rule about being engaged first is a bit old-fashioned, so I’m going to trust you and shack up with you. Throw my moral compass to the wind. But not until your season ends. We don’t need the press finding out there’s a moving truck in front of your house in the middle of the season.”

Damn. His chest tightened. The girl was making him soft. He’d need to crush a can or punch someone later. Make sure he still had his man card. “This is the best thing I’ve heard in a long time, Peaches. You sure you don’t want us to move into your condo?”

"No. The condo isn't good for Daisy. We can't really grow into it. I have some good equity though, and we can put the money into this house after it sells."

His head fell back on a laugh. "Oh, you're my sugar mama now?"

"I have to contribute, Maverick. Or I won't move in with you."

She could be so stubborn sometimes. He was learning to choose his battles. She'd agreed to move in. Progress. He wanted to tell her she wasn't stomping on her morals or her fairy-tale dreams by moving in with him, because he'd propose as soon as the season ended. But he didn't want to ruin the surprise.

"Baby, this house is paid off. I don't want your money. But I understand you want to contribute. What if we take the money from your condo and put it in a separate account we can build on and use to start your own business when you're ready?"

Her eyebrows cinched as she thought about his offer. "You make some good points. But I'm no kept woman. We can put it in a joint account and use however we see fit later. If we decide it's best put to use going toward my interior design company, I'll consider it. But we'll be fifty-fifty partners in it. And we're splittin' the cost of the new furniture. Deal?"

He shook her hand. "Deal."

She studied his face. "All right, you only have a few months of freedom before the ol' ball and chain takes up permanent residence here. You know, if you have any wild oats to sell."

Fucking adorable.

"First of all, it's not sell your wild oats, it's sow your wild oats. And I gave up my wild oats the day I hooked up with my ball and chain. She's got all my oats now."

He flipped her on her back and settled above her. She broke out in hysterical laughter.

"Ah, yes. I'm keeping all your oats, Wallace," she said, barely able to speak as she tried to catch her breath.

The doorbell rang, and Daisy went batshit crazy, per usual. His sister's voice filtered through the house, shouting something about getting his lazy ass out of bed. How the hell did she make so much noise standing on the front porch? He rested his forehead against Elle's. "Fucking. Naughty. Twin. She purposely shows up at the worst times."

She chuckled, and hurried off the bed, combing her hair with her fingers. "Yes, I'm sure Gigi plans her day around your sex life. Tell her I'll be right down. I'm going to get dressed."

"It's probably part of her evil plan," he said, pulling a T-shirt over his head.

"You're ridiculous, Wallace. Go let your sister in."

When he opened the door, Gigi huffed past him. "Took you long enough. Aren't you a professional football player? Shouldn't you be a little quicker, old man?"

What the actual fuck? Since when was twenty-eight old? He wouldn't waste his breath explaining the reason it took him a minute to get to the door. She'd only enjoy hearing she'd cock-blocked him.

"To what do I owe the pleasure of this early morning visit?" He dropped down on the couch.

She pulled off her ridiculously oversized sunglasses and stood in front of him tapping her foot like she was awaiting the detonation of a bomb. She rolled her eyes before taking a sip of her Starbucks coffee. His sister carried the white and green cup like an accessory. Pumped full of caffeine and ready to conquer the world. She'd been like this for as long as he could remember. As much as she annoyed him, he fucking loved her.

"I had a meeting a few blocks from here. Wanted to check on you. I called you yesterday about my friend and I staying here when our apartments get fumigated. You never called back."

He let out an irritated breath. "I talked to you yesterday."

"Dude. You talked to me earlier in the day. I called you later and left a message," she said, before falling onto the couch beside him.

"*Dude*. I'm a busy man. If I answered your every whim, I'd never get shit done. Tone down the attitude. Of course, you can stay here. Peaches and I will stay at her place."

"Where is your better half? I was actually hoping to see her."

"She'll be down in a minute. We were still in bed before you started screaming and banging on the door like a fucking hellion."

Gigi's head fell back with a maniacal laugh. "It's nine o'clock in the morning. Since when do you two sleep in?"

"I don't have to go to practice for two hours and Peaches wrapped up her project with the douchebag yesterday."

"Ah, yes. I thought we were calling him Count Asshat?"

"We are. I can't stand the fucker."

"Really? I'm shocked." She gasped and threw her hand to her chest like a fool. Sarcasm was Gigi Wallace's middle name.

He chuckled. "I speak the truth."

"*Hashtag no judgment*. I actually enjoy seeing you all worked up. It looks good on you."

"What does?" He crossed his arms in front of his chest.

"Caring. It's nice to see you actually love someone other than yourself. I mean, aside from the family, of course. I feared it would never happen, and you'd die a lonely, arrogant asshole."

He flicked her in the shoulder. "Thanks, G. Good to know."

"What's up with the nightmares? Have you had any more since Tahoe?" Her tone turned serious. She was all jokes and mockery until shit got real. And when it did, there was no one he'd rather have in his corner than Gigi.

"Only one since we've been back. Peaches wants me to see a shrink she found. Apparently, the woman specializes in night terrors. I can't risk going during season and having the press find out. I'll deal with it when the season wraps."

"Bullshit." She rolled her eyes at him.

"What the hell does that mean?"

"*Foolish, deceitful, or boastful language*," she said.

"What are you talking about?" His irritation always more prevalent when discussing his fucked-up nightmares. He hated his weakness.

"You asked me what *bullshit* means. I'm giving you the answer. But I prefer laymen's terms, which is, *you are full of shit, brother dear.*"

"Are you this annoying with everyone?" He sat forward and rested his elbows on his knees.

"On my good days, yes."

"If you don't believe the Miners quarterback seeing a shrink is news, you're crazier than I thought. They'd be all over it, and I don't want my shit out there."

"Who cares, Mav? I mean, everyone has something. Sure, they'd run with it, and everyone will forget about it in a day. It's not scandalous. You're human. You went through a lot when you were young. And look at you now. You overcame a learning disability, attended an amazing university, and you're playing professional football for one of the best teams in the league. You have nothing to prove. And I don't believe it's the reason you won't go see someone."

"Christ, now you know me better than I know myself. Let's hear it." He made a teepee with his hands and pressed them to his lips with irritation. He wasn't in the mood for her Dr. Freud shit.

"You don't want to get to the root of it. You don't want to remember what happened before Mom and Dad found you and brought you home. You're running from something, and it's going to chase you until you face it," she said. Her gaze wet with emotion only pissed him off more. He didn't want her pity.

"Jesus. Why do you always have to go there? Let it fucking go. I have."

"Sure, you have. Then why are we having this conversation if it's all fixed? You avoided sleepovers your entire life. It's not a remedy, it's a bandage, Mav. And now, you have this amazing woman you love, and your grand plan is for her to run to another room every time you have a nightmare? You don't think your plan is flawed? She won't be upset seeing you, the man she loves going through something, and being told to run down the hall when it happens? Would you hide from her if things were reversed?"

He pushed to his feet. "This conversation is over."

"You don't get to decide when it's over," she said, face flushed and angry.

"Hey." Peaches came bounding down the stairs.

Gigi hugged Elle, and his stare locked with his sister. In warning. She'd gone too far. She gave him a half nod, which was code for, *I got it*. He and the twins had always been able to communicate without speaking. Unfortunately, Gigi insisted on using her words most of the time.

"I'm glad I caught you, Elle. I stopped by to see if you wanted to meet for lunch today. And to give my brother a hard time, of course." Gigi flashed him a wicked grin. Her charm wasn't working. She needed to mind her own fucking business. But he'd always had a hard time staying mad at her for long.

"Sure. I'd love to have lunch with you," Elle said.

"Great. Have you been to Café Suzette? I've been dying to try it."

"I haven't, but I've heard it's fabulous."

"Okay. Meet you there at noon? We can do a little retail therapy after if you have time," Gigi said.

"Ooh, yes. There's a great furniture store up the street I want to check out." Elle winked at him.

"Something I should know?" His sister's wheels were already turning.

"Peaches and I are moving in together," he said, shooting her a look to keep her opinions to herself. Of course, she was going to lecture him about seeing a fucking shrink before moving in with Elle. But this wasn't up to her.

"Yep. We're shackin' up." Elle twirled around like a little kid. Damn, the girl had a way of lighting up a room.

"Awesome news, guys. Congrats," Gigi said, and slipped her gigantic sunglasses back on her face.

Daisy barked at the back door, and Peaches ran off to let her out while he held the door open for his sister.

"Moving in, huh?"

"Abso-fucking-lutely. If you have a problem with it—keep it to yourself." His tone came out harsher than intended.

"I wasn't going to say a word. I'm happy for you. And I'll be sure to help Elle pick out some new furniture for the guest room. At least until my brother gets his head out of his ass," she said and pulled the door shut hard.

He leaned his back against the door and tried to shake it off. He wasn't running from anything. He didn't want to live in the past.

Or think about it.

All the fucking time.

Chapter Twenty-Five

Elle's Tip of the Day
Once a snake...Always a snake!

"You look so handsome in a suit. Well, you look handsome in everything. And *nothing*," Elle said, adjusting his tie.

He laughed and slipped his hands beneath the hem of her skirt. Goose bumps spread across her legs as his fingers climbed their way up. "I can be naked in thirty seconds."

Her head fell back on a gasp, and his lips moved to her throat, peppering soft, insistent kisses along her neck. Lord, this man did crazy things to her. She couldn't get enough. *"Maverick."*

He pulled away, looking at her, and she already missed the contact. Their connection overwhelmed her at times. His dark gaze always studying and assessing her. She'd never felt so—seen. Exposed. This man loved her in spite of all her imperfection. Even in her wildest dreams, her silly fairy-tale fantasies, she'd never known a man could look at her this way. Like he saw into her soul and would do whatever he needed to protect her. To cherish her.

"What's the matter, baby?" His voice gruff. So manly and sexy. His mouth broke on a grin, and she melted all over again. She brushed back his gorgeous dark, wavy hair.

"You can't be late for your award," she said, her voice strained and breathy. Man, he had her all hot and bothered again, she could barely form a coherent sentence.

"You're such a sexy little rule follower." He wrapped two large arms around her and pulled her close. She reached up and nipped at his chin.

"Rules make the world go round. You're being honored tonight. I'm already upset I can't be there to support you, but I'll be damned if I make you late to your own award ceremony. We're meeting back here after, right?"

"Yes. And you promise to stay clear of Count Dickhead, right? I don't want you alone with him." He was all intense and serious now.

His hand slipped inside the front of her blouse. The man had no shame. He ran his finger over her lace bra, and she gasped. She wanted to strip down, right there in the foyer. So overcome with need, she couldn't think straight. "What are you doing to me?"

"Less than I want to be doing to you." He grazed her ear with his lips.

"Damn you, Wallace. We have to go, and now you've got me all flustered." She pushed up on her tiptoes and kissed him. Long and hard. So, he'd remember to hurry back to her.

"I like you flustered," he said, leading her by the hand through the door.

They left in separate Ubers, and she couldn't wait to get back home to him. A sick feeling settled in her stomach. She wished she could see Maverick receive his award and wished he was by her side tonight too.

Dani and Peyton were both on their way to meet her, willing to play interference if Edward didn't keep his distance. She hadn't spoken to him since their awkward encounter. She would focus her attention on his father. He was the reason they were doing this tonight anyway.

When she stepped out of the car, surprise flooded her. Camille stood in front of Efant Capital on a mini version of a red carpet with several photographers nearby, which was not the norm. The press didn't rally around design reveals for a financial institution. It was hardly big news. The Efants were in the press at times, but not flanked by paparazzi ever. This must have been set up in advance. Maybe Edward's father wanted it to be public?

"Isn't this spectacular?" Camille asked.

"Ummm, it's quite grand."

"What's all this?" Dani came up behind her with Peyton in tow.

Elle shrugged, as Edward stepped outside. He insisted she and Camille step in for photographs with him, the Efant Capital emblem the large backdrop. She shook hands with clients as they entered, and Camille made her way toward the entrance. Before she could find Dani and Peyton, two arms wrapped around her waist and pulled her close as flashes blinded her vision. Edward's head rested on her shoulder, and his grip held her tight.

"What the hell do you think you're doing? I told you not to touch me again. I'm not kidding. This is not okay," she hissed as she pulled away, trying hard to keep a fake smile plastered on her face.

He held both hands up in apology. "I'm sorry. I dipped in the Champs a bit early. Forgive me. I wanted a photo with my talented designer."

Her two best friends flanked each side of her, and they turned and walked away.

"He's sure not getting the message, huh?" Peyton asked, as they entered the lobby.

"Understatement of the year," Elle said.

"Typical rich guy. Thinks his wealth entitles him to take what he wants, and disregard people when he's done with them," Dani said.

Both she and Peyton chuckled. Dani had daddy issues, and Edward's attitude only fed her resentment. But she seemed edgier than usual.

"Easy, tiger. He's not worth the energy. What's with you tonight? Are you okay?" Elle stopped to look at her friend before they entered the chaos. The place was packed.

"She and Cam had a fight," Peyton whispered.

"Same fight. Different day." Dani shrugged, and grabbed a glass of champagne from the passing waiter.

"Oh boy. Someone wants to blow off some steam." Peyton chuckled, before leaning in close to Elle's ear. "Keep your eye on her. I need to call Jackson. Jojo wasn't feeling well when I left the house."

"Go. I've got this." Elle led Dani into the crowd, and they mingled. Camille introduced them to future clients, and Elle shook more hands than she could count. She kept a watchful eye on Dani, though they'd been pulled in different directions.

"What a huge success," Camille said. "You did an amazing job. This will garner you quite a bit of attention with the business world. You know how competitive they are."

Elle scanned the room once again, spotting Dani

sitting at a table with a few other Shine employees. Peyton paced in the corner on her phone, something was going on with Jojo. The lobby bustled with people dressed to the nines, taking in every little detail.

"Ah, the woman of the hour. I hoped we'd see you this evening," Tomas, pronounced toe-ma, Efant's accent was much stronger than Edward's. He was a regal man and had been polite to her the few times they'd met. His wife, Sabine, stood beside him. In her heels, she was the same height as her husband, which was quite a bit taller than Elle. She'd met Sabine only once and found her to be very intimidating. An observer by nature, she watched closely and didn't say much.

"Mr. and Mrs. Efant, it's so nice to see you both." She didn't expect to see Sabine, as she rarely visited the States with her husband. From what Edward told her, they lived separate lives most of the time.

"Please. It's Tomas and Sabine. You are dating our son, after all," Tomas said.

Elle sputtered her drink from her mouth, making a spectacle of herself. *What the hell?* He didn't know they weren't dating?

Sabine's gaze full of judgment as Elle juggled her clutch and cocktail while reaching for a napkin. Her purse hit the floor, and everything spilled out across the striking white marble. Edward hurried over and scooped up the items scattered around her feet. Her face heated, and she wished this night would end. Several sets of eyes turned toward her as she took everything from Edward and shoved it back in her purse. She dabbed at her hands and mouth with the napkin, while the haughty royals watched with disapproval.

"Your phone is wet, but luckily it didn't break

from the fall. There must have been water on the floor," Edward said. "Let me take it to the restroom and clean it."

Before she could respond, Peyton rested a hand on her back and leaned in. "I have to go. Jojo has a fever, and Jackson thinks we need to take her to the hospital."

"What? Oh my gosh. I can come with you," Elle said.

"No. This is your opening. She's fine. He's never been alone with her when she's had a fever. Once we get some Tylenol in her, she'll be okay. But she's not taking it from him, so I need to go home and give it to her." Peyton chuckled and rolled her eyes. The girl was made for motherhood. Elle looked forward to a time when she'd be hurrying home to her husband and baby.

Maverick.

She wanted to check in with him, but Edward ran off with her damn phone.

"Go. Text me as soon as you get the Tylenol in her and let me know how she is. I can meet you at the hospital if you have to take her."

"Okay, keep an eye on our girl. I think she and Cam had a bad fight this time. She's drinking an awful lot," Peyton said, keeping her voice down so only Elle could hear her.

"I will. Don't worry about a thing."

Tomas Efant was engulfed in a conversation with a man she didn't recognize, and Sabine watched her intently, causing Elle's palms to sweat. "Sorry for the interruption. My goddaughter has a fever."

Sabine nodded and sipped her champagne before speaking. "I'm glad we were able to switch our plans to be here tonight. I was surprised you changed the date on such short notice."

Luckily, she didn't have any liquid in her mouth to spatter all over the ice queen. What in the Sam Hill was she talking about? And why did she look like she was sucking on a lemon all the time?

"I didn't change the date, Edward did," she said, surprised by her own curt tone.

"Ah, I love finding my two favorite ladies together." Edward strolled over and returned her cell phone to her. *The weasel.*

"There seems to be a misunderstanding about who changed the date for this event on such short notice. Your mom thought it was me. I assured her it wasn't. Isn't your father leaving town tomorrow morning?" Elle wasn't going to let this go. She glanced down at her phone. There were still no messages or missed calls from Maverick. His event must still be going.

"We're not going back to France tomorrow. We just got here," Sabine said with annoyance. Her face twisted and bitter once again. Sheesh.

"Of course, you're not. This is a misunderstanding," Edward said, and he didn't meet Elle's gaze.

"Could I have a word with you, Edward?" She'd had enough. He'd lost his mind.

"Heeeeyyy." Dani moved beside her and almost knocked her over. Could this night get any worse? Her friend could barely stand on two legs, and Elle grabbed her arm to steady and shift her weight to support her. This was so out of character for her in-control bestie. The woman never acted on emotion. Ever.

"Are you okay?" she whispered so only Dani could hear.

"I think I'm going to be sick," Dani said, loud enough for both Sabine and Edward to raise their eyebrows in unison.

"Come with me." Elle faked a calmness while supporting the majority of Dani's weight. Thankfully, most people were making their way out. She kicked open the bathroom stall with her foot and pushed Dani in ahead of her. Her friend dropped to her knees and heaved for what seemed like eternity. Elle held her long hair back as she continued to dry heave.

"Elle? Dani? Are you in here?" Camille called out.

She locked gazes with Dani and put her finger to her lips, urging her to keep quiet.

"Yeah, we're in here. Poor Dani must have the same thing little Jojo has. She's got a fever and the stomach bug. I'm going to get her home in a minute, just making sure she doesn't get sick before we go."

"Oh my. Peyton said she needed to get home to the baby. Do you want my driver to take you both home?" Camille said, her red stilettos parked outside their stall. Dani's panicked gaze never left Elle's, but she stayed quiet. Camille Chadwick would not look kindly on her employees overindulging at a work event.

"No, you go ahead. We're leaving soon, but Cam's on his way to pick us up," Elle said. A necessary lie to save her friend's ass.

"Okay. See you ladies on Monday. Enjoy your weekend. Great job on this project, and the event went off without a hitch. Well done."

Dani covered her mouth, clearly ready to empty her stomach once again. How much champagne could she have downed in two hours?

"Okie dokie. See you Monday." Elle kept her voice

calm and flushed the toilet to mask the sound of Dani gagging.

When they heard the door shut, Dani proceeded to vomit over and over and Elle finally dropped down on the floor and leaned against the door. She didn't care about the lack of sanitation, she just needed to sit.

"I think I'm done," Dani said. Her makeup smeared under her pretty green eyes, and her pencil skirt was riding so high it was battling for real estate with her bra. Elle grabbed tissue, dabbed it on her tongue, and cleaned up her friend's face.

Gross? Sure.

Necessary? Absolutely.

"All right, let's get you up. Let me fix your skirt."

Dani hiccupped and wiped a stray tear rolling down her cheek. Elle had never seen her cry. Not once in all the years they'd been friends.

"I'm sorry. I don't know what happened tonight. Cam and I had a big fight, and the champagne was so good. Oh my God, do you think Camille knows I'm blunk?"

Dani laughed hysterically while Elle smoothed her skirt for her. There was vomit all over the front of her white silk blouse. Elle slipped off her jacket and put it on Dani, buttoning the front to hide what she could.

"Um, no. She doesn't know you're blunk." She was too tired to correct her.

"Wait. Blunk? Bllllluuuunnnkk. Blunk you very much. No such blunk," she said, and fell against the wall in a fit of giggles. *What the hell was happening?*

"Come on, my little blunkard. You're coming home with me." Dani lived alone, and there was no way in hell she could let her go home by herself in this condition. She reached for her phone and was surprised she still hadn't heard from Maverick. She sent him a quick text.

—So much drama tonight. Hope your evening went smoother than mine. Dani is three sheets to the wind, so I need to bring her home with me. Sorry to change the plans last minute. Can you and Daisy head over to my place instead? Love you—

She ushered Dani through the empty lobby and almost made it out the door without being stopped.

"Can my driver give you a ride home?" Edward said, standing closer than she'd like.

"No, I'm calling an Uber," she said in a huff, pulling up the app on her phone. She didn't even want to start with him. He'd lied about so many things tonight, and she didn't have the energy nor care to even resolve it.

"Don't be ridiculous. I know you're mad. I promise you it's not as twisted as you think. But now is not the time to discuss it. I have to stay here and finish. Let Raul run you home. Dani doesn't look well. The last thing you need is her vomiting in an Uber. He can come back and get me. Seriously, it's the least I can do." Edward kept his distance and appeared genuine.

"Speak for yourself Count Know-it-all," Dani said with slurred words, pointing her finger at him with anger.

"This just keeps getting better. Thank you for the offer of the car. I'll actually take you up on it." She pushed against Dani who leaned against her like a dead weight.

Edward was on his phone within seconds. "Bring the car around. Take Ms. Fiore wherever she wants to go."

He pushed the door open as his car pulled up in front of the building.

"Thank you, Edward. Take care." She walked past him and helped Dani into the car before climbing in behind her.

Sinking back against the black leather seats, she relaxed for the first time all night.

"Are we going to your house, Ms. Fiore?"

"Yes, Raul. Thank you for the ride. I appreciate it."

"I promise not to puke in your fancy car—because I'm no *fool, Rauuuul,*" Dani said accentuating the rhyme before bursting into a fit of laughter, slipping off the seat and landing on her ass.

"Sweet Lord, you are on one tonight." Elle pulled her back onto the seat.

They arrived at her place and thankfully Dani was exhausted, and Elle got her to bed in the guest room. She left a bottle of Tylenol and a glass of water on the bedside table. She was disappointed Maverick and Daisy weren't there and she retrieved her phone.

—Not going to make it over. Let's talk tomorrow—

This wasn't the norm for Maverick. They'd never spent one night apart when he wasn't traveling for a game. She dialed his number and after a few rings, it went to voicemail. She tried to calm the panic emanating through her like a freight train at full speed.

"Um, I hope everything's okay. I'm sorry I couldn't come back to your place, but Dani is really drunk, and I didn't want her to go home alone. I hate not being with you. I love you," she said to his voicemail before hanging up.

A sick feeling settled in her gut. Something was

off, and she hated being the last to know.

****

Maverick never returned her call but finally sent a text the next morning.

—I have a meeting with Coach to go over game tapes this afternoon. I'll be over at 5—

Her stomach churned and anxiety built. He'd never been so short, nor had he ever ended without saying *I love you.* She pushed it away when the guest bedroom door flew open.

"Did someone beat me with a sledgehammer last night?" Dani stumbled from the guest room. Her long, wavy hair looked like she'd just escaped a windstorm and last night's makeup was still in place but smeared a bit.

"You must have one mean hangover. I've never seen you drink so much," Elle said, sipping her coffee and pushing her laptop aside.

"I know. I was upset about Cam. I think we're going to break up." Dani took the seat across from her and pulled her feet up on the chair, wrapping her arms around her knees.

"Really? What was the fight about?"

"He gave me an ultimatum. He wants to move in together, get engaged, the whole shebang. I can't even be mad because it's the natural thing to do at this point. We've been together three years. Of course, he wants to move forward," Dani said, her gaze wet with emotion.

"You don't want to move forward with him?"

"I don't want the same things he wants. I'm not ready for marriage or kids, and I don't know if I ever will be. When he talks about it, I completely panic. I don't want a roommate, hell, I barely like when he spends two nights at my place a week. I see how you are with Maverick, and what we have is so different. I don't miss him when I'm not with him."

Dani's shoulders slumped, and she buried her face in her hands.

"Listen, not all relationships are the same. Trust me, I've never had what I have with Maverick with anyone else. But maybe Cam isn't the guy for you. It doesn't mean you don't love him. You just don't want the same things," Elle said, scooting her chair beside Dani's and resting an arm on her back.

"I really do love him. But he feels more like a friend than a lover. Ugh. This makes no sense. He's perfect for me. Everything I want. He's not pretentious, for starters—he's a really good, down-to-earth, guy. But the thought of moving in together or marriage makes me want to vomit. I don't know what to do."

Elle tried to contain her desire to chuckle. Dani rarely exhibited this much emotion. She was what you'd call even-steven. There weren't a lot of highs and lows.

"I think you have your answer, sweetie. I know it's hard, but if moving in and talking about marriage makes you want to vomit after three years of dating, well, it's a big red flag." Elle laughed a little, earning a small smile from her friend. "You don't want to settle, and he deserves to be with someone who feels the same way he does."

"I know. I keep trying to convince myself we're just in a rut. I love Cam so much. I don't want to lose him. What if he doesn't forgive me for not wanting the same things? He's wasted all these years with me," she said, sniffing and standing to get a tissue to wipe her nose.

"It will probably take him time to get over the initial blow, but eventually he will. You haven't lied to him. You've always been honest."

"Oh my God. We're supposed to go to his mom's for Thanksgiving in two weeks. We already bought the tickets," Dani said, swiping at the tears streaming down her cheeks.

"You really are out of it lately. Thanksgiving is *this* week. You can cancel the tickets. He's the one giving the ultimatums. You were happy going along the way things were."

Dani's face paled. "What did you say? Thanksgiving is this week? Are you sure?"

"You know me and my internal calendar. Don't be so hard on yourself. You have a lot on your mind."

"No, no, no. This isn't happening," Dani said, and then pushed to her feet. She hurried toward the front door and grabbed her purse.

"What's wrong? You can cancel a flight up to the day of departure. Relax. This is the least of your worries."

Dani pulled out her phone and studied it like it held the answer to all of life's problems. "Holy shit."

Elle moved beside her friend. "What's going on?"

"I'm late," she said, before dropping to the floor in a heap of hysteria.

"How late?" she crouched down beside Dani, rubbing her back and pushing her hair away from her face.

"Two weeks. I'm never late. What am I going to do? I don't want to move in with Cam. We're definitely not ready for a child." She leaned her back against the wall and pulled her knees up to her chest, in a little cocoon.

"You've been under a ton of stress, so you might have thrown off your cycle. Don't panic yet. You stay here and I'll go grab a pregnancy test, okay?"

"Thank you. Okay, I'll stay here." She broke on a sob.

Elle grabbed her keys and hurried to the drugstore on the corner, buying a pregnancy test and two pints of Ben and Jerry's cookie dough ice cream. Dani was in the exact same position when she returned home.

"Come on. No sense avoiding it. Let's do this." Elle pulled Dani to her feet and led her to the bathroom.

Three minutes felt more like three hours as they waited. They sat on the bathroom floor, hand in hand. "It's going to be fine either way. You're not alone. You've got Peyt and me, and we'll be there for you."

Dani didn't speak, just squeezed her hand harder. Elle's phone alarm went off and she moved to her feet.

"I can't look. Just tell me." Dani dabbed her nose with a tissue while she remained on the floor.

She moved to the counter. This little stick held Dani's future.

One pink line.

She bent down to face her friend. "Hells bells. It's negative. You're not preggers."

She hugged Dani while she sobbed for a good five minutes, the two of them huddled on the bathroom floor. When Peyton arrived, they spent the rest of the afternoon talking.

"I'm going to talk to Cam tonight. I think it's time for both of us to move forward," Dani said, picking at her salad.

"Listen, you're doing the right thing. He needs to go out there and find someone who wants what he wants. And it's time for you to do the same," Peyton said.

"And if this baby thing wasn't a wake-up call, I don't know what is. I'm definitely not ready for any of it right now."

Dani said she'd speak to Cam immediately. She would do the right thing. Elle glanced at her phone to see three texts from Edward, of all people, asking if they could meet. *Not happening.* She didn't respond. There was nothing more to say. No texts or calls from Maverick, which surprised her. They usually texted and talked throughout the day. Maybe she was reading into it. A dull ache settled in her chest. He'd be here in a little bit. She wanted to get to the bottom of whatever was going on soon. Her house phone rang, which usually meant the front desk was calling.

"Hello."

"Miss Fiore, we have Count Edward Efant here at the front desk, and I noticed you had him removed from your permanent list, so I didn't want to send him up without speaking to you," Bernie said, keeping his voice low, obviously trying to avoid Edward hearing. She couldn't believe he'd come to her house. He was proving relentless. She promised Maverick she'd stay away from him, so she wasn't about to invite him up. Both of her friends shared a puzzled look and Peyton mouthed, "What does he want?"

Elle shrugged. "I'll come down, Bernie. Thank you for calling."

"I can't believe he came here. The guy is an entitled jackass," Dani hissed.

"I have no idea what he wants. But I'm not about to invite him up after Maverick specifically asked me to stay away from him. We have nothing to discuss. He lied to his parents about our relationship, changed the date of the event, and used me as the reason. He's showed me who he is one too many times," Elle said.

"Well, we're coming with you. Give us a signal if we should stick around in the lobby," Peyton said.

"I will. Let's go."

Elle led them to where Edward sat on the white couch in the grand lobby of her building. Irritation grew with each step. He was pushing her limits.

"Edward, what are you doing here?" Elle crossed her arms. Dani and Peyton stood a step behind her in solidarity.

"You left me no choice. This is urgent. I know you and your mother aren't speaking right now, but I thought you should know what's going on," he said, his gaze met hers, and she saw genuine concern there.

"Did something happen?"

"It's Winston. He had a massive stroke, and he's in the hospital. They don't know if he'll make it through the next couple of days. It's quite serious."

Her legs wobbled, and she placed a hand on her churning stomach. Dani grabbed her hand, and Peyton fired off questions, "How did you find out? Which hospital?"

"Caroline let me know. I figured you would want to go home straight away," Edward said.

"Yeah, of course. I need to talk to Maverick. He won't be able to go with me with his game schedule these next few weeks."

"Do you want me to come with you?" Dani asked,

and Peyton offered to pack up little Jojo and go as well.

"No, I'm fine, thank you. You guys don't need to stick around. You've got a sick baby at home, and you need to go have a very important talk with Cam. Maverick will be here in a few minutes. I'm fine. I just want to get all the information, and then I'll book my flight." Elle hugged them both and insisted they head home.

She sat next to Edward and had him retell her the details of the stroke. At least what he remembered. Winston was taken by ambulance, and said they called it an ischemic stroke, and he wasn't able to speak at the moment. Her hands trembled as she wrote down the info in her phone. She wanted Maverick to get here now. She needed him.

"Edward, I really appreciate you coming here to tell me. I need to go book my flight."

He leaned over and hugged her. "I know how important he is to you. Keep me in the loop, and if you need me, I'll make myself available."

"Thanks for the offer, but I'll be fine. I'll let you know how he's doing when I get there."

"Safe travels, darling," he said, and she turned on her heels and hurried to the elevator.

She booked a ticket for first thing in the morning and sent her mother a text letting her know she was coming home. She didn't want to pick a fight with her mama over not having the decency to let her know what happened to Winston. Now wasn't the time.

She paced her living room. She knew she'd lose it the minute Maverick walked through the door. She texted him.

—I really need to talk to you. Please get here as

soon as you can—

Somehow, he'd become her rock. He knew how to settle her. Calm her. Put things in perspective. And right now—she needed Maverick Wallace something awful.

Chapter Twenty-Six

Maverick's Playbook
Watch your blind spot!

"Later, Mav. See you tomorrow," Brent said, walking out to their cars after meeting with coach.

"Yeah, get some rest. Big game coming up."

His phone vibrated, and he read the text from Gigi. She and her roommate, Mandy, were staying at his house tonight because their condo was being fumigated tomorrow morning. She'd mentioned it last week, but he'd forgotten. Hell, he had a shit ton on his mind and wasn't in the mood for thirty questions about the logistics. He sent her a quick response letting her know it was fine, he'd stay at Elle's. Gigi had a key and could let herself in.

The next text was from Elle, asking him to get there soon because she needed to talk to him. After the fucked-up way things went down last night, he'd expected it. He hadn't gone to her place last night because he didn't want to hash it out when he was pissed. His event went off without a hitch, until Ben, one of his teammates, sent him a screenshot of a photo of Elle with Count Asshat. Ben's girlfriend, Mia, worked in marketing for a local newspaper. She saw the photo on a table of lead stories to possibly run. Mia encouraged her editor to kill the story. The asshole's arms were wrapped around Peaches' shoulders. She didn't look comfortable in the picture, and she wasn't smiling, but he had his hands on her again. He'd asked her to stay the fuck away from the guy. It was a simple goddamn request.

Maverick saw red. And from there, the rest of the night went to shit. He called her to see what the fuck was going on, and the douchebag actually answered her phone. Her fucking phone. He offered no explanation as to why he had it. His exact words, "*You'll have to ask her yourself.*" Maverick wanted to drive over there and rip his fucking head off, but he had a speech to give. He put on a fake ass smile and took the stage.

When the event ended, there was a text from Elle asking him to come to her place because Dani was drunk. He didn't respond because he didn't trust what he'd say. He'd never been pissed at her. Not like this. He cooled down a little before driving over to her place with his goddamn goldendoodle sprawled across the passenger seat fighting to climb on his lap. When he pulled in front of her building, Edward Efant's goddamn car pulled out of her fucking building. He'd seen the ridiculous limo a few times, and there was no question whose car it was because the arrogant prick had his last name splattered across his license plate. Maverick turned his ass around and drove home. He'd been jerked around enough for one night. He couldn't think of a rational explanation for any of it.

Was the asshole in her condo? No fucking way. She'd asked Maverick to come over. But Edward had obviously taken her home. She clearly ignored his request. He'd been tolerant of Edward's bullshit and was at a breaking point. Was more going on than he knew? He'd walked in on the guy grabbing her arm, and yeah, she'd pushed him off, but how many times had it happened when he wasn't there? Was she being fucking honest with him?

He let out a breath and made his way into her building. He came to a halt, trying hard to rein his anger in.

"Mr. Wallace, are you ready for Monday's game?" Bernie, the doorman asked. The dude had to be pushing seventy-five, but he never missed a beat.

"Yeah, we're ready to get after it," he said to the older gentlemen, but his gaze never left the asshole talking on his phone in the corner of the lobby.

Edward fucking Efant.

"Good luck, we're all rooting for you."

Maverick patted Bernie on the shoulder before making a beeline across the lobby. "Is it possible for you to find your own fucking woman?" he growled.

The cocky bastard dropped his phone in his coat pocket and smiled. "Well, technically, she was mine before she was yours."

He wanted to crush his smug face. His slicked back hair and navy suit with a floral pocket square pissed him off even more. Douchebag.

"She was never yours, and she sure as shit ain't yours now. I'm going to tell you one more time, and I'll say it nice and slow. You need to hear me because this is the last fucking time I'm going to say it. *Stay. The. Fuck. Away. From. Her*."

"When she asks me to, I will. Until then, if she invites me over, which she does often—you'll probably see me again soon." He smirked, tucking his hand into his pocket.

"No fucking way she invited you here. Not now, and not ever. Not since we've been together. You're hanging out in her lobby like a goddamn stalker."

"Am I? I believe you're threatened by me, Maverick. And you have good reason to be. Because what we had never really ended. She was confused, yes, but the feelings are still there. We both know I'm a whole lot more likely to ride in on a white horse, while you're out there kicking a ball around a field with your friends. It bothers you, doesn't it? Knowing I'm better suited for her. You and I both know it, and Elle knows it too."

"If you're so good for her, then why'd she dump your ass, you selfish, arrogant prick? This isn't a conversation about who's better for her—she's with me. End of story. I don't give a fuck what you think."

"Yes, Elle and I hit a bump in the road as every couple does. You were a rebound until she comes to her senses. We've talked about a future together. About marriage and children. Have you? You've been with her for a few months and now she and her mother don't speak. You don't think it bothers her, do you? Well, it does. Then you come to my workplace calling out orders for me to stay away from her knowing it will reflect poorly on her professionally. What do you think she called me over to talk about today? I'll let you ponder the thought."

"You think you can get inside my head? I'm a fucking professional football player. I don't do head games—you manipulative fuck. Don't you already have children? Ah, yes, they're only a few years younger than Elle. Maybe you should put your energy there, old man. Now I'm going upstairs to spend the rest of the night with my girl. You can see yourself out, and I promise you this is the last time you're going to set foot in this building."

"Again, don't make promises you can't keep, Maverick. She invited me here. You can't stop me from accepting the invitation," he said in his haughty French accent, turned and headed for the door.

Maverick's blood boiled. He stepped in the elevator, replaying the conversation. Did she invite him here? He did see the guy's car here last night, along with the photo and the phone. Fuck, this wasn't good. But he knew her. She wouldn't fuck around on him, would she? Count Asshat sure seemed confident saying things never really ended with them. Maverick used his best poker face when he said the dude's head games weren't working. Nothing was further from the truth because right now, he didn't know which way was up. Running a hand through his hair he tried to get it together. He wanted to punch a wall. Kick something. Preferably a cocky French Count. The man's words replayed over and over.

What do you think she called me over to talk about today?

We've discussed marriage and children.

We both know I'm a whole lot more likely to ride in on the white horse.

Was he right? Edward did fit into her world better than Maverick. Was she calling him to vent about her problems? Planning a future with both of them behind his back?

He put the key in the door, anger radiating from every cell.

"Finally. I've been waiting," she said, her face

puffy and red. Was she crying? Had she cried to the Count earlier?

"Give me a minute," he growled, walking right past her and into the bathroom. He locked the door, which he'd never done, and bent over the sink.

Pull your shit together, man.

She looked dumbfounded when he moved past her. Seeing her upset nearly broke him.

Nearly.

But then he remembered he wasn't the first one to comfort her. He splashed water on his face before hitting his phone hard on the counter. His anger palpable. Unfortunately, his phone took the brunt of it. It crashed into the wall before landing in the garbage can. Normally he'd gloat about his impressive shot, but not today.

"Maverick. Are you okay?" she called from the other side of the door.

"I'll be out in a minute," he said, his irritation impossible to miss. He reached for his phone, noting the only other thing in the garbage can in the tidy bathroom.

What the hell is this? A white stick.

A motherfucking pregnancy test.

He bent down and pulled it from the trash can, and every muscle in his body tensed. His shoulders went stick straight. He barreled out of the bathroom with his cracked phone and the white stick in hand.

"What the fuck is this?" he said, his voice loud and angry. He flailed the goddamn thing in her face.

She blinked several times. Speechless. This was a first. It also spoke volumes. He'd never seen her at a loss for words.

Her gaze hardened. "What are you doing? Get that out of my face."

"I think we can jump ahead in this conversation. Is this why you're crying? You thought you were pregnant with someone else's fucking baby?" he said, his voice louder than intended. Everything bottled up was now at the surface, like a dam at its limits.

She crossed her arms, her face red and furious.

"Please, do me the honor of telling me who I've been impregnated by. Last I checked, you were the only man I'm sleeping with."

"But I'm not the one you called first to discuss this with, am I? And it sounds like your sidepiece doesn't wear a condom because you sure as shit make sure I do. Let me guess, you want to get pregnant by a fucking royal. Is this part of your fucked up fairy-tale?" It felt good to let it all out. He was done checking himself. She'd fucked him over, and he was damn well going out in a blaze.

Her glossy wounded gaze locked with his. He didn't miss the devastation. It almost made him stop his rant.

Almost.

But she'd cut him to the core, and he'd damn well have his say. He'd put up with this Edward bullshit for too long, and the whole time he'd been getting played.

"You think I'm sleeping with someone else? You're kidding, right?" It came out more like a squeak. Her voice broke, and tears streamed down her face. She still wouldn't own her shit.

"You bet on the wrong horse, Peaches. Your prince is an old douchebag. Probably can't even get it up. I don't think you're going to have any luck getting pregnant. I guess karma's a bitch, huh?"

"Get out," she said, and her voice trembled. Good. He wanted to hurt her the way she'd hurt him.

"My pleasure. *We're done.* Thanks for nothing." Bitterness rolled off his tongue with ease. Even he was shocked by his coolness.

"That's the first thing we've agreed on today." She held the door open for him to leave. His gaze locked with hers and something in his chest tightened. She looked sad. Broken. Why the fuck was she upset? She did this. This was on her. Where was the remorse?

"Have a nice life, Peaches." His tone laced with disgust.

She didn't respond, just slammed the door behind him. As the elevator moved down toward the lobby a sinking feeling settled in his stomach. They were done. She didn't make any effort to explain herself, defend why she'd been meeting with Edward behind his back, or tell him why the fuck she had a pregnancy test in her bathroom. He sat in his truck and leaned his head back against the seat. She'd fucking crushed him, and he never saw it coming. He knew better than to fully trust someone this way. He wouldn't make the same mistake twice. He'd bought a fucking engagement ring for her. Planned a future with her. Christ, she'd agreed to move in with him, all the while carrying on with another man behind his back.

He pulled in his driveway and slammed his fists against the steering wheel. "Fuck."

Mandy's car was in front of the house. She and Gigi were already here. *Jesus.* He sure as shit didn't need his sister grilling him right now, and he wouldn't stay at his house with them there. The way this day was going, he'd more than likely have a goddamn nightmare tonight. Betrayal had a way of dredging up bad memories.

"Mav, I thought you were staying at Elle's?" Gigi said, setting out enough Chinese food containers on the counter to last her a week.

"Yeah, just grabbing a bag. Do you mind feeding Daisy tonight and tomorrow?"

"Of course, no problem," she said, giving him a side hug when he walked past.

"Thanks."

"Hey, are you okay?" She studied his features as her roommate came walking out from the bathroom.

"Yeah, fine."

"Hey, Maverick," Mandy said. "Thanks for letting us crash here tonight."

"No problem."

He ran upstairs and threw practice clothes and toiletries in a bag and made a quick reservation at a hotel up the street. He used the back door to avoid his sister's inquisition, and yelled out for them to have a good night.

Driving to the hotel he made a conscious decision. No more distractions. Agonizing over why the woman he loved betrayed him included. Time to pull his head out of his ass and finish his season strong. He'd been caught up in a bullshit fairy-tale, and he knew better.

But why the fuck did it feel like someone cut his heart from his body and stomped it?

Maybe, because she did.

Chapter Twenty-Seven

Elle's Tip of the Day
Sometimes a prince is just a frog in fancy clothing!

"Take as long as you need," Camille said after Elle explained what happened to Winston.

"Thanks, Camille. I'll let you know when I find out more."

"Don't worry about us here. You deserve a break anyway. Take care of yourself."

"Thanks again," Elle whispered.

Her stepfather took a turn for the worse during the night. He was not responsive to the drugs they administered. Her father offered to take her to the airport, but she didn't want him to leave when he was on call at the firehouse. Peyton and Dani came over for a few hours last night after hearing what happened with Maverick.

Boy, when it rained, it poured. She'd wanted him to wrap her up in the safe little cocoon he'd always provided and comfort her after hearing about Winston. Instead he'd blindsided her. She could tolerate Maverick's occasional jealousy and his stubbornness about moving in together, but she wouldn't put up with being called a cheater or a liar. The man she loved actually believed she'd had sex with someone while they were together—it was inexcusable.

She thought he knew her. Knew who she was. She would never have been unfaithful. She'd been with someone who cheated on her, for goodness' sake, and she'd shared the gory details with Maverick. Maybe he was guilty like Will was. The guilty ones always pointed their fingers at the innocent ones. Nothing made sense anymore. They'd been so happy leading up to yesterday, she didn't know what changed.

And now they were done?

All because Dani threw her pregnancy test in the garbage can? It was ridiculous and offensive. She couldn't be with someone who believed she'd do something so shady. No. Maverick Wallace needed to check himself. She'd been there for him since the day they started dating, and when she needed him most, he'd gone fifty shades of crazy. It didn't stop the ache buried deep in her soul. He was her man. Her person. Now it was over? She couldn't wrap her head around it.

Rolling her bag toward the door, she nearly tripped over Daisy's stuffed giraffe. Damn. The giant pup loved this thing. Slept with it every night. She grabbed "Raffi" and the bag of dog treats on the counter. Maverick wasn't great about picking up the extras, and Daisy loved her Bully sticks. Stepping in the uber, she asked the man to make a quick stop before the airport, agreeing to pay extra to do so. Maverick's house was on the way. She'd leave it on the front porch. She had no desire to see him. At least that's what she kept telling herself.

"Can you please park across the street? I don't want to pull in front of the house. I'll run over speedy fast," she said, grabbing Raffi and the treats.

The perturbed Uber driver, Ricco, rolled his eyes

but nodded. She slipped on her sunglasses, looked both ways, and ran to the porch. An unfamiliar car sat in front of his house. Her stomach twisted. Who would be here at seven in the morning? It couldn't be a woman because Maverick never allowed anyone to sleep at his house. She'd been the first, and thought she'd be the last. Not to mention they'd been broken up for all of twelve hours, he couldn't possibly have met someone already, could he? She gazed back at the Uber, knowing she could make it to the car in about twelve seconds. She wanted to see his face from a distance. Maybe she could get on the plane with peace of mind if she got a little peek. She dropped the items on the doormat and rang the bell. Memories of her ding-dong ditching days resurfaced, and she sprinted for the car.

"What are you doing?" Ricco said in a huff.

"Shhh…" she whispered, ducking down on the floor in the back seat and peering out the window. "I just want to see if he gets it."

"You look kind of desperate, lady." He chuckled.

"Isn't there some sort of *hashtag-no-judgment-rule* in your profession?" she whisper-hissed and her heart raced when the front door opened.

The air left her lungs. Her mouth bone dry. There stood a beautiful woman, wrapped in a baby blue towel, and her dark, wet hair fell over her shoulders. She looked right and left before scooping up Daisy's things.

At seven o'clock in the freaking morning.

Oh. My. God. She'd been a fool.

"Drive, please," she said. Elle never spoke the rest of the way. Maybe she'd lost her voice. Lost her mind. She'd most definitely lost her heart. She'd given it to the wrong damn man. Never in a million years would she have thought Maverick capable of being so cold. So callous. Never. She gasped on a sob, holding her hand over her mouth, and trying with all she had to keep it together. Even Ricco seemed to empathize as he stayed silent as well.

The trek through security and boarding the plane were a blur. She couldn't believe it. For the first time since yesterday, she realized it really was over. He'd accused her of being unfaithful, and now it all made sense. He probably met this woman a while ago and wanted to be with her. Making Elle the bad guy was an easy out. Hell, maybe he'd been unfaithful all along. Her mind spun with what-ifs.

Before the plane took off, she blocked Maverick Wallace from her phone and all her social media. She didn't want him to call or text her. Nor did she want to sit around staring at her phone hoping he would. He'd lost all rights of knowing where she was or what she was doin'. She fought the tears for the first hour of the flight before dozing off. Turns out, broken hearts are exhausting.

****

Once she grabbed her luggage, she moved toward the exit. Mama sent a text and said Bernard, their long-time driver, would be at the airport to pick her up and bring her to the hospital.

"Elle." A familiar voice called out.

She thought seeing a half-naked woman open the door at Maverick's house this morning would be the most shocking thing to happen today. But lo and behold, Caroline Humphries was full of surprises.

"Mama?"

Two arms wrapped around her, speaking through

her sobs, "Yes, I came to get you."

Say, what?

First off, Mama hated the airport. She always sent Bernard. Second, she never left the house unless she looked impeccable. And she most definitely didn't look like Caroline Humphries, the darling of Savannah's social circle, right now. Lastly, she didn't believe in showing emotion in public, and she was currently a blubbering mess.

"Are you wearing *pajamas*?"

Mama intertwined their fingers and led her out to the street. Again, hand-holding was not the norm.

Elle gave Bernard a quick hug before jumping in the car.

"These are pajama bottoms, but the top is a blouse. It's Christian Dior. It goes with everything." Mama tucked her disheveled blonde hair behind her ears.

Well, hells bells. Never in her entire life had she seen her mother with a hair out of place. And last she checked Christian Dior didn't design blouses to pair with pajamas.

Elle faced her mother. "How's Winston? Are you all right?"

Tears streamed down Mama's face. "He's doing the same. I'm sorry I didn't call you. I'm sorry you had to hear about Winston from Edward. I'm sorry for being a terrible mother."

She'd woken up in an alternate universe because nothing made sense today.

"Wow. You've just covered a lot of area. Yes, I wish you had called. But I'm glad I'm here now." She wasn't going to touch the part about Mama being a terrible mother because it was a can of worms she didn't want to open at the moment.

"I was afraid. I didn't think you'd answer after the way I treated you. I don't know what's wrong with me, Elle. I'm so angry all the time. Mostly at you."

Elle tried to cover her mouth when she laughed.

"You're preaching to the choir, Mama. I'm quite aware of how angry you are at me. You have been for years. And for the love of Pete, I don't know why. I'm sorry I didn't win the stupid pageant. Not because it even matters to me anymore, but because things have been so much worse between us since I lost. If I could go back and change the outcome, I would. For you. I'd try to be the daughter you wish I was." Elle broke on a sob and tears streamed down her face.

Saying it aloud was both a relief and a heartache. A blessing and a curse. Admitting Mama was disappointed in who she was—it stung something awful, but at least she finally said it. Her heart couldn't take much more today. She was hanging on by a thread. Didn't expect to have such a heavy talk when she landed in Savannah.

"No, darlin'. It's not what you think. This is why I've failed you so terribly." Mama slipped off her oversized sunglasses and met Elle's gaze. "Winston and I have been in a fight since we met you for dinner weeks ago. We've barely spoken. I probably caused his stroke. He's so upset with me for how I treated you. How I've treated you for years. I'm so full of anger. And none of it was meant for you."

The car merged onto the freeway and she shook her head at her mother. "What is it about? I don't even know anymore. The pageant? Your legacy? My last name?"

"No. No. I don't even know how to explain it." She leaned back against the seat with a sigh.

"Try."

"I was engaged to Winston when I was nineteen years old. I was so young. Too young. Grandma and Grandpa were thrilled about the wedding. I mean, marrying a Humphries was a step up for me, of course. I loved him. I really did. But I was too young to even understand what it meant. And then I met your father. Winston was traveling all the time, as his career was taking off. He was more than a decade older than me. And Nick, well, he was so handsome and charming. I mean, the man was deliciously sexy. And I was selfish. I acted on attraction," Mama said, swiping at the tears falling down her cheeks.

"You can skip the part about how hot my dad was, please." Elle rolled her eyes.

"Oh, of course. Yes. Excuse my manners. Well, you know the outcome. The fling came to an end with Nick, and I thought it would be our little secret. Two days before my wedding to Winston I found out I was pregnant. Kept it a secret from everyone until I was almost five months along. I never told a soul it wasn't Winston's baby. I think a lot of people suspected with the rumor mill and all the whispers about me runnin' wild with some young boy a few weeks before the wedding. I think Winston always knew because we didn't have, hmmm, relations before our wedding night."

"Mama." Elle threw her hands over her ears. She knew how one got knocked up, she didn't need to hear all the gory details about their sex life.

"Sorry, but I wanted you to know I was a virgin on

my wedding night, you know, with Winston."

Elle's jaw hit the ground. Was she playing with a full stack of cards? How did one manage to get knocked up before their wedding, yet remain a virgin? Only Caroline Humphries.

"I beg to differ, Mama. You were pregnant. Kind of impossible to be a pregnant virgin," Elle said, studying her mother as she fell back in laughter.

"Right. But I hadn't slept with my husband, which made me a virgin on my wedding night." Mama crossed her arms in front of her, like she had the final say on the matter.

"Yeah, it's doesn't really work that way. But it's beside the point. No one is questioning your virtue on your wedding night right now."

"Anyhoo, I made a promise to myself back then to be the best mama to you. You know, since I'd sort of messed up with getting pregnant by another man and all. It's really all I ever wanted. But I got so caught up in this secret. And well, secrets have a way of coming out of the shadows when you least expect it. But I shouldn't have blamed you for my mistake."

"So, I *am* a mistake to you. I always have been." Elle shook her head and closed her eyes. Her heart had already been broken twice today and she hadn't even had lunch yet.

"No. You most definitely are not a mistake. You never were. I made a mistake. But it brought me my greatest gift."

Elle nearly choked on the water she'd just guzzled. She'd never referred to her as a gift. Not once in the twenty-seven years she'd been around.

"It's true. I know you don't believe me. I didn't

resent you, Elle. I wanted you to be mine. When your daddy came back into our lives and made his paternity a public spectacle, I was angry. But not at you. Not even at him. I was jealous because you fell in love with him right away. You two were so much alike. So natural together. I hated it. I know how ugly I sound, but I was green with envy. And I held on to you for dear life. But the harder I held on, the farther you moved away from me. I became obsessed with the pageants. With us sharing something Nick couldn't touch. Something that was just ours. When you lost the pageant, I knew it was over. There was nothing else holding us together. And you couldn't move to San Francisco fast enough. You left me and ran to him."

The car pulled in front of the hospital and Elle sat completely silent. Processing Mama's words, her jaw all but lying on the ground. Wow. Who would have guessed Caroline Humphries was jealous of Nick Fiore?

Elle grasped her mother's hands. "Mama, I've loved you my entire life. My earliest memories are sittin' on your bathroom stool while you had your hair and makeup done, and just watchin' you. You've always been the most beautiful woman I've ever seen. I was crazy in love with you. And when Nick came into my life, yeah, I did have an instant connection with him. But it didn't lessen the way I felt about you. Or Winston."

"I've made so many mistakes. About everything. And me wanting you to date Edward wasn't about your happiness, it was another way to hold on to you. Having control over who you dated or married. And Maverick. *Please.* He reminded me so much of Nick, it terrified me. I saw the connection you have with him, and it scared me. There's no excuse. I'm trying to be honest with you. I know it's foreign, but I have to start somewhere."

"I appreciate it. But this is a lot to swallow. How about we go inside and check on Winston, and we can continue this tonight at home. Let me digest it all for a bit," Elle said, completely caught off guard over the entire conversation. She'd never seen her mother vulnerable or insecure. But she liked it.

"Yes, we need to get in there. I'm sorry to lay all this on you. I'm sure it wasn't easy to leave Maverick during his season either," Mama said, as they got out of the car.

Elle didn't respond, but her heart squeezed at the mention of his name. She wanted to call him. Tell him everything. He knew how to calm her. Help her sift through her thoughts. But she couldn't go to him now. She'd have to figure this out on her own.

Chapter Twenty-Eight

Maverick's Playbook

If you get sacked—pull your head out of your ass and figure it out!

Coach insisted Maverick stop by his office after he showered. He didn't have a clue what it was about because they'd had a meeting two days earlier. He'd played well in his last game, even though his life was a pile of steaming shit. He'd fucked up bad with his girl, and he didn't know how to fix it.

Coach Romero's assistant, Carla, hung up the phone. "He's ready for you, Maverick. You can go on back."

"Thank you," he said, striding through the office decorated in sports memorabilia.

Coach sat in his chair behind his oversized cherry wood desk. "Thanks for stopping by. Take a seat."

"What's up?"

"I wanted to ask you the very same thing. What's going on with you? Everything all right?"

Was he for fucking real? Sure, his life was shit, but his game was exactly where it needed to be.

"Everything's fine. Is there a problem?" His tone came out harsher than intended, but he wasn't sleeping well, and he didn't want to talk about his personal life, or lack thereof.

"I'm not attacking you, Maverick. But after two years of working closely together, I know when you're off. And son, right now, you're off. And I'm not talking about the game. You're playing well, I have no complaints. But your head's not in it. You aren't leading the team right now."

Maverick scrubbed a hand over his face. He'd survived a tongue lashing from Gigi yesterday. She'd been ever so happy to point out all the mistakes he'd made in his relationship with Elle. The last thing he needed to hear was how he was failing the only area in his life that didn't suck right now.

"I'm sorry if I've let you down." He let out a long, frustrated breath. What the hell did Coach want from him? He showed up every day, pushed himself as hard as he could, and put the ball where it needed to go ninety-nine percent of the time. What was the fucking problem?

"Listen, Maverick, I've been around a long time. I've coached a lot of athletes over the years. You're special. You've got the talent and you've got the heart. It's a rare combination. You aren't just a player on this team, son. You're the leader of this team. You led us to the Super Bowl last year, and we have the potential to do it again this year. But it doesn't work without you. If you want to be a stubborn ass and pretend everything's fine when we both know it isn't—then it's on you. This is me offering my ear. We're a team, remember? This is what you do for family, and I consider you part of my family."

He wasn't prepared for an emotional talk. *Jesus.* Everywhere he turned people were trying to get him to talk. Well, with the exception of the one person he was desperate to speak to. Peaches wasn't taking his calls. And of course, Peyton wouldn't help him. She'd slapped him in the goddamn face when she thought he'd had a woman stay the night at his house. Peyton apologized and insisted she would make sure Elle was brought up to speed on who Mandy was. Like he said—his life was a shit show right now. He closed his eyes for a minute. Tried to sort out the mess he'd made of things. Didn't want Coach to see what a pussy he was when it came to Peaches.

"Just going through some personal shit. I don't mean you any disrespect by not talking about it. I don't like to bring my baggage to work," he said, locking onto Coach's hard stare.

"Well, I think you're about to find out you don't always have a choice. Life is messy sometimes. Tell me what's going on. You'd be surprised what a wise old man I am," he said with a chuckle.

Maverick ran a hand through his hair, stretched his legs out and crossed one ankle over the other. He'd need to get comfortable for this. "Okay, Mr. Wisdom. Have you ever fucked up really bad with Beverly?"

"You're making this far too easy. Yes."

"Well, I think our ideas of fucking up may be different." Maverick leaned forward and rested his elbows on his knees.

"Were you unfaithful?" Coach folded his hands on his desk and his gaze turned serious.

"No. Of course not. I'm an idiot, not a douchebag."

The older man laughed and blew out a breath. "Good to know. I think everything else is fixable. What did you do?"

"Accused her of being unfaithful because I was

jealous. Turned my back on her when she needed me most."

"I agree with you. You definitely behaved like an idiot. Have you apologized to her?"

"She left town and blocked my calls. I can't reach her."

Coach Romero leaned back in his chair and stroked his chin. "Do you know where she went?"

"Back home. Her stepfather had a stroke. He's in the hospital. Her best friend, Peyton won't tell me anything more. Elle won't speak to me right now, and there's not much I can do about it from here." Maverick's chest tightened.

It all made sense once Peyton gave him an ass kicking. Peaches looked devastated the day he'd stormed in her apartment. She'd just found out about Winston, and she'd needed to lean on him. But he'd been so caught up in seeing Edward in the lobby, he'd come in with guns blazing.

"Come on, Maverick. People have been messing up long before cell phones were invented. Just because you can't call her doesn't mean you can't apologize."

"And how do you suggest I apologize? I can't fly across the country in the middle of the season," Maverick said.

"Agreed."

"Okay? Then what are you suggesting?"

"Well, what do you do when you can't get the ball down the field. Or you've been sacked, and you can't seem to get away from the other team's defense?"

"I get pissed and make sure it doesn't happen again. And this helps me, how?" Maverick didn't hide his frustration. This conversation wasn't helping, which was exactly why he didn't like to talk about it.

Coach raised a brow and shook his head. "You get mad? Being mad gets the ball down the field? Being mad buys you time before a four-hundred pound man takes you down? Think, Maverick. You aren't one of the best players in the League because you get mad all the time."

He leaned back in his chair and thought about those moments in recent games. He wasn't sure how this had anything to do with what they were talking about, but he'd play along.

"Well, I get pissed, and then I come up with a new plan."

Coach's fists hit the desk, causing Maverick to jump in his seat.

"Bingo. You come up with a new plan. You don't get sacked and stay down. You fight. You figure out a way to make it happen. Relationships are no different. It's called the game of life. You can sit on the sidelines or get your ass in the game. You don't strike me as a guy who likes to sit the bench. And right now, you've been sacked."

This piqued his curiosity. "Do you have any new plays in mind?"

Coach chuckled. "If you can't reach her by phone, and you can't fly there—think of something else. Come up with a new plan. You're a smart guy—figure it out. On top of apologizing, you best show her how sorry you are for acting like a fool. And make sure you don't do it again."

"Okay. Maybe you're onto something."

"You're not a guy that gives up easy, or you wouldn't be the quarterback for the San Francisco

Miners, would you? How important is she to you?"

"She's the most important person in my life."

"Well, then, start acting like it. Stop sulking and fix it," Coach said.

****

"Tell me why you think you behaved the way you did." Dr. Sparrow said.

He'd been there for forty-five minutes, and this wasn't his first visit. He'd come three times in the last week and a half. She really took her time getting down to business. Dr. Sparrow was in her late thirties, tall and lean, dressed in a navy pantsuit. Her dark hair was pulled in a bun and red reading glasses hung from her neck—exactly what he pictured a shrink to look like. She didn't appreciate the word *shrink*, and she told him so on the first day. Dr. Sparrow didn't mince words.

"If I knew the answer to your question, I probably wouldn't be shelling out the big bucks to see you, now would I?"

She gave him half a smile and studied him. He noticed this each time he came to see her, and she continued to do it today.

"Do you always make jokes when you're uncomfortable?" she said, her head cocked to the side.

"Why do you think I'm uncomfortable?"

"You're deflecting. Let's stick with my original question. Why did you accuse the woman you love of being unfaithful, when you've repeatedly told me you trust her explicitly?"

He scrubbed a hand over his face. Damn, he hated this. Hated thinking about why his life was so fucked up. "The hell if I know."

"Listen, if you don't want to be here, no one is

forcing you. But if you want to figure out why you pushed away the only woman you've ever loved, and why you wake terrorized from something in your past, then you are going to have to take this seriously. Or it's a waste of our time."

"I want to figure it the hell out. I think I accused Elle of being unfaithful because Count Asshat got under my skin."

"The ex-boyfriend you spoke to in the lobby? Does he have an actual name?"

"Come on, Doc. I'm meeting you halfway, can't you give me this one?" He leaned back in his chair and stretched his legs out, crossing one ankle over the other.

"Fair enough. When Count—Asshat," she gave him one simple nod, "when he gets under your skin, what do you feel?"

"It feels like…he's trying to take what's most important to me. It feels like a threat."

"All right, good. What is he threatening to take from you? Elle?"

"Yes."

"Do you think she wants to be with him?"

"No. She can't stand the guy."

"Then how could he take her away? Do you think he'd physically take her? Against her will?"

He thought about the ridiculous question and rolled his eyes. "No. I don't think he's going to kidnap her."

"Then how could he take her away?"

"I don't know. I know he wants to. And for a minute I guess I believed it was possible."

"You think she was dishonest with you?"

"No. She's one of the most honest people I know. She doesn't have a dishonest bone in her body."

"So—then I'll ask you again. How could he take away someone who doesn't want to go?" Dr. Sparrow said.

He leaned forward and scrubbed his face with his hand. "Jesus. This is going nowhere. I don't know."

"Don't get frustrated, Maverick. This is how we get to the root of the problem. I'm sure you experience frustrations when you're playing football, but you don't just give up because it's not working, do you?"

For fuck's sake. Did everyone have to throw football in his face every time he got frustrated?

"No. Maybe for a second I thought I'd been wrong about her. That maybe she was blindsiding me. It can happen when you love someone, and I love her so damn much. It doesn't make sense, but it's how I felt in the moment."

"Good. It's an honest answer. Has Elle given you any reason to think she isn't who she said she is?"

"Never."

"When was the last time someone blindsided you?" Dr. Sparrow pressed.

"I don't get blindsided."

"Interesting."

"Why is it interesting?" he said, irritation coursing his veins.

"Because you thought it. About the woman you love. The woman who you say doesn't have a dishonest bone in her body. The woman you claim to love more than you've ever loved anyone. No one has ever blindsided you, yet you doubted the most important person in your life?"

He was fucking agitated. And Dr. Sparrow remained completely calm. It was as if he was watching this whole conversation go down from an outside seat. Something in him always shut down when he discussed his biological mother. And he knew this conversation was going there.

"I didn't say *no one ever* blindsided me. I said I don't get blindsided now," he hissed. Surprised by his own anger.

"Does talking about this bother you?"

"Yes. I prefer not to talk about it."

"And how's that been working for you?"

A bitter laugh rolled off his tongue. "I'd say not so fucking well."

"I'd agree."

He sat in silence for a moment, processing her words. Not ready to share more yet.

Dr. Sparrow broke the silence. "Do you think your mother blindsided you when you were a child?"

His head tipped back, and he looked up at the ceiling. Three. Two. One. "I don't know Doc, I'd say dragging your kid around with you when you're a fucking prostitute and then dying in front of him would fall under the definition of blindsiding someone, right?"

"Yes. But why do you say *dragging your kid* instead of *dragging me*? Or *blindsiding someone* instead of *blindsiding me*? We are talking about you, aren't we?"

"Of course, we're fucking talking about me."

"And those memories, from when you were young—tell me how they make you feel?" Dr. Sparrow said.

He let out a long sigh. "I have terrible pieces of memories. Like little flashes of things happening. It's sickening. Scary. Lonely. Unsafe. The list goes on and on."

"Good, Maverick. I know it isn't easy to talk about, but sometimes getting it out is how you start the healing process."

"I don't like dredging it up."

"Dredging it up often allows you to deal with it and then put it away. The hope is to stop it from haunting you. Most of the issues you're dealing with are all connected," she said.

"I don't really see how it connects to Peaches."

"Well, let's review what you've shared. You avoided sleepovers your entire life up until you started dating Elle. So, your past was impacting you pretty early on. Elle's also the first woman you've ever loved, and from what you've shared, it sounds like a deep love."

"It is."

"Maverick, your first experience with love was not a positive one. As a child, you instinctually attach to your mother, your father, your caretaker. You had only a teenage, single mother, who was living a pretty dark life. You were dragged into her world, and it wasn't a safe one. Though you got out at a very young age and were able to start over with a wonderful family, you can't erase what you did live through."

"I understand. But how does it affect me and Peaches?"

"You're an adult now, and you're finally ready to truly love someone. It can be scary for someone who's had their guard up most of their life. Sure, you love your family, you're a social guy on the surface. But what you have with Elle is different. You're putting a lot of stock, a lot of trust into one person. It can be a powerful thing, Maverick. And when you feel there's a chance of losing someone who means so much to you, well, it can stir up a lot of those fears inside you. You need to deal with the past so you can move forward in the future. Separate them. Losing your mom was out of your control, and out of hers, in all honestly. She was a young girl who didn't know anything different. She most likely did the best she could with you considering her circumstances. Elle is not an addict nor is she a teenager. She is educated, strong, and successful, and she has given you no reason to doubt her. You need to change the way you react to situations. Your instinct is to fight and attack and hold on tight. It's probably what you did as a little boy to survive. But this situation is different. Am I making any sense?"

He took a minute to digest her words. It did make sense, but it pissed him off. Made him feel weak. "Yeah. How do I fix it?"

"It's kind of like football. You work hard and you try different strategies. But Rome wasn't built in a day. This was a lot today. Let's have you sit with this for a bit and meet up again in two or three days."

"All right. I have to fix this, Doc."

"Well, when you have something motivating you to do so it's easier to work at it," Dr. Sparrow said.

"Agreed."

He'd do whatever it took to make things right. Because Elle Fiore wasn't something—she was everything.

Chapter Twenty-Nine

Elle's Tip of the Day
Love Trumps Everything!

"I think you've had enough sugar for a lifetime," Elle said, as Winston ate another cookie from her run to Miss Cherry's sweet shop.

"Don't tell your mama, okay," he said with a smile. Powdered sugar remnants settled around his mouth. "You know it's time for you to get back home, back to work, back to your life."

She dropped in the chair beside his hospital bed. "I know. I have Jojo's baptism this weekend. I told Peyton I'd be there, pending you get released Friday."

"You just watched me eat four pastries, I'd say I'm on the mend. They're only keeping me a few extra days as a precaution. You don't need to wait, but I sure do appreciate you being here this whole time."

"Nice try. I'm not leaving till you're released. This is where I want to be."

Winston's glossy gaze surprised her. He was a sweet man, but he didn't show emotion often.

"You know, sweetheart, I may not be your biological father, but *you* are my proudest accomplishment. You've grown into an amazing young woman. You're kind and thoughtful, and you charge through life with a whole lot of courage."

A lump formed in her throat. This trip home proved a milestone. She'd closed doors on past resentments, moved forward with Mama, as they'd spent every day over the past two weeks talking about *all the things*. They still had a long way to go, but for the first time in more than two decades, they were on the right path. And Elle was tired of living by so many rules and restraints. Perfection was overrated.

"You contributed to raising me as much as anyone. Blood isn't what bonds us—love is. And I love you. Always."

He cleared his throat and adjusted his pillow. "I love you too. Glad you and your mama have mended some of those old hurts. Now, let's stop with the sappy stuff and get ready for a damn good football game."

She chuckled. "Sounds good to me."

Maverick's game would be televised in twenty minutes. She'd watched every game since she'd been home and seeing him on TV left her heart heavy. An ache still resided in her chest, as it had since the last time she'd seen him.

"Game's starting soon, I hear," Mama said, catching her off guard when she entered the room. Winston coughed, as her appearance must have surprised him as well. Caroline Humphries didn't watch football or any sporting event. Ever. She waltzed in wearing a navy Dior dress and heels and stood out in the hospital like a sore thumb.

"You came to watch the game?" Elle tried to hold back her laughter.

"You love the man, so I thought I ought to take an interest in getting to know him too."

"You can get to know him without watching

football, Mama." Elle laughed.

"I know you're heading back home soon, and I want to be with the two most important people in my life. So here I am."

What in God's creation was happening? She didn't know, nor did she care. She wanted to mend her relationship with her mama, and this was as good a start as any.

They spent the next few hours watching the game. Her gaze never left the screen as he led the Miners to the win. She wished she could reach through the screen and touch him.

****

The last bit of sun made its final descent behind the horizon. Mama left after the game, and Winston dozed off. She leaned forward to stretch her back, turning her neck from side to side before searching for another episode of *Dateline*.

"Elle Fiore?" A male voice said.

She sat up. "Yes. Who's asking?"

The man wore a baseball cap and tinted sunglasses. Who wore sunglasses inside a hospital?

He moved into the room and shoved a large package at her. She looked down at the white box, it wasn't wrapped, and someone used a Sharpie to write her name. First and last. No address. What the heck was this? A flash lit up the room. The delivery guy snapped a photo of her looking at the box. What kind of shady business was this? She couldn't ask because he turned on his heels and was out the door before she could process what was happening. She tossed the box to the side and took off down the hall. He was a fast little bugger, because he was halfway to the elevator when she entered the far end of the long hallway. She took off in a sprint, determined to stop him. Her ballet flats allowed her to move at full speed. Nurses blurred in her peripheral, but no one said a word. After weeks in the hospital, they knew her well.

"Hey. Stop," she called after him.

He looked over his shoulder and ignored her plea as he hurried in the elevator. What in the Sam Hill? She entered the hall area outside the elevator and shoved her foot between the narrow space just before the doors closed.

"Dammit." She leaned down to rub her sore calf when the doors sprung open.

"What the hell?" the guy called out, sounding a lot younger than she'd thought.

"I'll tell you what the hell—get your butt off this elevator before I hit the alarm and alert security."

He stepped off, shaking his head in disbelief. "You're crazy."

"Am I? You haven't scratched the surface of crazy yet, so buckle up, you scoundrel." She crossed her arms in front of her as he stood against the wall.

"What is this? I gave you the box. What's the big deal?" The kid acted wounded.

She leaned forward and yanked his stupid sunglasses and hat from his body. Wow, he was young. He looked like a college kid with his overgrown sandy brown hair and nervous blue gaze.

"Oh, it's a big deal. Do you think I'm stupid? I've watched enough crime shows for a lifetime, and I know shady when I see it. And you're shady," she said, loud enough to draw attention.

"Crime shows?" His words wobbled. Did she feel

sympathy? Sure. Would she back off? *Hells to the no.* She'd already broken the poor kid. Now it was time for answers.

"Crime shows? Crime shows?" She mocked him in a high-pitched voice, before returning to her scolding tone. "You're damn straight, kid. You don't deliver a package to a hospital with no address if you're on the up and up. And you don't take a picture of me without permission, do you understand me? What did they ask for, proof of life?"

"*On the up and up? Proof of life?* What the hell are you talking about? Look, he asked me to take a picture when I gave you the package. It's the only way I get paid." His hands trembled as he held them up in defense.

She'd scared the bejesus out of this poor kid. And now she had him right where she wanted him. If only she had a bright light to shine in his face to make him sing like a canary.

"So, you are gettin' paid. I thought so. Who do you work for, the drug cartel? If you think I'm going to be your drug mule, you've got another thing comin'. You may choose unassumin' innocent girls to do your dirty work, but you knocked on the wrong damn door today." She poked her finger hard into his chest and studied his frightened features. She knew this guy. She'd definitely seen him before. But where? Had she seen him on *Dateline*? "Are you a wanted man? I've seen your face before."

"*Wanted?* Oh my God," he moaned. "You're batshit crazy."

"You bet your ass I'm batshit crazy. You can tell your boss, or your godfather all about my craziness.

Whoever it is you answer to. Now I'll ask you one more time. Who. Do. You. Work. For? You've got five seconds before I blow my rape whistle and bring you to your knees."

"Holy shit, lady. I don't work for a mobster. You know me because you've seen me at PBV Bistro a few times. I'm a *busboy*. I work for Jackson Vance, for God's sake."

Her stomach dipped. "Is Jackson in some sort of trouble? Has someone pulled him into something he can't get out of?"

Now the kid started laughing and shaking his head. "No one's in trouble. Christ. I just wanted to make a few extra bucks, and now I'm not going to get paid because you're insane."

"It always starts with a busboy, or a college kid—someone who wants to make a few extra bucks. But do you know how this story ends?"

He crossed his arms and rolled his eyes. She had to say—this kid was a lame excuse for a criminal. He'd buckled like a two-dollar lawn chair, and he had a bad attitude.

"I can't wait for you to tell me."

"It ends with you in an orange jumpsuit and four narrow walls closing in around you. Your roommates are cockroaches, and the food is terrible. So, I'm going to do you a solid and pay you double what your boss is paying you. Start singing, kid."

His head fell back in laughter. "My boss? Maverick Wallace hired me. But he's not my boss, or my godfather. No one is wearing any jumpsuits either. Peyton wouldn't tell him where you were, so he paid me to fly to Georgia and go to every hospital in

Savannah until I found you. I was supposed to hand you the package, take a picture so he knew I delivered it, and get out without answering any questions. He was afraid if you knew it was from him, you would throw the package out before you opened it."

Well, this was a huge relief. Unfortunately, she'd just tortured one of Jackson's employees. The package was from Maverick. Her heart raced. Did he miss her as much as she missed him?

"Why would I throw it out?"

"I don't know? Because you're a bit of a nutjob? Personally, I find you quite terrifying, so I'm probably not the right person to ask."

"Well, you should have said who you were, and we could have avoided this whole ugly situation." She laughed, and he did too.

"What's he paying you?"

"A first-class plane ticket here, a thousand bucks, and a suite tonight at the Marriott."

"Wow. Not bad for your first *undercover job*."

"I think he would have paid me anything I wanted. I picked the price, and he didn't waver once. He was desperate to get the box to you, and he couldn't leave because he has a pretty important job with the Miners." He chuckled.

"Shame on you." She reached over and pinched him hard.

"Ouch. What did you do that for?" He rubbed his shoestring of an arm.

"For preying on someone when they're down. Didn't your mama teach you any manners?"

He raised his brows. "Did yours?"

Her head fell back in a fit of laughter. "Touché.

Come on, let's see what's in the box. I've got some pastries in the room. You can have a snack before you go shack up in your suite."

"You're lucky you're hot, because you're one crazy ass woman," he said, walking beside her down the hall.

"You're lucky you aren't wanted because I was all set to take you down." She smirked.

She reached for the package and reminded him to be quiet while Winston slept. He dug into the box of pastries while she tore at the paper, and a gasp escaped when she opened the box. Maverick Wallace was full of surprises. Holding up his jersey, number seventeen, her jaw hit the floor. His number covered in gold Swarovski crystals, sparkled in the last remnant of light peeking through the window. His name also frosted in black stones. It was breathtaking. He'd teased her in the past about the ridiculousness of bedazzling a football jersey. Was this an apology? A peace offering? She dug further into the box to find a crown. She'd never laid eyes on something so regal. This put her pageant tiaras to shame. Clear stones surrounded it and the weathered gold gave it a vintage feel.

"The dude sure likes diamonds, huh? Never seen it on a jersey. What's the crown for?" he said, keeping his voice low.

"He doesn't like them, I do. And I don't know what it's for, but maybe this will explain?" She lifted the envelope lying beneath the tissue paper.

"Okay, well, I have a suite with my name on it. So, if the interrogation is over, I'm going to get out of here," he said with a chuckle.

"Thanks for coming all this way to drop it off.

Sorry for the confusion."

"No worries. Can I say something without worrying you'll drop-kick me?" he asked, standing in the doorway.

"Sure."

"The guy's been a mess. I don't know what he did, but he mopes around PBV all the time, and he begged me to fly out here and find you. Said he would do it himself if it were possible. He seems pretty desperate. People make mistakes, right? No one's perfect. Maybe you should hear him out?"

"Yeah, thanks."

"See ya," he said, leaving the room.

She settled into her chair and opened the letter from Maverick. She was surprised he'd written her, but since he was still blocked on her phone, technically this was the only way he could speak to her.

Peaches,

I don't normally write letters; in fact, I can't tell you the last time I did.

I've lost my way without you. Like all the light in my life has been snuffed out. Peyton refuses to tell me where you are, and I get it. I deserve to wallow in my own misery. I promise you I have. I fucked up. But maybe if you understand what was going on in my head, you can find a way to forgive me.

I need you to know I have never cheated on you. Since the day you showed up on my driveway in Lake Tahoe, I haven't wanted another woman. Only you. Always you, Peaches.

Peyton says she explained Gigi's roommate being at my house the morning you dropped off Daisy's shit. I stayed at a hotel alone the night we broke up, sulking like the asshole I am. Peyton told me to respect your wishes and give you space. I'm trying like hell to do that, but I need to tell you everything in my own words.

There will never be anyone else for me but you. I knew it the first day we met.

What I'm most sorry for is the way I treated you the last time we spoke. There is no excuse. I lost my shit and I own it. Everything went sideways when we went our separate ways the night of the opening. A teammate sent me a photo of you and Count Dickhead. The way he touched you in the photo—it did something to me. I saw red. My reaction was unwarranted. I called you right after I saw the photo, and the bastard answered your phone. Doubt crept in and jealousy won. I got your text a few hours later and I drove to your house. I saw his car pulling away, and it sent me over the edge. I felt like I was losing you. It's not rational, and I should have talked to you.

When I came to your place the next day, I hadn't slept much. Count Asshat was in the lobby. I shouldn't have approached him. But again, my temper won. He told me you invited him over. Said you were with him first. Insinuated it wasn't over. Hell, it's stupid now. I knew better than to take the bait, but I fucking did. I stormed up to your place.

Finding the pregnancy test was clearly my breaking point. The thought of you being tied to someone else, of you wanting someone else—hell, I don't know. I lost it. I said inexcusable things to you. All I can tell you is I didn't mean any of it. I lashed out. Apparently, it's what I do when I'm hurting. But I promise you I'm working through these things.

I see Dr. Sparrow twice a week now. Ironic, right?

You tried to get me to go for months, and I finally start seeing her after I ruin everything. You were right, she's good. We're digging deep, and it's not always fun, but you make me want to be so much fucking better than I am.

Not sure if you've been watching my games anymore, but the season is going well. I realized something with you being gone. I don't play any different when I'm in a relationship or out of one. I've had good games and bad games since you left. The difference isn't how I play, it's how none of it really matters. It's my job, and yes, I love it. But you don't affect the way I play football. You affect the way I feel before and after a game. Celebrating was better with you, and losing was a lot sweeter when I could come home to you. It's just a game. You are so much more to me. I miss you so much, Peaches. Your smile, and the way it lights up my life. It's like someone cut me open and tore out half of my heart. There's an empty space there now. No one can fill it but you.

Now I know, without question—YOU are the single best thing to ever happen to me. Because I found my heart. And nothing else matters without it. You are my family, my passion, my heart—my everything.

In case you're wondering, I had the ridiculously blinged-out jersey made for you before I went and fucked everything up. Do you remember our picnic at the park a few weeks before you left? We were lying on the blanket when you shot up to look around. You said you heard a cry. Sure enough, there was a little girl who'd lost her mom. I pushed up to watch you. You were so gentle, the way you bent down and talked to her. She stopped crying and you took her hand and walked off to find her mom. I was in awe of you, the way you fixed the situation. When you sauntered back to me, the sunlight shone around you, and I swear to Christ you sparkled. After we got home, I got on the internet and found some sort of rhinestone shop famous for putting the stones you like on clothing. Never thought I'd want to see my number covered in sparkles, but dimming your light is something I vowed never to do.

I broke my vow the last time we spoke. The jersey showed up a few weeks ago, and it only reminded me of my mistake. Whether you forgive me or not, this belongs to you. Nothing better than seeing my girl shine in my number. You once told me I was the first person who saw you, really saw you—and I sure as shit do. I know who you are, Peaches. What I said to you had little to do with you, and more to do with me. Dr. Sparrow happily reminds me of this every time we meet. It was my insecurity talking, and I give you my word it won't happen again. Sure, I'll make mistakes, but I promise I'll never doubt you or question you again.

A week or so ago, I passed a store with an old copy of Wuthering Heights propped on a table in the window display. I went inside to see about getting a copy because you told me it was your second favorite book. The man pulled the book from the window and rang it up and behind the counter, on a high shelf, there were all these crowns. There was one sitting in a clear case. I asked about it because it looked different from the others. He told me it was a replica of the crown belonging to Elizabeth 1, the only unmarried Queen of England. He said she's considered one of the greatest and most powerful queens in history because she helped

England carry out one of the greatest military victories against Spain. He personally believes she epitomized everything a queen should be. Strong, tenacious, powerful, and kind. I told him I knew someone who sounded an awful lot like her. He said anyone with her strength should be granted a crown. I agreed. You are so much more than any of the princesses from the fairy-tales you read growing up. You are my forever queen. I may not have a white horse, I may not be perfect, but I will spend the rest of my life showing you why you belong with me.

Please forgive me. Come home and let me make things right. I hear you're coming back for Jojo's baptism. I'll be wearing the gray suit my girlfriend bought for me. I hear it goes great with her pink dress. Please, Peaches, bring back the other half of my heart.

Maverick

Tears streamed down her face, and she hugged the letter to her chest. She grabbed the jersey and slipped it over her head. Somehow it made her feel closer to him. Studying the crown, she settled it on her head and reread the letter several times. His words meant everything to her. The room now dark, she sat in silence, as tears spilled down her face. She wanted to talk to him, but they needed to speak face-to-face. His words were better than any white horse, or any fairy-tale—because Maverick Wallace owned her heart.

And that trumped everything.

Chapter Thirty

Maverick's Playbook
Failing is not an option!

The collar on his dress shirt was annoying as shit. He undid the second button and cracked his neck. Hell, the thought of seeing Peaches—he'd never been so nervous. He hadn't heard from her since she left. The last time he'd seen her he'd said so many things he regretted. Elle all but tackled Seth when he delivered the package. God, he loved his feisty girl. He laughed his ass off hearing how she grilled him. Didn't surprise him one bit—only made him miss her more. He hoped she'd reach out, say something after she heard him out. Maybe she didn't care what his reasons were. A dull ache settled in his chest. He didn't know what he'd do if she didn't forgive him. He'd keep fighting till he wore her down, because life sucked without her.

"Dude, you look like you're about to pass out. Are you afraid you're going to catch the place on fire when the angels find out you're here?" Jackson's laughter boomed through the church. The high ceilings and stained glass were pretty damn spectacular if you were into this kind of shit. He wasn't, but his girl was, so he paid attention.

"You're fucking crazy, dude," he said.

"Okay, you two can't do this here. For goodness'

sake, you're in a church. Your daughter and your goddaughter is about to be baptized. Pull it together," Peyton whisper shouted.

They both straightened. She had a way about her. A simple glare could paralyze you in your tracks.

"Sorry, Peyt," they said in unison and laughed.

"Maverick Wallace, I swear on everything holy I will hunt you down and torture you if you do anything to upset Elle today. It's her first day back, and she's been through a lot, so watch yourself," Peyton said.

"Christ, I'm not going to do anything to hurt her. I miss her." He put his hands up in defense.

"Dude, you can't say *Christ* in church," Jackson said, winking at his wife like he'd done his good deed for the day.

"And why the hell not? It's his house, isn't it? Am I not allowed to say Jackson in your house?" Maverick asked with annoyance.

Peyton huffed and walked off. Her father and sister were in the Narthex with baby Jojo, while Jackson and Maverick stood outside Pastor Mike's office where he'd left them.

The door opened. "Okay, are you ready?" Pastor Mike looked to be in his sixties and wore a long white robe. He'd agreed to do a private baptism for them as Peyton wanted it to be close friends and family.

"Yeah, I think so. We're just waiting on the godmother. Her flight was delayed, and she's on her way from the airport now," Jackson said, raising one brow at Maverick.

"She's on her way now?"

"You're like a schoolgirl waiting for her crush to arrive in the lunchroom. You should see your face,"

Jackson said, tossing his head back with a laugh.

"Shut the—" He paused when he remembered Pastor Mike was walking alongside them.

"What? I didn't hear you?" Jackson said with a dumb ass grin on his face.

"Pastor Mike, should I be ashamed of being in love? My friend here seems to think so" Maverick said, as Jackson rolled his eyes and covered his mouth to hide his smile.

"One should never be embarrassed to love. It's what God wishes for all of us," Pastor Mike said with pride.

"Maybe you should lock Jackson in a confession room or make him say a hundred Hail Marys?"

The older man chuckled. "We don't say Hail Marys. This is a Christian church."

Before they could respond, Peyton walked up holding their little girl. She was the cutest kid he'd ever seen. Josephine Danielle Vance. Absolute perfection in a tiny package.

"Sorry, Pastor Mike. Elle will be here in five minutes," Peyton said. Her family sat in the front pews, along with Dani.

Maverick's stomach twisted. Would she acknowledge him, or ignore him? She'd iced him out for the last few weeks.

"Not a problem. Why don't we head up front, and she can join us when she arrives."

"Here, let me hold the squirmy, little noodle until you're ready," Dani said as they walked toward the front of the church.

"Thanks, have you heard from her again?" Peyton asked Dani.

"Yep. Her Uber just pulled up." Dani spun Jojo around in a circle to keep her entertained.

They stepped up on the stage and Jackson took Jojo in his arms. Everyone's attention turned to the back of the church.

"Holy shit," Dani whispered from the pew before covering her mouth.

A smile spread across Maverick's face at the sight of her. Elle's appearance sucked all the air from the room. Larger than life, and brighter than the north star. She left her suitcase at the back of the church and strode toward the stage.

"You're wearing quite the outfit," Peyton called out with a chuckle.

She wore the football jersey he'd had covered in stones, black leggings, high as fuck heels, and the antique crown on her head which probably weighed as much as she did. Her gaze locked with his, and that was all it took. He hurried down the steps, and she pulled the crown from her head and broke into an all-out sprint. Yeah, his girl could haul ass in sky-high heels. He met her halfway down the aisle, and she jumped in his arms, wrapping her legs around his waist and burying her face in his neck.

Jasmine and vanilla. Everything good.

"I'm so sorry, baby," he whispered in her ear.

She pulled back and placed a hand on his cheek. "I'm sorry too. I missed you so much."

"Umm, hate to break up this sweet reunion, lovebirds, but Pastor Mike has another baptism in a few minutes," Jackson said with a laugh.

"Leave them alone. We can reschedule," Peyton said, swiping at her cheeks to catch the falling tears.

"You will do no such thing. I just threatened an Uber driver to get me here in time. Come on, Wallace. First things, first." She slid down his body and her feet hit the floor. She grasped his hand in hers and led him to the stage, setting her crown down on a pew on the way there.

"Sorry, Pastor Mike," Elle said, before turning her gaze back to Maverick. Her smile so wide it nearly knocked the wind from him.

"No apology necessary. Shall we get started?"

Jojo reached for Elle, and she pulled the little beauty into her arms. He swore right then he'd have as many babies with this woman as she wanted. The sooner, the better. She was back, and he was never letting her go. She held the baby as they poured water over her little forehead. Jojo's gaze never left Elle's. She didn't cry or fuss. They took a couple pictures afterward, and Dani and Peyton flanked Elle's side, happy to have her back. He sat in the back of the church, waiting to have her all to himself again. He needed to know they were good, hear her say the words.

Everyone agreed to head over to PBV Bistro for lunch, and Elle caught him staring and smiled. He tucked his hands in his pockets. Didn't want to move too fast if she wasn't ready.

"Hey." She walked over to where he stood as everyone exited the church.

"Hey, Peaches."

"Thanks for the jersey and the crown."

"Of course. They look great on you," he said.

"The letter was my favorite part."

"Nothing I wouldn't do for you. I'm so fucking sorry for what I said to you."

She moved into him, wrapping her arms around his middle. "I know you are. I am, too. We both made mistakes."

"I hear Winston's doing well. I had dinner with your dad a few times while you were gone."

"He's doing much better. I'm going to have to scold my dad. What a traitor. He doesn't know where we stand," she said on a laugh.

"So where do we stand?"

"I did a lot of soul searching back home. I know we're going to fight and disagree, but it doesn't mean you don't know who I am. Things got heated, and we both made assumptions that we shouldn't have. But I do know one thing for sure."

"Tell me."

"I'm miserable without you. There's this empty space, and all I feel is sadness."

"My life doesn't work without you, Peaches."

"So, we're on the same page."

"Thank Christ."

"I'm not even going to correct your foul mouth in church because I've turned over a new leaf. I'm throwing all the rules to the wind. I mean, look at my outfit. Clearly, no one is following any sort of etiquette here." She laughed, and he intertwined his fingers with hers.

"Does this mean you'll still move in with me?" He said it on a tease, but the truth was he'd move in with her today if she was willing. But he knew they had some things to work out first.

"Slow down there, Cowboy. I'm not saying no, but I think we need to go back to the basics and work on our relationship," she said, pausing while he grabbed her rolling bag and they exited the church.

"It sort of sounds like a rule though? Didn't you give those up?" Damn, he'd missed teasing this woman.

"You make a good argument. What are your demands? Maybe we can meet somewhere in the middle."

He helped her into his truck and jumped in the driver's seat. "Meet in the middle, huh?"

"You heard me. I'm all about compromise."

"Okay. Well, I'd like to get married and have a dozen or so babies with you as soon as possible. You want to date me first. So I'm guessing the middle ground would be lots of sex? And only half a dozen kids to start with?"

"Hmmm…you drive a hard bargain, Wallace." She laughed. "I'll consider it. How about we go see Dr. Sparrow together a few times, and then we can reassess at the end of your football season."

"All right. It's a couple weeks, sounds fair. And you'll marry me at the end of the football season if all goes well?"

"Maverick Wallace, you just got your middle ground and you're already pushing for more. I've been home for an hour, and you're all in already?" she said with a laugh.

"I've always been all in, Peaches. If it means asking you every day until the day you say yes, I'll do it. You're it for me. Always have been. Always will be."

A pink hue spread across her cheeks, and she smiled. "You're it for me, too."

"I love you," he said, pulling in front of PBV. He paused and turned toward her.

"I love you too."

"Hey, what would happen if we didn't go in?" he asked, knowing she would insist they go to the luncheon. They were the godparents after all. But damn if he didn't want to hold her. Talk to her about the past few weeks. Hear about her time at home.

"It's a rule I'm willing to break. Let's go to your place. I miss my Daisy girl."

"Really? You're good with skipping it?" he said with surprise.

"I'm good with spending time with you."

For the first time in weeks, he felt like everything was going to be okay. Because nothing worked without her. He loved his friends, his family, and football. But Elle Fiore made him whole. He'd talked to Dr. Sparrow about it during the last couple of sessions.

"I'm glad. Did you know Dr. Sparrow thinks we're soulmates?" He pulled away from the curb.

"Really? She said it or you did, Romeo?"

"We talked about why I've never spent the night with another woman. It wasn't only about the nightmares. It was more about trust. She thinks being abandoned so young and in such a tragic way left me with some serious trust issues." He laughed because no one knew better than Elle.

"No kidding?" She gasped in dramatic fashion, sarcasm impossible to miss.

"No kidding." He laughed before continuing. "Anyway, she said a mother is usually the first person a child feels a strong connection to. I didn't get that with my mom. My parents adopted me and over time I gained a sense of safety and love."

"It makes sense," she said, as he pulled the car in

the driveway.

He turned to face her. "But until you, there was always a void. And somehow you manage to fill it. Dr. Sparrow agrees. You're the missing piece I've been searching for my whole life, Peaches."

Tears streamed down her beautiful face. She unbuckled her seatbelt and climbed on his lap, holding his face in her hands. "You do the same for me. I know it sounds corny, but I know I can be myself around you because you love me, unconditionally."

"You're damn straight I do." His mouth came over hers, and his fingers tangled in her silky hair.

Their kiss grew frantic, both trying to get closer. Make up for lost time. Her back hit the horn, startling them both.

"Oh my gosh, let's go inside," she said, hair all messy and cheeks flushed.

He lifted her out of the car, and tossed her over his shoulder, carrying her toward the door.

"What is it with you and this fireman hold?" she said with laughter.

"It's faster this way. Your little legs don't move as quick as mine."

"You're crazy." She slapped his backside.

"I'm so glad you're home. I've missed you. And so has my flaming baton," he said, setting her on her feet.

Her head tipped back with a big glorious smile. "You have a one-track mind, Wallace."

"Only when it comes to you."

Daisy galloped to greet them, and Elle dropped down on the wood floors while the oversized doodle assaulted her with kisses. He took a deep breath and enjoyed the moment. Hell, maybe Elle was rubbing off on him—because this sure felt like his own happily ever after.

Epilogue

Elle
Three months later

"So much has happened since we were last here. It feels like a lifetime," Elle said when he pulled into the driveway at the Lake Tahoe house.

"It does." He jumped out of the truck and came around to help her out.

"How do you feel about the season being over?"

"I mean, I would have preferred to win the whole thing, but I'm glad we made it to the Super Bowl," he said, before pushing open the front door. "Having you there cheering for me was the best part."

"I'll always be cheering for you."

"Damn, it feels good to be back. I forgot how awesome this place is. I've hardly spent any time at this house." He wrapped his arms around her waist, as they took in the magnificent view from the great room. Her back pressed to his front, and his chin settled on her shoulder.

"I know. It's been a while. With your season over, it'll be nice to come up here on the weekends."

His scruff brushed her cheek. The man's scent did crazy things to her. Mint and sandalwood awakened her senses. Every. Single. Time.

Since she'd returned to the city, they'd been

inseparable. Better than ever. They were solid. Like two broken pieces of a puzzle that fit together perfectly. She'd moved into his house a week after she returned. He never pressured her once. But after being apart those few weeks, she didn't want to be away from him when she didn't have to be. Edward had reached out once after she returned to the city, but she made it clear there would be no further communication as he'd caused enough trouble in her relationship with Maverick for a lifetime.

Maverick continued to see Dr. Sparrow and she joined him. He was making progress. He'd had two nightmares since she'd been back, but they were different. He no longer screamed for help or appeared terrorized by whoever haunted him. Something was working. His most recent nightmare left her cryin' something awful. He'd said goodbye to his mama. He told her he was okay. Somehow the terror she usually saw in his gaze wasn't there. His tone wasn't frantic or desperate. Maybe it was closure.

"We can come as often as you want, Peaches." He tickled her cheek with his scruff, and her head fell back in laughter.

"Have I told you how proud I am of you for sticking with Dr. Sparrow and diggin' into your past?" She turned in his arms and looked up at him. His wild dark hair tousled around his beautiful face, and his dark stare locked with hers.

"Nothing to be proud of, baby. Doing what I should have done a long time ago."

"You can't do things until you're ready. I know you were worried about the press findin' out, but they just looked like a-holes trying to force a story there."

The news of Maverick's therapy sessions blew over quickly. Teammates shared with the media how proud they were of him for dealing with his past and Maverick handled it with grace and humility.

"Did you really say *a-holes*? You can't say *asshole*, can you?" He tickled her sides and she fell onto the couch howling like a lunatic. He propped himself above her.

"I choose not to," she said, still breathless.

"You're perfect to me exactly as you are."

She put a hand on his cheek and met his gaze. "Right back at ya, Wallace."

And what else mattered? Loving someone so much their flaws became attributes. She'd strived for perfection her whole life and failed. But together, they were perfectly imperfect.

He moved to his feet and whistled for Daisy. "Come on, let's get out on the boat so we can catch the sun going down."

They'd stopped by Mimi's on their way into town, and she'd whipped them up a picnic basket so they could get out on the water.

"Let me grab a few extra jackets and a blanket. The temp is dropping as we speak," she said, jogging over to the closet.

"Okay. I'll grab a few waters and throw them in the bag."

The lake was so serene, especially this time of year. They pulled the boat around to their favorite spot on the water. She zipped her jacket over her hoody and pulled her knees up to her chest. Maverick turned off the boat and came to sit beside her, pulling her close and wrapping her up in his arms.

"This is fucking beautiful, isn't it?"

She tipped her head back to look at him. "Yeah, I love it here."

"I wanted to talk to you about something." He turned her so they faced one another.

"Okaaaay?"

"You know how there are some things you know? There's no question. No shadow of a doubt," he said, studying her.

"Yep. I know a lot of things. What in particular are you referring to?"

"How I feel about you."

She scooted forward and tangled her hands into his hair. "I most definitely know how I feel about you too."

He leaned down and kissed her hard. He pulled away, dropped off the bench and onto the floor of the boat propped on one knee.

"Maverick Wallace, what are you doin'?" She cupped both hands over her mouth and tried to catch her breath.

"What I've wanted to do since the first time I laid eyes on you. I knew you were meant to be mine even way back then, Peaches. And I've known every day since."

He paused, and she couldn't help herself. She dropped down on her knees and faced him. Tears streamed down her face. "I can't believe you're doin' this right now."

"We fell in love in Lake Tahoe. So, I wanted to do it here. And nothing says romance like a sunset, a boat, and a decorative goldendoodle," he said with a laugh. "But you were supposed to be standing or sitting on the bench. Why the hell are you down on your knees?"

"It's too far away up there." Her words broke on a sob.

Maverick swiped at her cheeks with his thumbs. "Elle Fiore, my heart belongs to you forever. You make me want to be a better man. I also want to put a shit ton of babies in you and spend my life making you smile. What do you say, will you marry me?"

"Did you just curse in my proposal?" Her head fell back with laughter.

"I sure as shit did. I want to give you the fairy-tale, Peaches. I want you to open the business you've always dreamed about, and I want to build a family with you." He pulled a box from his pocket and opened it to show the most beautiful ring she'd ever seen. All the air left her lungs. So much emotion stirred inside her.

"It's beautiful. I can't believe you did this," she said on a sob.

"Dying here, Peaches. Is that a yes?" He laughed, but his stare remained serious. Nervous. Maverick Wallace was actually nervous about asking her to marry him.

"Well, of course it's a yes. I'd marry you today if I didn't think our families would be devastated if we ran off and got hitched," she said, dangling her fingers in front of him, wanting him to slip the ring on.

He gently glided it on to her finger before letting a long sigh escape. "Thank Christ. You had me nervous there."

"You know I want to marry you, Maverick Wallace. Even when I hated you, I think I secretly loved you. You're my best friend. My favorite person. *The love of my life.* And your flaming baton ain't too shabby either." She winked, and he pulled her close, tilted her head back, and kissed her hard.

"I love you. And I don't give a shit about a wedding. Hell, I'd fly to Vegas tonight and marry you if I had my way. But I agree. My mom, your mom, and Mimi would never forgive us. And don't even get me started on the wonder twins. They'd kick my ass if they didn't attend our wedding."

"Yeah, and I couldn't do it to my dad and Winston. I know they'd want to give me away." She stared down at her sparkly ring. "This is the most beautiful ring I've ever seen. Did you design it?"

"It's Mimi's wedding band from my grandfather, engraved with the words, *forever mine*. I added the stone and the design with a little help from Peyton and Dani. You've got something old and something new."

She slipped the ring off and read the inscription, staring down at it in awe. "I absolutely love it. Thanks for being my fairy-tale."

"Thanks for making me believe in them."

They moved up to the bench, and she leaned back against his chest as they watched the sun disappear behind the horizon. Oranges and yellows and reds mixed together like a colorful canvas in the sky. His arms came around her, and she intertwined her fingers with his, still starin' down at her ring.

"I can't believe it. We're getting' married," she said, tilting her head back to look up at him.

"You happy, baby?"

"Happier than I ever dreamed I could be."

His laughter boomed, and he wrapped her up in his arms a bit tighter. "Love you, Peaches."

"Love you more." And she meant it.

Maverick Wallace didn't stride into her life on a

white horse. Or any horse for that matter. The man was a bull in a China shop. He was passionate and strong. Fierce and loyal. And he got her in a way no one else ever had.

She could retire her flaming batons, because this man set her world on fire.

And now that she found her happily ever after, she was never letting go.

Acknowledgments

Thank you so much for reading *Beautifully Flawed*! I hope you enjoyed your journey with Elle and Maverick as much as I enjoyed writing it. Please take a moment to leave a review on Amazon and Goodreads, as they truly help authors so much!!

Greg, Chase & Hannah, thank you for always supporting me and believing in me. I love you so much!

A huge thank you to the most amazing beta readers: Pathi, Natalie, Annette, Abi, Nicole, & Doo

Judi Mobley, thank you for all the time you put in to editing *Beautifully Flawed.* I'm so excited to have this story out in the world!

Willow Aster, thank you so much for your help, feedback and input with this story. You definitely got me over the last hurdle, and your support and encouragement mean the world to me!!

To my amazing parents…thank you for teaching me to never give up! That lesson has been invaluable in my life! I love you so much!

Thank you to my amazing siblings, who always support me with each release, Lisa, Julie, Eric, Jennifer, and Jim. I love you!

Steph, Pathi, Nat, Nicole, Sue, Thompson, Bell, Annette, Carol, Margy, Mindy, Kristin, Laura, Anne, Abi, Dina, Kelly, Maggie, Sammi, Liva, Leigh Anne, Julie, Nancy, Bev, Leslie, Florence, Tina, Renae, Cindy, Kelly & Kate, Darleen, Althea, Jess, Ariel, Heather, Shannon, Brandon, Logan, Brock, Caroline, Kennedy, and all of my friends and family who have supported throughout this journey…I am so thankful for you!! Xo

A word about the author…

Laura Pavlov writes sweet and sexy contemporary romance that will make you both laugh and cry. She is happily married to her college sweetheart, mom to two awesome almost-grown kids, and dog-whisperer to a couple crazy Yorkies. Laura resides in Las Vegas where she is living her own happily ever after.

laurapavlov.com

www.ingramcontent.com/pod-product-compliance
Lightning Source LLC
Chambersburg PA
CBHW051128030726
47504CB00004B/755
9781509232833